Under Your Spell

LAURA WOOD

Under Your Spell

SIMON &
SCHUSTER

London · New York · Sydney · Toronto · New Delhi

First published in Great Britain by Simon & Schuster UK Ltd, 2024

1 3 5 7 9 10 8 6 4 2

Simon & Schuster UK Ltd
1st Floor
222 Gray's Inn Road
London WC1X 8HB

Simon & Schuster: Celebrating 100 Years of Publishing in 2024

Simon & Schuster Australia, Sydney
Simon & Schuster India, New Delhi

www.simonandschuster.co.uk
www.simonandschuster.com.au
www.simonandschuster.co.in

A CIP catalogue record for this book
is available from the British Library

ISBN: 978-1-3985-2976-2
eBook ISBN: 978-1-3985-2977-9
Audio ISBN: 978-1-3985-2978-6

Typeset in Bembo by M Rules
Printed and Bound in the UK using 100% Renewable
Electricity at CPI Group (UK) Ltd

For the six-books-a-week,
just-one-more-page, trope-loving,
library-card-owning, smutty-audio-book-
in-public-listening, HEA-chasing dreamers.
This is a love letter.

PART ONE

Chapter One

Here's an insight into my life right now: my sister is standing on my doorstep clutching a dead bird, and that's not even close to the worst thing to happen today.

'Clemmie.' Lil's eyes fill with easy tears, her heavy black eyeliner already beginning to smear alarmingly, as she holds up the bundle of greasy feathers. 'He flew straight into my car . . . Do you think he'll be okay?'

I look at the bird. The very obviously dead bird.

'I don't think so, no.' I aim for gentle, but fall about a mile short. As I say, it's been a long day.

'For fuck's sake, Lil!' Our sister, Serena, appears at my shoulder, swigging directly from the neck of the champagne bottle she brought with her. 'What are you doing with that thing? It's disgusting!'

Lil glares at Serena, 'I'm trying to save its life. Do you think you can do mouth to mouth on a bird?'

'Mouth to beak, surely?' I muse as Serena makes loud retching noises.

'I can't just let it die,' Lil says again, stubbornly, and I'm standing firm in the doorway because I know that given half the chance the dead bird will end up inside my flat.

'I think that ship has sailed.' Serena pokes a well-manicured finger towards the thing. 'Pretty sure it's not supposed to be flat in the middle like that.'

Lil looks down. 'Oh,' she says finally. 'That's terrible.'

'Yes, well, maybe you can put the dead bird down and come inside?' I suggest.

'Just leave it *on the ground*?' Lil is horrified.

I can already see where this is heading and I am much too knackered to organize a bird funeral. I cast a desperate glance at Serena who rolls her eyes in response.

'Why don't you put it in the bin?' she suggests.

'The bin?!' Lil's voice climbs to a higher pitch.

'The *compost* bin,' Serena says quickly. 'Clemmie's got about sixteen different bins, hasn't she?' She looks at me.

'There's one for garden waste,' I shrug. Though 'garden' is a strong term for the scrubby patch of grass that came with the flat. I always meant to plant some bulbs, had great visions of myself wafting about with a wicker trug in the crook of my arm, smiling modestly when people praised my green fingers, but there was never the time. And it didn't really matter now.

'There you go, then.' Serena tosses her hair. 'That's perfect. You can return it to the earth.' Serena is a master at getting people to do what she wants, and right now she's dropping into Lil's language, her tone persuasive.

Lil wavers. 'It doesn't seem very dignified.'

'It's nature, Lil.' Serena waves a hand. 'You know, dead in tooth and claw.'

'It's *red* in tooth and claw,' I put in. 'And I don't think that getting hit by a Toyota Yaris driven by a tiny woman in an enormous pink coat was really the kind of poetic act of violence that Tennyson envisioned.'

'Whatever,' Serena dismisses me, getting warmed up now. '*Red*, *dead*, it's all part of the cycle, isn't it? From the earth we arise and to the earth we return, ashes to ashes, dust to dust. It's the circle of life . . . it moves us all . . .'

I absolutely know she's about to break into a lusty version of the song from *The Lion King* which I feel may undermine the impression she is taking this as seriously as Lil would like, and so I jump in quickly. 'Come on, Lil, it's freezing out here, and there's pizza inside. Your favourite vegan pizza, and wine. Lots and lots of wine.'

'Fine.' Lil nods reluctantly. 'But I think I should say a few words.'

'Say them quickly,' Serena says. 'Clemmie needs us more than that dead bird does. There *might* still be some hope for her.'

'Was that really necessary?' I mutter.

Serena doesn't reply, just takes another mouthful of her drink, her eyebrows raised, but her meaning is clear: my life is pretty much one big dead bird, and I can't exactly disagree.

Five minutes later, we are gathered around my open garden waste bin.

'Here lies Peter the pigeon,' Lil intones.

I'm not at all convinced that the bird lying dead in my bin is a pigeon but now does not seem the time to quibble over semantics.

'We don't really know how long you were alive,' Lil continues, 'but you were part of this big beautiful world, and it's sad that you're gone. I hope wherever you are you can feel the sun on your back and the air under your wings. I hope you are happy and free.'

I feel unexpected tears prickling at my eyes, which I try to hide from Serena.

'You two are as bad as each other,' she grumbles, but I hear the reluctant affection in her voice. '*Now* can we go inside? It is freezing, you know. Never mind this bloody bird; I'm about to perish of hypothermia.'

Lil swings the lid closed on the bin and with a sigh of relief I lead them both inside.

'What happened in here?' Lil asks, peering around at my flat which is admittedly looking a little spartan.

Serena scowls. '*Leonard* happened.'

'He took all your stuff?' Lil gasps. 'Your sofa? And your TV? And . . . where's all Tuna's stuff? Where is *Tuna*?'

Ah, yes. The cat. Can't think about that too hard, or I start crying again.

Lil blinks, the facts registering. 'He took your cat?'

'Len said it'll be better for him in the new place,' I say, trying to keep the words light. 'And he's right. It's a proper house and not near any of the main roads. Much safer.'

'He took your cat!' Lil repeats, and this time murder sparkles in her big blue eyes. 'He left you for another woman, took all your stuff and stole your cat?! I hate him.'

I look around at the near-empty open-plan kitchen/living room. Yesterday it was full of Ikea's finest flat-pack, neat and well ordered. Sure, it wasn't really to my taste – all the clean, contemporary lines and lack of clutter were a bit soulless, but it had been perfectly nice; it had looked like a home. Now, with the single armchair that I once found on the street (I'd told Len I bought it at an antique fair otherwise he'd have never let it through the door), the sagging, half-full bookcase, and the table lamp in the shape of a mermaid holding a seashell, without a table to sit on, it looks like the final few minutes of a car boot sale.

'It was his stuff,' I say with a shrug. 'He chose it, he paid for it. I suppose I just didn't realize how *much* of it was his until the movers came and took it away.' Which they had done, today, while I was at work. At a job I would soon no longer have. At that thought the headache I've been battling flares.

'I always knew he was the worst,' Serena says darkly, draping herself across the kitchen counter and flipping open the lid on the giant pizza box. 'I've been telling you this for years.'

'You said he was boring,' I reply, 'which, to be fair to him, you can hardly say now.'

Len and I had been together for four years, and then, ten days ago, he told me that not only was he leaving me for Jenny, a colleague from his accounting firm, but that the two of them had been seeing each other for the last eighteen months and that she was three months pregnant. Len, Jenny, their baby and my cat would all be moving to a four-bedroom cottage in the Oxfordshire countryside, along with all of our furniture. He was benevolently leaving me the flat in the city that I could no longer afford to pay rent on. It was all very tidy.

Prior to this experience, I had always been a little dubious of people who were blindsided by events like these. *How could they not know?* I thought. Well, let me tell you now – I had no idea. Not an inkling, not a single notion about any of this had so much as flickered on the edge of my mind.

When Len laid the facts out for me, standing portentously in front of our fireplace, like he was a detective in a bad Agatha Christie adaptation revealing who dunnit, my first thought was that he was joking.

That didn't last long because Len wasn't much of a joker, and frankly none of the words coming out of his mouth were very funny.

'I just think we've both been going through the motions for so long now,' he said, and his words had the stiff, practised quality of a rehearsed speech. (I found out later this was because Jenny had literally written him a script, which demonstrated good sense because Len does have a tendency towards vagueness and our breakup was nothing if not extremely clear.) 'You and I are too different. It's not really surprising given your background . . .' That, I felt, was a particularly sharp twist of the knife. 'We're not really in love with each other anymore, Clemmie. We're just used to being together. You'll see, this is all for the best.'

At which point I promptly threw up into the empty Quality Street tin I was clutching.

The fact that he wasn't wrong was of little comfort. I didn't miss him so much as the familiarity of having another person around, the worn-in routine of our lives which seemed so tightly entwined. I did, however, miss the cat. And the sofa.

'I'll admit, I was initially distracted by how boring he is,' Serena muses now. 'It's possible I hadn't realized that his boiled-egg personality masked the heart of a villain. But now, now I see.' Her voice is dangerous, promising retribution, her glower impressive. She helps herself to a slice of pizza and bites into it with unnecessary violence.

Lil hops up onto the kitchen counter and begins to pull the foil off another of the champagne bottles Serena arrived with. 'He *was* so boring though, Clemmie.' She tugs the cork from the bottle with a well-practised pop. 'You can admit it now.'

'He wasn't boring,' I protest. 'He was steady, reliable. I liked that about him.'

'Jesus, Clem,' Serena exhales in exasperation. 'He was your boyfriend, not a Volvo. You deserved way more out of a relationship.' She pauses heavily here before delivering the blow. 'Besides, we all know that this whole thing with Leonard was actually about the D-word.'

'No, it wasn't,' I snap, buttons instantly pushed. 'And don't say the D-word.'

'Got to agree with Clemmie on that one,' Lil nods, carefully pouring champagne into three mugs, despite the fact

Serena is still happily drinking from her near-empty bottle. 'The D-word sounds like you're talking about dicks.'

'Ew.' Serena accepts a mug that says 'accountants are great between the (spread)sheets', a gift from me which Len doesn't appear to have been as emotionally attached to as he was, say, to our good glassware or the vacuum cleaner.

'If I wanted to talk about penises,' my sister continues loftily, 'I would simply talk about penises. But fine.' She clears her throat and gives me a stern look. 'Clemmie – you know your whole relationship with Leonard was actually about Dad.'

'Speaking of penises,' I mutter, taking a long drink from my own mug. The champagne is cold, crisp, the bubbles rush through my blood. Serena only buys the best.

We all have our own relationships with our father – in my case it might best be described as a passing acquaintance. When your dad is an ageing rock god who managed to impregnate three women in the space of four months, things tend to get complicated.

'It's true that Len was the anti-dad,' Lil muses. 'It doesn't get less rock 'n' roll than an accountant from Surrey.'

'Not sure what you'd know about rock 'n' roll,' Serena scoffs.

'I'm a musician.' Lil crosses her arms, 'I know about all sorts of music.'

'Only music made by women who look like Victorian ghosts.' Serena smirks while Lil splutters, though it does appear that she is wearing a voluminous white nightdress underneath her giant pink coat.

'That mass-produced crap you put out at your label can hardly be called music.' Lil is indignant.

Serena flicks her curtain of subtly balayaged hair over her shoulder. 'Being popular isn't a crime. God forbid a song should have a beat, something people can actually dance to.'

'Can we not?' I interject wearily, the argument a familiar one.

Both my sisters followed in our dad's footsteps with careers in music, yet they manage to be two barely touching circles on a Venn diagram: Serena is a terrifyingly efficient executive producer at one of the biggest record labels in the world – polished, gorgeous, her fingernails constantly clacking over the screen of her iPhone, while Lil is a tiny angelic waif who wins over festival crowds with her sweetly rasping voice, acoustic guitar and flower-child energy.

'No need for you to wade in, Miss I-Haven't-Listened-To-New-Music-In-Two-Decades.' Serena huffs.

'It's *Dr* I-Haven't-Listened-To-New-Music-In-Two-Decades, thanks,' I reply, refusing to take the bait. There's no point in us getting bogged down in my parental issues, when there's plenty of other stuff to be upset about. 'And I was under the impression you were here to help with my problems,' I finish forlornly, clambering onto one of the stools at the small breakfast counter.

'We are!' Lil exclaims. 'Of course we are. So tell us what happened? I thought you said they were going to extend your contract?'

'I thought they were, that's what the head of the

department told me, but there have been cuts and . . .' I trail off, pinching the bridge of my nose to stop the tears from falling. I cannot keep crying or at some point I will simply disintegrate.

'If they told you they were going to keep you on then that's what they should do,' Serena huffs. 'You're brilliant, an expert in your field and all your students love you. This is bullshit.'

'I suppose being an expert in the field of obscure medieval literature doesn't mean I'm as in demand as you'd think,' I say into my mug.

Ever since I'd finished my PhD five years earlier, I'd taken one badly paid, short-term contract after another always hoping that the job would turn into something more permanent. Here in Oxford, I thought that had finally happened, but it seems that the universe wasn't done crapping all over me. Just when I thought I'd be able to catch my breath, to actually start adult life at the ripe old age of thirty-two, I find that I'll be jobless when term finishes for the summer. Jobless. Boyfriendless. Soon to be homeless. So much for adult life.

I drain the mug of champagne and hold it out to be refilled. Silently, Lil complies.

'So, we need to make a plan,' Serena says firmly. 'Find a new job for you.'

'Academic posts don't come up that often,' I say. 'And they all have about a trillion applicants because of that. Trust me, I know. And even if something *does* miraculously come up for next year, it won't be until the start of the autumn term, which leaves me a good four months totally unpaid.' I am feeling extremely sorry for myself now.

'How about a short-term loan?' Serena asks. 'Just until you get something sorted.'

I'm already shaking my head. 'I can't take money from you.'

'You know there's always Dad,' Lil suggests and then winces when I glare at her. 'I know you don't want to, but I'm sure . . .'

'I don't want his money,' I say, trying to keep emotion out of my voice.

'You're being so unnecessarily stubborn about this,' Serena says. 'He's a shitty dad whether you take his money or not, might as well let the old duffer do something to help out. And besides, he's not as bad as you—'

I cut her off with a wave of my hand. My sisters look at me for a moment and then sigh in unison. They know this is an argument they won't win.

'So what will you do?' Lil asks. 'Have you told your mum?'

I grimace. 'Not yet. She'll want me to come home.'

The three of us knock back some more of the champagne in thoughtful silence. I can barely feel the bubbles anymore, a pleasing buzz hums through me.

'*I* know what we should do,' Serena says finally, and her words are smudged by the alcohol, just a little soft around the edges.

'What?' I ask.

She grins. 'We should cast the breakup spell.'

Chapter Two

'The breakup spell?' I wrinkle my nose. 'Like when we were kids?'

Something suspiciously like a cackle rises on Serena's lips. 'The Weird Sisters fly again!'

I groan, dropping my head into my hands. The Weird Sisters was a game we used to play when we were about ten and it had its basis in our slightly . . . *unusual* family set up.

It started as a comment in the newspaper, referring to our family as a 'coven' and my mum had laughed and said, 'If the pointy hats fit!' Then Petty and Ava laughed too, so the three of us girls joined in, even though we had to look the word up in the dictionary later.

The papers wrote about us often in those days. When Ripp Harris was revealed to have impregnated three different women practically simultaneously, it was just the sort of salacious story the press could get behind. My mother, Dee – twenty-three years old and an up-and-coming musician herself – had the dubious distinction of being married to

Ripp at the time, and so the attention on her was relentless. *What would she do?* they asked breathlessly. *Would she stay? Would she fight for her man? Would she do so literally and preferably in front of a camera if the other two women came within fifty feet???*

In fact, my mum did none of those things. She packed up and left (with minimal protests from Ripp), and bought a farm in Hertfordshire with her sizeable divorce settlement.

Then she invited Petty and Ava to come and live on the farm with her, and the tabloids went wild.

RIPP'S EX OPENS BABY COMMUNE was Mum's favourite headline. She had that page framed in our downstairs loo. None of us were ever really clear what a baby commune would look like, but our real life was nowhere near as scandalous or exciting as the paparazzi outside our gates wanted to believe.

Mum gave up singing, and the press attention receded but never fully died down. The house was our safe place. Mum stopped performing and started an arts charity which she still runs from her home office. She and I lived in the middle section of the long, low, ramshackle building, which had been slapped together over several different centuries, while Petty and Lil lived in one converted side of the house, and Ava and Serena lived in the other. Everyone had their own space, but doors usually remained open, and we tended to congregate in the giant central kitchen, or the worn-in living room.

I don't know how Mum, Petty and Ava forged the relationship they did, especially under such circumstances, but for as long as I can remember it has been the three of them – best friends – and then the three of us – sisters – in and out of each other's houses, running around the acres of neglected farmland, growing up together in a happy, loving tangle.

Ripp didn't really feature in our lives. When asked about the whole three-babies-in-one-year thing, he would just shrug and say, 'Hey man, it was the eighties,' with a rueful smile, as if that explained everything, as if the fall of the Berlin Wall and a proliferation of leg warmers made it simply *impossible* for him to stop shagging everyone in sight, spreading his seed about. ('Ew, don't say *seed*,' Lil had said when I voiced this thought aloud.)

We were all born within four months of each other in 1990 and though Ripp could presumably have blamed it on the new decade, we were not blessed with any further half-siblings. It's hard not to take it personally when your dad gives a front-page interview about his vasectomy the week after you're born. (IT'S THE SNIP FOR RIPP!) That had really given my therapist something to get her teeth into.

Anyway, the general public consensus was that our home was a sort of cross between a cult, a commune, and a site for the practice of dark magic. The reality was of course much more mundane, but it became something of an obsession for my sisters and me, this idea that we were witches – like the three sister witches in Macbeth.

As the Weird Sisters we had dressed ourselves in Mum's Stevie Nicks-inspired wardrobe – tripping over long, spangled black dresses as we 'cast spells' over an old Le Creuset saucepan, cursing our enemies, and gifting one another with radiant beauty, numerous love interests, and – on one memorable occasion – 'much bigger boobs'.

Mum and Petty hadn't minded, but Ava said we should be asking for business acumen and stock tips because all that other stuff was for sale thanks to the Patriarchy. Patriarchy was another word we had to look up in the dictionary, and after that our spells got a lot . . . angrier.

Later, when we were teenagers, we had occasionally revived the tradition during periods of heartache.

'We're not kids anymore,' I say now, but Serena is already rummaging through her ginormous handbag and she pulls out a small wooden box.

'I thought we might need this tonight,' Serena says and my mouth drops open.

'Oh my God!' Lil exclaims. 'Is that . . .'

'The breakup box?' I finish breathlessly.

Serena nods. 'You know Petty's been renovating Granny Mac's house and she found it buried in the garden.'

Lil's eyes are wide. 'That is some spooky timing. It's like . . . *destiny*.'

I take the box from Serena and there's a needle of pain in my chest as I pry off the lid. Inside there are several envelopes – one for every time one of us had broken up with our teenage crushes. On the top is a black envelope with a silver star drawn on it. I know exactly what's inside . . . the last spell the Weird Sisters ever cast. The breakup spell.

It was right before I turned eighteen and a time of my life I don't like to dwell on. I had just gone through a breakup that made this one feel like a walk in the park, and Serena and Lil had talked me into a night of drunken witchcraft. We were up in Northumberland at the time, at Petty's grandmother's house, and after we cast the spell we buried the box in the garden. I didn't think I'd ever see it again.

Serena plucks the black envelope from the box and tears it open without ceremony. 'Three Wishes and a Curse,' she reads, then she looks up at me and Lil, grinning. 'Time to reawaken these bad boys, don't you think?'

'Yeeeeeeeeeessssss!' Lil shrieks, falling off the kitchen counter.

Serena starts opening the kitchen cupboards looking for a suitable pan. There's no aged Le Creuset – if we had any to start with, I'm certain it would now be safely ensconced in Len's new home – but she emerges with a dented frying pan which she seems to think will do the trick.

'I'll get the herbs,' Lil exclaims, and she makes for the front door, swaying slightly on her feet.

'Serena, this is ridiculous,' I say. 'I can't believe you're encouraging this.'

'Why not?' my sister shrugs. 'It can't hurt. It's not like your luck can get much worse.'

I groan again.

'Candles?' Serena asks.

'Do I look like I've got candles?' I gesture at the barren wasteland of my home. It is hardly an advertisement for Jo Malone.

With a *tsk*ing sound she starts opening and shutting drawers, eventually letting out a victorious yelp as she pulls out some half-melted birthday cake candles.

Lil bursts back in, her hands full of greenery. 'I wasn't sure if any of these were herbs,' she says, dumping a pile of weeds on the kitchen counter.

'I think that one's sage,' Serena says, poking at one of the leaves.

'That's a dandelion,' I reply.

'Never mind.' Serena waves an airy hand. 'Lil, put them all in the pan.'

Serena lights the candles and sticks them in the leftover pizza, which makes it look vaguely festive, while Lil dumps all the leaves in the frying pan.

'This is stupid,' I try again.

'Tell that to your bra size,' Serena snorts.

'That's called puberty, not magic,' I say.

'We've got a great track record,' Lil giggles tipsily. 'Remember when Cam and Serena broke up and we cast that spell?'

'That's right,' Serena says. 'And then her mum found her secret stash of Marlboro Lights under the bed and grounded her for the whole summer, and she missed seeing Shania Twain in Hyde Park. Who had the last laugh then?'

I blink. Maybe it's this compelling argument, or the unflinching support of my sisters, maybe it's the wave of nostalgia, or maybe it's the bottle of champagne I've drunk (who can say?), but I'm actually warming to the whole magic spell idea.

'Fuck it,' I say. 'Let's do it.'

'Yessssss!' Lil pumps her fist in the air and then staggers slightly, tripping over the hem of her nightie.

'What did we use to do first?' I frown, trying to remember.

'We need a salt circle,' Serena says, already liberally scattering Maldon flakes around the kitchen floor. She runs out halfway around, but, undeterred, grabs the pepper mill and starts cranking that instead. Soon all three of us are sneezing our heads off.

'Maybe sugar would be better than pepper?' Lil says, eyes watering. 'It feels like a sugar and salt circle would actually be really, like, symbolic of life – sweetness and . . . saltiness, you know?'

I'm in this now, and the champagne fizzing through my veins means that Lil's argument actually sounds incredibly sensible. I grab a bag of caster sugar and finish up the circle. 'Now what?' I ask.

Lil takes the pan of herbs and puts it on the floor in the middle of the wonky circle.

'We have to have music.' Serena grabs her phone and frowns down at it. 'Needs charging,' she mutters, digging around in her enormous handbag and pulling out a charger, which she plugs in. After tapping at the screen for a moment, the familiar sound of 'Sisters of the Moon' by Fleetwood Mac rings from the tinny speaker.

'Yesssss!' Lil exclaims again, already swaying from side to side. 'I remember!' She starts crooning along with the lyrics, and Serena and I join in. I close my eyes, imagining us back in our old kitchen, the music crackling over Mum's record player, the smell of lavender and mint pilfered from Ava's garden hanging in the air. Music was a simple thing for me then. Something that filled our house.

Serena shakes out the paper in her hand and begins to read from it: 'We are the Sisters Weird, and we come here today to ask the Goddess to grant our wishes three!'

She passes the paper to Lil, who reads the next line: 'We also ask that you curse our enemy. A man who has wronged our beloved sister.'

'Leonard,' Serena snarls, inserting his name here instead of the name written on the paper. The one I *definitely* don't want to think about.

'Yeah,' I nod, cranking the cork out of a bottle of red wine and slopping it into my mug. 'Len, we curse you!'

Lil hands the paper back to Serena. 'Leonard, we curse you! May you never satisfy another woman sexually, and may you get some sort of extremely itchy rash down there,' she cries.

'It does *not* say that!' I hiss, horrified.

Serena holds out the paper to me and I see the words written there in her handwriting.

'God, we were savage,' Lil says sunnily.

'Poor Jenny,' I murmur. Serena hands the paper to me and I read the next line, which is in my handwriting. 'May you learn the error of your ways and feel guilty forever for how you treated me.' I feel a dip in my stomach as I think about the girl I was when I wrote that. 'Hmmm, a bit earnest, maybe.'

'It's not earnest,' Lil jumps in. 'It's true! Len should feel guilty forever just like . . .' She catches Serena's glower and cuts herself off, before she brings up the ex we never mention. 'But the rash thing, too,' she says, flustered. 'Definitely the rash thing.'

With a nod, Serena plucks one of the candles from the pizza and throws it into the pan of leaves. The three of us cheer, and Serena cackles again.

'Now the wishes,' I say, looking at the sheet of paper.

'Three wishes for Clemmie,' Lil says. 'To heal her heartbreak.'

Serena immediately snatches another candle and throws it in the pan. 'Hot sex!'

'You didn't even need to look at the spell,' Lil says admiringly.

'I remember it well.' Serena smirks. 'Just what she needs. I don't know if it helped, Clem, but it certainly came true for me. A lot.'

'*I* remember pointing out that you could have given it a *bit* more thought at the time,' I say.

'That's your problem, Clemmie,' Serena exhales wearily. 'Too much thinking, not enough doing, and by *doing* I mean . . .'

'We all know what you mean.' I roll my eyes.

'You haven't been with anyone but *Leonard* for years,' Serena shudders. 'Frankly, I can't imagine anything worse.'

'It would be good to really embrace your sexuality,' Lil says more diplomatically.

'I embrace my sexuality,' I huff.

My sisters are suspiciously silent.

'Just put yourself out there a bit,' Lil pipes up in the end.

'Casual sex, Clemmie . . . it's great and you've never had any,' Serena says.

'There was Tom at uni,' I say indignantly. 'That was casual.'

'You were together for six months. It was only casual in that you found out he was shagging half the drama society.' Serena's tone is withering.

That's not exactly true. It *was* casual for me because I was still not over the aforementioned very devastating breakup and therefore not really invested in Tom.

'I'm just saying a one-night stand would do you the world of good,' my sister continues.

'I could do something casual,' I insist. 'But I'm not using any apps.' Last time I was single, Serena signed me up for all of them and made a profile describing me as 'A curvy redhead with a mind for business and a bod for sin', incorrectly assuming that this would attract men who could quote *Working Girl* (good), rather than a bunch of massive pervs who thought I'd be instantly enamoured by pictures of their penises (bad). 'Thank God I'm a lesbian,' Serena had said by way of apology.

Now she rolls her eyes. 'How are you going to find someone to have sex with otherwise? You're basically a hermit. You hang out in libraries and the only men you interact with have been dead for eight hundred years.'

'No. Apps,' I say.

'It's fine,' Lil interrupts soothingly. 'The spell will bring Clemmie someone to have hot sex with. She doesn't need an app. Now, Clemmie, do your wish.'

I look down at the paper. 'I wish for a job doing what I love,' I read. 'Wow. Thanks for that, past me. Looks like I'm no further on now than I was at seventeen.'

'That *is* unfortunate timing,' Serena grimaces.

'But the wish will help get you back on track,' Lil says firmly. 'That's the whole point.'

I feel a kick of pain as I remember I've only got a couple of months left in the job I love. I grab a candle and throw it in the pan.

With that, Lil turns and picks up the final candle in the pizza. She reads the words written in her own looping hand with a soft smile: 'I wish for big love – the unconditional, whole-hearted, soulmate kind. Just what Clemmie deserves.'

'Booooooo!' Serena jeers. 'I forgot how rubbish your wishes were.'

Ignoring her, Lil throws her candle in the pan. 'The three of us say the last line together.' She shows us the words.

'Into the darkness we offer light, from the ashes may we rise,' the three of us intone. Wow, we were really bringing the drama back in the day.

Then Lil looks at us both, and when we nod she drops the spell into the frying pan as well. The paper catches and smoulders around the edges. There's a sudden hiss, then a cloud of smoke as some of the dry leaves catch alight.

'Wait, Lil . . . are there sticks in there?' I ask.

'Maybe?' Lil says it like a question.

The tiny flames flicker to life, gobbling up the sheet of paper and licking higher, taking over the pan as all three of us watch in stupefied silence. A plume of thick smoke rises. Then the smoke alarm begins to wail above our heads. Seconds later, all the lights go off.

'WHAT IS HAPPENING?' Serena yells, her hands clamped over her ears.

'You've plugged your phone in the dodgy socket!' I shout back, tripping over things in the dark. 'The fuse has blown. There's a torch in the cupboard under the sink.'

Lil is on her feet waving a tea towel ineffectually at the smoke detector. Serena grabs the wine bottle and upends it on the fire, which puts out the flames but does little to decrease the smoke.

'My wine!' I yelp forlornly.

'WHERE THE FUCK IS THE FUCKING TORCH?' Serena growls from the shadows. There's more clattering, several loud bangs, and Lil manages to wrestle the back door open. Serena finally locates the torch and sends a bright arc of light around the room.

The smoke alarm abruptly stops its wailing but is replaced by a shrill ringing.

The three of us stand blinking in confusion over the steaming wreckage of the frying pan.

'It's my phone,' Serena says finally, grabbing her mobile and glancing down at the screen.

'Hi, Mum,' she says, picking up. 'It's not actually a great

time . . .' She pauses here and whatever Ava says has her eyes widening. 'Wait, slow down,' Serena breaks in. '*Who* died?'

'Oh my God, Clemmie,' Lil whispers, the tea towel still clutched in her hands. 'We are some seriously powerful witches.'

Chapter Three

Despite what Lil might think, we haven't killed anyone with our witchy powers. It eventually transpires that the person who died is Uncle Carl, and it was after his third heart attack, which took place hours before we were drunkenly setting light to a bunch of twigs. I am pretty sure that means we are in the clear.

Uncle Carl was not actually related to any of us, but was my mum's ex-music manager as well as still being Ripp's manager. Despite my mum giving up on her singing career, she and Carl had managed to stay friends over the years – largely, I think, because he acted as a sort of intermediary for Ripp, organizing everything from visitation days to extra money for school trips. Nothing was too much trouble for Uncle Carl, up to and including standing in for our dad when he inevitably forgot or slept through the days he was supposed to be looking after us – something that happened with predictable regularity.

Carl was a rake-thin man who smoked like a chimney

and had a mobile phone permanently clamped to his ear. I can roughly date every remembered encounter with him by the size of the phone. He talked out the side of his mouth and always had cherry cough drops in his pocket, which he doled out liberally in between telling us that he'd never had a filling and that the war against sugar was 'a communist plot'.

Now it's two weeks after the spell casting, and I am driving to his funeral. For some reason best understood by my mother, Carl's wake is being held at our house, after a service at a nearby church. I'm chugging down the M40 in my dilapidated old Ford Fiesta, cursing and running spectacularly late thanks to a mandatory staff meeting at the university that sacked me.

I only hope the car doesn't simply fall apart before I get there. At my last MOT the mechanic told me that if it was a horse he'd have shot it, a comment which I found unnecessary as I handed over an exorbitant fee for four new tyres and a lengthy list of 'amber warnings that should really be looked at'.

I take two wrong turns, and when I finally squeal up to the church I realize the hearse is right behind me. Grabbing my phone and my handbag, I sprint through the doors. The place is packed and hundreds of heads swing in my direction as I stumble in, pulling my coat over my too-tight black dress and casting around for my family.

A hissed 'Clemmie!' directs me to where Serena and Lil are saving me a seat, and I fall into the pew beside them not a moment too soon.

'Cut that a bit close,' Serena whispers as some sombre organ music starts up.

'Had a nightmare finding the place,' I say, slumping wearily in my seat. I don't have long to reflect because the signal is given that means we are all supposed to rise to our feet. I stand and turn with everyone else to watch the coffin being carried in.

It's hard to believe that Carl, who was after all a very *alive* person, is inside that small box. I feel a lump in my throat and tears sting my eyes. Lil hands me a crumpled tissue.

As the procession draws level with us I realize that my father is one of the pall-bearers and I feel my body tense. Even though he and Carl were close, I think part of me had expected Ripp to flake on the funeral.

I haven't seen him for at least a year – the last time had been the one and only occasion I introduced Ripp to Len. They had hated each other instantly. At the time I thought that was probably a good sign for my relationship.

Now he spots me and gives me a jaunty little wink. Of course Ripp Harris wouldn't let a little thing like the dead body resting on his shoulder interfere with his charm offensive. I keep my own expression stony, and my stomach sinks as I realize I'm going to have to see him later at the wake.

The discordant groans of the organ get louder, but suddenly I'm aware that there's another sound fighting for attention.

'YOU HAVE REACHED YOUR DESTINATION,' a

voice intones solemnly, cutting through the music. A few heads lift, and I exchange a look of confusion with Serena.

'YOU HAVE REACHED YOUR DESTINATION,' the voice thunders again, and it seems louder this time. More heads swivel.

'*God?*' Lil mouths, casting her eyes up at the high stone roof.

As the six of them continue up the aisle past us and the voice calls out, I notice a hitch in the step of one of the pall-bearers – a man with his back to me. I can't see anything apart from his broad shoulders, dark hair curling over the collar of his perfectly tailored suit.

'MAKE A U-TURN IF POSSIBLE,' the voice yells now, and the truth begins to dawn on me in painful increments.

'No, no, no,' I murmur, closing my eyes as if I can will myself to sink through the floor. As if ignoring the problem will make it go away.

'MAKE A U-TURN IF POSSIBLE,' the voice comes again.

'Fuck, fuck, fuck,' I mutter, fumbling with my bag.

There's a horrified gasp from the lady in front of us, who glares at me before rather pointedly looking at the enormous crucifix hanging on the wall in front of us. Frankly, I think Jesus has bigger problems. I know I do.

My hand closes around my phone and, as I pull it from my bag, the Maps app takes one last opportunity to scream, 'MAKE A U-TURN IF POSSIBLE' at top volume as though directing the coffin back towards the land of the living.

The organist stumbles; everyone in the congregation is looking at us now. The dark-haired pall-bearer's shoulders are shaking as the coffin finally reaches the altar.

'I'm so sorry,' I whisper, muting my phone with trembling fingers while feeling the sort of heat in my cheeks that could power a nuclear facility.

Serena and Lil have collapsed in silent giggles beside me – the occasional unhelpful snort issuing from them as I consider finding a nice open grave to fling myself into.

The service passes off without a hitch after that, not that I am able to pay attention to much of it. There is some music, and a reading from the Bible. Finally, Ripp swaggers up to give the eulogy.

He's tall, lean, with improbably dark shaggy hair, but his face looks more crumpled than the last time I saw him. His jaw, I notice, is softening, his whole face starting to sag, just a little. His black shirt is unbuttoned at least one – if not two – buttons too far for respectful funeral attire, but the disapproving lady in front of me doesn't seem to have an issue with that. Instead she is staring at my father with that look . . . the one that mixes adulation with awe and a stomach-churning pinch of lust. It's a look I am all too familiar with, having seen it on everyone from my own friends to my year-eight Maths teacher.

'Carl Montgomery,' Ripp says now, with a slow, sad shake of his head. 'What a guy. What a loss.' He doesn't speak loudly, but everyone shifts forward, hanging on his words, focussed on the rough rasp of his famous voice. Something happens to Ripp Harris when you give him an audience: he's absolutely magnetic. It's one of the things I've always found difficult about being around him – it feels like he sucks all the air out of a room.

'Some of you probably know who I am,' Ripp says with faux-humility, and the dragon-lady in front gives a breathy little sigh, clearly falling for it hook, line and sinker. 'But no one would have heard of me if it hadn't been for Carl. He *discovered* me, I suppose you'd say, in a pub basement in Sheffield many, many years ago.' He pauses here, flashing his perfectly even, white teeth. 'Although for the sake of our vanity, I'm sure Carl would want me to say "not *that* many".'

There's a quiet chuckle that moves through the crowd and Ripp goes on with the eulogy, which no one else seems to notice is actually all about himself. By the time he's reached his second Grammy win, my attention has drifted, and I find myself absently scanning the congregation looking for my mum.

My gaze snags instead on a man near the front. It's the pall-bearer again, though I don't know why I'm so certain when I've only glimpsed the back of his head – surely the backs of people's heads are all quite similar, nondescript things? He's turned to the person beside him, clearly saying something in a low voice, and I notice that his profile is even nicer than his back. I see a slash of cheekbone, the square edge of a jaw, soft, dark hair falling over his forehead, and curling around the shell of his ear.

Something hot and peculiar lances through my body and

it takes me a queasy moment to identify it as lust. It's been a while, and I'm actually going to have to give myself a stern talking to. Lusting after a stranger? In church? *At a funeral????*

While I'm sure Serena and Lil would be delighted by this turn of events, I am not. I tell myself I am *not* repressing my sexuality; I am demonstrating good manners as I fasten my gaze instead on the sad Jesus dangling from the crucifix on the wall. He looks a bit like a melted candle and there's absolutely nothing sexy about that.

On that thought, the organ pipes up again. This time it's playing something cheerier, as a pair of curtains close around Carl's coffin. I realize it's 'Here Comes the Sun' by the Beatles, and I feel another twist of sadness, but it's too late now – the funeral is over, and heaving a collective sigh of relief, the crowd begins to make its way out into the weak spring sunshine.

'How many of this lot are heading back to ours?' Serena asks as we join the throng.

I shrug. 'Mum said just a handful of close friends.'

Serena grimaces. 'So about two hundred gawpers then.'

'I guess so. Where are the mums anyway?' I ask, craning my neck.

'They were up near the front,' Lil says from behind me. 'They said to just meet them back at the house.'

'What on earth are you wearing?' My eyes widen as I finally take in Lil's full funeral attire.

'What?' Lil asks from behind the black lace veil she has pulled down over her face. The rest of her is swathed in an oversized black tent. She appears to be wearing elbow-length black gloves. 'We're all in mourning, you know.'

'She's cosplaying as a Mafia widow,' Serena whispers.

'I heard that,' Lil snaps. 'I don't understand why you two are so unconcerned with honouring the dead.'

'Lil, I swear, if this is about that bloody bird again . . .' Serena starts.

'He had a name.' I can only assume the expression behind Lil's veil is fierce.

'NO, HE DIDN'T,' Serena yells. 'I REFUSE TO REFER TO A DEAD BIRD AS PETER THE PIGEON.'

I smile wanly at the people around us whose interest is understandably piqued by this outburst. 'Come on, you two,' I say, my voice low. 'We've got a wake to get to. And our bloody father is going to be there.'

Without another word they link their arms through mine.

'I hope there's wine,' I mutter.

'I *know* there's tequila,' Serena smirks, opening her handbag and pulling out a bottle.

'God bless you,' I breathe as we head for the cars.

Chapter Four

When I reach the house, I pull up alongside Serena's sleek Mercedes and Lil's custom lilac Toyota hybrid. Unsurprisingly, they have both arrived before me. Chugging stoically along the motorway, watching them nimbly dip and weave around traffic and disappear into the distance had felt like a rather heavy-handed metaphor for my life.

The house, welcoming and lopsided, looks the same as it always does, apart from the mess of parked cars and the discreet security presence. I wonder if the handful of burly men with rigid posture – who are trying to blend into the bushes in the front garden like that Homer Simpson meme – are here with one of the guests, or if Mum organized them. Either way, I'm glad. At least the paparazzi won't feel it's an invitation with the front gate standing open.

The atmosphere is already carnivalesque, with guests spilling out the doors, drinks in hand. I reflect for a moment that aside from the fact that everyone's draped in black, it could be one of the coven's legendary happenings.

The mums didn't throw a lot of parties when we were little, but every once in a while something impromptu would occur – they'd have a group of friends to stay and then a few more people would join and suddenly there was music and dancing and pale green cocktails in empty jam jars. The crowd would always be an interesting mix of artists, musicians, writers and other creative types, and that made for extremely fun parties.

The mums didn't tolerate any really bad behaviour, and the odd joint or bit of skinny dipping in the river was the most scandalous thing we ever saw, though we were never left unsupervised so I can't speak to what else went on behind closed doors. I can say with confidence that it wasn't the RIPP'S LADIES' CULT SEX-ORGY that one headline claimed.

('Just say orgy,' Ava had sighed, shaking her head. 'The word sex is redundant here.' She tapped at the paper with one scarlet nail. 'Remember girls: words, when used precisely, are weapons. You don't need to *slobber* over them.')

Now, I see – as I push my way through the kitchen doors – that most of the people at Carl's funeral have taken the opportunity to get a look at the site of all those years of scandal. It makes my skin itch seeing them all here. I don't think it is my imagination that several faces I pass display disappointment. *Where*, I can almost hear them wonder, *are the sex dungeons and piles of Class-A drugs?* I see one man examine Mum's Orla Kiely sugar cellar hopefully, but after lifting a casual finger to his mouth his expression drops. It must be devastating to discover that Dee Monroe doesn't sprinkle her porridge with cocaine.

The kitchen is my favourite room, right at the centre of the house. It's massive and full of light, made up of three of the original rooms knocked together, with wonky stone walls, sanded beams on the ceiling, and a wall of French windows that open up onto the garden. There's an ancient Aga, glass-fronted cupboards bristling with mismatched china, two large, squishy sofas, and a wide oak kitchen table which has all our initials carved into the legs, as well as the word FUK emblazoned on the underside in wonky, sloping letters added by a daring six-year-old Serena.

Hidden, badly spelled swear words aside, this room is the opposite of rock 'n' roll. It's the centre of our family – it's where the six of us spent most of our time: it's where we shared family dinners, where we did our homework, it's where we played games on the floor, where we drooped over the sofas when we had tonsillitis while Mum fixed us steaming mugs of honey and lemon.

Speaking of Mum, here she finally is, drifting into the room shrouded in a black silk kaftan-style dress. She's holding a bottle of champagne in one hand, which she uses to top up people's glasses as she passes, pausing to commiserate and offer comfort.

'Clementine!' Her face lights up when she sees me. Dee Monroe is irresistible and even I, after so much exposure, am not immune. She looks like a pixie, full of mischief – heart-shaped face, huge grey eyes, a wide, infectious smile. She has pale, porcelain skin that burns easily, and her auburn hair is cut short, showing off her slender neck and killer bone structure. She moves like a dancer and has the husky singing voice of a French chanteuse who chain-smokes Gauloises.

When she wraps me in her arms she smells the same as she always does, of Pears soap and Diorissimo, a perfume she chose when she was eighteen because it made her feel like a character in a Jilly Cooper novel. She gives me an extra squeeze, which I know is because I finally came clean about the whole losing-my-boyfriend-and-my-job thing, and I hug her back, holding on for a long moment.

'Hi, Mum,' I say. 'I thought you said it was only going to be a few people?'

'Well, darling, I suppose Carl was more loved than we realized.' My mum looks around her, obviously pleased by the turnout.

'I still don't understand why you're the one hosting his wake,' I say in a low voice, and even I know I sound peevish.

'You know he didn't have any family,' Mum blinks, her face sad. 'It's what he wanted, and he was a good friend to us.'

Guilt churns in my stomach. 'I'm sorry,' I reply. 'You're right. I just hate seeing all these people in the house, but of course it was the right thing to do. It was a lovely service.'

Mum puts an understanding hand on my arm, but accepts the change of subject. 'It was, wasn't it?' she says. 'Although I think there was some sort of commotion at the back near the start. I didn't catch what was happening, did you?'

I shake my head innocently. 'No, no, I didn't notice anything.'

'There you are!' I see Serena and Lil pushing their way through the crowd. Mum embraces both of them.

'It's a fucking scrum in here,' Serena huffs.

'Love the veil,' Mum says, stroking the lace that hangs around Lil's shoulders.

'Where are Petty and Ava?' I ask, scanning the room.

'I think they're through in the sitting room with your father,' Mum says, and I try to keep the sour lemon wince from my face. 'Let's go and say hello. They're all dying to see you.' She lifts a hand to her mouth. 'Oops! Unintended funeral humour.'

We decide to cut around the side of the house rather than fight our way through the crowds, and so it doesn't take too long to find the rest of our parents.

Predictably, the room is heaving, with everyone crowded around them while pretending not to gawp openly. There are plenty of celebrities at the wake, not that I recognize many of them (Carl had worked very successfully in the music industry for over forty years after all), but the sight of Ripp, Ava and Petty sipping champagne together is admittedly a compelling one.

I catch the eye of one man trying to take a sneaky picture with his phone and scowl. He drops the device in his pocket like it has scalded him. My shoulders are so tense I have to force them down from around my ears. *I hate this, I hate this, I hate this.*

The furniture has all been pushed to the side of the room and people cluster in groups. Ripp's hand is round Petty's waist and she smiles up at him good-naturedly. Petty – short for Petunia – is the sweetest person on the planet, and she's never had a bad word to say about Ripp. She was only seventeen when she had Lil – Ripp was almost forty, so I'm really not kidding when I tell you he's the worst – and she always says she grew up in this house too. She works as a costume designer for various theatre companies, and is a talented artist. With her long blonde hair and blue eyes, she and Lil pretty much look like twins, though Petty doesn't have a musical bone in her body.

Ava on the other hand is looking at Ripp the way she always does, with a slightly dazed sense of *what was I thinking*? I stifle a laugh at the exasperation in her eyes, the arms folded across her chest. Ava looks like a supermodel – almost six foot tall, rich brown skin, ink-dark hair pulled into a smooth chignon, a wide, sulky mouth. She was in law school when she had Serena, and she's a top human rights lawyer now. Many better men have trembled beneath her flinty glare, but if Ripp picks up on the fact she doesn't like him much, he's not showing it. Then again, he always has been oblivious to subtlety.

'There are my girls!' he booms now, delighted to see us, and uncaring about the heads that turn in our direction, the interest from the crowd more shameless now that he seems to be inviting it. I have a sudden flashback to the time I was seven and we stopped at a motorway services. Ripp swanned in and yelled, 'Good morning, Watford Gap!' like he thought he was Robin Williams, then did an impromptu autograph signing. I got knocked down by the enthusiastic crowd and hid under a display of microwaveable burgers.

My father didn't notice until we were back in the car and my knees were bleeding. Carl cleaned up the blood with a handkerchief and slipped me a cherry drop while Ripp was on the phone with his girlfriend of the week.

Serena kisses him on the cheek. 'Hi, Dad,' she says.

'So sorry about Uncle Carl,' Lil adds, giving him a quick hug.

'Ripp,' I say with a cool nod. I keep out of his immediate reach, positioning myself beside Ava, who pulls me into a warm hug instead.

'Clemmie,' she murmurs in my ear. 'I've missed you.'

'I've missed you too,' I say, returning the hug. With my life swerving so spectacularly off the rails it's been a while since I've managed to drag myself home. I know that the mums want me to move back, stop wasting money I don't have on rent, let them fuss over me, but I'm thirty-two years old. It feels like coming home would be the final admission of defeat and I can't bring myself to do that yet. I am choosing to see this as a positive – it's possible that there is some fight left in me after all. A teeny, tiny drop anyway.

'It's been a while since I saw you, Clementine,' Ripp says. 'You're looking more and more like your mother every day.'

'Really?' I shrug. 'Must be the hair colour. I don't see it myself.'

'My *most* beautiful wife.' Ripp ignores my cold tone and focuses his sparkle on my mother, who grins.

'Ripp, I was your only wife,' she says.

'There was just no getting over you,' he sighs, pulling her hand to his lips.

That seems in rather poor taste seeing as he fathered children with two of the other women standing there, and he's probably being circled by no less than seven ex-girlfriends, but Petty and Ava are used to his theatrics and no one reacts. I always think it's strange in these situations, how everyone else seems content to *let Ripp be Ripp*, while I want to fling a drink in his smug face.

'As I recall, you got over me by getting under a vast number of women,' Mum says. 'They just had the good sense not to marry you.'

Ripp's smile only widens.

'Let's go and get out of our coats and have a real drink,' Serena says, putting her hand on my arm.

'Good idea,' I reply, happy to let myself be dragged back towards the wide stone entrance hall where a bar has been set up, complete with bartender.

I unbutton my coat and hand it to Serena. Her mouth drops open.

'Fuck, Clemmie! Good for you,' she says, taking in my outfit.

'Woah!' Lil agrees. 'Len who?'

I tug at my dress. 'Don't even start,' I say. 'It's my only black dress and I have obviously put on some weight since I last wore it.'

'Yeah, in the boob area,' Lil says gesturing to the low cut

of my dress where there is, I have to admit, a good bit of cleavage on display. 'Oh my God, do you think we, like, reawakened *all* our old spells the other night?'

I laugh. 'What, you mean my boobs are just going to keep growing exponentially because of the magic wish I made when we were twelve?'

'Smothered to death by her own boobs.' Serena shakes her head. 'What a way to go.'

'I think all of me has just got a bit bigger, and the boobs are part of that.'

'Well, you look super-hot and it suits you,' Lil replies, her eyes taking in the otherwise quite demure black dress. It's simple, short-sleeved, scoop-necked with a flared skirt that hits somewhere below my knee.

I would agree with that. I'm probably somewhere between a size 16 and 18, and while I obsessed over my weight as a teen, these days I'm quite happy with the soft, dimpled body I see in the mirror. I guess that's one of the gifts of good therapy.

'Now where are those drinks?' I say as Serena stuffs all of our coats inside the cupboard that still houses things like our childhood wellies and several broken tennis rackets (Lil is a surprisingly sore loser with a real John McEnroe streak).

We make our way to the bar and the bartender flashes us a smile. He's extremely good-looking – floppy blonde hair, soulful blue eyes, maybe late twenties. 'What'll it be?' he asks.

'Got any tequila?' Serena lifts a brow.

The man shakes his head regretfully. 'Sorry, ladies, I've got champagne, wine, beer, gin, vodka or whiskey.'

'I don't suppose the mums were expecting people to do shots at a funeral,' I say.

'That was their mistake.' Serena grabs the bottle of Patrón from her bag and hands it to the bartender like it's a precious newborn. 'Hide that in the fridge back there for me, will you? But give us three glasses with some ice first, please.'

He's more than happy to do so, especially because passing Lil her glass means their fingers can brush lingeringly. Lil's cheeks pink, and so do his.

'I'm Henry,' he chokes out.

'Lil,' my sister manages, and they look at each other as though there should be a halo of tiny blue cartoon birds circling both their heads.

'And I'm Serena and this is Clemmie,' Serena cuts in, oblivious to all the delicate romantic vibes buzzing in the air. 'You guard that tequila with your life, Henry. If these old soaks get wind of it, it'll be a massacre.'

'You can count on me,' Henry says gamely, pouring three extremely large shots of tequila into our glasses before hiding the bottle at the back of the small fridge behind him.

'Right.' Serena takes a fortifying sip. 'Should we go and see what the parents are up to?'

'Do we have to?' I whine.

'Would you rather make small talk with a load of people in the music business?' she asks slyly.

I remain mutinously silent.

'Didn't think so.' Serena sails forward. 'Come on, Lil,' she calls over her shoulder.

Lil and Henry are just standing, silently smiling at each other.

'Lil?' I shake her by the arm.

She turns to me, her pupils so wide she looks as if she's been taking hallucinogens. She makes a noise that sounds like, 'Waaa?'

I stifle a laugh. 'We're going back through.'

'Oh . . . yeah . . . right . . .' she says, visibly collecting herself. 'See you later, Henry.'

'See you later, Lil,' Henry whispers, and my sister melts like he's just quoted Shakespeare.

When we return to the sitting room it's to find Ripp centre stage – he's telling a raucous story that involves him and Carl and a stripper they picked up in Las Vegas, and everyone around him is laughing. I know this story because I remember seeing the paparazzi photos of my father stumbling out of a club with his arm around a topless woman. It was the same week he didn't turn up to my thirteenth birthday party.

'Why don't you give us a little tune, Ripp?' someone calls. 'Something for Carl?'

'Oh, Jesus,' I mutter under my breath.

'Oh no, I couldn't possibly,' Ripp says with a bashful wave of his hand, though his eyes drift towards the piano in the corner of the room.

'Yes, yes, go on!' more people start joining in.

'Dee?' Ripp says, looking at my mum, and there's a frisson of excitement, something electric that zaps through the crowd.

Mum rolls her eyes good-naturedly. 'I don't think so, Ripp.'

'You know Carl would have loved it,' Ripp wheedles. 'He was always on at us to sing together.'

'That's true, Dee,' Petty puts in.

Mum blinks, and I think there are tears in her eyes. 'Oh, all right,' she says. 'For Carl.'

With that, she makes her way to the piano, Ripp loping along behind. When she sits down in front of the keyboard, she doesn't hesitate, just lifts her hands and brings them down, a crash of chords as she starts singing 'Girl From the North Country'. Her voice is still beautiful: warm honey spilling through the room. Ripp joins in with her and, say what you like about the man, he can really sing. Their voices blend perfectly; something magic is happening and everyone here knows it. There's a collective holding of breath, a stillness.

'This was Carl's favourite song,' Petty whispers, her cheeks already wet with tears. 'God, she's wonderful.'

My hands are curled into fists, as I look at my mum, at Ripp. I see the flash of someone taking a photo. Finally, I pull myself away, take a step backwards, then another, and another, until I'm out of the crowd.

Until I back right into someone. Their hands come up to my arms to steady me, and even before I turn around I know who it's going to be. Perhaps it's the smell of his aftershave – he was always a little too heavy-handed with the stuff and it seems that habit hasn't altered – or perhaps it's the deep, apocalyptic sense of dread that tips me off, but either way, I know.

Slowly I turn around. 'Hello, Sam,' I say, and I'm relieved to hear that my voice at least is steady, even if the rest of me feels like I'm on a boat adrift in choppy waters.

'*Oh, my darlin' Clementine!*' He twangs the words in a faux-cowboy impression and if I didn't already viscerally hate that song with every fibre of my being then this moment would have done the trick. The man who almost broke me grins down with a lazy, lop-sided smile. It is a smile that once set butterflies loose in my stomach, a smile that made me feel giddy. Now there's just a dull feeling of nausea, that swooping sense of falling from a great height.

Of course he's here, in my house, today. It's as if that bloody spell has summoned him.

Sam Turner – the original victim of the curse, the boy who broke my heart at seventeen – is actually pretty famous now. He's still good-looking, with his long, sandy hair, and tall, rangy body, but he's more polished than the scruffy young guy I remember. I've seen pictures of him, but have managed to avoid meeting him in the flesh for almost fifteen years. It wasn't hard – we don't exactly move in the same circles.

'You're looking good,' he says, giving me a not-so-subtle once-over. 'But then you always were gorgeous.' The smile grows, his blue eyes crinkle at the corners, tiny lines that weren't there the last time I saw him.

Over the years I have imagined this – meeting Sam again.

Sometimes I imagine screaming at him, punching him right in the nose. Other times I imagine demonstrating an icy poise as he grovels in front of me. In none of my imaginings did I picture him acting as though nothing ever happened. I never thought that I would simply stand, frozen, heart pounding as he smirked and made small talk.

He leans casually against the wall, drink in hand. 'So how have you been? What have you been up to? You're a teacher, right? I was hoping I'd run into you. Your dad wasn't sure if you were coming or not.'

Something short-circuits in my brain. Even now, in this moment, I'm dimly aware that I'll regret running away. I can't do anything but gape at Sam, can't even begin to sift through the wild range of emotions that the sight of him, and the words coming out of his mouth, have set churning inside me. He's here, in my house. He's been talking to Ripp about me. Ripp is here too.

'I have to go,' I manage to choke out, and then I shoulder past him, through to the hallway.

There is only one thing for it now.

'Henry,' I say grimly, marching over to him. 'I'm going to need that tequila.'

Without a word he hands me the bottle and I snatch it, running upstairs and down the hall until I reach my bedroom door. I burst through, ready to throw myself face down on the bed.

'Hello,' a voice says. 'Are you okay?'

Chapter Five

There's a boy in my room. Those are the only words my scrambled brain can seem to latch on to as I stand with my back against the door, heart pounding, bottle of tequila clutched in my hand. *There's a boy on my bed.*

And he's the most beautiful thing I've ever seen.

'What are you doing in here?' I manage. I'm still reeling from the encounter with Sam, and now *this*? Someone is definitely messing with me. Just what exactly did Lil put in that frying pan?

'Sorry,' the boy (who is actually a man) says. 'I couldn't stand another minute of that lot. Do you live here?'

'N-no,' I say, because that is true, at least for the time being, and I'm clinging to the fact. I'm also trying to catch up with the scene in front of me.

Mum has left my bedroom untouched since I moved out and it's still the room of my childhood: a bookcase full of battered books about ballet dancers and pony clubs, a small dressing table crowded with crusty Rimmel nail polishes and dried-up tubes of mascara. Beside the single bed, a poster of Geoffrey Chaucer is pasted on the wall next to one of Ryan Gosling in *The Notebook*. The bed itself is currently occupied by the beautiful man sprawled across my soft floral duvet cover.

He moves now, swinging his legs so that his feet hit the floor and he's sitting up, his back against the wall, the top of his head brushing the bottom of the Ryan Gosling poster. He looks like he's in his late thirties, inky hair that curls slightly in a way that makes you want to plunge your fingers into it, dark eyes lit with mischief, which stops the rest of his face from looking too severe – otherwise he's a series of sharp corners, straight lines, perfectly symmetrical.

I realize he's the pall-bearer from the funeral, and once again I feel that keen-edged slice of lust. It's not helping with the shock of finding him in here. On my bed.

'I'm Clementine,' I blurt.

'Clementine?' The hard line of his mouth softens, and his smile causes all the air to leave my body.

I nod, before continuing inanely, 'My mum says she chose it because clementines are the friendliest fruit.'

The smile widens, revealing the ghost of a dimple in his left cheek. Not totally symmetrical after all. 'And why,' he asks, 'did you have to be any kind of fruit at all?'

'Believe me, I have asked that question many times,' I grumble, regaining a little of my poise. 'And the reasoning remains unclear. *Imagine* being a small ginger girl called Clementine.'

He laughs, and the sound zings through me. I instantly want to hear it again.

'My mum *still* calls me Teddy,' he says. 'If it helps.'

'It does,' I reply. 'If even a very sensible name like Edward can be got at by embarrassing mums, then maybe I don't need to feel so bad.' His mouth opens as though he's going to say something, but I press on nervously. 'Most people call me Clemmie, anyway.' I hold up the bottle of tequila. 'Would you like a drink?'

He pats the bed next to him. 'I won't, thank you, but do you want to join me? We can hide out together?'

'Who says I'm hiding out?' I take a step closer. 'Maybe I was having a great time down there.'

'The giant bottle of tequila suggests otherwise.'

'Fair enough.' I take a deep breath and plonk myself down on the bed beside him, careful to leave space between us so that we're not touching. I undo the bottle and take a short swig, wincing.

'So, how did you know Carl?' Edward asks.

'He was an old family friend,' I say. I sit back underneath the poster of Chaucer, lean against the cool wall, my feet dangling off the side of the bed.

'I'm sorry,' he replies. 'Were you close?'

'I actually hadn't seen him for a long time. He was a nice man though, from what I can remember.'

Edward smiles. 'Yeah, he was a good guy.'

'You were a pall-bearer, weren't you?' I ask awkwardly. 'I mean, I think I saw you in the church. How did you know Carl?'

He shifts a little. The sleeve of his shirt brushes lightly against the side of my arm and my brain empties apart from the sound of white noise. I notice that he's taken off his dark suit jacket and tie – they're folded over the back of my pink desk chair. The top button at his collar is undone, and my gaze snags on the tiny triangle of skin I can see at the base of his throat.

'We'd known each other for years,' he says finally, and I drag my attention back to the conversation. Good grief, where's a good crucifix to focus on when you need one? Staring at an earnest and lovelorn Ryan Gosling is simply not going to have the desired effect.

'But I was surprised to be asked to be a pall-bearer to be honest,' Edward admits. 'I guess I just didn't realize he didn't have any family or anything. It's sad.'

'Yeah, it is,' I agree, 'but there were tons of people at his funeral, and hundreds here at the wake. He obviously touched a lot of lives.'

Edward is silent for a moment, and his mouth is firm again, the humour gone from his eyes. He looks unhappy and I hate that.

'And at least you didn't drop him,' I say, the words coming out quickly before I can think about them too much.

That surprises a crack of laughter out of him. 'Exactly.' He turns so that he's looking straight at me. 'I was so worried about that. You know when you just get a terrible thought stuck in your head? I should have been concentrating on feeling sad about Carl, this big honour or responsibility or whatever, but inside my head there was just this chant going,

Do not drop the dead man, do not drop the dead man. And then that sat nav started going off . . .'

I groan, my hands flying to my face.

'No!' He sits forward now, voice gleeful as he gently pulls my hand away. His fingers wrap around my wrist and I half expect my skin to start throwing off sparks. 'That was you?'

'Of course it was me.' I groan again. 'My life is just one giant disaster at the moment.'

'Oh God, that was so funny,' he chuckles. 'I mean, I know it was a funeral, but when that voice started yelling *Make a U-turn*, it took everything I had not to burst out laughing. I had to focus all my attention on this giant Jesus hanging on the wall who looked like an Action Man figure who'd been put through the microwave . . .'

'That's exactly what he looked like!' I exclaim. I realize he's still holding on to my wrist, and his face is closer to mine now. He's grinning at me, and the dimple has deepened. I can't look at him straight on; it's like looking at the sun: so dazzling it hurts. I shift, pulling my hand away and taking another sip from the tequila bottle. It burns down my throat.

'So why is your life one giant disaster, Clemmie?' Edward asks.

'Oh, you know, the usual story,' I say, fiddling with my skirt. 'Got dumped by my cheating boyfriend who is having a baby with the other woman, lost my job, soon to lose my flat.'

'Oof!' Edward winces, his head falling back against the wall. 'That is very, very shit. Your boyfriend is clearly an idiot.'

'He took my cat,' I say in a small voice.

'Bastard,' Edward says flatly.

'Yup.' I close my eyes. 'And as if that's not enough, I've just bumped into *another* ex.'

'Another bastard?'

I laugh, but it's a hard sound. 'The king of them, actually.'

'Ah,' Edward says knowingly. 'First love?'

'Something like that. I didn't handle it the way I would have liked . . . I know I'll regret that later. And then I've got to deal with my family situation and that's . . . complicated.'

'Family can be complicated,' Edward agrees. 'My sister once played an extended prank on me where she pretended to be a poltergeist called Colin who lived in my bedroom.' This surprises another laugh out of me, a real one this time, and I'm grateful for the change of subject.

'Do you have siblings?' he asks.

'Two sisters,' I smile. 'And we've all played a fair amount of tricks on each other, though I don't think any of them were poltergeist-related.' The slight buzz from the tequila triggers a rush of warm affection for Lil and Serena. 'We *are* possibly magic, though. We did a spell.' I don't know why I say that last bit, but there's something about Edward and being in my old room that has me feeling comfortable.

'What do you mean you did a spell?'

'It's something we used to do when we were kids, pretending to be witches, and when my sisters came round the other night we dug out an old spell we had cast. The breakup spell. We set fire to a frying pan and cursed Len.'

'Len?' There's a quiver in Edward's voice.

'My ex-boyfriend,' I explain. 'We read out the same spell from when I was seventeen and cursed him, which was extremely cathartic, and then we made three wishes for me, one each.'

'What were the wishes?'

'The wish I'd made back then was for a job I love, which actually felt a bit like the universe playing a mean joke given the current circumstances.' When I glance at him, he's already looking back at me. His eyes are so dark, but now I see there are flecks of a lighter, golden brown around his irises. 'I've been working really hard to get to where I am in my field, and it constantly feels like one step forward, two steps back.' I feel a soul-sucking weariness crash over me at the thought of more job applications in my future. 'But I guess focussing on your career is the best course of action when your love life is in the toilet,' I say, like I'm trying to convince myself.

'And what were the other wishes?' he asks.

'Oh, um, one of my sisters wished I'd fall in love – big, soulmate love. She's the optimist in the family.'

'And the other one?'

I feel a flush rising to my cheeks. 'She wished for hot sex.'

'Hot sex?' His eyebrows lift, but otherwise he seems unaffected.

I nod, trying to appear equally nonchalant. 'I've been with Len for a long time,' I shrug. 'I've always gravitated towards serious relationships. And my sisters, they think I need to be a bit more . . . sexually adventurous, I suppose, a bit more casual. Have the odd one-night stand.'

'I see,' he murmurs. And there's something in the way he says the words that has heat unspooling in my belly. 'And is that what you want?'

'I don't know,' I whisper. 'Maybe.'

We're so close together now that it would only take the tiniest movement for my mouth to be on his. I don't know how that has happened, we must have been leaning towards each other, increment by tiny increment, without my noticing.

But I'm noticing now. I can smell him, and he smells delicious, like cool, clear sea air cut through with something citrusy and what must presumably be a shit ton of super sexy pheromones because my whole body feels like it's lighting up. I want to bury my face in his neck and just *inhale* him, and something of that crazy desire must show in my face, because there's a change in the air around us, crackling like the feeling before a thunder storm, and he stills.

'Maybe we should find out?' he asks quietly.

My heart is hammering, and I see his gaze drop to my mouth. Before my courage can desert me I lean forward and press my lips to his. It's a quick kiss, hardly anything, the softest brushing of lips, and yet I feel it all the way down to my toes. I jerk back.

'Sorry,' I blurt. 'I'm so sorry, I shouldn't have done that. Not without asking. It was rude, bad idea, I—'

'Clemmie,' he interrupts. Then he plucks the tequila

bottle from my hand before placing it carefully on the nightstand. 'I think it was a very good idea.'

Then – so gently – he cradles my face, his thumb stroking along my cheekbone before he pulls me in and kisses me.

And he *really* kisses me. It starts slowly, as if there's all the time in the world. Lazy, drugging kisses that melt into one another, leaving me dizzy. I can feel him smiling against my lips. I'm floating out of my body, *delighted*. My mouth opens under his and I let out a sound like a sigh.

The angle changes, and the kiss suddenly deepens. I grab onto his collar, his fingers spear through my hair, and then I'm climbing into his lap like I can't get enough of him. The way he tastes, the way he feels – in my mouth, under my hands.

Desperate, urgent want, like nothing I've ever experienced, is barrelling through my body in waves. My teeth nip his bottom lip and he growls, kissing a light trail from the corner of my mouth round under my ear, and down the side of my neck. He pauses on my collarbone and I have never previously realized what an erogenous zone that is but now it's all I can do not to scream. I yank him back, wanting more of him, wanting this wild, electric kiss that's searing into my bones to carry on forever. I twine my hands around his neck and press myself against him, the pressure of my chest against his sending us both further over the edge.

Finally, we pull apart. We are both breathing hard. His pupils are blown wide, and I'm sure mine are as well. Two more of his shirt buttons are open though I have no memory of undoing them. His hair is deliciously rumpled. He has my red lipstick smeared across his face.

'I-I—' I stutter. 'I mean that was . . . I . . . we . . .'

'Yeah,' he breathes. 'Yeah.'

His eyes are on my mouth again, and then they drop to my chest which is actually *heaving* like I'm the lusty heroine in a spicy regency romance novel.

'Where are you staying tonight?' I ask him.

He shakes his head, as if trying to clear it, frowning at me in confusion. 'Er – some hotel in town.' He manages. 'Why? Where are you staying?'

'With you?' I try to throw the words out confidently, like a statement, but they come out a slightly quavering question.

Edward's eyes widen and that smile takes over his face again, the blinding one that shows off his dimple and does strange things to my insides. 'Yes, Clemmie,' his voice is husky, kissed rough as he pulls me to him again. 'With me.'

Chapter Six

The sound of running water wakes me up the next morning and I sit bolt upright thinking my flat is being flooded. But this isn't my bed, these aren't my sheets twisted around me, and this definitely isn't my flat. Instead, I'm in a very nice hotel room, and the running water I hear is the sound of the man I had mind-blowing sex with last night, having a shower.

I pull the one-thousand-thread-count white sheet to my chest and flop back against the goose-down pillow, a wild, unmanageable grin spreading across my face as I let it all flood back in – the kissing, the touching, the *heat*. So many images fluttering through my mind like sexy confetti.

Like when I ripped his shirt open and got my hands on his beautiful chest, my fingers running over the flat, hard muscle there, and then when I pushed the shirt off his shoulders and it revealed that both his arms were covered in tattoos from shoulder to wrist. I don't know why it was so insanely hot, to pull away that crisp, white shirt and find all that surprising, swirling ink underneath, but it was. I had stopped then, straddling his lap, spent time trailing my fingers over biceps and forearms, finding scrolling acanthus leaves weaving through geometric patterns, punctuated with hothouse flowers open and blooming, until Edward had groaned and I realized he was watching me with hungry, horny eyes.

There was more kissing. Greedy, desperate kissing. Sinking back into this bed with his weight pressed into me, the full, hard length of him just where I wanted it.

There was the moment when he had wrenched himself away, carefully, so carefully, and asked, 'Are you sure you want to do this? We can stop. We can stop any time.'

I blinked up at him, my lust-dazzled brain struggling for words.

'Yes, please,' I said. 'More now. Yes. Please.'

He laughed and returned to kissing me until I was light-headed.

There was the image of his beautiful hands, his long, clever fingers touching me, cupping me, teasing me, the rough, sandpaper feel of his jaw against my chest, my stomach, my thighs.

There was the first orgasm – the one that tore through me, left me seeing stars, panting and giggling like a maniac. My confession that I could only ever finish once and I personally thought all this talk of multiple orgasms was a fairy tale.

I hadn't meant it to sound like a challenge, but he'd taken it that way, taking his time using his mouth, his fingers, whispering sweet, dirty words until I came apart again, even more violently.

Exhausted, the last thing I remember is curling against him, resting my head on his chest while he smoothed the hair away from my face. The steady thump of his heartbeat under my ear.

And now he is in the shower.

I have never had a one-night stand before and I have no idea about the etiquette.

I turn my head towards the bathroom but the shower is still running. Levering myself out of bed, I realize my muscles ache like I've been to the gym and I know I'm still grinning because my cheeks are starting to hurt too. I scoop up my underwear and my clothes from where they are scattered around the room and quickly get dressed.

Then I stand awkwardly in the middle of the room. Should I stay? Staying seems to imply expectations. Breakfast and cuddling and all those other things which are part of being a couple, all the things that I usually do after sleeping with someone. But not now, that's the old Clemmie talking. So do I sneak out? Is that rude?

I bite my lip in indecision and catch a glimpse of myself in the mirror. My hair is sticking out all over the place, my cheeks are pink, my mouth swollen, my eyes look huge and my expression is one of dazed bewilderment – basically the night of carnal activity is written all over me. Reaching inside my handbag I find a hair bobble and scoop my long, tangled hair up into a sloppy bun. I rub underneath my eyes to remove the panda smudges of mascara, and dig out a slightly dusty extra-strong mint which I pop in my mouth. *There*, I think, *practically human*.

My phone is also in my bag, and I realize the battery is about to run out. There are messages from my sisters and from my mum, from after I texted them to say I was going home early and that I'd talk to them later. My WEIRD SISTERS group text has gone wild:

Serena: Ugggggg how could you leave us here?? The olds are getting wasted.

Lil: Henry says he saw you earlier and you were leaving with a man????

Lil: And you two looked v cosy???

Serena: WTF Clemmie??? When you said you needed an early night I had no idea . . . 🍆🍆🍆 👀 😏

Lil: The hot sex spell is ALREADY WORKING!!!!!!

Serena: You're welcome.

Lil: Omg. Henry invented a new cocktail and called it 'the Lil' 🖤🖤🖤

Serena: Meet you by the booze shortly.

Lil: Wooooo! The Lil is STRONG. Vodka, gin and white wine. About to havE my third!

Serena: The Lil is disgusting. I do not think Henry is a real bartender.

Lil: ShuT up, tastes reall good. Henry is a carpernter like JESUS. Henrys face is a poet.

Serena: Lil is practically mounting Henry on the

bar. I cannot believe you left me to deal with this. This better be in aid of some 🔥 sex. At least there is tequila to numb the pain.

Serena: CLEMMIE

Serena: WHERE IS THE TEQUILA???

Serena: CLEMMIE

Serena: CLEMMIE

Serena: CLEMENTINE GRACE MONROE

Serena: I take it all back. May you have incredibly mediocre sex.

Lil: HenrY kiss Lil kiss !!!!!!!!!!!!

Serena: Lil puked in your old wellies. I hope you're happy now.

There's also a notification reminding me of my appointment today. Oh, shit. In a turn of events that is entirely in keeping with my life at the moment, I am going to be late for therapy, unless I run out on my one-night stand *right now.* That feels like a sign from the universe, right?

I grab the notepad and pencil from the desk and chew my lip for a moment.

Dear Edward,

I write,

Thank you very much for a lovely evening. I really appreciated your time and effort.

What am I doing? Why do I sound like an elderly woman thanking him for cleaning out my attic? (I can already hear the joke Serena would make here – *'More like your basement, Clem.'*)

I crumple up the sheet of paper and try again.

Edward,

I had a great time, thank you.

Clemmie x

That will have to do. Before I can think better of it, I gather my belongings and creep from the room, pulling the door quietly shut behind me. I hurry down the hallway, scrabbling in my bag for my car keys. Thank God I had the sense to have Edward drive us here in my car last night so that I could make a speedy getaway.

I take the lift down to reception and keep my eyes on the ground as I push through the revolving door.

FLASH!

A light pops in front of my eyes, followed by another and another. My body instantly revolts, heart hammering, throat tightening.

Cameras. Cameras everywhere.

'Oh, sorry, love,' a man shouts as the camera flashes suddenly cut off. 'Thought you were someone else.'

I grasp wordlessly at the collar of my wool coat, pulling it tight around me. Blinking against the bright dots still swimming in front of my eyes, his words register and I realize they're not there for me. Air starts to filter back into my lungs. It's been a long time since I was exposed to the paparazzi, and that moment of blind panic leaves me dizzy.

I wobble along on unsteady legs in the direction of the underground car park, concentrating on pulling in slow, deep breaths. I remember Edward saying something about a lot of the people at the wake booking rooms in this hotel, so it makes sense for the photographers to descend on a spot where multiple celebrities are likely to be appearing a little worse for wear the morning after.

For all I know my dad is staying here and they're going to get eight hundred photos of 'brave Ripp' grieving his dear friend. The thought makes me queasy for more than one reason. It's definitely time to jet out of here because I think being caught sneaking away from a man's hotel room by my famous father in front of a wall of cameras might be my own personal worst nightmare.

I reach the safety of my car and press play on my audiobook, feeling the exhilaration of earlier creeping back in. I can't believe I did that. I can't believe that I, Clementine Monroe, had a one-night stand with the most gorgeous man on the planet, and it was *so* good. So good that it's possibly ruined sex for me forever, but that's a whole other issue. Serena and Lil are going to be unbearable.

It starts to rain and my windscreen wipers squeal across the window. I tap the steering wheel, full of an unfamiliar sense of energy and genuine elan. Who knew that casual sex could be such a mood booster. (Again, I hear Serena's voice: '*Everyone, Clemmie, literally everyone knows this.*')

Just under an hour after leaving the hotel, I pull into the outskirts of Oxford, up to the practice where my therapist, Ingrid, has her office.

She buzzes me in and even though I'm only a couple of minutes late I feel flustered into a rambling apology, which Ingrid observes in silence.

'I'm so sorry,' I huff, flopping into the spotless white silk armchair, and dropping my bag on the floor. 'I overslept after the wake last night and I had to rush back here.' I proceed to ramble about the traffic, about the hotel, about the fact that I spent the night with a man I had just met and how I had to extricate myself from my first one-night stand. All of this comes out in one breathless wall of speech.

Ingrid doesn't even blink. 'Would you like me to take your coat?' she asks.

'Yes, please,' I say, standing up and unbuttoning it. I hand it to her and she calmly hangs it up on a coat stand next to her own navy Barbour jacket, before taking the seat across from me.

There is a table between us with a jug of water and two glasses on it and Ingrid pours me a glass, which I accept gratefully.

I've been seeing Ingrid every couple of weeks for almost two years now, and I don't really want to focus on the fact I may not be able to afford her much longer. She's in her late forties, with short silver-white hair and wide green eyes behind thick-framed glasses. Her sense of chilly detachment gives her incredible cool-head-girl energy. I want her to like me with a rabid passion that is presumably part of the reason I am in therapy to begin with.

She dresses like a member of the British royal family on their days off – as if she's about to go hop on a horse at a moment's notice, sort of vaguely tweedy, with knee-length boots and the occasional gilet. I know very little about her, except that her husband is English and she has a daughter in secondary school.

Ingrid's accent has a Scandinavian edge, and her face is so still that I'm never sure if it's been pumped full of Botox, or she's simply incredibly good at her job. Possibly, it's both.

Like Ingrid, her office radiates a sense of intense calm. There's minimal furniture: a huge, modern-looking glass desk with a sleek computer, a notepad and a single pen all at perfect right angles; a bookcase full of alphabetized books; and the coffee table between two chairs. Everything is gleaming white, with soft grey accents, and it always smells like those candles no normal person could possibly justify spending money on.

Ingrid is, as I mentioned, unflappable, and for some reason this often makes me want to get a reaction out of her. Now, as always, she displays no signs of shock at all.

'So,' she says after a moment, 'you spent the night with a man?'

'Yes!' my head is bouncing like a nodding-dog toy. 'And you know, that's so out of character for me, but it was great.'

'I'm glad to hear that. How do you feel about it this morning?'

I frown down at my glass. I've been having therapy for years, and I do enjoy the chance to sift through my emotions – the way that I can speak to Ingrid without filtering things first. It's a strange way of talking to someone, verbalizing thoughts and feelings that seem to shimmer vaguely at the edge of your mind. 'I feel good,' I say slowly. 'Sort of elated. It was . . . nice, very, very nice, and I had to make a choice to do it, when I could have just played it safe and gone home alone, which is definitely what I would usually have done. It felt . . . weirdly brave?'

Ingrid nods.

'And I thought this morning I would feel guilty or . . . I don't know, a bit regretful. But I don't, I really don't. I'm starting to wonder if we actually did make Serena's wish come true!' I laugh.

Ingrid does not. 'This would be in reference to the wiccan ritual you and your sisters performed?'

'Ha!' I exclaim, but Ingrid's look is one of mild inquiry. 'I mean . . . yes? I'm not sure the drunken breakup spell we cast could really be described as a *wiccan ritual* . . .'

'But you refer to Serena's wish for' – Ingrid consults her notes here – 'hot sex?'

There's a pause. I clear my throat.

'Right. Hot sex. Which it was. The only thing is . . .' And I trail off here.

We sit in silence for a while. Ingrid wields silence like a

weapon, a ninja assassin highly trained in the art of stillness. It would not surprise me if MI5 used her to break terrorists this way. I'm certain people would be falling all over themselves, giving her nuclear codes left and right while she sat quietly and sipped from a glass of water.

'I feel a bit sad about not seeing him again.' The realization hits me with full force even as the words are forming. 'Even though I don't really know him.'

We sit with that for a moment, and Ingrid writes something in her notebook.

'When you write in your notebook, I feel like something important has happened,' I say, happy to change the subject.

'These are just my notes, Clemmie,' Ingrid says neutrally.

'I know,' I agree, 'but of course everyone wants to know what their therapist thinks about them, don't they? And sometimes, when I say something and you write it in your notes, I feel like I've made a good point and you're, you know, noticing that.'

'You think my notes are me marking you?' she asks carefully. 'Like a teacher marks homework?'

I nod. 'Yes, like you're writing down when I'm doing well, being really good at therapy.'

'Clemmie.' If I didn't know better, I'd say there was a touch of weariness in Ingrid's voice now. 'We have talked about this before. You aren't being graded. You can't be good or bad at therapy. It's a process.'

'Sure, sure,' I wave my hand, 'but obviously *some* people can reach breakthroughs quicker, can be more in touch with their feelings, more honest with themselves about things. I don't think it's unreasonable to want to be *the best* at therapy. You're always saying it's good to set goals.'

Ingrid makes another note in her book. Presumably about how insightful I'm being.

'Do you want to talk about the funeral?' she asks. 'I know you were anxious about possibly seeing your father.'

'Seeing him is always hard. He acts like everything is fine between us when we have no relationship at all. It makes me feel like I'm going mad – like I imagined everything, all the different ways he let me down.'

I slump down in my chair. 'What is there to say? The man is a terrible person. Being related to him is a nightmare and I wish I never had to see him again.' Now *there's* a wish I should have been making.

Ingrid's pen scratches against the page.

I suppose it's possible I'm not the best at therapy after all.

Chapter Seven

Any belief that we have unleashed the decades-dormant power of the breakup spell is quite firmly quashed by the events of the next few weeks.

First, there is no more hot sex. As predicted, Serena and Lil were delighted about Edward and demanded many more details than I was comfortable with giving. Since that night there has been no communication between the two of us, obviously. And while that was the plan, and it's not like we knew much about each other, I can't help but think that if Edward really wanted to he could have tracked me down. After all, how many Clementines were at Carl's funeral?

Second, my job comes to an incredibly anticlimactic end.

Third, there is certainly no big love/soulmate on the horizon. Nor is there likely to be seeing as I have basically retreated to my flat (which I have had to give notice on), where I am living like a grumpy, unwashed hermit subsisting on packets of ramen and share-size bars of Dairy Milk.

And fourth, and the real low point of low points: Len appears to be flourishing in a thoroughly uncursed-like way.

'I don't know why you keep looking at it,' Lil says as I drape myself dramatically across her sofa. 'Who cares what that idiot is doing?'

I stare at the photo on Instagram – Len and Jenny are on a beach, he has his arm around her, their faces squished together, close to the camera, beaming. Her hand is held up, showing off her diamond ring.

'Len hates the beach,' I grumble, sitting up to better show Lil the picture. 'He tells people he's allergic to sand. Remember when I tried to get him to go on that all-inclusive holiday to Menorca and he acted like I'd suggested a romantic escape to Mordor?'

'What's Mordor?' Lil asks.

'Never mind.' I sigh.

'It's irrelevant, anyway,' Lil says, striding back and forth from her bedroom to the living room with armfuls of shiny, colourful fabric which she dumps beside me. 'This is just further evidence of what we already know: Len is the worst. What I want to know is why you're still following him on Instagram anyway?'

This is quite a good point, so I decide to ignore it.

'It's not like *I* want to be with Len,' I say, 'but it's very galling to have my life fall so spectacularly apart while he waltzes off into the Instagram-filtered sunset with another woman.'

'And I get that,' Lil replies soothingly, 'but I can't let you waste your time dwelling on Len, when we have a fabulous party to go to.'

I moan, flopping back on the sofa. 'I'm not really in the fabulous party mood.' It's been a rough few months and I think I'm *entitled* to a bit of dwelling, a good old sulk. I didn't even tell my sisters about my run-in with Sam at the funeral, reluctant to open up that can of worms, and they haven't mentioned him either so it's possible their paths didn't cross. I'd love to say that the encounter didn't throw me, but it did, and I've spent quite a bit of time thinking about exactly what I *should* have said to him. It's been a really fun little addition to the running list of regrets that plays on a loop while I try to go to sleep.

Lil ducks down beside me, her face close to mine. 'Clemmie,' she says in the voice of someone talking to a small, truculent child. 'Do you think Serena is going to let you miss her birthday party? Is that something you think our sister would be very calm and accepting about? Or do you think she would be very, very angry and make the lives of both you and your entirely innocent younger sister a total misery?'

'The second one,' I say flatly. 'The misery.'

We all tend to celebrate our birthdays in different ways. Serena's way involves a big party, and has made a natural progression from the Powerpuff Girls and ice cream sundaes to nightclubs and themed cocktails. (Although she did still make us dress up as the Powerpuff Girls for a Halloween party last year.) Attendance is absolutely mandatory, as are presents.

'Correct.' Lil is brisk now, standing up and gesturing to the piles of clothing. 'The misery. So stop sulking and help me choose something to wear because I've invited Henry tonight, and I need to look spectacular.'

'Henry would think you looked spectacular if you were wearing a black sack and a ridiculous veil, because that is *literally* what you were wearing when you met him, and you spent the night superglued to his mouth.'

Lil smiles coyly. 'I know, but I haven't seen him all week and I want to wow him.'

Lil and Henry have been pretty inseparable since the funeral, and it would be easy to hate them if they weren't so adorable. 'You really like him, don't you?' I ask.

Lil fiddles with the dress in her hands. Her smile is shy, like she's keeping a secret. 'Yeah,' she says softly. 'I mean, it's early days, but I really do.'

'Ugh. *Fine,*' I groan, pulling myself to my feet. 'Show me the outfit options.'

'Yay!' Lil's eyes brighten and she dives for the pile of clothes. The next ten minutes are spent cat-walking several different ensembles across her tiny, but dazzlingly expensive central London flat. We finally settle on a rainbow-striped silk jumpsuit which looks amazing on her.

'Hair up or down?' she asks.

I tip my head, considering. 'Down.'

She nods. 'I'll curl it a bit, I think. Loose waves?'

'Perfect,' I agree.

Lil hands me a sheet mask to put on my face while she

curls her hair and does her make-up. Her eyeshadow is bright pink and sparkly, and while I do the back of her hair, she sticks little star-shaped gems around her eyes. When she's done, she beams at me. She looks like a glamorous My Little Pony. 'Now, what about you?'

'Oh,' I gesture towards the bookshop tote bag that I shoved all my stuff in. 'I've got jeans and a nice top in there.'

Lil's look is withering. 'Jeans?'

'And a nice top,' I say defensively. After all, I even showered for this event.

My sister rolls her eyes. 'It's a good job I took matters into my own hands.'

I am instantly suspicious. 'What does that mean?'

Lil flicks me a quick grin and then disappears into her bedroom, emerging triumphantly clutching a whisper of fabric covered in gold sequins. 'I made you a dress!'

'Nope,' I say, shutting this down immediately. It's not that Lil can't sew – Petty taught her how to make her own clothes when we were teenagers – it's that her taste has always been significantly more daring than mine and this led to some *questionable* fashion choices in the mid-noughties.

'Come on, Clemmie.' Lil sticks out her bottom lip, big blue eyes looking at me all hopeful. 'At least try it on, I worked really hard on it.'

I feel like an ungrateful, heartless witch and cave immediately. 'Okay.' I hold out my hand. 'I'll see if it fits.'

Lil's face lights up with victory and I'm reminded yet again that she has us all wrapped around her little finger.

People think Serena is the one to worry about, but Serena has the subtlety of a steamroller. Our whole family will tell you that Lil is much more likely to talk you into doing her bidding without you even realizing the whole thing wasn't your own idea.

'Oh, it will fit,' she says confidently now. 'I made it to show off all those curves. Just trust me, you're going to look ridiculously hot.'

I strip off to my underwear and then tangle with the dress, which I'm pleased to see has a decent amount of stretch in it. When I finally get it over my head and tug it over my chest, the material slithers softly down my sides. It fits like a dream.

Lil starts squealing at a pitch only dogs can hear. 'Oh my God, amazing!' She takes my hand and pulls me over to the mirror.

I look doubtfully at my reflection, tugging at the hem of the dress. 'It's really beautiful Lil, but don't you think it's a bit short?'

The dress is lovely, completely covered in gold sequins, with long sleeves and a sweetheart neckline that sits wide on my shoulders and shows off a decent amount of cleavage. It hugs every curve, clings lovingly across my soft belly, over my hips. It's also the sort of length that we used to roll our school uniform skirts up to, in order to scandalize our teachers.

'You look gorgeous,' Lil says firmly. 'And honestly you'll blend in much better at this party in that dress than you would in a pair of jeans. Don't forget it's going to be all

Serena's super-glam work friends, and they don't know the meaning of the word casual.'

I am well aware that my sister knows how to manage me, but this is exactly the right thing to say. If she thinks dressing me up as a disco ball will help me fade into the background, then I'm all for it.

'Okay,' I sigh. 'If you're sure.'

'Of course I am. Now let me do your hair and make-up and then we can call an Uber.'

I don't bother arguing as Lil twists my hair, braiding it up in a loose crown on top of my head and leaving a few wavy tendrils to fall on my bare shoulders. She puts some magic stuff on my skin that makes it smooth and shimmery, pencils in perfect flicks of black eyeliner, and then paints my lips a dark, vampy crimson.

'There,' Lil says, finally satisfied as we stand side by side in the mirror. 'Let's take a picture.' She snaps a photo of us on my phone and swiftly uploads it to Instagram.

'Len's not the only one moving on, Clemmie,' she says softly.

I take the phone from her outstretched hand and look at the post. She's captioned it with an orange emoji and a flower emoji, and we look great. Arms around each other, matching heart-shaped faces and clear-eyed grins. I feel my spirits lift.

It occurs to me then that this is precisely why Lil insisted I come round to hers to get ready first, so that she could work her magic and give me a pep talk. I feel a lump in my throat and pull Lil back into my arms again. 'Thanks,' I say a little gruffly into her shoulder. 'The dress is so beautiful, and I know I've been wallowing lately. It's nice to get dressed up. You were right.'

'It's going to be such a good night, you'll see.'

I try to share in Lil's optimism as I slip on my shoes and we gather our stuff, ready to head out to the Uber that's waiting downstairs.

Chapter Eight

Our driver, Marcus, doesn't even blink as Lil and I wrestle two giant number-3-shaped helium balloons into the backseat of his very small car. The two of us end up in hysterics, me inside with the balloons and Lil trying to pretzel her way into the gaps.

'I should have ordered a six-person car,' Lil pants. 'No offence, Marcus!'

Marcus smiles the infinitely patient smile of a man who has dealt with an extreme amount of nonsense. 'Maybe you should just sit in the front?' he suggests.

'Oh my God, Marcus! You're a genius. I can't believe we didn't think of that. I mean I can believe *I* didn't, but Clemmie is supposed to be the clever one.'

'Hey!' I protest as Lil shuts the door on me and my inflatable friends. 'I was distracted.'

Lil scoots round to the front, and Marcus delivers us without further ado to the swanky bar that is hosting Serena's birthday party.

The venue is located down a small side street in Mayfair,

and I know Serena well enough to be certain that the discreet black-on-slightly-darker-black sign and unassuming building are not an indication of what we'll find inside. Having been checked off the guest list by a woman in a sleek black dress, and having bypassed the beefy security guards, we find ourselves ushered through to a dimly lit bar that is part nightclub, part botanical garden – full of beautiful people, vibrant green palms and pastel-coloured orchids. The air is warm and scented with something spicy.

A huge, square-shaped bar is in the middle of the room; a dance floor has been cleared at one end, and at the other there are candlelit booths with deep green velvet banquette seats. We're quite early, but there are already plenty of people here, and something with a pulsing beat pumps through the speakers, drawing people out to dance.

As a girl drifts past me wearing what looks like a halo and a bin bag full of snakes, I'm filled with gratitude towards Lil for her intervention, because the vibe is definitely less 'jeans and a nice top' and more 'what if a Bond girl joined the circus'.

Serena spots us straightaway (though the giant balloons are surely a help) and emerges from the crowd in a flowing red silk dress, an elaborate gold crown resting on her head. No hats or badges for Serena, who somehow manages to be both more subtle and way more ostentatious than that at the same time.

'Happy birthday!' Lil and I screech.

'Thirty-three!' Serena shakes her head as we hug and hand over the balloons. 'Almost a third of the way to my first centenary. I've been waiting for you two to get here.'

'It looks like you've got plenty of people to keep you company.' I gesture to the crowd.

'Oh, them.' Serena wraps her fingers around my arm and starts tugging me towards one of the booths, Lil following in our wake. 'Yeah, the label invited a bunch of people – not that I mind because they're picking up the drinks tab, but that's not why I wanted you to arrive.'

'No?' I ask, sliding carefully into one of the seats, Lil alongside me.

'No!' Serena stows the balloons in the corner and turns to me with a wide grin. 'I've solved all your problems.'

'What do you mean?' I ask.

'Have you seen Henry?' Lil asks, twisting in her seat. 'He texted me to say he arrived a while ago.'

Serena snaps her fingers. 'Lil! Focus! You're about to bear witness to my genius.'

'Oh God,' I groan, 'whenever you start talking about your genius it never ends well.'

'Yeah, like with the guinea pigs,' Lil puts in. 'The ones you said we could keep as secret pets, hidden from the mums.'

'I was eleven. And the guy told me both those guinea pigs were male. How was I supposed to know they'd start reproducing at such a rate?' Serena blazes indignantly. 'But you're both about to eat your words. Clemmie, I've got you a job.'

'A job?' I repeat. 'Doing what?'

Serena wiggles in her seat. 'That's the best bit. It's the jammiest gig you'll ever have. We've got this artist at the label who's really, really overdue delivering his new album, right?'

'O-kaaaaay,' I say, drawing the word out.

'And so I've come up with this brilliant plan to get him off the grid so that he can have a writing retreat, really knuckle down and get it done.' Serena leans forward. 'And I don't mean "celebrity off-the-grid" where he's in some mansion surrounded by his entourage and the press camped outside. I mean really off the grid. Petty has said we can borrow Granny Mac's house.'

My stomach swoops. Granny Mac's house. High up on the Northumberland coast, it was the place we spent all our long summers while growing up, running wild, living half-feral. We loved it. It was also the site of some of my most painful memories, the place where we cast the final breakup spell. I haven't been there since, but it seems as though that part of my life won't leave me alone at the moment.

'Oh yeah, Mum mentioned that,' Lil says. 'Such a good idea. That space will be, like, a creative *haven*.'

'I know.' Serena looks pleased. 'It works out perfectly with the timing. Petty doesn't have anyone renting it right now because she's just finished the renovations, and it's in the middle of nowhere with zero distractions and no one who will freak out over him being there. There's literally nothing for him to do but work.'

'Serena, I'm very confused about how any of this is leading towards a job for me,' I say.

'Is that Henry?' Lil suddenly shrieks, clambering all over me. 'Henry! Henry!' She breaks off. 'Oh, no, wait. That's not him.' She slumps back in the seat, not moved by my complaint that I have now lost the hearing in my left ear.

'Right, so the label want to send someone to Northumberland to keep an eye on things, and act as a sort of housekeeper, but one who reports to us. Not his friend or his assistant, someone who *we* employ. That's part of the deal,' Serena says, completely ignoring Lil's outburst. 'And I suggested you. You practically grew up in the house after all, and you know the area really well.'

'You want me to babysit a musician in Northumberland?' I ask, vaguely horrified by the whole idea. And not just the musician part. There's a reason I haven't been back there.

She nods and holds up a hand. 'Before you say no, hear me out. The job is a piece of cake; you'll probably hardly even see him. It's for six weeks starting the week after next and the pay is *incredible*.' She drops a figure that has the blood draining from my face, and then starts ticking things off on her fingers. 'You wouldn't have to move in with the mums; you could work on that dreary book you've been writing for years, and apply for jobs – all while getting paid and building up some savings. It's a no-brainer, Clemmie.'

When she puts it that way it does sound pretty perfect. Like the answer to many, many of my problems in fact. But surely this was all too easy? And I haven't exactly had the best experience when it comes to rock stars.

'Who is it?' I ask.

'Theo Eliott,' Serena says, and Lil gives up looking for Henry long enough to turn and face Serena, her mouth hanging open.

'Holy shit, Serena! Theo Eliott?' Lil's voice is breathy.

'You're going to *pay* Clemmie to shack up with Theo Eliott for six weeks?' She grabs a bar menu off the table and starts fanning herself. 'You lucky duck. That man is gorgeous.'

'Who's Theo Eliott?' I ask.

Serena rolls her eyes and Lil lets out a groan. 'This is why you're perfect for the job,' Serena says. 'You're way too much of a grandma to be starstruck by him. He's only one of the biggest musicians on the planet, Clemmie. Used to be in The Daze before they split up, then had a massive solo career? Fourteen number-one singles? Sell-out world tours? Eight Grammys? Theo Eliott!'

'Oh yeah,' I say. 'Actually, the name does sound familiar. And The Daze, I remember them. Didn't they have that one song about the girl who worked at the Post Office?'

'Coffee shop,' Serena sighs. 'But yes, anyway, this is another reason you'd be good for the job. Theo's great, but he has a bit of a reputation and we need someone who won't be too charmed by him, to keep things on track.'

'What do you mean a bit of a reputation?' I ask, instantly on guard.

'Oh, no, no, nothing bad,' Serena rushes in. 'I'd *never* ask you to do the job if I thought he wasn't a good guy. I just mean he sort of . . . dazzles people into doing what he wants. But we need him focussed, and you won't let him slack off.'

'Hmmm. I suppose I'm not easily dazzled. And certainly not by a famous musician.' I shudder.

'See!' Serena grins. 'It's your daddy issues that make you the perfect candidate!'

'That's not funny,' I grumble.

'He's coming along tonight,' Serena says, her tone wheedling. 'Just meet him and then decide.'

'I don't know . . .' I say, still hesitant.

'I think it could be really good for you to get away,' Serena says, and anxiety threads through her voice. 'And you'd be doing me a *huge* favour. Getting this record done is a big deal. There's a lot of pressure on me from my bosses, and I have to make sure Theo delivers. I've worked really hard to sell them on this plan so I need things to go without a hitch. Please, I need you.'

I exchange a look of concern with Lil. This is deeply unusual. As the oldest – even if it is only by a matter of months – Serena has always been the problem-solver of our trio, and if history is anything to go by, she has to be pretty desperate to ask me for a favour. 'Of course I want to help you,' I say, biting my lip, 'but I don't know the first thing about making an album – I can't possibly be the best person for the job. You shouldn't be worrying about me and my employment status; you should do what's best for you.'

'This *is* what's best for me. You're smart, organized, and used to dealing with anxious undergrads on a deadline,' Serena points out. 'I don't need a musician; I need someone who I know and trust to handle this. Whatever happens I know you'll do what you can to keep him focussed, and that you'll tell me the truth about how he's getting on. Anyone working for him would be worried about *him*, but you won't. Getting good information that I can feed back to my bosses is the whole point.'

'You should meet him, at least,' Lil pipes up. 'I know him a bit and he seems really nice. What do you have to lose? Remember, Clemmie . . . you're moving on.'

I gnaw on my lip. 'You're right. Sure, I'll meet him.'

'Perfect,' Serena exhales, some of the tension leaving her body. 'I'll go and see if he's arrived yet.'

'And I'll go and get a drink,' I say. 'I think meeting my potential new super-famous roommate calls for a cocktail.'

'And I'm going to go and find Henry and drag him off to a dark corner,' Lil puts in brightly.

'You two have been at it non-stop.' Serena grimaces.

'It's the hot sex spell.' Lil's eyes are round. 'I told you we were some seriously powerful witches. The magic has, like, spilled over.'

'Can't say I've noticed,' Serena says with a feline grin, 'but then I'm always having hot sex anyway.' And on that note we go our separate ways.

I notice the crowd has grown considerably as I weave my way through, squeezing by with plenty of muttered 'excuse me's' until my elbows rest on the bar.

I lean my chin on my hand, expecting a long wait, but one of the bartenders makes a beeline for me straightaway.

She's very pretty with long dark hair, and a lip piercing. 'What can I get you?' she asks me.

'Um, Martini please,' I say. 'Dirty.'

'Sure, and for your friend?' Her eyes slide to the person next to me, her smile widening into something predatory.

'Oh, I don't—' I begin, turning to follow her gaze, but the

words die on my tongue and my heart stutters in my chest because standing there, smouldering down at me, is Edward.

We stare at each other for a beat, and I swear the music stops and all the other people in the bar just melt away. He looks good. Really good. His hair is a bit longer and his face is unshaven, his jaw covered in dark stubble. He's wearing black trousers, a black shirt open at the collar, and a black silk jacquard jacket covered in a pattern of red roses. There are silver rings on all the fingers of his right hand. There's something piratical about him that is deeply attractive, and given the attention he's drawing I'm not the only one who thinks so.

He turns to the bartender, offering her an easy grin. 'I'll have a soda water with lots of ice please,' he says, before his attention returns to me. 'Hello, Clementine.' His voice is velvet, the smile he gives me setting off some sort of nuclear reaction in my blood stream.

I'm sure my mouth must be hanging open.

'Edward!' I finally manage. 'What are you doing here?'

'Ah,' he grimaces, 'about that . . .'

'There you are!' Serena is suddenly beside me, having elbowed her way through the crowd. 'I see you beat me to it.' She beams at Edward and then at me. 'Clemmie, have you introduced yourself to Theo?'

I blink. 'Theo?'

'Yes.' Serena gestures to Edward. 'This is Theo Eliott. Theo, this is my sister, Clementine.'

Chapter Nine

'This isn't Theo,' I say, confused, at the same time as Edward says, 'Clemmie is your sister?'

The bartender places our drinks on the bar and leans forward to make sure Edward gets a good look down her black tank top. He keeps his eyes on me and I'm not proud of the smirk that puts on my face, but some cavewoman part of my brain wants to wrap myself around the man and hiss at her like a cat.

My God, Clemmie. Calm down.

My sister is frowning at me and for a moment I worry she can read my mind. 'What are you talking about, Clemmie?' She puts a hand on Edward's arm, tugging him forward. 'This is Theo Eliott.'

'No,' I say, putting my hand on his other arm. '*This* is Edward.'

'Clemmie,' Edward interrupts softly, putting his hand over mine. 'I was just trying to tell you: my name's not Edward, it's Theo.'

I'm so thrown by the way my body reacts to his warm hand covering mine that it takes a beat too long for his words to reach me. 'W-what?' I ask when they finally do.

Theo-not-Edward says nothing, but removes his hand and sips from his drink. I think he looks nervous.

'Edward?' Serena's face is baffled for a moment, then her eyes round in shock. 'As in Double-O Edward?' she hisses.

Theo splutters into his glass, and I wonder if I have perhaps died and am in some sort of previously unwritten-about circle of hell. Dante would absolutely love this shit.

'Double-O Edward?' Theo repeats, and there's a slow, delighted grin spreading across his face.

'Don't you dare smile at me,' I snap, flustered. The reality of this bizarre scene is starting to sink in and I feel queasy. I poke him in the chest with my finger. 'You're really telling me you're not called Edward?'

A look of chagrin passes over his face. 'Yes. I mean no,' he says, 'I'm not called Edward.'

'And you are, in fact, this Theo Eliott person who is a famous musician?' I continue, my voice deadly calm.

'Um, yes,' Theo says meekly.

'So why did you tell me your name was Edward?'

'Actually I didn't,' he says, and the smile flickers back to life, though it's more muted now. 'I told you my mum calls me Teddy, which she does, and you extrapolated from there.' He looks pleased with himself.

I think back to our conversation, try to remember if what he says is true. 'Teddy is short for Theodore?'

He nods.

'But why didn't you correct me?' I ask, and I can feel that my calm is slipping now, but I cling on to it for dear life.

'That's hard to explain,' he says.

'Try,' I grind out.

He runs a finger round the rim of his glass. 'I suppose at first it was because you didn't know who I was, and that was something of a novelty. And then . . . I got distracted.'

'Distracted!'

'Yes, and I honestly forgot about the whole name thing until the morning when I saw your note. I would have told you the truth then . . .' – he pauses here and treats me to a stern look from under his brows – 'but you had already disappeared. Snuck out while I was in the shower.'

'You're not going to make me feel bad about anything when you—'

'Hold on,' Serena jumps in here. Up to this point she's been silently observing our back and forth like she's watching a tennis match, but she seems to have gathered her wits. 'I think we need to move somewhere more private for this conversation.'

She glances over her shoulder, and I notice that several people are showing interest in our little group. At the moment they're all at a polite distance, and the music is quite loud, but that might not last. And there's also every chance that I'll end up shouting.

I glance at Theo's handsome face. Oh yes, there will definitely be shouting.

Stiffly, I follow Serena as she cuts through the crowds, very aware that Theo is walking close behind me. At one point someone steps out in front of me and tries to talk to him. Theo mutters something, his hand on the small of my back as he guides me past, his body curving protectively around mine. I shake him off as soon as possible, trying very hard to be unaffected by the tingling feeling that insists on running up and down my spine.

We duck through a door that says EMPLOYEES ONLY and climb a flight of stairs, eventually ending up in a small office that presumably belongs to the manager.

As soon as we're over the threshold, Serena whirls on Theo. 'Let me catch up here. Are you telling me that you slept with my sister?'

'I didn't know she was your sister,' Theo says, holding his hands up in front of him.

Serena whacks him on the arm. 'Not the point, Theo! You are an absolute liability. Do you have to sleep with everyone?!'

Something flickers across Theo's face at that, something that looks almost like hurt, but it's replaced by that charming smile so swiftly that I wonder if I imagined it. He leans back against the wall, his arms folded. 'I would say that what happened between Clemmie and me was just between the two of us, but it seems you've already had a thorough report.'

'Oh my God,' I mutter, swigging from the Martini glass still gripped tightly in my fingers. (At this point they would pry the booze from my cold, dead hands.) 'How can this be happening? I slept with someone and I didn't even know his name? And he's a *famous rock star*?'

'Your tone is confusing,' Theo says. 'Which of those two things is worse?'

'The rock star thing.' I take another long drink. 'Definitely the rock star thing.'

'Huh.' Theo sounds nonplussed.

'Put it together, genius,' Serena snaps, throwing herself into the chair behind the desk. 'If Clemmie is my sister . . .'

'If she's your sister then . . . she's also Ripp's daughter,' Theo says slowly. 'Oh shit.' He looks at me. 'You're Ripp's daughter?'

'And you know my father,' I groan. 'Of course. This just gets better and better.'

'Clemmie, you are the only person in the world who could pick up Theo Eliott and not know about it.' Serena rubs her forehead. 'This is what comes of being a cultural recluse.'

'I'm not a *recluse*!' I exclaim hotly. 'I hardly think knowing or not knowing a guy who makes a living singing about Post Offices is an indicator of how culturally engaged a person is.'

'Post Offices?' Theo frowns.

'She means coffee shops,' Serena says. 'Clemmie doesn't acknowledge the existence of music made past 2003. It's a whole thing.'

'I'm not living on another planet,' I break in, as Serena and I fall into the familiar argument. '*Lots* of people prefer audiobooks or podcasts or . . .'

'Boring people. *Elderly* people,' Serena snorts.

'Podcasts are the fastest growing media format in the world!' I hiss. 'Michelle Obama has her own podcast, Serena. Michelle. Obama.'

'I'm confused.' Theo looks bewildered. 'Why are we talking about Michelle Obama now?'

'Well, this has thrown a fucking spanner in the works,' Serena says, tapping her fingernails along the edge of the desk. She clearly recognizes the introduction of Michelle for the conversational checkmate that it is, and has therefore decided to pretend none of the argument ever happened. 'The whole point of Clemmie going to Northumberland was supposed to be so there'd be no distractions.'

'Clemmie is the babysitter you want to send with me?' Theo's face lights up. 'Suddenly, I don't hate the idea after all.'

'Well, I do!' I say firmly. 'I'm not spending six weeks trapped in a house with you.'

'Worried you won't be able to keep your hands off me?' Theo sighs lustily.

Now it's my turn to sputter into my drink. 'Absolutely not,' I hiss. 'I don't want anything to do with you!'

'Then I don't really see the problem.' Theo turns to my sister with a shrug.

'Theo,' Serena chides him. 'This isn't a game, and you're in deep shit with me for upsetting Clemmie.'

'Hey!' Theo objects. 'I'm the injured party here. I'm the one who got dumped with a three-line note while I was having a shower.'

'You didn't get dumped,' I say stiffly, putting my empty

glass down on top of a filing cabinet. 'It was a casual thing, remember.'

'And there was me thinking I was special.' Theo straightens up, stepping towards me. My traitorous body reacts to his nearness, heat washing over me. 'But now that we've found each other again,' he continues in a softer voice, 'are you going to let me buy you a drink?'

'The drinks are free,' I croak, staggering back like I'm trying to break away from some sort of sexy-rock-star tractor beam.

If flirting were a professional sport, then Theo Eliott would take home the gold. I realize, with a sinking feeling, that the chemistry I had with Edward – the chemistry that I thought meant we had a connection – is just something Theo has with everyone. He's a flirt, a womanizer, and I fell for the whole act like an idiot. You'd think I'd know better.

'You might as well stop that right now,' Serena says to Theo, as if reading my mind. 'I can absolutely guarantee that you'll get nowhere with my sister. It doesn't matter if you turn the charm up to eleven; she'd rather chew off her own foot than go out with a flirty rock star.'

Theo pulls back, a flash of surprise in his eyes. He glances at me.

I nod, cross my arms. Serena is completely right: whatever small fantasies I'd been quietly nurturing about running into Edward again are dead and buried in the face of the revelation that the man is actually Theo Eliott.

If Theo really is initially surprised by this, he shrugs it off almost instantly. When he speaks again his voice is soft, more serious than it has been. 'Then there really shouldn't be a problem with Clemmie taking the job.'

Serena starts to speak again, but Theo holds up his hand. 'Can I have a word with Clemmie, alone?'

My sister eyes him narrowly. 'Why?'

Theo's poise slips a little, and he snaps, 'For fuck's sake, Serena, I'm not about to ravish her; I just want to talk in *private*.'

Serena's eyes dart to me and I nod. 'You should get back to your party,' I say. 'I can sort this out myself. People will be wondering where you are.'

She gets to her feet and pushes away from the desk. 'Fine.' She points a finger at Theo. 'But you'd better be on your best behaviour, or I swear I will . . .'

'Curse me, I know.' Theo holds up his hands.

'Actually, I was going to say methodically destroy your entire life.' Serena smiles back at him, showing her teeth. 'But yeah, the curse thing too. Don't know if you're aware of this but my sisters and I are some pretty powerful witches. If you ask Lil she'll tell you we killed a man.'

Serena sweeps out of the room, pulling the door shut behind her, and Theo exhales loudly. 'Your sister scares the shit out of me,' he says.

'I'm sure she'll be delighted to hear that.' I move to perch on the edge of the desk, wishing I had another drink which would at least give me something to do with my hands.

'Look,' Theo starts, coming to stand in front of me, 'I'm sorry about the whole name thing. I didn't think about it from your side, and that was really selfish. I hope you can forgive me, but I understand if you can't.'

I'm thrown by the simple sincerity of the apology. 'Oh,' I say. 'Okay.'

'And about the job . . .' Theo clears his throat. 'You should take it. If you want to. I absolutely promise to leave you in peace. Despite what your sister seems to think, I am 100% in control of my own libido. You're not interested, I get it, and totally respect that.'

'I don't think us working together is a good idea,' I say, my brain trying to catch up with his words.

'Have you found a new job?' he asks gently.

I shake my head.

'And I take it Len hasn't come to his senses?'

I forgot how much I had told him. 'He got engaged.' I try to keep my face and voice neutral but I'm not sure I succeed.

Theo mutters something under his breath that doesn't sound complimentary.

'And if I hadn't been me,' he starts, then breaks off with a frown. 'I mean, if Theo Eliott and Edward weren't the same person . . . would you take the job?'

I tug at the hem of my dress. 'I think so, but—'

'Then you should take it. I know you've had a shit time recently, and I'm guessing this job could help you out. I have to be in the UK for a family event anyway so I'm staying either way. Who knows, maybe Serena is right and this will be good for me. We'll forget anything ever happened between us and it will be completely professional.'

I look up at him. He's not wearing his usual winning smile; instead his face is serious. His dark eyes bore into mine and he seems utterly genuine. *Forget anything ever happened between us*? How can I, when the night we spent together is branded on my brain? Would it really be so easy for him to ignore what had happened between us?

Of course it would. He's a rock star. You know a bit about that. He has women throwing themselves at him all the time, a constant stream of one-night stands. Serena said he dazzles people, and you were just another person who fell for his charm. That night probably barely registered for him.

It is this thought that reawakens the spark of pride in me, and I'm so grateful for it. If he can forget what happened between us then so can I. It wasn't real. I didn't even know who he was. Of *course* I shouldn't let a silly, insignificant thing like that stop me from accepting a job. I'm hardly going to let him think that I'm pining for him, unable to move on.

My spine straightens and I pull myself up to my full height. 'Fine,' I say crisply, holding out my hand. 'Completely professional. It's a deal.'

'A deal,' Theo replies, and he wraps his hand around mine to shake on it.

I only imagine him pulling me in for a scorching kiss for a fraction of a second.

A new job with the man I had hot sex with. If I didn't

know better, I'd say the universe certainly has a sense of humour when it comes to those wishes we made.

This will be fine. Six weeks alone together. In the middle of nowhere. Completely professional.

I glance up at Theo's face, then down to where his fingers gently rest against the pulse in my wrist.

Who am I kidding? This is going to be a disaster.

PART TWO

Chapter Ten

I change my mind about working with Theo approximately one thousand times over the course of the following week. My first mistake is looking him up online, which I do as soon as I get back to Lil's flat from Serena's party.

Theo Eliott.

About 372,000,000 results, Google tells me. Right. Fine.

And there he is. The man I met at a funeral, the man I spent the best night of my life with. There he is, all over the internet.

There are so many photographs, so many articles about him, interviews, fan sites, videos, blogs, tweets, photo shoots. I start clicking through but soon feel sick. It's just too much, way too familiar. The frantic headlines, the shitty paparazzi pictures.

There's plenty of speculation on his love life, and from what I can see a long, long list of models and actors and musicians who he's dated or hooked up with. Headline after headline about *Theo Eliott, the Heartbreaker*; *Theo Eliott, the*

Womanizer, and each one makes my heart sink further. Do I know better than anyone how many lies get printed in the newspaper? Yes. But do I know that the papers probably haven't covered even half of my own father's toxic behaviour? Also yes.

I told Theo I'd take the job. More importantly, I told Serena I'd take the job, but as I shut down all the tabs on my laptop I just don't know if I can do it.

By the time I have my next session with Ingrid I'm a seething, writhing mess of indecision.

'Your sister has offered you a job?' Ingrid asks, pen poised over her notepad.

'Yes, but it's not so straightforward.' I squirm. 'You remember the man I had the one-night stand with a couple of months ago?'

Ingrid nods.

'It involves working with him. *For* him I suppose. Just the two of us alone for six weeks in the middle of nowhere.'

Ingrid's head tilts thoughtfully. 'And you're concerned that your history may make things . . .' – she pauses for a moment – 'awkward?'

'Yes!' I exclaim. 'Extremely awkward. And not just because we . . .'

'Had sex,' Ingrid supplies.

I huff. 'Yes, had sex. But also because it turns out it's a bit more complicated. He isn't who I thought he was. He's . . . he's a musician. A famous one. His name is Theo Eliott.'

A muscle in Ingrid's cheek twitches. In any other human

being this would be the equivalent of falling to her knees, screaming, crying, and throwing up. I have never seen this happen before. I hadn't even been sure she *had* muscles in her face before this. I feel my own mouth drop open.

'Oh God,' I slump in my chair. 'You know who he is.' This is the biggest reaction I have ever got from my therapist and I feel weirdly jealous that it's Theo who has elicited it.

Ingrid's facial muscles are fully under control when she replies, coolly, 'Yes, I know of him. He's quite famous, Clemmie.' Her tone is mildly reproving but still, there is the faintest tint of pink on her cheekbones and I am fascinated and horrified in equal measure. I think it's possible my therapist has a crush on the man I slept with.

'So,' Ingrid continues after clearing her throat (another thing she has literally *never* done), 'I can see why this revelation may trouble you given your history with your father and your relationship with . . .'

'Yes.' I cut her off before she can bring up Sam, because there's only so much a girl can take. 'It does trouble me. He lied to me. Maybe not on purpose,' I add grudgingly, 'but he did. And before I found out who he was I thought there was some . . . connection between us. Now I know he's just like my dad, and' – I swallow, steeling myself – 'you know. The other one.'

'But Clemmie, as I remember it, you were the one who established the boundaries of your encounter with Theo.' This time Ingrid manages to say his name neutrally.

'That is true,' I agree.

'And that this encounter made you feel' – she consults her notebook – 'brave and elated.'

I wish she'd stop saying *encounter*, like Theo was an alien and our night together had involved some sort of cross-species probing.

'Mmm,' I murmur in agreement.

'But you also said that part of you was sad you wouldn't see him again. Do you have feelings for this man?'

'No!' I say quickly, squashing the traitorous flicker of something like disagreement in my chest.

Ingrid treats me to a long, narrow look. The silence stretches until it becomes a living, breathing thing threatening to crush the life out of me. Ingrid looks like she could do this all day.

'Fine,' I snap gracelessly. 'Maybe I had some small, *possible* feelings for him when I thought he was just some nice stranger at a funeral. But not anymore. I couldn't . . . I can't even imagine . . . there's no way . . . with how things have been for me that I'd ever, ever be in a romantic relationship with a famous musician. Never.' This time my tone is definite, not a hint of room for disagreement. 'Not that he'd want that, either,' I add quickly. 'He doesn't seem the type to be looking for anything serious. It was just a one-night thing for both of us.'

Ingrid's pen flicks across the page and I crane my neck, trying to see what she writes, but I can't make it out. 'If that is the case then what are your qualms about entering into this business arrangement with him?' she asks.

'I . . .' I stop, considering. 'I'm not sure. I freaked out when I saw all the articles about him. It felt so familiar; he's part of that world, the one I don't want to get pulled back into.'

'And is that something you think this job could lead to?' Ingrid asks.

'No?' I say, like it's a question, but then with more certainty I add, 'I mean I suppose not. It's sort of the opposite actually, being away from everything.'

'Tell me more about the job.'

So I do; I explain how it would work, what I'd need to do, how it would be helping out Serena, who never asks for help, how it would solve my housing and financial problems, and as I talk I feel some of the anxiety slipping away. Somehow, laying it all out like this for Ingrid is helping me to see more clearly what a good thing this could be. It's six weeks of my life, nowhere near the paparazzi or the parties or the crowds. And if there really is nothing between Theo and me – which there *isn't* – then there shouldn't be a problem. Annoyingly, this is exactly what he said last week. I guess it has just taken me longer to get there.

'I'm going to do it,' I say after a few more minutes of Ingrid's gentle questions. 'It's a good opportunity for me.'

'I agree,' Ingrid nods, surprising me. She rarely ventures her own opinion. 'I think this could be good for you in lots of ways. It will give you the space and time to think about what you want to do next, and perhaps now is a good time to revisit this place from your past and find some closure. I imagine it may bring up quite a lot of thoughts and feelings so I will be happy to continue our sessions online if that would help?'

And thanks to this job I'll be able to pay for them, I think as Ingrid and I discuss setting up our next appointment in a couple of weeks. *Just another reason this is a good idea.* I'm not sure I love the idea of having a lot of thoughts and feelings brought up, but I leave her office feeling more optimistic than I have in a long time.

Pulling out my phone I dial Serena, whose calls I have been dodging.

'I'm in!' I exclaim when she picks up.

'I should bloody hope so,' my sister huffs. 'I knew you'd spend the week dithering, but I've already told everyone you're doing it and I've got a list of emails as long as my arm from Theo's assistant that I'm forwarding you as we speak. He's your problem now, go with God.'

And on that note she hangs up.

Ping! goes my phone.

Ping! Ping! Ping! Ping!

I experience a brief moment of panic as the phone keeps chiming with notification after notification.

I get back in my car and open up the first of the emails. It quickly becomes clear to me that David, Theo's assistant, is having a major meltdown about leaving his side and I feel as if I will be pet-sitting someone's beloved and extremely fussy little Pekinese.

One email simply says:

NO KIWI FRUIT

The majority of them read like bizarre, middle-class haikus.

YUZU KOMBUCHA
SHIPPING ONCE
FERMENTATION IS COMPLETE

Aside from an extensive amount of dietary requirements there's also: a list of exercise equipment that's being shipped to Northumberland (Where am I going to put it all? Perhaps David expects me to erect some sort of private gym with my bare hands?); an insane list of vitamin supplements and the times of day Theo is supposed to take them; information about transporting precious musical instruments, and all this is before he moves on to a series on Theo's likes and dislikes beginning with films (the cryptic 'NO NICOLAS CAGE!!!!!!!!!!!!!!!!!' with seventeen exclamation marks raises some questions for me) and TV series ('HE FINDS GREAT BRITISH BAKE OFF SOOTHING'.)

I'm not even halfway through the list when my phone flashes up with a call from an unknown number.

'Hello?' I answer.

'Clementine?' A slightly pissed-off, incredibly posh-sounding voice comes down the other end. 'Clementine Monroe?'

'Yes, that's me.'

'This is David, Mr Eliott's assistant. Your sister passed on your number.'

I close my eyes and lean back, hitting the headrest with an audible thump. 'Oh, David, hello. I was just making a start on your emails . . .'

'Right, yes,' David cuts in. 'That's good, I'm glad the lines of communication are open. I have to tell you, I am quite . . . *concerned* about this trip, and about making sure that Mr Eliott has the support he's used to. In order for us to make the transition as seamless as possible I think it's important that we cover all our bases. Perhaps we can organize a video call tomorrow so that I can talk you through the dossier I'm preparing?'

'Right,' I say weakly. 'The dossier. I mean, of course. If you think it's necessary.'

There is a dangerous pause. 'So far the document in question is eighty-six pages,' David snaps. 'I imagine you're going to have some questions.'

'Eighty-six pages,' I repeat in a daze.

'Mr Eliott is a busy and important man,' David continues. 'Our job is to make sure his life runs seamlessly so that he can focus all of his creative energy on the process of making this album. I'm sure your sister has already made it clear to you that the stakes are very high. There are multi-million-pound contracts at risk here, and for whatever reason the wellbeing of Mr Eliott is being placed in your hands. I assume you are planning on taking the job seriously?'

I straighten at that. I hadn't, in fact, considered the multi-million-pound contracts, the weight of expectations pressing down on Serena. I'd been too busy thinking about my relationship with Theo and what that meant. I have a brief flashback to Serena's pinched face when she first asked me to help and guilt twists in my gut. 'Of course,' I say firmly. 'I'm going to take it very seriously. Let's schedule a meeting.'

'I have a window at six forty-five tomorrow,' David says.

'In the morning?' I manage.

'Will that be a problem?'

'No, no.' I already feel like I'd rather die than disappoint this man. Something to raise with Ingrid, perhaps. 'Six forty-five it is.'

'Good, I'll email you the link.'

And then, without any further niceties, the call cuts out.

Ping! Goes my phone.

Ping! Ping! Ping!

I let out a long breath. Okay then. I can do this. I'm a responsible, functioning grown-up. Babysitting a rock star. How hard can it be?

Chapter Eleven

To: Clemmie.Monroe@livemail.co.uk
From: David@Eliottmgmt.com
Re: re: re: re: re: re: re: Milk

YES, it does need to be Andalusian almonds. YES, you do need to make it. No, he cannot have 'whatever they sell in a carton'. YES, he will be able to tell the difference and YES, I WILL KNOW ABOUT IT.

To: Clemmie.Monroe@livemail.co.uk
From: David@Eliottmgmt.com
Re: re: re: re: re: re: re: re: re: Milk

Mr Eliott's bowels are none of your business.

To: Clemmie.Monroe@livemail.co.uk
From: David@Eliottmgmt.com
Re: re: re: re: re: re: re: re: re: re: re: Milk

I have arranged delivery of the almonds from a private producer in Spain. In order to circumnavigate some minor issues with customs they will be arriving in a box marked 'Cleaning equipment'.

To: Clemmie.Monroe@livemail.co.uk
From: David@Eliottmgmt.com
Re: re: re: re: re: re: re: re: re: re: re: re: re: Milk

The almonds will arrive whole, not ground, so no, I do not anticipate you being 'implicated in a drug smuggling racket,' however, I am happy to pass on details of our legal department should you find yourself in difficulty.

I plan to arrive at Granny Mac's house in the afternoon so that I have time to set things up nicely and go to the shop to get the extensive last-minute list of 'essentials' that David has emailed to me, and some real human food for myself. I don't know why I thought, given my current success rate, that things would simply work out the way I wanted them to.

First of all there's an accident on the motorway involving spilled oil, and I sit in four hours of stationary traffic, hoping my car doesn't die. Then, when we're finally moving again, my car *does* die and I have to wait another two hours for the roadside assistance van to come. The driver works in grim silence for a while before finally getting the car started again.

'Not going too far, are you?' he asks hopefully.

'Up to Northumberland,' I reply.

The air whistles out from between his teeth. 'Might want to keep us on speed dial, love.'

On that reassuring note he departs, and I chug the remaining 150 miles while holding my breath, lest the smallest movement should make the car collapse. When I finally do reach the house it's after ten o'clock at night. I had forgotten how light it stays this far north in the summer, so for the last hour of the drive it has felt as though I was keeping pace with the sun, which still hovers ember-orange just above the horizon.

I unfold myself from the car with an audible groan, and gather the carrier bags from the local supermarket, which certainly don't include Theo's specific brand of mineral water or lychee juice, or 90% of the other things on my list. I am already braced for several hundred icy emails on the subject from David.

As if I am a character in a police procedural being asked to identify the body, I steel myself to look at the house, drawing my shoulders back, taking a deep breath, lifting my eyes.

It looks the same. I don't know why I expected it to look different . . . I suppose because I knew that Petty was having work done on it, but – at least from the front – it's just as I remember, and the nostalgia that hits me is so intense it knocks the air out of me.

Looming up above the driveway, the high grey stone wall, punctuated by irregularly spaced, different-sized windows, isn't exactly welcoming. It looks hewn from the landscape, like it was made to withstand the wind, the rain and the waves that I can hear crashing down to the side of me. An old converted mill, the house is perched on the edge of a low cliff, and round the back there are views out across the water to Holy Island. If you scramble down the footpath from the back garden you find yourself on a private stretch of beach, hemmed in by dark, craggy rocks. It's the beach where Serena, Lil and I spent our summers swimming and playing pirates, and eating crab rolls, gritty with sand and somehow more delicious for it.

Awash with the memories of arriving here so many times before – the giddy excitement of another wild summer stretching out in front of me, of singing along to ABBA, of reading smutty romance novels and wearing coconut-scented sun cream – I walk up to the front door. It's the same pale green it always was, but cleaner now, shiny where the paint had once been peeling off in strips. I punch the code that Petty sent me into the key safe on the wall and let myself in, flicking the lights on as I go.

Inside it's a lot more obvious that changes have been made. Gone is Granny Mac's clutter, the fussy floral wallpaper removed in favour of muted greys and pale blues. It's different, but the bones of the house are the same, and it's like I'm seeing double – overlaying the image of what was with what is now. Off to the left of the front door is the living space, which is long and light – thanks largely to another of Petty's changes: the entire back wall has been replaced with sliding glass windows that frame the view of the sea.

I know that the record company had Petty put everything in the house in storage and they sent a bunch of furniture, so everything is – as you might expect – extremely expensive-looking. There's a *giant* TV, a couple of bookcases and a small four-seater dining table with an elaborate glass light fitting hanging above it that looks like something from Picasso's nightmares. I manoeuvre around the enormous L-shaped sofa – petrol-grey velvet, draped in snuggly blankets – and stand in the window taking in the view.

Unsurprisingly, this view has also stayed the same, and I find it comforting. I can hardly begin to sort through everything I'm feeling. Memories pepper me so hard and fast that I can't even separate them – my sisters, Granny Mac, that last summer, *all* the summers. I've been so busy worrying about Theo and staying here with him that I haven't really let myself imagine what this part would feel like.

I take the bags through to the kitchen, which is off the living room and all sleek and modern now, and unpack the groceries, fill the enormous American-style freezer with ice. David had sent me a one-line email that simply read, '*There MUST always be ice on hand*', as though Theo might keel over if forced to drink a room-temperature beverage.

I poke my head into the small study and find that – per David's instructions – this has been purged of any remaining furniture and instead contains a collection of gleaming gym equipment. Stacked neatly against one wall are a lot of boxes of various sizes which I know are some of the orders placed by David. As with the gym equipment, he liaised with Petty to make sure everything was delivered properly. 'He's quite the character' was her placid response to the organizational force of nature who has quickly become the bane of my existence.

I can't even bring myself to start sorting through the boxes now – I'll do it in the morning before Theo gets here. The thought of his arrival brings another rush of nerves.

I go back out to the car and collect the rest of my bags before stomping upstairs to my bedroom. When we were little, Lil and I always shared, but now the bunk beds that were our pride and joy have been replaced by a small double. I stick my head in what would have been Serena's room, across the hall from mine, and find to my delight that Petty has kept the walls that we painted midnight blue unchanged.

Next door to my room is Granny Mac's room, which Petty told me would be all set up for Theo. I push the door open tentatively, but again, the space is unrecognizable. There's a new, bigger window that offers a beautiful view over the bay. The bed is enormous, and the bedding is crisp, white and about a million thread count, spun by nuns in some remote mountain convent or something similar – honestly, I lost track of the bedsheet conversation thirteen emails in and just agreed with whatever David said.

I run my hand over the bed and instantly feel my skin prickle with heat. Great, now Theo Eliott is turning me into some sort of bedsheet-obsessed pervert. Why does it matter to me that the man will be sleeping in here? I have no feelings about that at all. None. It is just a bed.

Against one wall is a rack that holds several gleaming guitars, instruments that I know from David have been shipped with great care and at great expense. I check that everything is clean and tidy, and grab some fresh (Egyptian cotton) towels out of the linen cupboard where – when I read and reread *The Pursuit of Love* at aged fourteen – Serena, Lil and I used to pretend to be Mitfords, 'but without the fascism', as Lil was always careful to add. Here we sat practically on each other's laps – it was not a large cupboard – and talked about sex, a subject with which we, as the love children of Ripp Harris, were significantly more au fait than the Radletts, but about which we still had many, many interesting questions.

Fortunately for me, the cleaning company that Petty employs has done an excellent job, and so apart from laying out the towels and arranging some sweet peas from the garden in a jam jar on his bedside table, there's nothing else to do. I think the flowers add a homey touch that is currently missing – it looks too much like a hotel room right now: beautiful but soulless. And that seems wrong in Granny Mac's house.

I drag myself off to bed, sinking into the very ordinary, slightly worn cotton sheets with a great sigh of relief. Perhaps I'll have time after I unpack the boxes in the morning to drive back down to Newcastle where the bigger shops may help me cross more items off my list.

On this reassuring thought I fall into a deep and dreamless sleep until I am awoken by a loud banging noise.

As I sit up, my groggy brain takes a moment to catch up with my surroundings. Then I realize the banging is someone knocking on the front door. I stumble out of bed and down the stairs, rubbing the sleep from my eyes. I guess it's the online order David placed for weird Japanese energy drinks.

I'm almost at the door when my phone starts ringing shrilly in the bedroom.

'Oh God, hang on, hang on,' I mutter, wrenching the door open.

Standing on the other side is Theo Eliott, a phone held up to his ear. He's wearing jeans and a grey T-shirt that looks soft and worn but that probably cost more than my entire wardrobe. His dark hair is mussed, his face unshaven.

'Gah!' I say, succinctly.

He has a pair of sunglasses on so I can't really see his reaction, but his mouth kicks up at the sound. 'It's okay, David. She's here. I'm in,' he says into the phone. There's a brief pause, and then, 'Yes, you've made your feelings on the matter very clear, thank you. I'll speak to you later.'

He hangs up the phone and then nudges his sunglasses down his nose a little so that I can see his eyes.

'Nice jammies,' he says.

I look down at my seasonally inappropriate pyjamas which are covered in tiny pictures of dogs wearing Santa hats. Fantastic. I run a hand over the wild mess of my hair, trying to smooth it.

'What are you doing here?' I blurt, and the words come out more hostile than I intended.

'In the middle of bloody nowhere?' Theo sighs. 'No idea. Ask your sister.'

'I mean,' I say with forced patience, 'what are you doing here so early? I wasn't expecting you until this afternoon. What time is it anyway?'

Theo looks at the disgustingly expensive watch on his wrist. 'Almost seven.'

'In the morning?!' I croak, horrified.

'Not a morning person,' Theo nods understandingly. 'I get it. I've just come in from LA so it's almost midnight for me.'

'From ... LA?' I manage. 'I thought David said you were driving up from London. How did you even get here?'

'Plans changed. I flew.'

My eyes widen as I lean forward and search the driveway, half expecting to see a helicopter parked next to my Ford Fiesta.

'To Edinburgh, Clemmie.' Theo's tone is mildly exasperated. 'Then I drove the hire car down.'

'Oh, right, yes,' I notice the gleaming Audi which is doing a great job of making my car look even more dilapidated. 'Sorry, I think I'm still half asleep.'

We stand awkwardly on the doorstep for a few more seconds. He pulls off the sunglasses and hooks them into the collar of his T-shirt. His eyes look tired, and he runs a hand through his hair. I follow his tattooed forearm as it moves, his fingers with their silver rings running through hair that I know is silky soft. My mouth dries. God, is the man actually moving in slow motion??

'Come in!' I finally say, sounding like a jolly-hockey-sticks school teacher as I belatedly remember why I am here, why he is here, and what my job is supposed to be – the one I'm being paid huge amounts of money for. *Professional, Clemmie. Be professional.* 'Do you need help with your bags?'

Theo shakes his head. 'I'll come and grab them out the boot later.'

'Okay then.' I move aside so that he can get through the door. He brushes past me and I get a brief, delicious hit of his aftershave. My toes curl and my stomach swoops. I will my stupid body to behave itself, and lead him through the downstairs of the house.

'This place is nice,' Theo says, looking around with interest.

'Yeah, Petty has done a really good job with the renovations. That's Lil's mum.'

Theo nods. 'Serena mentioned.'

'So let me show you around. Through here is the study – well, I call it the study but I guess it's the gym now.' I lead him into the room and again he glances about and nods.

I notice his eyes linger on the boxes and I flush. 'I haven't had a chance to unpack all the stuff David shipped yet. I'm sorry. I arrived late last night. Car trouble.' The words tumble out of my mouth, and I see Theo's lips thin, but he only makes a noise between a grunt and a murmur.

He's being very quiet. Perhaps he's just tired? Or is he annoyed that I haven't got everything perfectly ready for him? I've been having trouble squaring the Theo I met with the tyrant David works for, but maybe this is the real him now he's not trying to charm me.

'Okay!' I say brightly. 'And through this way . . .' I turn

to move past him back through the door and stumble over a piece of equipment straight into Theo – or I would stumble into him if he didn't rear backwards as if I had a highly contagious skin disease. As it is, my arm barely brushes his and he clatters back against a set of dumbbells, a pained expression on his face.

'Sorry about that,' I say quickly.

He just makes that strange humming noise again and avoids my eye, but there's a muscle ticking like mad in his jaw.

I take him through to the kitchen. Everything about this feels so awkward. When imagining this part, I thought I was going to behave like a consummate professional. I had plans! A checklist! I was going to be calm, in control. I did not think I would be bleary-eyed in my novelty pyjamas, trying desperately to remember the gazillion emails David and I exchanged.

'Um, so this is the kitchen,' I say unnecessarily. 'I'm afraid I haven't been able to find all the things on the latest list David sent me yet. Obviously I need to unpack all the boxes, and there are a bunch of deliveries scheduled for this morning and then I'm going to head into Newcastle later. So there's sparkling water in the fridge,' I hesitate, 'but I'm afraid the brand is just whatever they had in the local Co-op, and there's fruit and eggs and bread and cheese.' I rifle through the checklist I've been carrying around in my head all week. 'There's a coffee machine coming later today and David set up a weekly delivery of organic veg. I'm sorry it's not all in place already . . .' I ramble nervously.

Theo's mouth is flat, and his jaw clenches again in annoyance. 'It's fine,' he says, but clearly it isn't. Clearly I've already failed the first test and David is going to feed me to his goldfish.

'Are you hungry?' I ask weakly. 'I could make you a cheese sandwich? Or a cup of tea? I haven't unearthed the almonds yet but I have ordinary milk?'

'I'm fine,' he says, and again it feels like 'fine' is code for 'extremely disappointed'. 'I think I'd just like to go to my room if that's okay?'

'Oh, sure,' I say, 'let me show you up.'

I take him up the stairs and hesitate outside my own room for a second. The door is still open from when I rushed downstairs and you can see the rumpled bed and my suitcase lying open. 'So this is my room,' I say. 'Just in case you need anything. I mean not that you need anything in my room, but if you need me.' I break off, feeling myself flush. 'Not *need* me, but if you need me to do something for you and you can't find me downstairs then I will be here.'

I expect a flirtatious response, at the very least a smirk and a sighting of the dimple, but Theo only clears his throat and frowns.

'And this is your room.' I push the door next to mine open, but hover on the threshold as he walks inside. 'There's a bathroom through there with a shower, but if you want a bath then there's another bathroom across the hall.'

Theo wanders in, sticks his head in the door of the en suite and then stands in the window looking out at the view. He doesn't say anything but his eyes move to the jar of sweet peas.

'I know it's probably not what you're used to . . .' I start.

'It's great,' Theo says, his tone flat but polite.

Great. Well, I suppose that's an improvement on 'fine'.

'Okay then,' I take a step back, 'you know where to find me, and I'll be going into Newcastle in a bit so let me know if you need anything else.'

'I'm good,' Theo says, 'thanks.'

And then he closes the door in my face.

Chapter Twelve

I spend the rest of the morning sorting through the boxes and soaking vast quantities of almonds as per David's meticulous instructions. I don't see or hear anything from Theo. I guess maybe he's sleeping.

At least now the kitchen is looking better stocked – I've been back and forth to the front door signing for endless parcels. David even sent me loads of clear plastic containers and a label maker so that I could organize everything in a way that made it easy for Theo to find things. He also sent me a detailed plan for precisely how the kitchen cabinets should be arranged so that they mirrored the ones at Theo's house in LA. While I may have rolled my eyes that *heaven forbid* the rock star has to rifle through a cupboard for his organic seaweed crackers, I have to admit the label maker is extremely satisfying and soon I find myself labelling everything in sight.

When Theo finally makes an appearance, I am leaning over the kitchen counter sorting his many, many supplements into little days-of-the-week pill organizers that I ordered from Amazon. Unlike David, I draw the line at trailing after him on an hourly basis with fistfuls of vitamin-B and electrolyte water. *Surely* he is a grown-up who can take some responsibility for himself? I hear the front door open and close, the thud of bags being dropped in the hallway, and then Theo appears in front of me.

'Here,' he says gruffly, throwing his keys at me, which I immediately deflect with a squeak, leaving them to fall to the floor with a clatter.

Theo scoops them up, placing them carefully on the counter beside me. 'They're car keys, not a hand grenade. You said you had car trouble so if you're going out, use mine. Use it whenever.'

His voice is a bit rusty and his hair is rumpled. He looks like he's been asleep. He's still not smiling at me, but I'm touched by the gesture. I hadn't expected him to think about me at all. He yawns then, raising his arms in a stretch which lifts the bottom of his T-shirt, revealing a sliver of muscled, golden stomach. I tear my eyes away. Nope. Not thinking about it. Keeping everything professional.

'Are you sure?' I ask, focussing once more on the pills. 'About using the car?'

He grunts. 'Don't want you breaking down in the middle of nowhere. That death trap of yours is held together by nothing but hope and Sellotape.'

'Hey!' I exclaim. 'It's duct tape actually and that's just for the wing mirror. One wing mirror. The other one is *fine*. Mostly.'

Theo only makes a scoffing sound as he heads to the

fridge, pulling the door open and helping himself to one of the bottles of the weird green juice that got delivered in a special cooler like they were organs ready to be transplanted.

He takes a swig and then peers at the bottle with a frown. Probably reading the label that says THEO'S WEIRD GREEN JUICE. Then he closes the door and eyes the sticker that says FRIDGE.

He looks at me and his brows lift. 'What's with the labels?'

I shrug. 'David sent me a label maker so that I could organize things for you and I got a bit excited.'

His mouth reluctantly tugs up at the side and his eyes drop from mine towards my chest, where they linger. Is he checking me out? I feel my cheeks warm, and a strange mixture of outrage and adrenaline thunders through me. Then he gestures with his juice bottle and says, 'And you thought I'd forget your name?'

I glance down and remember that there's a label on my chest that says CLEMMIE.

Theo is pressing his lips together like he's trying to keep himself from laughing at me, but those dark eyes of his are crinkled at the corners. I grab the label maker and punch at the buttons.

'I don't think you're one to talk about people's names,' I say, peeling off the sticker that the machine spits out and stepping forward to slap it on his chest. 'If anyone needs to wear a name tag, it's you.'

Theo looks down at my hand, my fingers splayed across his shirt, which is just as soft as I'd imagined. And it's stretched across a body that is hard and warm. For a second our eyes meet and I think there's a flash of something in his gaze, something wild and hungry that does strange things to my knees, but in an instant it's gone. He takes a step back, folding his arms across his chest, and I drop my hand to my side, leaving the label behind on his shirt, the one that says THEO.

'Not Edward,' he says quietly, his voice husky.

'Definitely not Edward,' I agree. A reminder that is worryingly necessary. I may have liked Edward, but he never existed. I need to stop getting confused by Theo's nearness. I need to remember that this is a professional situation. I need a really, really cold shower.

There's a long and extremely awkward pause.

'Right,' Theo says, and all the light has gone out of him, leaving behind nothing but a stiff politeness in his face and his voice. 'Better get on with this writing. That's why we're here. I'm sure Serena will be checking in on me soon enough.'

'I'm sure you're right,' I say. 'I'm going to the shops now, is there anything you need?'

'No, no,' he says briskly, already backing away. 'And you don't have to . . . you know . . . run around after me.'

'That's my job.' I give him a fixed, bright smile. 'And I think we both know David will come here and murder me very efficiently if I don't do it well.'

The smile Theo gives me doesn't reach his eyes as he lifts his hand in a little salute and then he's gone.

*

It's early evening by the time I get back from Newcastle, clutching yet more bags. At least now I'll be able to email David telling him I have everything Theo could possibly need. And driving Theo's big, expensive rental car made the whole journey much less of a hardship. I cruised along, listening to a Judy Blume audiobook which satisfied my nostalgia craving perfectly, air conditioning blasting, and not even a little bit afraid that the car would suddenly combust.

I call out a greeting when I let myself in the front door but there's no response from Theo. Hopefully he's deep in the creative zone. I unpack the bags and then set about making myself some dinner – spaghetti and a pretty basic veggie sauce, garlic bread warming in the oven. It smells great and my rumbling stomach agrees. I'm a decent cook but I'm very grateful I don't have to prepare meals for Theo. His private chef has sent over a freezer full of perfectly balanced, organic, sugar-free, dairy-free and gluten-free dinners that just need to be reheated in the oven. The most I have to do is blend the odd kale smoothie while thanking the Lord I don't have to be the one to drink it.

Speaking of Theo, there's still no sign of him, but I guess there's no reason to expect we would eat together or anything. Still, it feels strange with him in the house. Is it impolite to eat without him? Should I offer to put one of his fancy meals in the oven? I dither and decide against it.

David was very clear that Theo needs space when he's working and shouldn't be bothered unless he asks for something himself. And when I say 'very clear' I mean he brought it up a hundred times and warned against what he called 'idle chatter', and suggested that I should try to be neither seen, nor heard. When I told him that made me sound like a Victorian chambermaid, he made a distinct sound of approval.

So I don't bother Theo. Instead, I press the button to lower the blinds and sit on the sofa with my pasta, ready to watch the next instalment of my favourite teenage vampire drama, *Blood/Lust*, on Netflix. Four episodes later, I have washed up the dishes and made inroads on a tub of mint choc chip ice cream, but I still haven't seen or heard Theo.

I tidy up and leave a Post-it note on the fridge, telling him his dinner is in there and how long he needs to heat it for. After a moment's thought I add, *Or there's leftover pasta and garlic bread if you'd rather. Help yourself.* And I draw a smiley face.

I make my way upstairs and pause outside my bedroom door, my eyes skating towards Theo's room. There's no sound, no music, no strumming of a guitar, nothing. Perhaps he's already asleep?

I lie awake for a long time. Something about knowing Theo is not only in the house but on the other side of the wall behind me makes me feel agitated. I stay very still, picturing him lying only inches away, and it has my entire body on high alert. I'm troubled by the fact I don't seem to be able to turn off my reaction to him. It doesn't matter that my brain knows perfectly well that he's not for me, when several of my other body parts seem to vehemently disagree.

Whenever I'm near Theo, all I can think about is getting my hands on him. Or getting his hands on me. What is wrong with me? It's clearly some residual reaction to our night together. *It will get easier*, I tell myself, and that's the thought I am clinging to when I finally do fall asleep.

Chapter Thirteen

The next morning I go downstairs and open the fridge. Theo's meal is untouched, but the pasta and garlic bread is gone. So is my Post-it note. Otherwise I wouldn't know he's even been here.

I sigh.

Small victories. I guess we made it through day one and I've kept him alive. Only forty-one more days and one genre-defying, award-winning album to go. Nothing to worry about.

I spend the morning on edge, waiting for Theo to appear, but he doesn't. I drift around the kitchen, cleaning the already immaculate surfaces. I consult the lists that David sent me but I've checked off everything. There's nothing left to do except clean Theo's room – tricky when the man is currently inside it.

Perhaps Serena was right and this is going to be an easy job. Maybe I will hardly see him. That can only be a good thing given the starring role Theo Eliott played in the restless hours of graphic sex dreams that I enjoyed last night. My subconscious clearly did not get the memo about professionalism.

I'm sitting at the kitchen counter, staring into space, when I finally hear footsteps thumping down the stairs. As Theo doesn't appear in the living room I creep out and stick my head around the door to the hallway.

Theo stands with his back to me. He has ear pods in, and whatever he's listening to is loud enough that I can hear the thump of the bass. He hums along, a low rumble in his throat. He bends over to pull a pair of trainers on and I am treated to a delicious view of his rear end, clad in grey jogging bottoms. There's that white noise in my brain again.

I panic, slam my eyes shut. I've already spent the night fantasizing about him, now I'm objectifying the man, like some sort of pervert lurking in the bushes. *Get a grip, Clementine.*

'Shit!' Theo yells loudly. My eyes spring open to find he's turned around and is looking down at me. He holds his hand over his heart, pulls an ear pod out. 'I didn't know you were there.'

A dozen images flash through my brain in high definition and my blood sizzles.

Do. Not. Think. About. The. Dreams.

I smile, brightly. 'Yes, here I am.'

Neither of us say anything.

'Um. Can I get you something?' I ask at last.

'No,' he all but snarls. 'I'm going for a run.'

'Oh, good. Running is good.' I guess the charmer who wanted to get me into bed is long gone.

As if to underscore the point, Theo grabs a baseball cap and tugs it on, pulling it low over his face, then he strides towards the front door and leaves without another word.

'Bye then!' I say to the empty air. My shoulders slump. I suppose entitled rock stars really are all assholes when you get down to it. I shouldn't be surprised, but I can't help feeling disappointed.

I return to the kitchen where I keep my fat binder full of notes. The Theo Bible. One thing that David and I can absolutely agree on is a strong interest in good stationery. When I told him about my coloured tab system, I'm sure I heard the man purr.

'Running, running, running . . .' I mutter under my breath. Yes, there they were, David's instructions.

> After his run, Mr Eliott requires AT LEAST one of the high-protein snacks from addendum B, as well as one serving of the vegan recovery sport drink mixed with 300ml electrolyte water (served chilled between 2.5–3°C), and a fresh pressed kale and apple juice (see section 4, paragraph 7 for recipe. NB: Juice delivery does not include this post-run juice as it is Mr Eliott's preference to have this freshly pressed. Do NOT try to give him the other juice to 'see if he notices'. Just make the juice).

Whenever I drag myself out on a run (rare), I make do with a glass of tap water and a banana afterwards, but I suppose rock stars breathe rarefied air. I track down the juice recipe and set about getting the ingredients out, then remember that first I should go and clean the bedroom while he's safely out the way.

I traipse upstairs, ready to change the sheets that Theo spent one night in and find myself hesitating at the door. I know that it's my job to go in there, but it doesn't feel right to just barge in. *Be professional*, I tell myself sternly. *It's just a bedroom. It's not snooping. It's cleaning.*

Taking a deep breath, I push the door open. Despite my big talk I still creep in like a very mediocre cat burglar. This definitely feels like trespassing.

The room looks the same as I left it, apart from the unmade bed. I open one of the drawers a crack and find it full of Theo's neatly folded clothes. I'm pretty sure I was supposed to unpack for him, but it seems he's done that himself. The wardrobe is the same – everything hanging tidily, his empty cases stored underneath.

I move to strip the bed and tell myself I'm imagining things when the sheets feel like they are still warm from the heat of his body. Unfortunately, I'm definitely not imagining the smell of his aftershave, which clings lightly to everything and wraps itself around me as I wrestle with his bedding. Why does he smell *so* good? It's not fair. It's distracting. I make the bed as briskly as possible, waging war with the giant, puffy duvet and just about coming out the winner.

I am fluffing up the pillows when I notice that the label I made yesterday with Theo's name on it is stuck carefully to the wall next to his bed, the wall that separates our rooms. I run my fingers over it, wondering why he's kept it.

I double-check everything is perfectly smooth and neat, before heading back downstairs. I have no idea how long Theo will be running for, and according to David he's going to want everything waiting for him when he gets back. It's time to tackle the new giant, shiny juicer, which looks less like a kitchen appliance and more like a piece of industrial cleaning equipment.

After carefully reading the instructions, my first effort sends green gunk spraying all over me and the kitchen and ends with a dribble of unappealing sludge in the bottom of a glass.

'You are not going to be defeated by a juicer,' I mutter, scrubbing violently at everything with antibacterial spray. 'You have a doctorate. You can juice a piece of kale.' I'm not sure who I'm trying to kid – even without the machinery I wouldn't previously have identified kale as a particularly *juicy* vegetable. Perhaps David is hazing me.

My second attempt goes much better. I mean, *I* wouldn't drink it, but I have produced a glass of swampy-looking liquid, and I suppose that's the best I can hope for, given the circumstances.

I'm just transporting my precious glass of juice to the fridge to keep it chilled (a risk, as this is not specifically mentioned in the instructions, but seeing as everything else has to be well below room temperature I'm making an educated guess) when I hear the front door open.

Yes! Perfect timing. I sweep out of the kitchen, triumphant, headed towards Theo and ready to deliver a freshly pressed juice into his hands on his return like a good little housekeeper. Instead, on the threshold of the living room I smash face first into a very hard object.

'Shit!' I shriek, flinging juice into the air.

'Fuck!' the hard object yells.

Lifting my eyes, I find Theo scowling down at me. Kale juice drips from his hair, covering most of his upper body. His completely naked upper body.

'Why aren't you wearing a shirt?' I blurt, my eyes lingering on the perfectly defined chest I have just crashed into. I'm pressed firmly against him, meaning I am covered in my own share of juice and the thin layer of my now wet T-shirt does not feel like enough of a barrier between our skin. Not if I'm going to retain my sanity. I peel myself away, but he is still holding on to my forearms. He must have grabbed them to steady me when we collided.

'I was hot,' he says, but his voice is very, very cold. 'Why are you throwing green slime at me?'

'I was bringing you your kale juice.' I say miserably, clinging to the now-empty glass. 'It says in the binder that's what you have after a run.'

He squeezes his eyes shut. 'Of course there's a fucking binder,' he mutters.

'Shall I . . . make you another one?' I ask.

'No.' Theo looks down, notices he still has his hands on me and lets go as if he's just realized he's holding a burning coal. 'I don't need anything, thanks. I'm going to go and take a shower.' As he turns and stomps away I hear him mutter, 'A long, long shower.'

'Sorry,' I call after him.

I survey the destruction around me and sigh. Not what you'd call a great success so far. My phone rings and I pull it from my pocket.

'Hi, David,' I say brightly. 'No, no, everything's perfect. Smooth sailing here.'

I don't see Theo for the rest of the day.

Chapter Fourteen

I have barely interacted with Theo for seven days. I am the absolute worst music industry spy in the world. Is he writing the album? I have no idea. All I can tell my sister is that he's clearly enjoying unfettered access to carbohydrates.

'It's been a week, Serena,' I whisper at my phone screen. 'It's just getting weird. It feels like I'm living with a hungry ghost.'

Every single morning when I've come downstairs it has been to find that Theo has eaten the other half of the food I prepared the night before, rather than the work of the expensive Michelin-starred chef David hired. I have started making double now because I get it: frozen pizza probably *does* taste incredible if you haven't eaten actual bread for years. In fact, all my 'normal-person' food supplies in the cupboards have been disappearing.

Obviously I haven't mentioned this arrangement to David – I feel like I've accidentally become Theo's dealer, sneaking him refined sugar. Today I realized he's demolished an entire packet of chocolate Hobnobs and I think he's using the semi-skimmed milk too. I might have to stage some sort of intervention.

'You haven't seen him at all?' On the screen my sister scowls back at me.

'I mean I've *seen* him,' I say. 'I can offer you proof of life. Yesterday he came in the kitchen and I made him one of those disgusting slimy drinks – I've actually got the hang of the juicer now. I reckon I could juice *anything* . . . But he said maybe half a dozen words and then left again to barricade himself in his room. He barely even looked at me. Any time I ask him if he wants anything he practically snaps my head off. He's being really weird.'

I don't mention the night I overheard him on the phone. Having not seen him for seven hours I was just about to crack and knock on his door to see if he needed anything, when I heard him say my name. Knowing that I shouldn't eavesdrop, I did it anyway and, leaning forward, caught his words loud and clear.

' . . . absolute fucking disaster. Why did I ever think this was a good idea? This is torture. I should have made them let me bring David.'

'You're spiralling. Just try and act like a normal human being,' an amused female voice had answered, the sound tinny through the phone speaker as Theo moved around. Something about that voice and the husky way she laughed seemed vaguely familiar.

Theo let out a deep groan of frustration.

I'd snapped back, scurried away, pissed off by the whole situation. I didn't think I was doing a bad job; *he* was the one with the attitude. I have no idea what his problem is or how to fix it.

'Hmmm.' Serena continues to look deeply annoyed. 'And you haven't heard anything to suggest he's writing?'

I feel strangely disloyal when I shake my head. 'But how would I know what the process of writing an album sounds like?' I ask quickly. 'He could be writing things down in a journal or something.'

Serena sighs and rubs her forehead. 'You'll just have to ask him straight out,' she says. 'Try and get some sort of update. My bosses are really breathing down my neck on this one. If it doesn't work then I'm going to be seriously fucked.'

'It will work,' I say with more confidence than I feel. But looking at my sister's worried face has me convinced I will wring ten miserable songs out of Theo Eliott with my bare hands if I have to. After all, I control the flow of biscuits in this house and I'm not above bribery.

'At least it must be making life easy for you,' Serena continues. 'If he's making himself scarce.'

'Oh, yeah,' I agree a little glumly. 'There's really not much for me to do at all.' In fact, other than keeping all the cupboards stocked, cleaning his room, sending David thrice-daily updates, and sharing my dinner, there's been nothing.

Especially because Theo seems to barely tolerate my presence whenever we are forced together. I know I was worried about having to spend a lot of time with him because of all the fluttery feelings of attraction, but somehow living with Theo as a distant stranger is so much worse. I'm glad he's not around flirting with me all the time, *I am*, but it's like now that there's no possibility of a physical relationship between us, he doesn't want to bother with me at all, like he's going out of his way to avoid me. That's pretty dickish behaviour in my book.

I spend my days walking by the beach or staring at the screen on my laptop, half-heartedly filling out job applications or struggling to summon up some enthusiasm for the years-long project of turning my PhD thesis into a book. I think there was a time when I was excited about this work, but I'm finding it hard to remember. The pressure to publish is pretty intense in academic circles and I know that it would really help me to secure a position, but at this point the pages of notes make me feel strangely claustrophobic.

I'm a natural introvert, but even for me this much isolation is unsettling. I've been reduced to making small talk at the supermarket just to experience a bit of human connection. I had forgotten how far away from everything Granny Mac's house feels, and while that had always been part of the adventure with Lil and Serena, now I just feel . . . lonely.

And that's before we even get into the minefield of being back at the site of my seventeen-year-old self's deepest emotional trauma. Every time I go for a walk, I see something that reminds me of how I felt that summer, how angry and betrayed and heartbroken. Even though it's only an echo of those feelings, it's still a rush of pain that is almost physical.

As I do every time the spectre of Sam raises his head, I shove the thought aside. I'll save it for my session with Ingrid . . . maybe. Or maybe I'll keep ignoring it and hope it goes away. That seems like a good option.

'Are you okay?' Serena asks, fixing me with a beady stare. 'You're all mopey and actually, now that I look at you properly, you look like shit.'

'Gosh, thanks,' I mutter.

'And you're a bit croaky.' Her voice is accusatory.

'I think I might be coming down with a bit of a bug,' I admit, shivering a little and pulling the duvet up and over my head, clasping it under my chin despite the warmth of the day. I can see myself in the corner of my screen and I look like a clammy little caterpillar. *This* is what comes of making small talk with people.

'Don't you dare get ill,' Serena warns. 'You know you're useless when you're ill. It's because you pasty academics don't get any vitamin D. Have you been using that spray I sent you?'

'What is it with you lot and your supplements?' I grumble. 'Theo's on about seven hundred a day. And what is ashwagandha anyway? I thought that was what Lil drank in that tent when she had a vision of a giant version of herself eating a tiny version of herself and then everyone shit their pants?'

'That's ayahuasca, you idiot,' Serena says. 'Ashwagandha is to help with stress.'

'Don't know what he's got to be stressed about,' I reply sulkily, because I'm not feeling very charitable towards Theo at the moment. 'I'm pretty sure David brushes his teeth for him. Spoilt little rock star.'

'Well, that spoilt little rock star is your problem now, Clemmie, yours *and* mine. Just do what you can, will you?'

'Of course,' I agree instantly, because for Serena to even ask me to do something for her again tells me how stressed she is. 'I'll get you a full report, I promise.'

'Thanks, Clem.' Serena's voice softens. 'And I'm sending you some echinacea tablets right now. HARRIET!' I hear her call to her own poor, maligned assistant. 'WE NEED TO SEND CLEMMIE ECHINACEA ASAP.'

Just as I'm feeling a wave of affection towards my sister, she ruins it by adding, 'SHE'S A LITTLE BITCH WHEN SHE'S SICK!', and then she cackles, blows me a kiss and hangs up.

With a sigh I drag myself off the bed. Actually, my whole body is feeling a bit achy. Maybe it's just all the sad, lonely walking I've been doing.

I head down to the kitchen and pour myself a glass of orange juice because I might as well get in on these vitamins everyone is raving about, and then, as if my conversation with Serena has summoned him, Theo appears too.

'Hi!' I say, wiping the juice from my top lip with the back of my hand.

'Hey.' Theo's eyes flick towards me from under his lashes. He doesn't exactly sound thrilled to see me.

'Can I get you anything?'

'No.' He sounds frustrated, almost angry. 'I was just going

to get a bottle of water and go for a walk. Got to get out of that room for a bit.'

'Sure you don't want some orange juice?' I pick up the carton and hold it out towards him.

He actually takes a step back, away from my hand, as if he's afraid I'll touch him. That now familiar muscle in his jaw ticks. 'No,' he says again.

'Okay,' I reply, trying not to sound bothered. I can't work out why he's being so rude. I'm doing everything David asks me to do. I don't think I've committed any major errors apart from not having everything perfectly ready for him that first day, but he still seems vaguely pissed off by my presence.

I know what I promised Serena and I don't want to give myself time to chicken out so I blurt, 'I just got off the phone with my sister. She wanted to know how it's all going.'

Theo's back is to me as he reaches in the fridge, but I see his shoulders tense. 'It's going fine,' he says tightly.

'So, writing is happening?' I ask, wanting to confirm.

'Sure.' Theo closes the fridge door with an unnecessary amount of force. 'What do you think I've been doing all week?'

'I just wanted to check. Serena seemed . . . a bit anxious.'

Theo snorts. 'The studio will get their pound of flesh; you can tell them not to worry. After all, that's why you're here, to keep an eye on me, isn't it? Report back to the label. That's why it had to be you here instead of David, so they could send in a spy?'

'I'm not your mum nagging you about doing your

homework,' I snap, stung. 'You owe them an album and you're making other people's lives difficult. I'm just here trying to do a job.'

'So am I,' Theo snaps right back.

'Good.'

'Good.'

'Fine.'

'*Fine.*'

With that, he sweeps out, and I hear the front door open and slam shut. I slump back against the counter and press the cold juice glass to my forehead. I've got a headache coming on and I feel knackered. I try to remind myself that this is better than being unemployed and stuck back at Mum's house, but then at least Theo wouldn't be there, and I wouldn't be completely, utterly alone and feeling like crap.

I'm probably just tired. I glance at the clock and see that it's midday already. I'll just take some paracetamol and go and have a quick nap. That will sort me out. I knock back the tablets and then make my way upstairs, crashing wearily into bed and falling asleep almost instantly.

When I peel my eyes open it's dark. Properly dark. I'm completely discombobulated and also freezing. Teeth chattering, I pull the duvet tighter around my body and lift myself up on one elbow to look at the clock. The room tips around me for a moment before I can focus on the numbers. Almost midnight. Did I just sleep for twelve hours? Why do I feel worse than before?

Gingerly, I swing my feet out of bed, hissing when they

hit the cold floor. Right. I'm ill. But I'm a grown-up. I can deal with this. I just need to be sensible. What do I need? The ache in my head is a dull thump behind my left eye. My throat feels dry and scratchy. Water, I decide. That seems like a good bet. Water and painkillers and maybe something to eat.

With that mental list made, I shuffle downstairs, still swathed in the duvet. All I have to concentrate on is putting one foot in front of the other, but unfortunately the floor refuses to behave, tilting occasionally from side to side.

I have to sit on the stairs for a minute to have a little rest, my face pressed against the banister, but eventually I make it down to the living room. There, sprawled on the sofa, the glow from the TV kissing his perfect profile, is Theo. He looks up guiltily, and I see he's eating my mint choc chip right out the tub with a spoon. He reaches for the remote and pauses what he's watching, which is an old episode of *The Great British Bake Off.*

'Clemmie!' he exclaims, getting to his feet. 'I'm glad you came down. Look, about earlier . . . I didn't mean to be short with you. I'm sorry. I know you're just doing your job. I am working on the music. You can tell Serena, all right?' He says the words quickly, breathlessly, as if he's been waiting to get them out for a while, and I'm dimly aware that I should care about them, but I'm having to focus all my energy on not face-planting on the rug at my feet.

'Are you okay?' he asks, his voice wobbling from far away. Then suddenly his face swims into view, so close to me that

I jump, tripping on the edge of my duvet. He wraps his hand around my arm, which is the only thing that keeps me from falling.

'I think,' I say ponderously, 'I think I'm going to be very sick.'

And then I drop the duvet to the ground and run on shaking legs towards the kitchen, where I promptly throw up into the sink.

'Oh my God, Clemmie.' Theo's voice is aghast and I hear his footsteps behind me. I feel a vague sense of unprofessionalism as I vomit some more.

Theo makes a gagging sound, like he's trying not to be sick himself. Then a hand pulls my hair back from my face, while another hand rubs circles on my back. 'Okay, it's okay,' he murmurs.

'It's not okay,' I manage forlornly, my legs trembling as I lean heavily against the sink. 'David's going to be so disappointed. I'm not being a good Victorian chambermaid *at all*.'

'Are you finished being sick?' Theo asks, ignoring this.

I consider the question seriously for a moment, then shake my head and throw up again. After that things get a bit blurry. Theo cleans me up and I find myself sitting on the floor, my back against the cabinet, a famous rock star crouched in front of me holding a glass of water.

'Drink this,' he says firmly. 'Just little sips.'

I try to reach for the glass but my arm is so heavy. 'Why is my arm so heavy?' I ask Theo, bewildered.

He presses his fingers to my forehead and it's just *lovely*.

His hand is so cool and as it travels down to cup my cheek I can't help but nuzzle into it, only a little bit.

'You've definitely got a temperature,' he says. 'Right. Can you drink some water if I hold the glass for you?'

I squint up at him. It's so bright in here, and the kitchen light hangs over his head like a halo. He holds the glass to my lips and I take a few small sips.

'Good,' Theo says. 'Now let's get you some paracetamol and get you back to bed.' He hesitates. 'I don't actually know where the paracetamol is.'

'There's some in that drawer over there.' I gesture with my extremely heavy arm.

Theo feeds me the tablets and we have a small, wobbly moment where I'm not sure if I'm going to keep them down, but it seems safe for the time being. Then he puts his arm tightly around my waist and helps me get back upstairs and into bed.

'I'm sorry I didn't make dinner,' I say.

'Don't be stupid,' Theo snaps. Then he huffs a deep breath. 'That doesn't matter, Clemmie.'

'Don't tell David about all the food,' I whisper. 'I told him you're eating raw vegan sushi rolls and hemp muffins.'

'It will be our secret,' he agrees, his voice softening. 'I'm leaving the water here,' he says then, gesturing to the nightstand. 'And some more tablets which you can take after four, okay?'

'After four,' I mumble obediently.

He disappears for a minute and comes back with my

duvet and also a flannel soaked in cold water which he lays across my head.

'Ahhhh,' I say. ''S nice.'

'That's what my mum always did for me,' he says softly, stroking the hair away from my face. 'Anyway, I'm sure you'll feel better in the morning after some sleep.' He hovers uncertainly for a moment. 'And I'm just next door, so if you need anything, yell.'

'Mmmm.' I'm too groggy to make words.

He stands looking at me for another beat and then stuffs his hands in his pockets and leaves, pulling the door not quite shut behind him.

'Thank you,' I mutter, but I don't think he hears. He's already gone. And then my eyes drift closed once more.

Chapter Fifteen

I dream there's a burglar in my room. But it's not a dream, it's real, and the burglar is crawling on the ceiling and he has red eyes behind a mask and they're staring at me and when he reaches towards me he has long, grasping arms like a satanic Mr Tickle.

'Don't let him get me, don't let him get me,' I pant, grabbing on to the (thankfully normal-sized) arm beside me on the bed.

'I won't let him get you,' a gentle voice reassures me. 'I promise, Clemmie, you're safe. Go back to sleep.'

I look back at the burglar but he's gone and I feel panicked. *Where is he?* Then Theo is there, right in front of me, and he cups my face between his hands while he says slowly, carefully, 'There's no one here but me, sweetheart. You're safe, I promise.'

'Okay,' I agree, closing my eyes. 'You won't let him get me.'

When I next wake it's because someone is touching my face and I don't like it. I bat the hand away with my own.

'Get off.' I try to wiggle away, but it seems that my whole body is made of lead and even prying my eyelids open is a struggle.

'I'm trying to take your temperature.' Theo's face comes into focus above me and he sounds annoyed. 'Just stay still.'

'You have to point it at her forehead and press the button until it beeps,' a disembodied voice floats through the air.

'Oh no!' I moan hoarsely. 'It's David! He's here! He knows the secret!'

'What secret?' David's voice is suspicious and I peer around wildly, trying to find him. Perhaps he is under the bed? That seems a reasonable assumption.

'Don't listen to her,' Theo huffs. 'She's hallucinating, doesn't know what she's saying.'

'That's good,' I whisper with approval. 'Don't let him find out about the biscuits. Maybe we should just keep him under the bed?'

There's a beeping noise. 'It says 39.4 degrees,' Theo says, talking over me. 'And it's flashing red. I take it that's not good?'

'She's definitely got a fever.' David's voice sounds even more pissed off than usual. 'You need to—'

Theo picks up his phone and holds it to his ear. David's voice stops and I close my eyes in relief.

'Yeah,' Theo nods. 'Yeah. Okay. Yeah, put her through if you can.' There's a pause before he says, 'Doctor Swain, thank you for getting back to me.'

I sit up and sneeze. Once, twice, five times. Each time it

jars my whole body. Theo hands me a tissue out of the box on the nightstand and I blow my nose. *Ow.*

'That's right,' he carries on talking into the phone. 'Over thirty-nine degrees and she's been having nightmares, hallucinating I think. She was sick last night but nothing so far this morning. Now she's sneezing and she looks' – he eyes me consideringly and I try to stretch my mouth into a smile – 'awful. Really pale and clammy.'

Charming.

Theo listens for another moment, a frown on his face. 'How would I know what her glands feel like?' He casts me a nervous look. 'Right, right, I'm going to put the phone on speaker.' He places his mobile carefully on the nightstand and advances on me like I'm a horse he doesn't want to spook. 'I just need to feel your neck a moment, Clemmie.'

'I don't think I want your hands round my neck,' I say.

'Believe me, if anyone's going to throttle you it will be David,' he grimaces. 'He definitely heard that biscuit comment.' And then his fingers start pressing up the side of my neck, under my chin.

'Not really sure what I'm doing here, Doc,' he says, louder.

'You want to press just under her jaw, either side of her throat,' an American woman's voice comes through the speaker.

'Owwwwww!' I whimper moments later.

'I think that means they're swollen,' Theo says, and he looks all grim and shaky like he's had to perform some kind of intense medical procedure rather than simply touch my neck. I would roll my eyes if I didn't think that would make me pass out.

'Clementine?' The woman's voice cuts through the air. 'Can you tell me a little about how you're feeling?'

'My head hurts,' I manage. 'And my throat hurts. And . . . my bones hurt.'

'Okay, well, it sounds to me like it's a virus, possibly the flu. Theo, if you take me off speakerphone I'll give you some instructions.' The doctor is calm, business-like, and while Theo walks away talking to her in a low voice, I slump back against my pillow, closing my eyes again. God, *everything* is aching. I can feel every millimetre of my skin that is being touched by my heavy, scratchy duvet and suddenly I understand Theo's obsession with his bedsheets. Why am I sleeping in actual *sandpaper* like an idiot? The doctor thinks I have the flu, but I don't know, it seems more likely that the bubonic plague is staging a comeback. My head throbs and I feel the hot trickle of tears coming from under my eyelids.

'Are you crying?' Theo's horrified question alerts me that he is off the phone and back in the room.

'I don't feel good,' I sniffle, my voice small. I don't even have the energy to put a bright face on it. Serena was not wrong: I am a useless ill person. Absolutely the world's biggest baby. I am almost thirty-three and I want my mum and a McDonald's strawberry milkshake.

'Okay, I need you to get up,' Theo says firmly.

I crack one eye open. 'Is that a sick joke?'

'No. I just need you to get from here to my car. I have

to go and get things and I don't know how long I'll be and I don't want to leave you here on your own. You can bring your duvet.' He says this last part like he's tempting me with a special treat.

'I don't want my duvet. I hate it. It's hurting me.'

There's a gusty sigh. 'Right, then let's go and escape from the evil duvet.'

When I don't reply his tone gets sly. 'Clementine Monroe, if you don't get your butt out of bed right now, I'm going to call David and tell him you've been feeding me frozen chicken nuggets.'

Oh crap. I forgot about the nuggets. I don't even like them, but I had shoved some in the trolley correctly suspecting that Theo would love them. I was going to get him the ones in the shape of dinosaurs next.

With a lot of swearing on both our parts I let Theo lever me out of bed and then he basically carries me to the car. I'm too ill to even appreciate the feel of all those muscles wrapped around me.

He straps me into the passenger seat and my head lolls against the headrest. I'm wearing my pyjamas and a pair of fluffy socks that Theo put on my feet while I watched in detached silence. The daylight is too bright and I whine about it until he slips his sunglasses onto my nose. He also tucks a blanket over me. I think he's nervous.

It's another thing I should care about, but when the car starts moving I decide instead that my energy is better spent focussing on not throwing up again. We drive in silence, except for the drone of the sat nav, directing Theo to wherever we are going. I turn my head and decide to distract myself by focussing on the man beside me. I'm wearing sunglasses and he's concentrating on the road so I know I can look my fill for once.

I start at the top. His hair is messy, all rumpled, and not in an artful way. There's a little tuft sticking out at the back. His eyebrows tip down in a frown but his profile is just as beautiful as that first day I glimpsed it in the church: long eyelashes, a perfectly straight nose, full, soft lips. His unshaven jaw sports a couple of days' worth of dark stubble and it makes him look like one of those models in a razor advert. I imagine him, stripped to the waist, dragging a blade slowly up under his chin the way they do, rinsing the razor off in the sink. I shiver because the image is the most powerfully erotic thing that's ever entered my head.

His collar bones are visible above the top of his shirt. He's wearing a black T-shirt today, one of those collarless ones with the little buttons at the top that looks like it's been sprayed on. It stretches tight over his biceps and I follow the line of his arms down to where his hands are on the steering wheel. Long fingers wrapped around the leather.

I think my fever might be getting worse. It's so hot in here I can feel a trickle of sweat running down my neck.

'We're here,' he mutters, breaking the spell, and I gaze blearily out of the window. We're in town, outside the pharmacy, and Theo parallel-parks the car on the street.

Holy shit. Forget the imaginary shaving advert ...

effortlessly parallel-parking a car on the first go? One hand spinning the steering wheel, while the other braces on the headrest next to my face? Apparently that's my kink, because this is the most turned on I have been in my life.

His forearm is right there in front of me. Muscles and ink and soft, gold skin.

'Ow! Jesus, Clemmie! Did you just *bite* me?' Theo exclaims, and I snort, ready to deny such an outlandish accusation.

Only now that I look again there does seem to be the perfect pink imprint of two little rows of teeth pressed into his skin.

'Huh,' I mumble in confusion. 'Sorry.'

Theo turns off the ignition and pulls his arm away, holding it in front of him to look at it more closely. 'Let's hope this isn't the start of the zombie apocalypse.'

I snicker, but actually it feels like it could be true.

'I'm going to go and pick up the stuff Doctor Swain ordered,' he says with a sigh. 'I'll be right back, okay? Don't move.'

'Not really an option,' I agree.

He gets out the car, and I must drift off because it seems like it's only seconds before he's back clutching four bursting carrier bags.

'Did you buy everything they had in there?' I ask blearily.

He gives me a look that says he doesn't need to hear it from me right now, and pulls a bottle of water and a packet of tablets from one of the bags. 'Take these,' he says, putting two pills in my hand.

'What are they?' I ask suspiciously, because I'm not about to go popping any old thing a rock star asks me to.

A muscle by Theo's eye twitches and I get the impression he's trying very hard not to shout at me. 'Some anti-viral medicine the doctor prescribed. Just take them.'

I do, as well as the extra-strength painkillers he offers me next.

Theo exhales heavily and pulls his seatbelt across his chest. 'Right. Let's get you back to bed.'

'Thank you for looking after me,' I say after we've been driving for a few minutes.

He just shrugs.

'But why are you being so nice to me?' I ask, the words muffled from where I've burrowed back under my blanket.

I peek over at him. He looks offended. 'What do you mean? I *am* nice.'

'Not to me,' I say forlornly. 'Not anymore.'

Theo frowns. 'I'm not *not* nice to you,' he says carefully.

'I suppose,' I agree. 'But you've been ignoring me. I don't like it. You think I'm bad at my job.'

He grips the steering wheel harder, keeps his eyes ahead. He doesn't say anything for a long time and I can feel the pills he gave me starting to kick in. The sharp edges of the pain seem to dull and I feel woozy, heavy-eyed, everything seems softer now – me, the car, Theo, we're all blurring gently together.

'I'm sorry.' Theo's voice is soft too. I look over at him and he offers me a small, wry smile. His lips curve, his dimple flashes. 'I was just trying . . . it doesn't matter. I was an idiot. I'm really sorry, Clemmie.'

I want to lick your dimple, I think, only it's possible I don't just think it because Theo makes a strange choking sound.

'You'll feel better when we're home,' he says firmly.

And even though it doesn't really mean anything at all, the way he says 'we' and 'home' has me smiling like an idiot as I fall back to sleep.

Chapter Sixteen

I am not a great patient and Theo is not a great nurse. In his defence, the man hasn't had to take care of himself, let alone another person, for two decades. At first he hovers, anxiously, waking me up every ten minutes to ask how I feel and to take my temperature.

After the twelfth time, I summon the energy to throw my pillow at him and tell him in no uncertain terms that if he doesn't leave me alone to sleep, the zombie apocalypse will be the least of his worries. I use a lot of swear words. His eyes get bigger and bigger and at one point I think he's going to laugh, but the glare I send his way has him swallowing the impulse.

'Fine,' he huffs, leaving the room with a muttered, 'you know where I am if you need something.' I can already hear him speed-dialling David but I don't care and I crash out into an oblivion that lasts through to the next morning.

I'm woken by a lot of ominous banging noises from downstairs and the smoke alarm briefly blares. I later learn this is because Theo tried to make soup. He tells me this crossly, as if it was my idea, and I notice that three of his fingers have plasters on them.

'You should have just heated some up from a tin,' I say.

'It *was* from a tin,' he sulks.

Giving up on the soup plan, he brings me plate after plate of slightly burnt toast and forgets what medicine he's given me and when. I groan and complain and tell him there's this thing called a pen and he can write that stuff down. He tries to make me drink some of the green slime juice and there's more swearing from both of us. Like I said, I'm not at my best.

Once I start feeling a bit better, I apologize. 'I'm a horrible ill person,' I wince. 'Ask any member of my family and they'll tell you. You should have run for your life the second my temperature started rising.'

'You didn't give me much notice before you started projectile vomiting,' Theo says, rearranging the pillow behind my head. 'But I'll certainly bear it in mind for next time.'

'I'm just trying to warn you,' I mumble. 'We're not out of the woods yet. I'm going to be a whiney grump for a while.'

'I can handle it,' Theo says with what I consider to be misplaced confidence.

'You say that now . . .' I trail off, weakly. 'I need to phone David. Shouldn't we be organizing someone else to come here and look after you? Maybe I should just go home.'

'I don't need someone to look after me,' Theo huffs. 'I'm not a houseplant, I'm a grown man.'

I remain suspiciously silent but the look I give him obviously speaks volumes.

'I am,' Theo insists, clearly torn between outrage and amusement. 'You and David make me feel about three years old, but I promise you, I am almost forty and capable of functioning in the world without a nanny.'

I raise my brows. 'How much is a pint of milk?'

'I don't know. Two pounds? Three?' he hesitates. 'Wait, is this one of those trick questions to show how out of touch I am and it's actually 50p?'

'How do you pay a gas bill? How do you log in to your Netflix account? How does the washing machine work?'

He looks annoyed now. 'Just because I *don't* do those things doesn't mean I *can't* do those things,' he insists.

'Fair enough.' I slump back, closing my eyes, far too tired to carry on that conversation. I wonder distantly why it feels normal for Theo to sit on my bed, arguing with me. 'But it doesn't seem right that I'm getting paid to do a job I can't do. Not that there was much to do in the first place.'

'Because I'm so low-maintenance,' Theo insists, stretching his long body out beside me, hands clasped on his stomach. 'And just shut up about it. You're ill, it's not your fault. You'll be better in a few days and then everything will be back to normal. You don't need to lose your job just because you've got the sniffles.'

'The sniffles,' I snort, my head resting on his shoulder of its own accord. 'More like the Black Death.' And then I fall asleep again.

*

Two days later I'm feeling much better; wan and tired and coughing like I smoke forty a day, but my temperature is normal, my body has stopped aching, and I treat myself to a long, hot shower, changing into real clothes. Sure, they're a pair of yoga leggings and a crop top which is – at the very least – bra *adjacent*, but that is all anyone can ask for at this point. I top this off with a sloppy T-shirt that used to belong to Len but which I kept because I had broken it in perfectly. It may not be a huge step up from pyjamas but they're still clothes, *outside* clothes.

When I make my way gingerly downstairs, I find Theo sprawled on the sofa.

'Hey,' I say, suddenly weirdly shy. I've spent the last two days sleeping and sneezing. I have been a sick, sweaty, cross little gremlin that whole time, and he's looked after me. There's not really any reason to start feeling shy now. That ship has sailed. That ship is way over the horizon, tangling with sea monsters.

'Hey!' He turns to me, a pleased smile spreading across his face, and the dimple is out and it feels like someone has flipped a light switch inside me. 'You're up!' Then he sneezes four times in a row.

'Oh, no.' I take a step towards him.

'I don't feel too bad,' he insists, though his nose is pink and his eyes look a little glassy. 'Just some sneezing and a bit of a headache. Nothing life-threatening.' I lean over him, touching my hand to his forehead.

'You're not hot,' I sigh, relieved.

'That's a matter of opinion, thanks,' he replies, his voice muffled. I look down and realize that I'm standing bracketed by his long legs, pressing my chest right next to his face.

'Oops, sorry!' I take a sharp step back.

'Didn't hear me complaining,' he murmurs, but I ignore that. Flirty Theo has returned, it seems, and I remind myself not to read too much into things, that any feelings of a warm, tingly nature need to be firmly quashed.

'Let's get some of those vitamins in you,' I say over my shoulder, going to grab a bottle of juice from the fridge. When I come back into the living room I throw it at him. He catches it easily, cracks it open to start drinking, and I try not to watch the movement of his throat.

'Someone sent you something.' Theo gestures to the coffee table where he's left a small box addressed to me. 'There's another one too, I shoved it over there.' He points by the window and there's a giant box sitting on the floor. I can't believe I missed it. Too busy looking at Theo, which, I chide myself, is not a good idea. Does he have a pretty face? Yes. Does he have the body of an underwear model? Yes. Is he also surprisingly sweet and caring? Sure . . . I'm losing track of my own point here and I blink, focussing on the boxes instead.

I tackle the giant box first and Theo gets up to help me. It's an enormous, floppy stuffed unicorn, the kind a child could use as a beanbag. It has a rainbow-coloured mane and it's wearing a homemade sash, beauty-queen style, that says, GET WELL SOON, CLEMMIE!

'From Lil,' I smile. The most perfectly Lil gift, ever.

Theo is still examining the unicorn ('Can we call him Corny?' he asks) when I open Serena's gift. If the unicorn was perfectly Lil, then this is certainly Serena. It's a jumbo-sized bottle of echinacea and an extremely expensive-looking, all-the-bells-and whistles, also jumbo-sized, purple vibrator.

I snort, reading the card.

Orgasms make everyone feel better. Hope this stops you being a moody cow. No reason wish number 1 can't still come true. Xx Serena

I look up at Theo and see him notice what's in my hand. For a second there's a look in his eyes that feels like it's about to burn the clothes off my body. Then he clears his throat.

'From Serena, I'm guessing?' he says, and his voice is steady, amused.

'Of course,' I reply, shaking my head as if I can physically dislodge the decidedly not-suitable-for-work images that are flashing across my brain.

'Nice,' he nods, and he sounds so mildly interested that I think maybe I imagined the look altogether, maybe it was just me. I really don't think he's been affected after all, not until he turns and walks straight into the wall beside him.

'Ow!' he groans as I collapse helplessly into laughter.

Theo sneezes again. And again, and again.

Finally he crashes out face down on the sofa. 'My head hurts,' he mumbles.

'I need to call David.' I am already pulling out my phone.

'No, you don't,' Theo says firmly. Then he sneezes again.

'Are you kidding? What if you get worse? I'm already on the thinnest of thin ice with him. I need to tell him right now.'

Theo's response is to close his eyes and moan into the sofa cushions.

David answers on the first ring.

'Clementine.' He sounds as annoyed by my existence as ever. 'I trust you are feeling better.'

'Yes, thank you,' I reply nervously. 'Um, but Theo seems to have developed a bit of a cold.'

There's a dangerous pause. 'Is it affecting his voice?'

Oh God, I hadn't even thought about that. 'Is your throat hurting?' I ask Theo. He shakes his head. 'He says no,' I tell David.

'Put him on the phone, please.'

I hand the phone to Theo, who sits up reluctantly. 'Hey,' he says, resigned. Then he is quiet for a while as David talks. A frown pinches between his eyes. 'Fly the doctor in from LA?' he repeats incredulously. 'It's just a cold, David. Calm down.'

What follows makes Theo's cheeks flush. 'That was a totally different situation and you know it!' He casts a glance in my direction and huddles lower, speaking softer, but I still catch the sulky teenage tone. 'I'm not totally out of touch with reality, you know.'

Even I hear the bark of laughter David makes and I press

my lips together to keep from smiling. The way David acts about my job, I thought he would be incredibly obsequious with Theo, but it sounds like he's happy to give him as hard a time as he does me.

'Give it a rest,' Theo says. 'You know I'd let you fuss if it was something serious, but it's not. I don't have to perform for twenty thousand people tomorrow so I think we can give the doc the night off.'

This must be enough for David because after another couple of minutes of conversation Theo hands the phone back to me.

'Clementine, listen to me very carefully.' David's voice is serious. 'Mr Eliott's vocal cords are worth a fortune – an *actual fortune* – and they are in your care. Think of him as a Stradivarius. Your only job is to protect this precious instrument. I am going to send you a list of throat treatments that he needs to strictly adhere to, and if he shows any sign of getting worse, *any sign at all*, you contact me immediately.'

I can feel my eyes growing wider and wider as he talks. 'Yes, David,' I say meekly.

When he hangs up a few minutes later, I look over at Theo. 'What did he say?' he asks suspiciously.

'He said . . .' I swallow. 'That your vocal cords are in my care. He called you a precious instrument. He called you . . . a Stradivarius.'

Theo lifts his hands to his face. 'Oh my God,' he whispers, like a kid whose parents have just mortified them.

I start giggling then.

Theo drops his hands. 'And you can shut up as well,' he grumbles, but even though his mouth stays in a flat line, his eyes crinkle.

I laugh harder and my laughter almost immediately turns into a wheezy, honking cough that has me bracing both hands on my knees.

'Right,' I say, once I've got myself under control. 'I hope you like lemon and honey because according to David you're going to be basically swimming in the stuff.'

Chapter Seventeen

Things take a turn for the worse the following morning when Theo's temperature hits just over thirty-eight degrees. My phone is already out in my hand when Theo's fingers wrap around my wrist.

'Don't,' he says. I am temporarily distracted by this, the first time he has touched me when I haven't been too ill to pay attention. He has such good hands and the warm pressure of his fingers, the cold touch of the silver rings he wears against my skin . . . let's just say I'm definitely paying attention now.

I swallow. Gather my wits. 'I have to,' I say unsteadily. 'You're ill.'

'I just don't want the fuss.' He sighs, lets go of me. 'I don't feel too bad, really.'

'I don't know,' I say slowly. 'Your temperature is going up. And you're so pale and snotty.'

'But I haven't been sick,' he wheedles. 'And I don't have a sore throat. Your oath to protect my precious voice is still intact.'

When I still hesitate, he sighs. 'Look, we know exactly what it is and how to deal with it. I obviously don't have it as bad as you because I'm not currently vomiting all over your shoes.'

'I didn't vomit on your shoes!' I exclaim, outraged.

'There was splatter,' Theo says firmly. 'My shoes were compromised.'

'You're being ridiculous,' I grumble. 'I kept all my vomit neatly in the sink like a *professional.* I don't think you were even wearing shoes.'

Theo waves this away. 'Whatever, the point is that all I need to do is take some of the pills the doctor gave you, rest and drink water. If you call David, that treatment won't be any different, but do you know what he'll do?'

I shake my head. I actually *don't* know what David would do if his precious Theo was sick, but I imagine him smashing in through the window with a war cry and a sack of Sicily's finest lemons tucked under his arm.

'First of all, he'll fly a doctor – or multiple doctors – over from LA.' Theo looks at me from under his brows. 'Think of the earth, Clemmie. The environment. The unnecessary carbon footprint.'

I huff.

'Then,' Theo holds up a warning finger, 'he'll come himself, and – I cannot stress this enough – he will *never leave.* He will somehow blame you for this situation and then he will hover over you for the next four and a half weeks making sure you're following his instructions precisely and he will drive us both insane.'

'Is this all because you don't want to lose access to my junk food?' I ask suspiciously.

Theo looks shifty for a moment. 'I've just rediscovered Mini Cheddars,' he whispers finally, a broken man. 'Please don't take that away from me.'

I laugh – I can't help it – and Theo's eyes light triumphantly. He also follows this up with what I know is his trump card. '*And* he'll report to the label and then they'll all be going mad, fretting over the album, and it will just make things more stressful for Serena.'

Air hisses between my teeth and I know that *he* knows he's got me. 'Fine,' I say grumpily, 'but you're going straight up to bed; we're going to fill you up to your neck with medicine, and if you do start feeling worse you have to tell me.'

'So bossy,' Theo murmurs, walking ahead of me. 'I love it.'

'Are you all right taking these painkillers?' I ask him a little awkwardly once he's lying on his bed.

'Because of the drinking you mean?' he asks. I nod. I know he doesn't drink, and David specified the house should be kept clear of alcohol. I hadn't thought too much of it. I know plenty of people who don't drink for one reason or another – though I will admit that, given his job, I have my own suspicions, fairly or not. Let's just say Ripp and his friends aren't exactly squeaky clean . . . far from it.

'Yeah.' Theo leans his head back against the pillow. 'I gave up the drink a few years back. Not because I had a problem, exactly, but because I could all too easily imagine a future where it *would* be a problem. I've seen way too many friends heading down that road and I was lucky that one or two of them saw the signs and pulled me up on it before that happened. It was easier just to give it up altogether.' He groans. 'But painkillers are fine. Now I know what you were babbling about with your achy bones.'

I dole out the tablets and enter the time and what he's taken into the Notes app on my phone, which Theo says is 'smug and obnoxious behaviour', and which I tell him is simply the action of a functioning adult. I force him to drink some water, check his temperature again and then make to leave.

'No, don't go,' he says softly.

I turn back to face him.

'Who will protect me if I have demonic Mr Men hallucinations?' he asks, forlorn. 'What if I feel the need to chew on someone's arm?'

I feel my cheeks flush. 'I told you before that you definitely imagined that.'

'Please?' He tilts his head, patting the bed beside him. 'Don't leave me on my own.'

I eye his bed, tell myself this is a bad idea, but I think we both know it's for show. 'You need to go to sleep though,' I say, climbing up next to him.

'That's fine.' Theo's eyes are already closed. 'There are some books on the bedside table if you get bored of watching my beautiful face.'

I lean over him. There are three books stacked next to the bed: an Agatha Christie novel; the Judy Blume book I pulled off the bookshelf in my room last week, the one that has CLEMENTINE MONROE written in a round hand inside the cover; and a copy of *The Canterbury Tales*.

'Chaucer?' I ask, surprised.

'You've got a poster of him in your bedroom.' Theo doesn't open his eyes. 'I was jealous. Wanted to know what the fuss was about.'

I grab the book and get comfy on my side of the bed. 'You want all the girls to have Theo Eliott posters in their bedrooms?' I tease.

'Not *all* the girls,' he mumbles. I feel my cheeks warm, remind myself that he doesn't mean anything by it.

'I'm more of a Ryan Gosling fan,' I say lightly.

Theo groans.

We're quiet for a bit. I leaf through the familiar pages, smile as I notice Theo has been making notes in the margins, trying to translate the Middle English, underlining the rude bits. I think he must have fallen asleep, but then he snuggles closer to me.

'I like your bed better,' he says, his voice drowsy and a little slurred as the tablets kick in.

'Your bed is the one with the fancy gazillionaire sheets on it,' I remind him.

He sighs. Moves his hand until his fingers brush up against my arm.

'You're so soft,' he says dreamily. 'I'd like to bite you too. Like a peach.'

The noise my brain makes is like a rusty chainsaw revving

to life. *It's the tablets. We all get a bit loopy when we have a temperature. Remain calm.*

'I guess I don't mind which bed I'm in,' he manages after a moment, 'as long as you're in it too.'

What am I supposed to say to that? I stay frozen, trying to find the words.

But I don't have to find them, because a light snore lets me know that Theo has fallen asleep.

For the next couple of days I make sure Theo has a constant stream of lemon and honey, force him to inhale steam, gargle warm water, take his pills. I tick off every duty David has given me and it seems to do the trick.

Chalk one up for the ten thousand supplements because Theo's illness never gets worse than that day he had the higher temperature, not that it stops him complaining about it.

'I just think *maybe* I should ask David to send someone with an IV vitamin drip for us,' he whines when we are sitting on the sofa watching TV.

'Be quiet and drink your Lemsip.' I throw a kernel of popcorn at his face, but he catches it in his mouth and flashes me a smug grin.

I can't get over how easy it is being around him. I've even learned to tamp down the relentless electric crackle of physical attraction that I feel towards him. Well, partly. A little bit at least. The snot helped for a while.

And yes, he's a flirt. He's ridiculously, eye-wateringly charming, but I simply have to remind myself that that is who he is. The fizzy feeling I get sometimes is just a result of being caught in the orbit of someone with the charisma to woo stadiums full of fans. It's as natural to him as breathing; I'm not sure he can actually turn it off. And as long as I remember that, remember who he is, it actually feels like we're starting to be . . . *friends.*

The cold, distant Theo of last week has melted away, and now I lie under a blanket as we watch *Blood/Lust* together.

Days ago, Theo told me in no uncertain terms that he had no interest in watching this 'crap', but I paid no attention, silently hitting play on the first episode. Now we're halfway through season two. We've been living like mole people, eating ice cream and keeping the blinds shut. Theo is fully invested, researching his favourite pairings, reading bits of smutty fan fiction aloud to me from the browser on his phone.

'I can't believe you read fan fiction,' I say.

'Oh yeah. There's loads on this site about me, you know.' He sounds delighted with himself.

'No!' I am aghast. 'And you've read it?'

'Some of it.' He looks at me, widens his eyes innocently. 'What? There's no need to be so puritanical about it. I have talented fans. Nothing wrong with a bit of finely crafted erotica.'

I make a sort of spluttering noise while trying to convince myself that I won't be looking any of these stories up later.

We go back to watching the show, and we're just reaching one of my favourite bits – a pivotal romantic moment and the first kiss between the two main characters – when Theo makes the sort of high-pitched sound that I would previously have only attributed to a teenage girl.

'What?!' I ask, startled.

'This is my song!' he beams, gesturing at the TV. He grabs the remote and turns the volume up, and there – in the background – is a raspy, velvet voice singing seductively over a slow, pulsing beat. Then that raspy, velvet voice isn't just on the TV, it's in the room as he sings along and all of my skin breaks out in goosebumps. *Oh, shit.* The characters on the screen kiss, and I think, *Of course you're kissing, you dummies! Listen to that man's voice! I can't believe you've still got any clothes on!*

Fortunately, Theo doesn't notice my meltdown, too busy enjoying the moment, his eyes glued to the screen. 'My favourite show used one of my songs. That's pretty cool,' he says happily.

The spell is thankfully broken by this declaration, and I burst out laughing. 'Your favourite show? A couple of days ago you wouldn't even let me put it on.'

'I'm older now, Clemmie,' he says earnestly. 'Wiser.'

'You're an idiot,' I snigger, throwing another piece of popcorn at him.

He doesn't dignify that with a response, but as he settles back on the sofa he pulls my feet into his lap. Maybe it should feel like a strange thing to do, but it doesn't. It feels easy, natural.

'Hey, Theo,' I say, almost idly.

'Mmm?' He doesn't look away from the TV.

'Why were you so weird with me when you got here? Did I do something to upset you?'

I feel him tense, but when he turns to look at me his face doesn't give anything away. 'No, you didn't do anything.' He pauses for a moment, his mouth turned down. 'I'm sorry if I made you feel that way. I was stressed. I've been a bit . . . anxious.'

I think about that. 'About the album?' I venture.

He nods, a quick dip of his chin. I let the silence stretch between us. Ingrid would be proud. 'I haven't written anything in a long time,' he says finally. 'This album is two years overdue, did you know that?'

'I didn't know it was so long,' I say. No wonder the label is having kittens.

'Yeah.' He starts rubbing my foot almost absently, and I feel every cell in my body respond but strive to keep my expression neutral.

'My last record didn't do as well as the ones before,' he explains with a wince, sounding pained by the admission. 'I want this one to be special. I know I can do better, but for some reason I can't seem to get started. The longer it goes on, the more pressure there is and now it feels like this huge, impossible obstacle.' He sighs.

'This is the label's last-ditch attempt to get me to focus, then they're going to want to bring other writers in. I've never liked working that way. We did it for years when we were in the band, and I get that it can be great, but for me, that's the whole point – to make music that's totally personal. For it to come straight from me, from what I'm feeling.'

I am pretty out of my depth here. What do I know about making music? I might come from a family of musicians, but I've done my level best to avoid conversations like this. Already there's a queasy sensation that this feels too close to things I heard Sam say, but I shove that to the side. Theo is obviously upset. 'I know it's not the same thing,' I say tentatively, 'but when I'm writing something, I have to try and concentrate on just the little bit in front of me. If I think about the whole thing, it's too overwhelming.'

It's the most trite, obvious advice, but Theo smiles sweetly, squeezes my foot in his warm hand. 'Yeah,' he says. 'I guess I just need somewhere to start. It doesn't have to be perfect.'

'Right,' I agree.

He looks at me for another second, his gaze intent on mine, and for some reason my heart rate ratchets up. He takes a deep breath, like he has something important to say, then his eyes slide away.

'Anyway, it's your turn to fetch the ice cream,' is what comes out of his mouth. 'And don't even try and fob me off with that sorbet nonsense again.'

Chapter Eighteen

The next day we finally leave the house for a walk on the beach. It's Theo's idea, but I am quick to agree. It's a beautiful, sunny day and we emerge blinking into the light. I hiss like a cat and Theo chuckles.

'Come on, Drusilla.' He shakes my elbow. 'A bit of vitamin D will do you good.'

'Ugh, you sound like Serena.'

We head through the rickety gate at the bottom of the back garden and down the steep path. Winding through the dunes of fine golden sand punctuated with clumps of feathery green grasses, I am hit by that familiar blast of clean salt air. It feels so good, it must surely be medicinal.

'So you and your sisters used to come here for the summer?' Theo asks.

'Yep,' I nod. 'It belonged to Granny Mac, Lil's great-grandma. I mean, she was related to Lil by blood but she always saw Serena and me as family, too.'

'What was she like?'

'She'd have made mincemeat of you,' I laugh. 'She came from Peebles, and when she and her husband moved here, her family called her a soft southerner, even though it's only about thirty miles south of there. And she agreed with them! She lived here for most of her life and you'd think she'd retired to the south of France the way she talked about Northumberland.'

We've reached the beach now and the sand stretches out, the tide is low.

'Lil's grandparents didn't want much to do with Petty when she got pregnant, but Granny Mac did. Her husband died before we were born so she lived here alone. If Petty hadn't moved in with Mum, she and Lil would have come up here. We visited for every summer holiday for as long as I can remember.' I think about the woman who was a grandmother to us all.

'She hated my dad, *hated* him, but she loved us.' I smirk. 'I remember the only time she met Ripp she called him an over-sexed idiot and told him it was a relief to us all that his genes were so pathetic because luckily there wasn't a bit of him in *her girls*. Then she said she thought his music was pure shite, too. Ripp looked like he was going to wet his pants.'

Theo's laugh bursts out of him and I grin back. 'Yeah, it was great.' I think about it a bit more, about how best to describe Granny Mac. 'She was kind,' I say, swallowing hard. 'Gruff and bad-tempered and a bit intimidating I suppose, but under it she was so kind. She never made me and Serena feel like there was any difference between how she felt about us and Lil.'

'She sounds great.' Theo's hands are dug in the pockets of his jeans as we amble towards the sea. The tide is right out and the water is a perfect, clear blue.

I nod. 'I miss her a lot. I haven't been back here since she died.'

Theo stops in surprise, turns to me. 'You haven't?'

'No, not since I came back for her funeral when I had just turned eighteen.'

He blows out a long breath. 'I had no idea. How is it? Being back I mean.'

I twist my foot in the sand. 'It's strange. A bit sad. It helps that the house looks so different inside, I guess, but being down *here*,' I gesture around us at the beach. 'This is where the three of us lived. Granny Mac used to open all the doors and let us loose for the summer. The first thing we'd do is run down and write our names in the sand, claiming it for our own. We were wild for six weeks, just lost all sense of civility. Tangled hair, bare feet, sunburn, sand everywhere, never showered. We swam and played and climbed over all the rocks. It was wonderful.' I look around at the site of so many of our adventures and feel that particular, sweet mix of nostalgia and sadness that comes with memories of Granny Mac and those magic, uncomplicated summers.

Theo's white teeth flash. 'A sort of feral Famous Five?'

'That's right.' I smile back at him. 'I don't think Serena could ever pull off anything as wholesome as Enid Blyton. None of us could. One of our favourite games was seeing which one of us the others could pin down and force to eat the most sand.'

Theo hums with amusement.

'At least until we hit puberty and then it was sunbathing, Jilly Cooper novels and sneaking up the coast to watch the surfers in their wetsuits. And better personal hygiene, thankfully.' I gesture to the rocks that hem in this private cove. 'Do you want to keep going? We have to climb over the rocks but then we join a long stretch that's good for walking.'

'Yeah,' Theo agrees easily. 'This is nice.'

We scramble over the rocks past the 'private property' sign. Well, I scramble; Theo lopes gracefully over them on his long legs like they're nothing at all. Once we reach the other side I'm reminded that it's early summer and that it's not just the two of us out here at the end of the world. The long sweep of the public beach is dotted with people – families playing in the water, couples stretched out sunning themselves, excited dogs tearing about through the sand.

I glance over at Theo, but he doesn't seem worried. He's wearing his sunglasses and a baseball cap and his scruff has grown in so much it almost constitutes a beard. I guess it's unlikely anyone will recognize him. We walk for a bit, and he bends down, picks up a pretty, pale pink seashell. He turns it over in his hands then hooks his finger in the pocket of my shorts, tugging me closer as he drops the shell inside.

'So, why haven't you been back here since you were eighteen?' Theo asks.

I scrunch up my nose. 'I didn't leave the place on the best

of terms. I came here after a breakup, a bad one, and then it was only a few weeks after I went home that Granny Mac passed away. She had a heart attack and no one found her until it was too late.' I feel my eyes sting, blink rapidly.

It was just another thing that made me furious with Sam . . . and with myself. I'd been too busy thinking about my own drama to spend time with her. Heart-broken Clemmie was even less fun to be around than sick Clemmie, and I hated the thought that those last, precious memories were mired in a cloud of misery and me being the very worst version of myself.

Most important of all was the guilt that I might have missed some clue about her health, something that could have changed the outcome. I don't say any of that, but for a second I want to. I want to spill my guts to Theo, and I don't know when and how he started slipping past my defences.

'The last time I came up was for her funeral,' I say instead. 'She left the house to Petty in her will, but none of us could face being up here without her, so Petty lets the place out as a holiday home.'

'That's rough,' Theo says quietly. 'When my gran passed away no one told me until after the funeral. I was on tour in the States and they didn't want to bother me.' There's a bitterness in his words that I haven't heard from him before.

I suck in a breath. 'Ouch, that's awful.'

'Yeah,' he agrees, 'I was pretty angry about it. I would have wanted to be there. I loved her.' We come to a stop at the edge of the water and he turns his face, looking out to the horizon. 'Also, I guess I felt like, what does it say about me that my family did that? That they thought I'd treat her death as . . . an *inconvenience*? I don't know what I did to make them feel that way, but I must have been pretty shitty.'

'I'm sure they were only trying to protect you. I know from Serena's job what the big record labels can be like; they were probably thinking you wouldn't be able to come and then you'd feel awful.'

'I would have made it work,' he says, his voice low. 'I'd have been there to say goodbye. I'd do anything for my family.'

'I'm sure they know that,' I say, matching his tone.

'Excuse me,' a nervous voice says from behind us. Theo and I both turn and there's a woman standing there. She's in her twenties and she looks as if she's about to pass out, pale and shaking.

'Are you,' she starts, barely above a whisper. She closes her mouth, then opens it. Tries again. 'Sorry, but are you Theo Eliott?'

I freeze. It's not like we aren't allowed to leave the house or anything, but the plan is very much to keep Theo's exposure to people as low as possible. Serena had a long talk with me about security risks if the paparazzi and his fans found out where he was staying. It's not like Granny Mac's house is exactly Fort Knox.

But Theo is relaxed, smiling. 'No, sorry,' he says, slipping effortlessly into a Californian drawl that I don't recognize. 'I get that all the time, and my wife thinks it's hilarious.'

Here he picks up my hand and gives it a little squeeze.

My mouth opens and it takes a second for any words to come out, for me to realize he's using me as normal-person camouflage. I think it's because the word *wife* has short-circuited my brain. 'Yeah, he wishes,' I manage to croak in the end.

Behind his glasses I know exactly how Theo's eyes are sparkling. 'Don't I just? That Theo Eliott is one good-looking guy.'

The woman slumps in disappointment. 'Yeah, I thought it couldn't be him. I mean, what would he be doing here, right?'

'He's probably off doing goat yoga and drinking kombucha somewhere,' I agree.

The woman laughs. 'Yeah. Well, sorry to bother you,' she says with a shy smile, her eyes sliding back to Theo for another look before turning and running back to her friends who are watching us with interest.

We keep our backs to them, walking away.

'I feel bad,' I say. 'She was so excited.'

'Yeah, me too,' Theo agrees. 'I don't want to disappoint people, but sometimes it's more important to protect my little corner of normality, and the other people who are there with me. It took me a long time to get my head around that, that I wasn't obliged to give every piece of myself away. Boundaries and everything.'

Something warms in my chest. It's the sort of thing I have never, ever heard Ripp Harris say. I can't even imagine him *thinking* it, worrying about boundaries or wanting to protect me, and I'm his actual daughter.

In fact, I don't need to imagine it, do I? I've been there with Ripp, begging him to save me from the storm around him, and he didn't do a thing. Didn't even understand there was a problem. My stomach clenches at the memory.

'I've never done goat yoga by the way,' Theo says.

I roll my eyes. 'Tell it to the bottles of organic kombucha fermenting in our kitchen cupboard.'

'I'm not saying I'm against the idea,' he muses. 'Those baby goats are pretty cute.'

I laugh, a big, sunshiny laugh, and we carry on walking. I think about the seashell in my pocket and how I'll put it on my bedside table when we get home. And as my hand stays wrapped in Theo's all the way up the beach, I tell myself it's just part of the charade. It doesn't mean anything. Nothing at all.

Chapter Nineteen

I'm sitting at the dining table, staring at my laptop in something approaching despair a couple of days later, when Theo sticks his head around the door.

'Do you mind if I join you?' he asks, casting a glance at my computer.

'Of course not,' I say quickly. 'I'm trying to work on this stupid academic book and getting nowhere. Do you want me to get out of your way?' I start gathering the pages of notes that I have spread across the table.

'Don't be an idiot,' Theo says, moving into the room. 'I like you being here. If I wanted to be alone, I'd have stayed in my room.'

'Okay,' I say warily, because I've noticed the guitar he's holding in one hand. It's the first time I've seen any sign that he's working on his music since we arrived.

He strolls in and sits down on the sofa, pulling a small notebook out of his pocket, which he drops down beside him, his feet up on the coffee table.

He's wearing loose grey jogging bottoms and his hair is damp like he's just got out the shower.

I know for a fact that he spent the morning working out because I walked in on him in the office/gym while looking for a package that David sent while I was ill. He was lifting a heavy-looking dumbbell in a way that made his bicep curl and all the muscles pop out, and I had to go and lie down on my bed for ten minutes while thinking extremely pure thoughts.

'Do you need anything?' I ask.

'Nope.'

Theo doesn't say anything else and so I force my attention back to my work, reading over the chapter notes I've written for the hundredth time. Since we've been here, I've made precisely zero progress. It's funny how little I've been thinking about work.

Out of the corner of my eye I see Theo looking out the windows, his guitar in his lap. Finally, he starts playing.

He plays quietly, so quietly, and it doesn't seem like he's playing a song or anything, just strumming gently, absently, his fingers drifting over the frets. Occasionally he'll play the same thing – the same few notes – over and over again, and then he goes back to drifting. At one point he leans forward, pulling a pencil from behind his ear, and scribbles something in his notebook.

I feel like I'm holding my breath, like I don't want to do anything to distract him or let him know I'm watching. I start tapping at the keyboard in front of me so that he'll think I'm working, typing anything that comes into my head.

Table
Laptop
Chair
Legs
Hands
Hair
Smile
Teeth
Dimple
Dimple
Dimple

When I finally focus on my screen and observe the wild ramblings of a stalker that have appeared there, I backspace frantically, the cursor gobbling the words back up. If only it were so easy to delete the thoughts from my brain.

'Is something wrong?' Theo asks. 'Your face has gone pink.'

I smother a groan. 'Just stuck on something.'

'I know the feeling.'

My eyes slide towards him. He's slumped back in his seat, practically horizontal. The guitar is cradled in his lap.

'You're making a start, though,' I say. 'That's something.'

'I guess.'

'I like that bit you were playing. The bit you played over and over again.'

'Yeah?' He sits up at that, a pleased smile on his face. He plays it again, louder now, the handful of notes that rise and fall, sweet and melodic.

I nod. 'It's pretty.'

'Pretty?'

I laugh awkwardly. 'I mean, if you're looking for musical insight you've come to the wrong person.'

'No, pretty is good,' he says, looking down at the notebook. 'Pretty is actually just right.'

'Oh,' I say. 'Well, good.'

We both fall quiet then and I go back to staring at my screen. This time I don't risk letting my subconscious take the wheel. Especially because my subconscious seems to have an unfortunate interest in the man who is my *friend*, my work acquaintance. Nothing more.

'Can I ask you something?' Theo asks.

'Sure.'

'What is the whole thing with you and music? You had that strange argument with Serena about it on her birthday.'

'Ah.' I clear my throat. 'That.'

'Yes, that.'

'It's a bit hard to explain. I know it's sort of weird . . .' I trail off.

Theo pats the sofa beside him. 'Step into my office,' he says. 'You tell me your weird and I'll tell you mine.'

I can't help smiling at that. 'You're supposed to be working,' I remind him.

'I am working,' he says. 'Talking helps. It's all . . . simmering in the background.'

I decide not to question why I'm so happy to accept that reasoning, to pick up the cold cup of tea I've been nursing and take it over to the sofa. I don't sit right next to him – extremely proud of myself for establishing such a boundary – and I pull my feet up settling cross-legged, almost across from him on the corner seat.

'So,' he says, strumming his guitar dramatically, 'Clementine Monroe and music. The true story.'

'I mean it's not very interesting.' I begin hesitantly. 'I don't like listening to music. I'd just never come home and put the radio on, or go and listen to live music or anything like that.'

'What happens if you hear music?' Theo asks.

I laugh. 'It's not like kryptonite. Nothing happens. I don't have a meltdown if I hear music. I hear it all the time, obviously. Music is everywhere, I just don't . . . seek it out or pay attention to it. I know Lil's music and I've been to see her play a few times, but otherwise . . .' I shrug.

'Mmmm.' Theo tilts his head. 'Glad to hear that my playing isn't going to strip you of your superpowers. But there must be more to it than that? Did you always feel that way?'

I shift uncomfortably. 'No. When we were growing up there was music in the house all the time. My mum was a singer and she plays the piano.' I look at him and he nods.

'I know your mum,' he says. 'I mean I don't *know* her, but I know who she is. I'm a big fan of hers, actually. It's gutting that she stopped so young – her first album was brilliant.'

Theo can't know that his words hurt, but something in my face must give it away because he frowns. 'What did I say?' he asks.

'Nothing.' I shake my head, fix a smile on my face. 'She was a wonderful musician; it's great that you like her music.'

'Okaaaay,' Theo draws the word out, clearly unsure what is going on.

I clear my throat. 'Anyway, thanks to Mum there was always music. She loved Fleetwood Mac, Simon and Garfunkel, Bob Dylan, Joni Mitchell . . . you know, anything with that sort of folky, story-telling feeling. She wrote her own music too.'

'She definitely had a Stevie Nicks vibe,' Theo muses.

'That's why Stevie was our favourite,' I agree. 'Serena, Lil and me, I mean. We used to love listening to Mum's album best – the one she made – but her Stevie Nicks and Fleetwood Mac records were a close second.' I smile. 'They were the soundtrack to all our witchy happenings.'

Theo's own mouth lifts in response.

'Anyway, Mum listened to all sorts and so did we. Petty was basically a teenager and she was in a real grunge phase, mad about Nirvana; Ava's always been into classical music, and they made sure we had all Ripp's albums too, that we knew what our dad did. That we were . . . proud of him.' I clear my throat. 'Me and music, it was uncomplicated for a long time. Normal.'

'So what changed?'

'My dad,' I say, fiddling with the sofa cushion. 'It's not that much of a mystery. My relationship with him deteriorated pretty sharply when I was a teenager and could finally see his bullshit for what it was.'

'I know he was pretty wild. I'm guessing Ripp Harris wasn't exactly a model father?'

I give a humourless laugh. 'You could say that. I actually saw more of him splashed across the papers than I did in real life. I remember once – I must have been nine or ten – I had a role in the school play, some tiny part, but I was thrilled and nervous. Ripp promised he'd come but of course he didn't turn up. Afterwards I was frantic, crying, insisting to my mum that something bad must have happened, that he'd *promised* he'd be there. She tried to calm me down but I was hysterical, convinced he'd been in a horrible car accident and no one was looking for him.' I still remembered the tang of fear from that night. Being on stage, searching for his face, baffled later that no one would listen to me.

'The next day there were photos of him in the paper with his tongue down the throat of some actress. He was in Milan, I think. Somewhere sunny and glamorous, anyway, somewhere far away from a school play in a draughty assembly hall.'

I blink. I haven't thought about that in a while.

'I'm sorry,' Theo says quietly.

I wave my hand. 'Don't be. The point is, it was only one of many, many disappointments. Death by a thousand cuts, that was my relationship with Ripp. I think at first I blamed the music for taking him away from us, which is . . . ridiculous, but it was how I made sense of it at the time. I suppose I felt like the music industry spat out my mum, and corrupted my dad, and I just didn't want anything to do with it. It was a sort of reverse teenage rebellion, turning my back on my parents' world. Giving up rock 'n' roll and turning to Chaucer instead.'

'I can see that.' Theo rubs his jaw. 'I'm just surprised it lasted so long.'

'It didn't exactly,' I shrug. 'A year or so. Then I turned seventeen, and fell totally in love with a musician.'

Theo's relaxed posture remains the same, but there's nothing sleepy about his eyes now.

'We were together almost a year. That's a lot at that age, isn't it? A week before my eighteenth birthday we broke up.' I continue. 'It was . . . bad.' That was an understatement. I was pretty sure most seventeen-year-old's breakups didn't get covered by the national press, but I wasn't about to get into the details with Theo.

'Let's just say he ended up confirming all my worst opinions about musicians and the business they're in. It wasn't a conscious decision after that, to cut music out my life; it just happened. At first everything reminded me of Sam – then I suppose it was habit, and yeah, it's a petty little dig at Ripp too, a way of showing I'm not interested in anything he has to offer. Music and heartache – they're wrapped together pretty tight for me.'

'Is this the ex you ran into at Carl's funeral?' Theo asks, then his brows lift. 'Wait. Seventeen? Is it the same breakup you were talking about yesterday? The one where you came here afterwards?'

'Yes, to both those things,' I say, and then, after a pause, 'That was Sam. Sam Turner.'

'Sam Turner?' Theo frowns. 'As in the drummer Sam Turner?'

'The one and only,' I agree.

'But isn't he . . .' It's Theo's turn to trail off.

'Ripp's drummer?' I keep my tone light. 'Yep. And if you're trying to do the maths, he got the gig right before we broke up.' I don't feel the need to clarify that it was actually the same day, but the anger that is still there, fifteen years and a ton of therapy later, must show.

'Shit,' Theo whispers, obviously drawing some conclusions that aren't precisely wrong. 'What a dick!'

'Ripp or Sam?'

Theo slumps back. 'Both, I guess.'

'Can't disagree with that.'

'So that's why Serena said that thing about you and rock stars? That you'd never be in a relationship with one?'

'What?' I start. I'm surprised by the question, but when I look at him his face gives nothing away; he's just watching me closely again. 'Er . . . yes, that's why. I've already had two of them smash my heart to pieces. You know, *fool me once* and all that.'

Theo is silent and I have absolutely no idea what is going through his mind. Judging by the look on his face, whatever it is isn't good.

The quiet makes me feel awkward. I hadn't realized he even remembered Serena's comment. *I* don't even remember Serena's comment, not exactly. I think back, something about me chewing off a body part before going out with a rock star. Perhaps Theo's been feeling bad about that, the fact that I slept with him without knowing what he did for a living.

'But you don't have to worry,' I say finally, and Theo blinks, looks at me like he'd forgotten I was there. 'What happened between us. You and me. Maybe I should have said something earlier. There are no hard feelings.'

'No hard feelings?' Theo repeats.

'I mean, I didn't know you were . . . *you*, when we slept together, but now that I do, I still don't feel like you've been . . .' – I flounder – 'added to that list.'

'The list of rock stars who smashed your heart to pieces?' he says slowly.

'I think this is coming out wrong.' I twist my fingers together. 'I'm just saying we never talked about it and things were awkward at first but I'm glad we're friends now. I never expected that night to turn into anything more, so it's not like I can be disappointed you turned out to be a rock star with a . . . *vibrant* sex life.' I wince. *Did I really just use the words 'vibrant sex life'? Oh God, I am so deeply, deeply uncool.*

'I get that you're all about keeping things casual,' I push on, desperately, 'and I was the one who said I wanted to try a one-night stand first and then you said you did too. Consenting adults. Boundaries. Crystal clear. I don't want you to think that I hold anything against you. I mean, it wasn't great that you didn't tell me who you really were, but I do get it: I get why that must have been nice for you, that I didn't think of you as *Theo Eliott.*' I'm rambling now.

Theo just looks at me coolly. 'I didn't say I wanted a one-night stand.'

It is literally the last thing I expect him to say. 'What?'

'I didn't say that. I asked you if a one-night stand was what *you* wanted, you said maybe, and I said perhaps we should find out.' He ticks the points off on his fingers.

I blink. How did he even remember all of this? And what was the difference between what he said and what I said?

Theo gets to his feet then, the neck of the guitar clasped loosely in his hand. He comes to stand in front of me and with his free hand he reaches out and gently tips my chin so that I'm looking right up at him, right into his eyes. There's no hint of sparkle there now.

'Clemmie.' His voice is rough, deeper than usual. So deep it sends a shiver over my skin. 'Let me clear up a misconception that you seem to be labouring under. I will admit that that wasn't my first one-night stand, but it was the first one in over a decade. And *I* wasn't the one who left the next morning.' He lets those words hang between us for a second before continuing. 'So don't tell me that I'm the one who wants to keep things casual, okay? You feel however you feel, but don't put words in my mouth.'

He just looks at me for another beat. Then his fingers move from my chin, drifting up along my jaw in the lightest touch before his hand falls away.

'I'm going to go and work now,' he says calmly. As if nothing momentous has happened at all.

'Okay,' I manage. 'I'll see you later?' It comes out as a question.

'Yes, you will,' he responds, and I don't understand why the words sound heavy, weighted with something. It's not until later that I realize they sound like a promise.

Chapter Twenty

'So he's definitely writing?' Serena asks, her eyes narrowing.

I nod. 'Yes, he has been all week. He told me to tell you he thinks it will end up somewhere between ten and thirteen tracks based on what he has so far.'

On the screen Serena's face relaxes, her shoulders slumping. 'Thank fuck for that. And? Is it any good?' Before I can say anything, she carries on. 'Actually, don't bother answering that. You wouldn't have a clue.'

'Right, I'm going to put your especially charming mood down to stress,' I say. 'And what I've heard *is* good, I think.'

I'm not going to tell her that I've only heard little snatches of music here and there, that Theo is being pretty cagey, spending most of his time in his room again. That neither of us have talked about what he said the other day. Or what it meant.

No, that's just been my own personal, private form of torture – lying awake replaying the conversation over and over and trying to work out what the hell happened.

I return my attention to my sister. 'He said it's going well, that he's feeling good about it. Obviously it's still early, but he seems really genuine.'

And that's true too, because even though I have been seeing less of Theo now that he's writing, he hasn't gone back to the moody, distant man who arrived here.

No, he's positively cheerful, still as funny and flirtatious as ever. We're still friends. And even that is messing with my head. What he said . . . had it been anyone else, I'd think they were saying they were interested in me – and not in a one-night-stand way. But it isn't anyone else; it's Theo Eliott, literally the Sexiest Man Alive, according to *People* magazine, and Biggest Womanizer Alive according to everyone else.

But, my brain whispers, *he said he hadn't had a one-night stand for over ten years. Ten years.*

And I believe him. Maybe that makes me an idiot, but I know Theo wouldn't lie to me. Not about that. So that means . . . what, exactly?

'This is such good news,' Serena breathes, and any lingering vulnerability in her face or voice is banished when she crows, 'I knew this would work! Two years! No one has got anything out of him, but then I come up with a plan and BAM! God, I'm good.'

'And don't forget humble,' I say.

'Women don't need to be humble.' Serena's smile is sharp. 'It only furthers the agenda of the patriarchy. Wait,' – she leans forward, suddenly suspicious – 'this sudden burst of creativity . . .' Her eyes drift over me on the screen. 'You'd better not be sleeping with him.'

'What?' I splutter. 'Of course I'm not sleeping with him! I would never.'

'You already have.' Serena folds her arms.

'Yes. *Technically*,' I manage. 'But I barely even remember it.' *Liar, liar.*

'You barely even remember the night you described as "an experience that transcended the boundaries of space and time when you looked upon the face of God and she was beautiful"? *That* night?'

I clear my throat. 'I don't think I said that.'

'You definitely said that.'

'Right, well, regardless of who said what and when, there is absolutely nothing going on between me and Theo now. He's probably just feeling creative because of all the . . . sea air.'

'The sea air?' Serena lifts a brow. 'I suppose so. Notoriously hard to find the stuff in *California*.'

I maintain a stony silence.

She sighs. 'All right, I believe you. Just make sure it stays that way. You know I wish you nothing but hot sex, but Theo Eliott is not for you, Clemmie. He'd chew you up and spit you out.'

'I wish we'd never made those wishes,' I grumble. 'Not when you and Lil keep bringing them up.'

'Baaaaabe!' a voice calls from somewhere off-screen behind Serena. A woman's voice. A woman in Serena's flat. Calling her babe.

We freeze, just looking at each other for a moment. Serena's eyes are enormous. A muscle in her jaw twitches.

'Babe?' The voice again. 'Have you seen my gold bracelet anywhere? I thought I left it by the bed.'

'Serena!' I hiss. 'Who is tha—' But I don't get to finish my question because my sister cuts the call off.

I stare, blinking at the blank screen.

'What just happened?' I ask aloud. I contemplate calling Serena straight back but I already know she won't answer, so I do the next best thing and call Lil.

'Sweet Clementine!' she coos when she picks up, her face close to her camera, beaming at me.

'Lil!' I get straight to the point, breathless. 'I was just on the phone with Serena and there was a woman with her in the flat and I heard her in the background and . . .' I trail off.

'And what?' Lil asks, a worried frown on her face.

'She called Serena "babe",' I whisper.

Lil's face turns blank. 'She . . .' she starts. 'What?'

'She called Serena "babe". *Twice.*'

'Fuck me,' Lil says succinctly, and the phone screen goes blurry. 'I'm ordering an Uber right now. I'm on my way. Do you think it's possible she's in some sort of hostage situation? Was this a cry for help? Was she blinking a lot? Like she was trying to communicate with you in Morse Code? I saw a film where someone did that once.'

'No, she was blinking a normal amount,' I say. 'There was something about it . . . I think . . . I think maybe Serena has . . . a girlfriend.'

Lil's face is back and she's on the move, heading down the stairs from her flat, panting into the screen. 'Serena?' she says like it's ridiculous. 'The woman who said that relationships were exclusively for people of below-average intelligence?'

'Remember that time Len called me "babe" in front of her and she mimed throwing up so realistically that he panicked and pulled the car over on the side of the A1, and then she had that twenty-minute rant about the infantilization of women and made him donate money to Women's Aid in front of her?'

'To be fair, that might be more of an "I-hate-Len" thing than an "I-hate-pet-names" thing,' Lil points out, folding herself into the back of her Uber and greeting the driver with a delighted, 'Oh, hello, Marcus!'

'So, tell me exactly what you heard,' she continues.

I do, and Lil frowns. 'So whoever this woman is she has *things* in Serena's flat? I don't believe it. Serena doesn't even have coat hooks because she doesn't want people "making themselves too comfortable". She sleeps diagonally across her bed. She only has one coffee cup.'

'There was a vibe!' I insist. 'The woman's voice was all sweet and relaxed and Serena flipped when I heard her, and put the phone down.'

Lil makes a humming sound. 'Suspicious. I'm pulling up to her place now.'

'Keep me on the phone,' I say, desperate to know what's going on.

'Of course.' Lil says her goodbyes to Marcus and rides the lift up to Serena's flat, before pounding on our sister's door. 'Serena!' she shouts. 'Open the door right now!'

There's a long pause.

'She's not answering,' Lil says. 'But I can tell she's in there. I can hear her *skulking*. Hang on, I need both hands.' Then she stuffs the phone down her top, treating me to an extreme close-up of her cleavage.

'Turn the camera around!' I shout.

'Oops!' Lil does, then puts the phone back in her top, so this time I am facing the door. Then I hear her digging through her bag until she finds Serena's front door key, which she slips into the lock.

'Hellooooo!' Lil calls out, moving through the hallway towards the living room. 'Serena?'

'Oh for fuck's sake!' I hear before Serena appears on screen, looking belligerent. 'Did Clemmie call you the *second* I put the phone down, that rat? How did you even get here so fast?'

'I took an Uber,' Lil replies.

'I'm here too, actually,' I call, presumably from the direction of Lil's boobs.

Serena's eyes bore into the camera. 'Good, then I can tell you to your face that you're a rat.'

'Lil thinks you're in a hostage situation,' I say.

For a second there's a look on Serena's face like she's considering agreeing with that, as if it were the better option.

'I'm not a hostage,' she finally admits, grudgingly.

'That is the most romantic thing you've ever said,' a voice

comes, the one I heard earlier, and a woman steps into the living room. She's drop-dead gorgeous. Tall and willowy with deep brown skin and braids that fall almost to her waist. She's about the same age as us, and her wide brown eyes shift nervously to my sister.

Serena sighs, but even over the camera I can see her face soften. She holds out her hand to the woman, who takes it shyly. 'Bee, this is my sister Lil, and my other sister Clemmie is shoved in her bra for some reason. Lil, Clem, this is Bee.' There's a pause and Serena manages to get the words out. 'My girlfriend.'

'OHMYGODDDDD!' Lil launches herself at Bee, which means I do too and the next few minutes are a series of increasingly bizarre camera angles and Lil's excited squeaking.

Eventually, my sister fishes the phone out of her top and hands it to Serena, dragging Bee off to the kitchen to make coffee and very obviously grill her on her intentions.

'You really are a pair of nosey bitches,' Serena huffs.

'We just love you!' I insist. 'How long has this been going on?'

'A few weeks,' Serena admits, and I can tell she's trying not to grin. I feel my heart squeeze, and I just look at her, beaming.

Serena rolls her eyes. 'Calm down. This is why I didn't tell you. I'm still me. I'm not turning into some gooey, cutesy little half-person, all right? I'm a whole person.'

I can hear the thread of anxiety in her words.

'S, you are the most whole human being I know. Being in a relationship doesn't mean losing a single piece of you. Not if it's with the right person.' As I say the words I realize the truth in them – and that I've clearly never been with the right person, because with Sam and with Len I gave up pieces of myself left and right like we were in an emotional game of Operation. It's a moment of epiphany and it's actually pretty overwhelming.

Clearly Serena comes to the same conclusion because she waves a finger at the phone. 'Don't you dare get upset,' she says firmly. 'Just stop going out with dickheads, all right?'

'Sure,' I nod. 'Though it would be easier if they wore signs around their necks or something, so I could give them a wide berth.'

'. . . And that's when we cast the spell for Clemmie, but now it's all coming true for me and Serena too!' I hear Lil explain sunnily as she and Bee come back in the room.

'I'm going to kill her,' Serena mutters.

Lil appears on my screen, right next to Serena, the two of them squished together looking at me, their faces as familiar as my own, and suddenly I miss them so much it's a physical ache in my chest.

'You'll see, Clemmie,' Lil says confidently. 'The three wishes are coming for you! Even Serena couldn't escape the big, soulm—'

'That's enough, Lilian,' Serena cuts her off, sounding so panicked that I have to stifle a laugh.

'I'll leave you to it,' I say reluctantly. 'But, Lil, you call me later.'

'Oh, I will.' Lil waggles her eyebrows to subtly communicate that I'll get the full lowdown as soon as possible.

'Jesus,' I hear Serena mutter wearily in the background.

'So, Bee, tell me literally every single thing about yourself—' Lil chirps before she hangs up the phone.

I sit for a moment just staring at nothing, trying to sort through the mess of feelings I'm experiencing.

Big love, the unconditional, whole-hearted, soulmate kind. Lil's wish echoes in my head. The fact that my thoughts turn almost instantly to Theo is enough to have me screaming silently into the void. What is wrong with me? Why am I doing this to myself?

I guess it's time to make an appointment with Ingrid.

Chapter Twenty-One

Theo decides to go out for a walk the afternoon that I'm scheduled to have my Zoom session with Ingrid, so I set up my laptop at the table in the living room and make myself a glass of iced peppermint tea. The teabags are Theo's fancy Moroccan ones and I've developed a taste for them which I'm sure is going to prove financially disastrous when we go home.

It's another blissfully sunny day and I've got the windows open, trying to encourage a bit of air into the sticky heat of the house. Distantly, I can hear the waves crashing outside and it triggers the urge to run down and splash straight into the water, a sound so tangled up in my memories of this place that it's all I can do not to rush out the door immediately, but instead to sit calmly, grown-up-ly, at the computer.

Despite being here for three weeks, I haven't spoken to Ingrid since arriving at Granny Mac's house. I know I should have done, but I've been putting it off. And I don't want to look too closely at why that is.

When she greets me, as unruffled as ever, sitting behind her immaculate glass desk, I feel a sense of relief at seeing her face.

I tell her how strange it is being in this house without my sisters or Granny Mac.

'Does it make you sad?' Ingrid asks.

'Sometimes.' I rub my nose. 'I didn't realize that after she died, I sort of . . . actively tried to stop thinking about her. It was too painful. But, now, *that* makes me sad, because it's like I've forgotten her. Being here after so long . . .' I glance around the room, the one that is still part of Granny Mac's house, and yet also not, also somewhere different now. 'It's like all the memories rush up sometimes. So fast I can't keep up, like they all come at once. It's noisy. Not bad, but noisy.'

Ingrid tilts her head. 'Perhaps you could start writing them down,' she suggests. 'I know that writing has often helped you to process things in the past. Would that give you a chance to untangle things? To sit with each memory more fully?'

'Maybe.' I chew my lip. 'It might. I just don't know if I want to . . . remember everything.'

Ingrid makes a humming noise in the back of her throat. 'And why do you think that might be?'

I fidget. 'Because she died. And I wasn't here. Because I *had* been here, just before and I wasn't so nice to her. I feel ashamed of that now. I didn't know it would be the last time, but it was.'

'Often we don't know when the last time will be,' Ingrid

says. 'You were only eighteen, Clemmie, and going through a very difficult time. Do you think your great-grandmother resented your behaviour?'

'Not resented it, no,' I shake my head slowly. 'But maybe she was disappointed?'

'I think you may be projecting your own feelings onto the situation. From what you have told me, the two of you had a very strong relationship. If you were hurting then I'm sure she understood. Do you think you can find some compassion for yourself? For the young woman who wasn't perfect but who was doing her best?'

I feel my eyes fill with tears. 'God, Ingrid,' I sniffle, reaching for the tissues that I had wisely placed beside my elbow. This was not my first therapy session after all. 'Why do you do this to me?'

'Fucking hell!' Theo's voice makes me jump as he crashes through the front door. 'It's hot as balls out there. I couldn't keep walking without risking desiccation. I brought you back a Magnum though, one of those almond ones you like . . . Oh, shit, sorry!'

He's in the living room now, and his cheeks are pink from the sun, his thin T-shirt clinging to his chest and stomach. He looks at me over the top of his sunglasses, taking in my tear-stained face, Ingrid on the screen in front of me.

'I'm interrupting,' he says slowly. 'I'm so sorry. Are you . . . okay?'

I give him a watery smile, wave the tissue in my hand a bit

awkwardly. 'I'm fine, just having a session with my therapist.' I'm not at all ashamed of having therapy, but I have to admit that Theo walking into the middle of it is a bit jarring. I have no idea what the protocol is. 'Er, this is Ingrid. Ingrid, this is Theo.'

Theo lifts his hand to wave, but frowns. 'Oh, I think the screen has frozen.'

I glance down, and he's right; Ingrid's face has frozen mid-word, her mouth slightly open. 'Oh typical,' I grumble, annoyed. 'David had them install that super-swanky router thing with eight thousand green lights on just for you. It looks like it could power a small nuclear facility and it can't handle one little Zoom call.'

'Let me have a look,' Theo says. 'It might be your laptop rather than the Wi-Fi.'

'Let's hope so or we're not going to be able to stream to the TV later.'

His expression is stricken. 'But . . . *my vampires*,' he whispers, anguished.

He leans over the computer, that beautiful face of his filling the screen. Theo Eliott in high definition.

That's when I hear it, the high-pitched squeaking sound. And it only takes me half a second longer to realize the sound is coming from Ingrid, who is not frozen in any technical sense of the word but is having some sort of Theo-Eliott-induced episode and staring out of the computer like a rabbit caught in a pair of extremely handsome headlights.

'What's that sound?' Theo says in confusion. 'I swear, I didn't touch anything! I only opened the settings.'

'Yeah, yeah,' I say, pushing him quickly to the side, trying to get him away from the screen and maintain Ingrid's dignity. 'It's a thing my laptop does sometimes. It's old. Don't worry about it.'

'Ingrid,' I say firmly. 'Can you hear me now?'

I see her blink.

'Yes, Clemmie, I'm here,' she says haltingly. 'I think there was a technical issue on my end.'

'There you go,' I say to Theo. 'No threat to your TV viewing.'

'Thank God for that.' Theo lifts his hand to Ingrid, who raises her own (is it *shaking*?). 'Nice to meet you, Ingrid. I'll leave you guys to it.'

Theo leaves the room, and Ingrid and I just look at one another for a long moment.

'I'm sorry, Clementine,' she says. 'That was very unprofessional of me.'

I smile sympathetically. 'Don't worry about it. He has that effect on people.'

'I would imagine so.' Ingrid seems to have regained her composure now and she's watching me closely, keenly. 'Is that . . . difficult for you?'

'Why would it be difficult for me?' I say unconvincingly. 'It's nothing to do with me.'

It would seem that Ingrid doesn't need to be in the same room with me to use her Jedi silent treatment effectively.

'Fine,' I exhale slowly, listening to make sure I can hear the sound of Theo's guitar coming from his room. I snatch up the ice cream he has left for me and tear off the wrapper. 'But I hope you've got time for a double session.'

'I'll clear my diary,' Ingrid says.

Around an hour after Ingrid and I say goodbye, Theo knocks on the doorframe before coming in the room. 'Are you all finished?' he asks, clocking that I'm sitting on the sofa with my laptop.

'Yeah, we finished a while ago,' I say. 'I was just doing some writing.'

'On your book?' he asks.

'No, I still can't face that. This is actually something Ingrid suggested.'

'Ah. I'm really sorry I interrupted your session like that.'

'It's fine.' I smile up at him. 'I should have done it in my room but it's so hot in there.'

Theo drops onto the sofa. 'Have you been seeing a therapist for long?'

'I've been seeing Ingrid for about two years now, but I've had therapy for a long time. It's sort of mandatory if you come from my family.'

'I wish it had been mandatory in mine,' Theo huffs. 'I had loads of hang-ups about it at first.'

'You've had therapy too?'

He lifts a brow. 'I do live in LA, you know. Talk about mandatory.'

I laugh and he does too. 'It helps a lot, actually,' Theo carries on. 'I've spent twenty years doing this very weird job that comes with a lot of challenges that aren't exactly typical. My whole adult life I've been famous. Public property. I was only a teenager when I joined the band so it's honestly like, at this point, I don't know anything different. This is my normal, and that actually doesn't make for great mental health. It seems like a good idea to get some help with that.'

'Wow,' I say. 'That's . . . incredible.'

Theo looks surprised. 'Really?' he asks. 'It feels like the absolute bare minimum amount of self-awareness to me. Something I'm working on, honestly.'

'Let's just say that the bare minimum is light years ahead of where Ripp Harris is on the self-awareness scale. And he's been doing that job for over forty years. I'm not sure there's even a *person* left inside him anymore. I can't tell you how different my life would have been if he'd done what you're doing.'

'Jesus, that's bleak.' Theo leans back against the sofa, but his head stays turned towards me, his eyes on mine.

'Yeah. You know, when I was eleven, there was this whole chunk of time . . . I didn't see him for eight months.'

'Why not?'

I lean back, mirroring Theo's posture. 'He'd taken me to see one of his gigs,' I sigh, remembering. 'Which was just about the highlight of my life up to that point. Then he got drunk, got high, forgot I was there and left me in the green room with a handful of people who were as out of it as he was while he went to some afterparty.'

'What? Seriously?' Theo looks shocked.

'Mmm,' I nod. 'I must have fallen asleep on the sofa in the end. By the time I woke up it was dark and the place was empty. I was scared, I remember that. Eventually Carl found me and drove me home. My mum was absolutely incandescent.'

'I'm not surprised.' Theo sounds pretty furious himself.

'She stopped Ripp's visitation rights for a while and I was devastated, hated her for keeping me from him.' I feel a pang of guilt. 'The next time I saw him was after my twelfth birthday. I was ready for this great reunion and he acted like nothing had happened. Not a thing. I wasn't even sure if he noticed I hadn't been around. It killed me.'

I blow out a slow breath. 'God, sorry, I'm on that post-therapy, feelings-at-the-surface wave right now.'

'I know it well.' His voice softens. 'But that's a lot. You seemed upset when I came in as well. Do you want to talk about it? It's fine if not.'

I close the computer and lay it on the sofa beside me. 'I was just talking about Granny Mac and being here. All the memories with my sisters and her and how strange it is being back. How I've avoided the place and thinking about her for so long. I feel pretty guilty about that last summer.'

'From what you've told me about her, I don't think she'd want you to feel guilty.'

The words bring a lump to my throat. 'That's pretty much what Ingrid said. She suggested I write down some of the things I remember about being here. That's what I was doing when you came in. It's nice actually; there are good stories. Most of the time when I was here it was . . . magic.'

'I like hearing about you here.' Theo looks around the room.

'In a way it feels like the last time I was really *me*. I didn't realize until I came back how much I'd closed myself off to things. How small I made myself.' I glance at him, and he's just watching carefully, giving me space to talk. 'It's like when I broke up with Len,' I carry on, 'and he had the movers come and take away all his stuff. It was pretty much everything in the flat, and I hadn't even *noticed*. I was just living inside someone else's life. I feel like I've been a, I don't know, a shadow for so long.'

'Huh,' Theo frowns.

'What?' I ask.

'It's just,' he hesitates, 'I'm surprised. The first time I saw you, I thought you were . . . luminous. Literally, like a light walking into the room. I never would have described you as a shadow. More like a candle in the dark.'

It's an incredibly lovely thing to say, and I have no idea how to respond to it.

'Sorry,' Theo clears his throat, looking like he didn't mean to say so much. 'That came out a bit weird. I just . . . I'm really sorry. It sounds like you've had a tough time.'

'No, no.' I feel embarrassed, like I've sold him some sob story when actually what's been bothering me is more how flat my life has been. 'I mean, things haven't been great, but they haven't been so bad either. And I've had Lil and Serena through it all.'

'Man, you and your sisters . . .' Theo grins, clasps his hands behind his head, ease returning. 'That relationship is pretty incredible.'

'Yeah, it is,' I agree, happy to change the subject. 'Most people don't get it, but it's like we're not just sisters. We're triplets. Not technically, but we never knew a life before there were three of us. And growing up the way we did, with the attention and the Ripp of it all – of course they have their own collections of Sad-Dad stories – they're the only other people in the world who will ever fully get it.'

'You're lucky,' Theo says, and there's something like envy in his voice.

'I am. With my job I've had to move around loads to different universities. I haven't got a big circle of friends and the ones I have, they're very spread out, but I never really needed a lot of friends – because I have Serena and Lil. For better or worse, they're the voices in my head.'

'Who's the oldest?' Theo asks.

'Serena,' I say. 'She's two months older than me, then Lil is almost two months younger than me.'

'Mmm,' Theo tips his head thoughtfully. 'I think I would have guessed that. You have real middle-child energy.'

'What's that supposed to mean?'

'Like you're the peace-keeper, trying to keep everyone happy,' he says, smug about having it all figured out.

'I'm working on the people-pleasing,' I huff. 'What do you think all the therapy is about? Anyway, you've got a sister, right? Any other siblings?'

'Nope, just Lisa.'

'And I bet you're the youngest.'

'Why would you think that?' he frowns.

'Because *you* have real baby-of-the-family energy,' I grin.

He throws a cushion at my face. 'I think you just called me spoilt,' he grumbles.

'Hey, if the handmade, Italian loafer fits.'

'You're the worst,' he says, but he can't hide the smile on his face.

'You love it,' I shoot back at him, the same way I would at Serena or Lil. I get to my feet, ready to make us both some dinner.

'Yeah,' I hear him sigh as I walk away. 'Yeah, I do.'

Chapter Twenty-Two

Ingrid's idea to write down my memories of being in the house quickly spirals in an unexpected way. It starts off like that, sure. I find myself giggling as I recall the time Lil became utterly convinced she'd seen a mermaid and the three of us went out with peanut butter sandwiches and the fishing nets we used in the local rock pools to try to catch her. The peanut butter sandwiches had been my idea because I thought it must be extremely sad that you couldn't grow peanuts underwater.

This led to a rather fraught conversation about what mermaids *could* eat. When Serena suggested fish, Lil's face had paled. 'Like *Flounder*?!'

All our future viewings of *The Little Mermaid* had taken a dark turn as Serena yelled, 'DO YOU THINK MERMAIDS INVENTED SUSHI?' at the screen.

Only, when I'm writing it down, the story changes into something else. Something about three sisters with magic. Ones who really do find a mermaid and bring her home to meet their grandmother. I hardly even know what I'm writing, just that it's fun and it's funny and it makes me think of my sisters and our time here.

The next morning I wake up and am surprised that I'm looking forward to working on it again. Dimly, I have an idea that I will finish it – whatever it is – and share it with Serena and Lil, that they'll get a kick out of this twisted version of our past. I like the feeling of *making* something. It's a million miles from the book outline I've been staring at and tinkering with for years. I suppose it's just another act of procrastination, but it feels nice, it feels *light*.

I'm still haunting all the job listing websites, so it's not like I'm not doing anything. It's more like a sabbatical for my brain. For the first time in five years the pressure of hustling for academic work is lifting off me, and until that happened, I don't think I realized how crushing it had been, grinding me down inch by inch.

As we move firmly into the second half of our six weeks in Northumberland, I'm no nearer to a plan over what I'm doing next, and though I still find that scary if I let myself think about it too much, it's certainly not the full-blown panic I was experiencing before. I have money in the bank, thanks to my job here and the zero expenses I've had. I know I can go and stay with Mum while I keep filling out applications, which – while not ideal – is a soft place to land and regroup.

After a couple of days, clearly noticing how absorbed I've been, Theo asks me how my work is going.

'It's . . . going okay,' I say, shifting in my chair.

'Why do you look guilty?' Theo asks, amused.

I hesitate. 'Because I'm not exactly working on my research.'

'What are you working on?' Theo asks, and I squirm again. The laughter lines around his mouth deepen. 'Ahhhh, I know. You're writing smutty fanfic, aren't you?' There's a pause and he asks, hopeful, 'Is it about me?'

'No!'

He sighs heavily. 'Well, I don't think I like the idea of you writing smutty fanfic about anyone else, Clemmie.' His bottom lip juts out in a pout. 'It's the vampires, isn't it? I get it, I do. Damn them and their chiselled jawlines.'

'It's not fanfic,' I laugh. 'It's . . . actually, I don't know what it is. It started off as the exercise Ingrid gave me to write down some of my memories of being here, and now it's . . .' I trail off, hesitate again. 'Why don't you just read it?' I turn the computer screen towards him.

'Really?' His eyes light.

'Why not?' I say awkwardly, because I suddenly realize that I *want* to share this with him, and isn't that the strangest thing of all?

Theo pulls out a chair beside me at the table and sits, bends over the laptop, eyes already scanning the screen. I try not to watch him read, but what else am I going to do? There are moments when I think he's smiling, and there's definitely one point where he chuckles under his breath, a rich hum of laughter.

I don't realize that I'm nervously jiggling my leg until his hand comes down on my knee. 'Stop,' he murmurs, and he leaves his hand there, his palm warm against the bare skin exposed by my shorts.

This at least proves to be a distraction from freaking out over him reading my silly story.

'Clemmie,' he says finally, his voice serious, dark eyes sober. 'This is so good.'

'What?'

His smile is slow and lovely. 'It's *so* good. It's properly funny; it's charming. It's totally weird. It's *you*.'

'Er . . . thanks?' I say, flushing. 'I think that's a nice thing.'

'It's the nicest thing.'

'I don't really know what it is.' I feel flustered by his praise, by the earnest way he delivers it. I don't think I had expected him to take this, *me*, so seriously. 'I'm just putting off doing my real work, but I thought maybe I'd finish it and give it to Lil and Serena as a gift.'

'You should definitely do that.' Theo rubs a hand across his jaw. 'They'll love it. But I know exactly what it is.'

'What?'

'It's a book, Clemmie. It's a children's book.'

'What?' I say again.

'It's the beginning of a children's book. I love it.'

'You do?' I am not being eloquent, and I know that, but my brain feels like a stuck record, skipping across his words, over and over.

'Yes,' he says firmly. 'I do. And other people would too. You should do something with this, something real.'

I rear back. 'Don't be an idiot,' I say.

Theo shrugs. 'I'll stop being an idiot when you stop belittling yourself and how talented you are. I see how you try to protect yourself, I'm even starting to understand why you like to play it safe, but it's okay to put yourself out there once in a while, to throw yourself into something.' He leans in and, hypnotized, I find myself leaning in too. He reaches out and carefully tucks a strand of hair behind my ear, his touch gentle. We're so close that I can see every golden freckle in his irises. We're so close I can feel his breath across my own lips. For a second I think he's going to kiss me and my body thrums with something painfully close to desperation. His eyes roam my face. 'It's okay to take risks, Clemmie,' he says quietly. 'Creative or otherwise. Remember that.'

And then he stands and strolls off, like he hasn't just absolutely obliterated me.

My hands are trembling and I ball them into sweaty little fists. I force my attention back to the computer screen, to the words there.

A *book*.

I don't know what I think about that, but I let the idea settle around me, and after a few more minutes I go quietly back to writing.

Chapter Twenty-Three

The days slip by faster and faster now as Theo and I settle into a nice companionable routine. I sit and type at my laptop – not quite acknowledging that I'm working on a book, but not exactly denying it either – and he sits on the sofa and writes. Sometimes he doesn't have his guitar, just the notepad and a pencil. Other times he plays quietly, hums something. It's all still fragments. Bits of something. But I can tell it's going to be good. You don't have to know anything about music to know Theo Eliott has *it*.

These moments feel special. Both of us creating, making something – not together but in the same space. When we pause for breaks, chat over a drink about how our work is going, it feels like I'm taking myself seriously, throwing myself into it. Just like Theo said.

About a week after I start writing, Theo sits at the kitchen counter reading *The Canterbury Tales* while I cook dinner. Spread on the surface beside Theo are the shells and bits of sea glass we just picked up on our walk. Later I'll add them to the jar on my bedside table which is already half full – each shell a reminder of the time we've spent together.

'Hey, Clemmie.' Theo lifts his head from the book. 'What does "queynte" mean?' He chokes on a laugh. 'Wait, never mind, now I say it aloud I think I've got it.'

'How are you and Chaucer getting on these days?' I ask, grating some cheese into a dish. Theo leans over and pinches some between his fingers, stuffs it in his mouth. I notice he's not so bothered about the piles of raw vegetables I've already chopped.

'I love it,' Theo grins. 'I wish they told us when we were kids how filthy it is, then I'd have paid attention much sooner.'

'Philistine.' I shake my head.

We're interrupted by Theo's phone ringing and when he pulls it out of his pocket I see the name of the caller flash up on the screen: Cynthie.

'Sorry,' Theo says. 'I need to take this.'

I try not to react as Theo picks up the call but makes no move to leave the room. Cynthie. My casual internet search of Theo had been more than enough to fill me in on his on-again-off-again relationship with Oscar nominee Cynthie Taylor, an actress with the delicate features, luminous porcelain skin and waif-like figure of an elf-princess (in fact, she's played two). I know Theo and Cynthie were together for years – and there are plenty of fans who still love the idea of them as a couple.

'All right, trouble?' Theo smiles as he speaks into the

phone. 'I thought you were living it up in the South of France.'

Whatever Cynthie says has him guffawing. 'Sure, I believe you.' His eyes flicker over to me and I busy myself with measuring out the flour for the bechamel. It's none of my business. *None. Of. My. Business.*

Should I leave the room? But I'm the one cooking. Why doesn't *he* leave the room? Why am I listening to him having a conversation with his ex-girlfriend? Not that he can't have a conversation with her, or whoever he likes. God, why am I spiralling about this?

'Not much, just reading Chaucer while a beautiful woman cooks me some carbohydrates. Living the dream,' Theo says, pinching some more cheese. He pauses as she says something. 'Yeah, of course Clemmie. She's right here.'

My hand freezes. Did it just sound like Theo had told Cynthie Taylor about me, like she asked about me by name? That's when it hits me that she was the one he'd been complaining to on that phone call weeks ago – I knew I recognized that voice.

Theo pulls the phone away from his ear. 'My friend, Cyn, says hi.'

'Say hi back,' I reply mechanically.

He does and I seem to be the only one finding this whole thing surreal. 'Anyway, how's filming going?' Theo asks.

The two of them chat for a bit and I manage to largely tune out, focussing very hard on putting the lasagne together.

'Wait, what do you mean they called you?' The hardness

in Theo's tone has me looking up. His gaze meets mine, and I see annoyance flicker in his eyes as he listens to what Cyn is telling him.

He huffs out a long breath. 'What a load of bullshit. They must be desperate. Well, thanks for the heads up. I guess David will pass it on to the label and they can handle it from there.'

I stir the sauce.

'No, we don't need security, Cyn. No one knows where I am. It's quiet here. No one recognizes me. I like it.'

My heart squeezes at the way he says the words. A minute later he puts the phone down. I stay where I am at the hob and the silence stretches between us.

I feel him come and stand behind me. After a moment, he puts his hands on my shoulders. 'Aren't you going to ask me what that was about?'

'I don't want you to think I was listening in on your phone call,' I say primly.

He laughs. 'If I was worried about that I wouldn't have had the conversation in the room with you, would I?'

He tugs gently at my shoulders, pulling me around to face him.

'Okay,' I roll my eyes. 'What were you and two-time Golden-Globe-winner Cynthie Taylor talking about, Theo?'

'Put that together, did you, Poirot?' Theo cocks an eyebrow.

'Let's just say it wasn't one of the world's great mysteries. And I prefer Miss Marple.'

'So you maybe know that Cyn and I were a couple once upon a time?'

'That's none of my business.'

'God, you're stubborn.' Theo's hand runs down my arm from my shoulder. He closes his fingers around mine and takes the spoon from my hand, gently bumping me aside so that he can stir the sauce himself. 'How about we just say that friends know things about each other? And we're friends, aren't we?'

I don't even know what I'm feeling right now. 'Of course we're friends.'

'Right,' Theo nods. 'So Cyn and I, we dated for about five years. It was a long time ago now. We're still good friends. Just friends. I think the two of you would get on really well.'

'That's nice,' I say, trying not to be thrown by this bizarre image. 'I'm not sure I've ever managed to stay friends with an ex.'

'I'm guessing you've been going out with the wrong kind of men.'

'Not sure there's a right kind at this point,' I grumble.

Theo treats me to a simmering look.

'Focus on the food, please,' I say. I don't think he can go too wrong with stirring, but with Theo you never know what culinary disaster will occur next.

'Anyway,' Theo says, 'Cynthie wanted to give us a heads up: she had a call from one of the tabloids, reaching out for comment on a story about me being in rehab.'

'Rehab?' I feel my eyes widen in surprise.

'Apparently the fact I've been totally off the grid for four weeks has people speculating. They don't know where I am so they've decided I've been shipped off for treatment somewhere. Probably got a "source" claiming to be a close friend to say how sad it all is.'

'That's outrageous!' I exclaim. 'They can't just print whatever they want . . .' I trail off, and my stomach lurches because I know first-hand that they absolutely can. They can and do print lies about people all the time. They did it to me.

'It's not a big deal,' Theo shrugs. 'If they want to write that, it's fine with me – let them think I'm in rehab if it means they leave me alone, but the problem is that the paparazzi have got a little mystery on their hands and I'm worried they're going to put some effort into solving it.'

'You're worried they'll find you here?'

He stops stirring. 'Let's just say, I'd rather they didn't.'

'Yeah, me too.' I shiver.

'So we'll just be a little more careful, right?' Theo says, and I hear the edge of anxiety in his voice.

'No leaving the house without your false moustache,' I say weakly.

I'm glad when he smiles. 'And my rubber nose.'

'Okay,' I agree. 'Now move out the way because somehow you actually are managing to burn the sauce.'

With that we go back to our evening. Although we don't talk about the paparazzi again, the conversation about them lingers like a bitter taste on my tongue. The thought of them intruding here, into this place, this magic slice of time Theo and I have somehow carved out together – it stings.

We have less than two weeks left here now, and I don't like how sad that thought makes me. I don't like how much, if I'm really honest with myself, I'd like to stay here, in this bubble, for a long, long time. I don't like how much of that is about being with Theo. So I push those feelings firmly aside and do what I do best: pretend nothing is wrong.

Chapter Twenty-Four

The next day we're both working in the living room, complaining about the heat, when the doorbell goes. 'Must be a delivery,' I say, getting to my feet.

'Oooh, I hope it's those Pop Tarts we ordered.' Theo's head lifts.

'*You* ordered,' I say. 'If David ever finds out about those, I already told you: I'm not going down for your crimes.'

'You'd take a bullet for me, Clemmie. Don't pretend otherwise.'

'A bullet? *Maybe*. The wrath of David?' I lift my eyebrows. 'Think again, sucker.'

Honestly, I am slightly concerned that introducing him to the online American grocery store was a mistake. I tried not to freak out too hard when he put over £300 worth of extremely unnatural flavourings in his basket, paying for it with a black credit card that looked like it was made of some material mined from an alien planet.

But when I cautiously check the door cam, it's not a Pop Tart delivery, it's Lil.

'Surpriiiiiiise!' she yells, throwing herself at me.

'Lil!' I exclaim, squeezing her tight, all wrapped up in her familiar sandalwood perfume. 'What are you doing here?'

'I had a gig in Newcastle last night,' Lil says, moving past me and looking around herself with interest. 'I thought I'd come up and say hi in person. I missed your face.'

'I missed yours, too.'

'Wow, look at this place, it's so different.' My sister wanders through to the sitting room ooh-ing and ahh-ing over the remodelling before she spies Theo on the sofa. 'Theo! Hey, it's so nice to see you!'

'Lil!' If Theo is surprised to see my sister, he doesn't show it. Instead he gets to his feet and wraps his arm around her shoulders. She kisses him on both his cheeks.

'Oh, right,' I say, suddenly awkward, 'you two already know each other.'

'We've played a couple of festivals together,' Theo says, still standing close to my sister. 'When was the last one? Reading, I guess? A couple of years ago.'

'That's right.' Lil beams up at him. 'How's Sidney doing?'

'Oh, you know Sid,' Theo groans and Lil laughs.

'Fully recovered, then?' she asks.

'Of course.'

'I'll put the kettle on,' I say, my voice too bright. I don't know why this is weird for me – I knew that Lil and Theo moved in some of the same circles.

'No, no.' Theo moves then, standing close to me so that my shoulder is pressed against his chest. He lifts a hand and rests it on my back, looks down at me with a crinkly-eyed smile. 'I'll do that while you guys catch up. But it's so hot, do you want some of that disgusting iced mint tea you've been guzzling? I made a jug of it this morning and put it in the fridge.'

'Oh, that would be nice,' I say, 'and it's not disgusting; it's just wasted on you.'

'It tastes like cold toothpaste water and you know it,' Theo calls over his shoulder, already headed for the kitchen. 'Oh!' he stops suddenly, as though remembering she exists. 'Sorry, Lil, what do you fancy?'

'Cold toothpaste water sounds great,' my sister says, her gaze flicking between me and Theo.

'No problem,' he replies.

Lil is quiet until I ask her about Serena and Bee, and then she shakes her head and smiles. 'I can't believe it. I never thought I'd see Serena so smitten. She's acting like it's a personal failure. I can't work out if she's happy or devastated by it.'

'You know how independent she is. It's hard for her to be vulnerable like that,' I say.

Lil hums in agreement as Theo returns with two glasses of iced tea.

Lil and I settle ourselves around the table and after a moment's hesitation, Theo returns to the sofa and picks up his guitar. 'I'll just head to my room.'

'No, don't bother on my account,' Lil says quickly. 'Not if this is where you usually write. I promised Serena I wouldn't interrupt.'

Theo looks at me. 'Are you sure?' he asks.

'Of course,' I say. 'That's why we're here.' I don't know why the words hang in the air.

'Wow,' Lil exclaims, her eyes lighting on Theo's guitar. 'Is that a Martin D-45?'

'Yeah, 1940.' Theo holds it out to her. 'I've had this one a while now. I've brought a bunch here with me, but I like writing on this one best.'

Lil nods. 'Serena said you're working on your new album,' she says, strumming lightly at the guitar. 'Beautiful,' she breathes, reverent over what must, I suppose, be an incredibly expensive instrument.

'I'm trying.' Theo grimaces. 'The writing has been slow. But it's coming on now.'

'It's really good,' I say quickly, and then I flush when they both turn to me. 'I mean, the bits I've heard are anyway. Not that my opinion counts for much.'

'I think your opinion counts for a lot,' Theo says softly.

Lil has that furtive, darting look about her again.

'So, how's Henry?' I ask, and she swoons back into her chair.

'I'm in so deep, Clemmie. He's *everything*. He's like . . . the sun and the moon all at once.'

'Ah, the smoon,' I nod wisely.

Theo chuckles while Lil pretends to be outraged. 'You mock me, but I'm telling you those three wishes we made . . .'

I groan. 'Lil, you and those wishes!'

'Remind me, Lil,' Theo calls from the sofa, where he's plucking at the guitar, making all these fancy, frilly notes run up and down. (I don't know the lingo, okay, we've already covered this.) 'What was your wish again?'

'Big, unconditional, soulmate love,' Lil answers promptly, squeezing her clasped hands between her knees, wriggling like a little kid. 'And I swear, we have unearthed some, like, deep dormant magic in our veins. The wishes were supposed to be just for Clemmie but *clearly* our power spilled over. It's like we summoned Henry into existence, and now there's Serena and Bee . . .'

'Sounds like you're next, Clemmie,' Theo says lightly. 'Watch out, your soulmate is coming for you.'

I clear my throat. 'I think I'm the proof that we don't, in fact, have magical powers. But I'm so happy for you and Serena,' I say to my sister.

'We'll see,' Lil replies mysteriously, 'but if it's such a coincidence, get this – last night after my gig I ran into an old friend and she's opening a new music venue in London and she wants me to be a part of it. It's going to be small and arty, something that supports upcoming artists.'

'You've been talking about something like that for ages,' I exclaim.

'I know!' Lil squeals. 'How's that for doing a job you love?!' She turns to Theo. 'That was Clemmie's wish.'

Her words take something in me by surprise. When we made those wishes, I was so sure I'd just lost the job I loved, but over the last few weeks I haven't missed it at all. Well, maybe teaching my students, but the rest of it? The truth is it's been a relief. That thought sends a wave of panic through me and I push it roughly aside.

'Oh, I know *all* about Clemmie's wishes,' Theo is saying. 'And I'm sure she'll get everything she wants.'

Lil grins impishly. 'Yes, because it's like we've tuned into the vibrations of the universe or something. Honestly, I've never been so happy, and it's making me feel so creative. And as for Serena's wish . . . let's just say that I'm having the best sex of my life. Henry does this thing where—'

'Yes, all right,' I cut her off. 'We don't need to hear about that, thanks.'

'Don't be such a prude, Clem. I'm trying to give you all my top tips here.'

'We don't need any tips!' I say and then freeze, totally aware of how that sounded. 'I mean I don't need any tips and Theo *definitely* doesn't need any tips.'

Lil is giggling, but Theo just winks at me. 'Thank you, sweetheart.' He's using his gravelly voice again. 'I'm glad to hear it.'

'I meant,' I say, feeling the hot red flush creeping up my neck, 'that you don't need to be subjected to the details of Lil's sex life.'

'Of course you did,' Theo replies soothingly and I glare at him while Lil snort-laughs beside me.

'*Anyway*,' I say firmly, changing the subject, 'back to the job thing. I've been keeping an eye on the academic job sites and there was a position that came up this week that I might apply for.'

'You don't sound very enthusiastic,' Lil remarks.

'Of course I am!' I say quickly. 'This is what I've been working towards for years. Of course I'm enthusiastic. It's just . . . you know, job applications. They're so daunting and there's no guarantee I'll even get an interview.'

'They'd be absolutely mad not to hire you,' Lil says staunchly and absolutely without basis.

As she tells me more about this venue her friend wants to open, her eyes keep darting away and I can tell I don't have her full attention.

Finally, it gets to be too much for her because she bursts out, 'Oh my God, Theo, I love that riff.'

I've got so used to Theo playing in the background that I hadn't really noticed he was doing it, but clearly Lil had. She's glowing with enthusiasm, half out of her chair, as if it's a struggle not to move closer to the music.

She sings the notes in her lovely, clear-bell voice, the same notes I had told him I liked that first day he played.

'Really?' Theo looks so pleased it squeezes at something in my chest.

Lil nods. 'Are you building something around it?'

'Yeah, I'm trying to.'

'I'd love to hear some of it,' she says. 'Only if you want?'

I wonder for a second if Serena has put her up to this. Meeting Theo's eye, I can tell he's having the same idea.

'Sure,' Theo shrugs, and I'm surprised by how casual he

is when he's never offered to play anything for me. Maybe it's different because Lil's a musician too. I try not to let that bother me.

Then Theo starts playing and all other thoughts empty out of my mind. 'I don't have lyrics yet,' he says, but he hums a melody while he plays. His long fingers dance over the strings, and the music soars, filling the room. And it's *beautiful.* It's just him and the guitar but somehow it sounds bigger than that. I can feel it all the way through me. I can feel it in my teeth.

'That's all I've got,' he says, coming to an abrupt stop.

'Oh my God, Theo,' I manage. I'm breathing like I've just run a marathon.

He looks at me and whatever he sees on my face has his cheeks turning pink. 'It's not done,' he says gruffly.

'I can't believe all of that . . . is *in* you,' I say disjointedly. I am in so much trouble here. What a massive cliché, going weak at the knees over a handsome man playing the guitar.

'It sounds incredible,' Lil enthuses, saving me from further mortification. 'I love it. What else do you have?' And now I know she's not asking because of Serena; she's asking because she's absolutely caught up in the moment.

Theo grins. 'I've got a couple of other things on the go.'

And then Lil's sitting on the sofa beside him and they've got their heads bent together while Theo plays something else. And eventually, after a while, Lil starts singing along and he nods and plays some more and then she grabs the guitar from him – grabs it without asking, like she's hanging out with a friend, all reverence of the fancy instrument gone – and Lil starts to play, changing what Theo was doing very slightly, in a way that I don't understand. Then Theo is the one who gets enthusiastic, and before any of us know it . . . they're writing a song. *Together.*

I watch silently. Watch these two people I care about, completely lit up with this thing that they love, and I feel a messy swirl of envy and tenderness and loneliness and joy.

I remember what Theo said, about how he only likes to write alone, but now he's here with us and he's writing with Lil, and he looks so happy and unguarded, there's none of the anxiety I've felt coming off him over making this album.

When he looks up and catches me watching, he smiles at me, a sweet smile that knifes through my heart because it's full of something I don't know how to interpret. Or perhaps I just don't want to. And so I look away, and let the music wash over me instead.

Chapter Twenty-Five

I wake up on my thirty-third birthday to what must be the hot-blooded fantasy of a decent percentage of the population. A shirtless Theo Eliott is in my bed, and he's singing 'Happy Birthday' to me.

More precisely, he's not *in* my bed but on it, sitting on top of the covers, playing his guitar next to my ears. Very loudly.

'Jesus, Theo,' I groan, turning and pressing my face into the pillow. 'What time is it?'

'It's seven thirtyyyyyy,' he sings, strumming the guitar.

'Why . . . is . . . anything?' I mumble.

'It's your birthday!' He nudges my arm. 'I was so excited I couldn't sleep.'

I sit up, rubbing my bleary eyes, and glare at him. 'And yet, I was managing just fine.' My eyes flicker over his bare chest and I will myself to feel nothing about the rippling muscle, those two little grooves at his hips, disappearing down into his pyjama bottoms. *Nothing. I am ice.* 'And why are you half-naked?' I ask, waving my hand vaguely in the direction of *all of that*.

'I spilled stuff on my shirt while making breakfast,' he explains patiently.

I groan. 'I thought we agreed that you were not to be let loose in the kitchen unsupervised. Remember the scrambled eggs? We had to order Petty a whole new set of pans. I didn't even know you *could* melt eggs. Like, I think it defied the laws of physics.'

'As I pointed out at the time, I think if you had been a more patient and understanding teacher, that incident wouldn't have occurred . . .'

'I *was* a patient and understanding teacher!'

'You threw a spatula at my head.'

'It was silicone,' I grumble. 'And it was in a panic, when you hurled a pan of fire towards me.'

'I think you're really overreacting,' Theo says. 'I know loads of chefs and they're always setting fire to things.'

'Oh my God.' I flop back down and close my eyes. 'Why are you in my bed, arguing with me at seven thirty in the morning?' I ask weakly.

'It's nice, isn't it?'

I crack open one eye and he's looking down at me with such warm affection that the corners of my mouth lift all by themselves.

'It's *not* nice,' I say firmly. 'It's too early for anything to be nice.'

'Anything?' Theo lifts an eyebrow, and for a second it flashes in front of my eyes, the image of him leaning down, pressing those warm lips to mine, the weight of that hot, hard body on top of me, my hands in his hair, his hands under my pyjama top.

I blink and the image is gone, but the way Theo's looking at me makes me think that the whole fantasy was written all over my face.

'I meant presents, you little perv,' he says, his voice rough. 'And a nice breakfast. Though I'm very open to your suggestions.'

I feel the blush travel up my body from my toes to the roots of my hair. 'I do like presents,' I manage.

'Then get up and meet me downstairs.' He jumps off the bed.

'I will if you put on a shirt,' I yell after him, because, honestly, there's only so much a girl can take.

When I shuffle downstairs, still in my pyjamas, yawning and combing my fingers through my messy hair, I find that Theo has laid the table. There's a jar full of Michaelmas daisies, glasses of fresh orange juice and a plate full of warm pastries as well as a small pile of wrapped gifts.

'I'm just making coffee,' he calls from the kitchen.

When he walks in, I'm still staring at the table. I blink hard, but my eyes won't stop tearing up.

'Hey!' Theo exclaims, striding towards me and wrapping his arms around me in a hug. 'What's this about?'

I press my face into his chest and sniffle into the T-shirt he is now, thankfully, wearing. He holds me tighter, rests his cheek on the top of my head. It's the greatest hug I've ever had, by a factor of a thousand, and I give in and let myself cling to him. Call it a birthday treat.

'This is just really nice,' I say finally, breaking away with no small amount of reluctance. 'How did you even know it was my birthday?' I certainly hadn't made him aware of the fact.

'I knew it must be coming up because you said you were a couple of months younger than Serena, so I asked Lil when she was here last week.' He pulls out a chair for me. 'We've been scheming.' He looks so boyish and pleased with himself that it honestly feels like an attack. It would be the most natural thing in the world to lean over and kiss him, and even acknowledging that feels dangerous. Neither of us have discussed the fact that in four days we'll be going our separate ways. It's like we're just pretending it's not happening at all, and that's making everything even more confusing.

Which is why, instead of kissing him, I sit and return my attention to the table. 'And you really did make breakfast,' I say. 'Without burning the house down or anything.'

'I had some help from Mrs D,' he admits, taking his own seat across from me.

Mrs D is approximately one hundred and fifty years old and she owns the general shop in the nearest village. She has absolutely no idea who Theo is, but she's known me since I could walk and she insists on calling Theo 'Clemmie's nice young man'. Theo never corrects her, and the two have become unlikely friends, bonding over their shared love of Mini Milk lollies and muscle cars.

'She made the pastries and all I had to do was heat them up in the oven.' Theo's brow creases. 'Which was actually a lot harder than she made it sound because some of them started burning around the edges before the others were warm, but I don't think I did too badly.'

'They're perfect,' I say, biting into one, and they are, but at this point I think I'd eat a lump of charcoal if he'd got up early to make it for me on my birthday. Aside from my family, no one has ever made a fuss before. Not Len, who said birthdays were 'not something to be celebrated by people over the age of thirteen'; certainly not Sam, whose big gift was breaking up with me right before my eighteenth birthday; and I don't think Ripp even knows when I was born, not exactly. He might have sent the odd card, but come to think of it that was probably Uncle Carl.

'Okay, okay,' Theo says impatiently. 'Now open your presents.'

He doesn't have to tell me twice, and I rip into the paper.

There's a sunny yellow hardback first edition of *Are You There God? It's Me, Margaret* by Judy Blume; a bottle of my favourite perfume; a voucher for two people to take a goat yoga class; a poster of the Chaucer painting I have on my wall at home but with Theo's head superimposed on top ('I got David to make it in Photoshop and now he thinks you have a really weird kink.'). And, most impressively, a signed and framed photo of the cast of *Blood/Lust*.

'I asked them to do one for me too,' Theo says, starry-eyed. 'I'm going to put it on my wall next to the platinum records.'

I'm laughing so hard that there's orange juice coming out of my nose and I don't care.

'And that's not all,' he says when we've finished breakfast. 'You have to go and shower and get dressed. We're not done with birthday celebrations.'

'Why are you doing all this?' I ask, bewildered.

Theo groans. 'Honestly, Clemmie. For someone so clever, you can be very, very dumb. If you need to ask that, then you're *really* not paying attention.' He ushers me from the room.

I try not to think too much about what *that* means as I shower and get dressed. Theo tells me not to worry about getting dressed up so I pull on my denim shorts and a loose, cropped black T-shirt which is a variation on a theme of what I've worn since we got here as it's been so hot, but I take my time doing my hair, scrunching product in to make the waves more defined, and I put on make-up, trying with middling success to recreate the cat's-eye flicks Lil is so good at, and painting my lips a bright red because it feels vaguely festive.

The perfume Theo bought me is the kind that comes in an old-fashioned bottle and I'm usually pretty stingy with it, but today I dab it liberally on all my pulse points, enjoying the sweet, heady scent of it.

'You look nice,' Theo says when I finally come back down. His eyes linger on my mouth for a long moment. The smile he gives me is slow and wicked and the air temporarily leaves my lungs. He steps closer, brushes the hair away from the side of my neck and leans in to me. 'You smell nice, too.' The words rumble across my skin.

'So,' I say nervously, taking a step back for the sake of my sanity. 'Where are we going?'

He looks shifty for a moment. 'Er, actually, there's been a very slight change of plans so we're going out for coffee first.'

'Oh,' I frown, unsure what plans he's talking about. 'That's okay. We can just hang out here if you want, we don't need to do anything special.'

'No!' Theo exclaims. 'I mean' – he collects himself – 'no, I really want to go and get a coffee. I checked the tides and we can get over the causeway to Holy Island for a walk if you like?'

'Do you think that's a good idea?' I ask. We've been so careful about keeping a low profile since Cyn's call.

'It's still too early for crowds. We haven't heard anything to suggest anyone knows where to find me. We're only here a few more days – where's the harm?' He looks at me, his eyes soulful, his smile winning. 'Please? I can't leave without seeing the place.'

'I guess that's true,' I agree, softening because I absolutely love Holy Island, and I want to share it with him.

We get into Theo's car and drive with the windows down. It's the end of June and the world is clear, clean blue: pastel-blue skies dipping lovingly into turquoise water. The sun is shining and the breeze through the window is ruffling Theo's hair, making my own fingers jealous.

We travel over the long causeway, past the signs urging visitors to check the tides, not to try and drive if the road is unsafe. As a tidal island, when the water is high the place is cut off. For now, the tide is out about as far as it can go, and aside from the small puddles of water that punctuate the side of the tarmac, you'd never guess how quickly the whole road can be swallowed up by the sea.

Theo wants to stop and look at everything, and I don't mind. I know how special this tiny island feels, separated from the rest of the world half the time. It's still morning so the place is quiet, not yet overrun with tourists, which means that he was right and there's little chance of him being recognized, but he pulls his cap down low and keeps his sunglasses on anyway.

We wander the cobbled streets, grabbing a cup of coffee from the local café. I think maybe the woman serving us does a bit of a double take, but she doesn't say anything, and I hope I've imagined it, that I'm just being over-sensitive.

'Birthday girls get second breakfast,' Theo insists, stopping at the ice cream counter.

'Don't you want one?'

'No, it's not my birthday.'

I choose a strawberry cone and he complains that this is the worst flavour, despite me pointing out that he doesn't have to eat it and can order his own ice cream in any flavour he likes.

We meander down the beach towards the castle, which juts out dramatically, a dark, huddled shape against the sky.

'What's that noise?' Theo asks, tipping his head. 'At first, I thought it was the wind, but it's not that windy. It sounds more like . . .'

'Ghosts?' I say innocently. 'The wailing spirits of the undead?'

'Yeah, actually.'

'It's the seals,' I say with a smile. 'They sing.'

'What?'

'It's seal song. If we climb up the hill there, you'll be able to see them all.'

'Seals do *not* sing,' Theo insists, a slow, delighted grin spreading across his face.

'In fact, they do.' I reach for his hand, tugging him gently back towards the village. Swallows arc over our head as we walk a path cut through a meadow of wildflowers, the ruins of an abbey looming to one side. Theo just shakes his head over it all.

'This is a dream,' he murmurs. I pretend I haven't noticed that we're still holding hands, his fingers tangled carelessly with mine.

When we reach the top of the hill, I gesture out to the sand dunes with my ice-cream cone to where a long, huddled line of seals are just hanging out, making their haunting, whistling sounds.

'I want to live here,' Theo breathes.

'You might struggle getting your Pop Tarts delivered,' I reply.

'Please, Clemmie?' he widens his eyes. 'Let's move to Holy Island and I can sing with the seals.'

'That sounds like a euphemism, like "sleep with the fishes",' I say, trying to ignore the zing that comes with his casual mention of us living together. Honestly, his Theoness is relentless. I think I deserve a medal for holding out this long – I don't doubt that, had I not been the only person around for the last five weeks, he'd have moved on long ago, but as things stand, every day that passes it's becoming harder and harder to cling to all the reasons I *must not* fall for him.

Theo laughs, puts on an exaggerated mobster boss voice. 'Clementine Monroe, if you don't hand over the ice cream, you'll be singing with the seals.'

'I knew this would happen. I *told* you to get your own.'

'I don't want my own. It tastes better when it's yours.' The dimple peeps out and I roll my eyes but hand him my cone, which he polishes off in a few bites.

'I'm glad we came here before we have to leave,' I say quietly.

Theo frowns but before he can reply, his phone dings and he pulls it out of his pocket, looking at it in a way that I think is supposed to be furtive. 'Right,' he says brightly. 'I think we should go home now. Not for any specific reason.'

'You do know you're being weird, right?' I ask.

'You're the weird one,' Theo replies, already tugging me back towards the car.

We get home without incident, but Theo keeps glancing at me, a secret little smile on his lips.

'What?' I ask, half-laughing after he does it the fourth time.

'Nothing,' he says. Then he reaches over and grabs my hand, lifts it to his mouth and presses a soft kiss across my knuckles. 'I'm just glad you were born,' he says, then he gently places my hand back in my lap and returns his to the steering wheel like nothing happened.

'Oh' is what comes out of my mouth.

'Oh?' The dimple flickers.

'I mean, I'm glad you were born too.'

'You can tell me that on *my* birthday,' he says.

'I don't know when that is.' I flex my fingers, trying to get them to stop tingling.

'October 7th.' Theo pulls the car into the drive.

He'll be back in LA by then, I think as I get out the car. *He won't even remember telling me about his birthday.* There will be a big party, one full of models and millionaires, and he'll probably be on a yacht, actually. Maybe he even has his own yacht? He could have his own yacht and I don't even have a flatshare. Serena's words echo in my head as they have so many times of late: *Theo Eliott is not for you, Clemmie.*

While I'm busy spiralling, Theo has raced ahead of me, letting himself in the house.

'Let's go down to the beach,' he suggests.

'Oh, Theo, I don't know,' I hedge, 'I'm pretty tired.'

'Please?' he asks. 'Just humour me?'

I follow behind him, and I wonder if he has any idea how I feel, how I'm all tangled up over him. Would he be mortified if he did? Or is it just something he's used to? All the girls with their Theo Eliott posters, swooning over him.

We have less than a week left here; I just need to keep it together for a few more days and then we can go our separate ways. And I can pretend the thought of that doesn't crush me, just a little bit.

We make our way down the path, and then through the dunes, and right when we're about to crest them, right before the beach comes into view, Theo reaches for my hand again.

'Happy birthday, sweetheart,' he says, and then he turns and I follow, and there, standing on the sand, are my family.

Chapter Twenty-Six

'Ahhh!' I squeal, already sliding down the sandy slope towards Serena and Lil, who are running forward. We tumble to the ground together in a untidy heap, laughing and screaming, especially when Serena starts trying to push sand into Lil's mouth.

'Ugggg, Serena! Get OFF!!!!' Lil wails, which is an extremely basic error as it only gives Serena more opportunity to cram sand in her.

Behind me, I can hear Theo laughing, the sound happy and soaring, and I pull myself up and out of the scrum, moving towards Mum, Petty and Ava, who wrap me in a much more dignified group hug.

'Happy birthday, sweet Clementine,' Petty whispers in my ear.

'Our girl,' Ava coos, kissing my cheek.

'What are you all doing here?!' I exclaim.

'Theo organized it,' Mum says, and then she's walking towards him, her arms stretched out in front of her, kissing him loudly on the cheek. 'You lovely boy,' she says. 'Our girls have been telling us all about you. I'm so happy to finally meet you in person.'

Theo's cheeks are pink and he looks utterly starstruck as Mum continues to grip him just above his elbows, beaming up at him. 'Th-thank you, Ms Monroe,' he manages thickly. 'It's nice to meet you too. I'm a big fan . . .'

Mum waves a hand, 'Oh, don't you dare Ms Monroe me. It's Dee. And you haven't met Petty or Ava either, have you?' There are more greetings, and then I notice two other figures: Henry and Bee hovering at the side.

'Hi, Henry!' I give him a little wave, which he returns.

'Happy birthday, Clemmie,' he smiles shyly, tucking his hands in his pockets.

'Thank you,' I say. 'I can't believe you're all here.' I turn to the woman beside him. She's even more beautiful in real life. 'You must be Bee?'

She nods. 'It's nice to meet you properly.'

'You mean not just as the disembodied voice echoing from Lil's bra?' I say, and Henry doesn't look at all fazed, only smiles bigger at the sound of my sister's name.

Bee laughs. 'Yeah, you're much taller in real life.' I grin at her and she grins back. Then Serena appears beside her, rumpled and sandy but not as sandy as Lil, which I think means she won.

Serena's arm slips round Bee's waist, easily, as if it belongs there. Henry and Lil are holding hands. I can't believe how much things have changed in the last few months, and I try to ignore the pang of jealousy I feel.

'So, what do you think?' Serena asks, gesturing around. I take it all in. A huge wooden gazebo strewn with patchwork bunting has been erected in the middle of the beach. There are giant, confetti-filled balloons tied to weights and bobbing on long ribbons, and under the gazebo is a fire pit and piles of pretty, brightly coloured picnic blankets and giant, squishy cushions. Off to one side an entire tiki bar has been built and stocked with drinks and there's a barbecue beside it, the coals already glowing orange.

'It's incredible,' I say, dazed. 'How did you pull this off?'

'It was Mum and Theo,' Lil says. 'They arranged it all.'

'With a bit of help from David, of course.' Theo comes and stands beside me. 'He says happy birthday, by the way. He sent you some flowers. They're inside.'

'David did?' I ask, stunned.

'I think he's warming to you,' Theo says. 'I'm trying not to be jealous. He's never bought me flowers before.' He looks down at me. 'So? Do you like it? Are you surprised?'

'I'm *so* surprised,' I say honestly. 'And I don't think I could like anything more.'

We just stand there, staring at each other for a moment. I don't know how long, but long enough for Lil to clear her throat, and for Serena to grumble, 'Well, fuck. Lil was right for once.'

'Right about what?' I ask.

'Right about you and—'

'Shall we get a drink,' Bee interrupts quickly, squeezing Serena's hand and tugging her away. My sister goes with her, but turns and glares at me over her shoulder. Then she lifts two fingers and points them at her eyes before pointing them at Theo in the universal symbol for *I'm watching you.*

'I keep forgetting how scary your sister is,' Theo says.

'So scary,' Henry whispers, and he and Theo exchange a look of solidarity.

The rest of the afternoon passes in a happy blur. Mum and Ava take charge of the barbecue, and Petty goes up to the house, pulling big bowls of bright salad, rice mixed with creamy green pistachios and slick pomegranate seeds, and platters of sweet, charred roast vegetables out of the fridge.

Theo lights the fire using way too much lighter fluid and nearly takes his eyebrows off.

'Oh my God, Theo!' I gasp, pretty sure I am suffering cardiac arrest. 'Imagine if I had to explain that to David. He'd have some Californian plastic surgeon flown in to perform emergency eyebrow transplants.'

'*Mr Eliott's eyebrows are worth a fortune, Clemmie, and you have failed them,*' Theo says in a spot-on David impression.

'It's no joke. You're not allowed anywhere near the barbecue,' I say firmly.

Theo only laughs and pulls me down to sit on one of the blankets.

'How did you keep all of this a secret?' I ask.

'Honestly, Petty and David did most of the hard work. I just had to keep you out the way. And then your family were held up in traffic, hence our impromptu coffee trip.'

'Well, I love it,' I say happily, fishing a piece of strawberry out of my drink and popping it in my mouth, relishing the sweetness. 'It's my second best birthday ever.'

'*Second* best?'

'When I was seven, I had a Power Rangers party, and the pink Power Ranger made a special appearance.'

'Oh, well, no chance of competing with that.' Theo tugs me against him, his arm sliding around my waist. 'If it had been the blue or red Power Ranger, then *maybe* . . .'

'Exactly,' I say. 'But I don't know. This is pretty close.'

'Yeah?' His lips tug up.

'Yeah.' The word comes out soft, an exhalation. His fingers tighten, brushing the thin strip of bare skin between the top of my shorts and the hem of my shirt, and I have to fight so very hard to resist the urge to press my face into the place where his neck meets his shoulder.

Whatever has been simmering between us for weeks seems, to me at least, as though it has been turned up to its boiling point. My whole body feels too tight, like I'm aching – not just for him to touch me (though definitely that, too) – but aching for something more, something that I definitely have no business wanting.

Only, the way Theo is looking down at me now makes me feel like maybe he wants it too. And that's the most confusing part of all.

'Food's ready,' Ava yells, and the spell is broken. I turn away, Theo removes his arm, and I take a deep breath, steadying myself. *A few more days*, I chant in my brain. *Just a few more days.*

As everyone scrambles to fill up their plates, arguing over

who gets first choice over what's on the barbecue (somehow Lil, despite the fact it's *my* birthday), I let it sink in that my family are here at Granny Mac's together. The hum of their voices, the familiar warmth of their laughter, even the sound of Lil and Serena squabbling, it feels right that it's happening here. I glance up at the house, and it's as though any remaining demons have been banished. I feel nothing but pure goodness about being here, tinged with a sweet sadness at the thought of leaving. And that seems like the biggest gift of all.

After we eat, my sisters drag me off for a walk on our own. It's not that I've been avoiding this situation precisely, but I have a feeling I know what's coming and I'm having enough arguments with myself without throwing their opinions into the mix.

'Right,' Serena says once we're far enough away from the others, her hands going to her hips. 'What. The. Actual. Fuck?'

'What?' I ask.

Lil and Serena exchange a look and Lil says, 'I told you so.'

'You and Theo, Clemmie,' Serena says with exaggerated patience. 'I didn't believe it when Lil told me what was going on, but here we are.'

'I don't know what you're talking about,' I say unconvincingly.

'It's like you're . . . together.' Lil puts a hand on my arm. 'Like, *really* together. Are you? Why wouldn't you tell us?'

'I—' I start, then stop, avoiding their eyes and trying to collect my thoughts. 'We're not. We're just comfortable together. I suppose being stuck here alone, just the two of us, we've become pretty close. We've become . . . friends.'

'I do *not* look at my friends the way you look at him,' Serena says.

'Not to mention the way he looks at you,' Lil pipes up.

'Yeah,' Serena exhales slowly. '*That.* I've known Theo a long time and I've *never* . . .' She trails off, bites her lip, clearly worried.

'I don't know what you're talking about,' I say again, trying to sound firmer this time.

'He's *always* looking at you, Clemmie,' Lil exclaims. 'All soft and twinkly, like the friggin' heart-eye emoji come to life. I don't think he's even *trying* to hide it, from us or from you, it's so obvious. He's totally in l—'

'Stop.' I cut her off with a wave of my hand. My voice is shrill. 'I know why you think that, but you need to understand. That's just Theo being Theo. It's what he's like. He's charming; he's a six-foot-tall bag of muscles and charisma; he's tactile and flirty. He's like that with *everyone*.'

My sisters look at me. Lil looks sad. Serena is frowning.

'Do you really think that?' Serena asks.

'Of course I do! You're the one who told me he was a terrible flirt, that he dazzles people, that he sleeps around, which, you know, no judgement, but that's just not what I'm looking for. If I was looking for anything at all. Which I'm not.'

Serena shifts uncomfortably. 'I know what I said, and I still haven't exactly changed my mind on all of that, but you really need to know that whoever *that* is,' – she gestures over her shoulder towards the beach where Petty seems to be trying to organize an egg-and-spoon race while Henry and Theo elaborately stretch their muscles like they're preparing for the Olympics – 'is not the Theo Eliott I was talking about.'

'Right,' I say, 'so you're saying this isn't the real him, this is just . . . I don't know, *holiday Theo*, and we've been in a little bubble, the two of us on our own. And when he's back in the real world, then he'll be the man you know, the man you've known for years.'

'Or, maybe this *is* the real him, Clemmie,' Lil says, determined as always to see the best in people. 'He seems so genuine. This doesn't feel like a performance to me. Does it feel that way to you?'

I stare at the ground. 'No. But maybe that's what makes him so dangerous.'

They both fall quiet again before Lil speaks. 'Clemmie,' – her voice is gentle – 'you're not the only one who would have issues trusting someone in Theo's position. It's not like Serena and I have been falling over ourselves to date people in the industry, and we're *in* the industry. We know better than anyone that there are plenty of Ripp Harrises out there.'

Serena lets out a snort of agreement.

'But Theo?' Lil reaches out, takes my hand and squeezes it. 'He isn't one of them. I can feel it.'

Serena looks less convinced, but for whatever reason she chooses to stay silent.

'And what about Sam?' I say, and they both flinch at the name. 'I didn't think he was like Ripp either, and look how that ended up. I honestly don't think I could go through anything like that again. Not just the breakup, but everything around it, the whole circus.'

'Sam was a vicious little dickhead,' Serena spits out. 'Whatever doubts I might have about Theo, I can tell you for a fact they are not in the same league.'

'It doesn't even matter,' I insist. 'I get what you're saying and why you think it, but Theo is a rock star who lives in LA. We're only stuck here together for a few more days. The list of reasons we would never work is as long as my arm. There's not going to be anything between us regardless of how I may or may not feel or what may or may not have happened in the past. He's not for me. That's what you said, Serena, and you were totally right.'

For once, my sister doesn't look pleased to be told she knows best. 'These just sound like excuses,' she says slowly.

'They're not excuses. They're facts.' I wish I didn't sound like I was trying to convince myself as much as them.

'It's just that . . . you're different, Clemmie,' Lil says slowly. 'I don't know if it's being here or if it's breaking up with Len, or if it's Theo, or some combination of all of those things, but something has changed. In a good way. You seem . . . *lighter.* I don't want to see you talk yourself out of something that could be wonderful because you're scared.'

'I'm not scared,' I insist. 'I'm just being realistic. Practical.' Before they can protest further, I say, 'Now, can we go back and finish celebrating my birthday, please? Because before you leave, I am going to absolutely destroy you both in an egg-and-spoon race.'

And with that, the interrogation ends, because, as I know very well, even when they're busy worrying about my love life, neither one of my sisters is physically capable of resisting such a challenge.

Later, when Theo and I wave goodbye to everyone, I have mostly managed to push the conversation with my sisters out of my mind.

I have mostly managed to ignore the long, beaming looks from not just my mother, but from Petty and Ava too when they thought I wasn't looking.

I have mostly managed to resist leaning into Theo's touch like a besotted Labrador. Mostly.

'Shall we go down to the beach and watch the sunset?' Theo asks. 'We should make the most of the fire pit before David's guys come and take it away tomorrow.'

I eye him narrowly. 'You've got more marshmallows, haven't you? I thought you told Serena we'd run out.'

'I kept a stash back, just for us, birthday girl.'

'How selfless of you to be thinking only of my happiness.'

'Always.'

We head back down to the beach and Theo makes for the bar, pulling out a bag of marshmallows from behind the fancy, fruity, alcohol-free beer.

'I knew your sister would never look here,' he says gleefully.

'She's more of a clear spirits girl,' I agree.

'When she's not drinking the blood of her vanquished enemies.' Theo's smile looks slightly haunted.

We throw a couple more logs in the fire pit and thread our marshmallows on metal skewers before sitting down side by side on one of the blankets. It's gone ten o'clock, and a burnished rose-gold light begins to spill across the sky. My name is scrawled in the sand in front of the fire pit next to Lil's and Serena's, all of them held inside the giant heart Lil drew with her fingertips.

'I cannot believe that last race.' Theo shakes his head with a wince. 'I think Lil might have broken a couple of my ribs. How can someone so tiny slam into you like she's a defensive player for the All Blacks?'

'I tried to warn you,' I laugh, while carefully rotating my marshmallow. 'You should have noticed everyone else was giving her an extremely wide berth.'

'Honestly, I thought Serena would be the vicious one.'

'Nope, Lil's always been a competitive nightmare. She once got suspended from school for breaking another girl's nose during a hockey match. She said she didn't do it on purpose, but I don't know . . . there's this red mist that descends.'

'Henry was loving it, though, wasn't he?' Theo smirks. 'She was busy trying to trip people up – *including him* – and he looked at her like she was an angel who fell out the sky.'

'True love,' I smile.

'Why is your marshmallow so perfect and mine always look like this?' Theo grumbles, blowing out the flames that are engulfing his marshmallow, leaving behind a blackened lump.

I examine my own evenly golden, gooey treat. 'It's because I am careful and patient, something that you know very little about.'

'Clemmie, I can be *very* careful and patient if the occasion calls for it,' Theo replies, and something low and serious in his tone has me looking up at him. His gaze is steady, open, and it makes my skin heat.

I smile, trying to cover the nervous feeling in my belly. 'I'm sure. Tell it to the half dozen eggs you broke today.'

Something like disappointment flickers in Theo's eyes at my response, but he lets it slide, arranging his face in faux outrage. 'I'm not saying the game was fixed, but did we test Serena's egg to make sure it hadn't been boiled? I swear she dropped it once and that thing *bounced*.'

'Here,' I say, handing him the marshmallow. 'I toasted this one for you anyway.'

'You did?'

'Yes, I did, because I know how rubbish you are at cooking them and that you would burn yours, but I also know how much you like eating them, you sugar junkie.'

'You toasted a marshmallow for me.' Theo takes the skewer from my hand and just sits, looking at it for a moment.

I laugh, inexplicably nervous. 'It's just a marshmallow, Theo.'

'Mmm.' He makes a noise like he disagrees but doesn't want to tell me so.

'And it's to say thank you.' I draw my finger through the sand, not wanting to look at him for some reason. 'For my best birthday ever.'

There's a beat. 'You mean I'm even better than a pink Power Ranger?' His body relaxes, the easy smile returns.

'I mean watching Lil rugby-tackle you to the ground then trample over your prone body towards the finish line was even better than meeting a pink Power Ranger.'

'I *knew* there was trampling. Having her mother referee was a clear violation of egg-and-spoon-race regulations.'

It feels like we've successfully navigated away from something too serious, back to familiar ground. We tease and bicker some more, and Theo eats his marshmallow slowly, like it's the most delicious thing in the world.

When he's finished, Theo picks up his guitar, and if you had asked me before this if I could think of anything cringier than a grown man appearing at a camp fire with an acoustic guitar, I'd have been hard pressed to give you an answer. But with Theo it's not an affectation. Or embarrassing. It's perfect. Probably because of how talented he is, but also because I realize now that Theo with a guitar in his hand is Theo in his natural state.

He starts to play softly, absently, in the background while we talk. That lovely melody he played for me and Lil first, and then other things, bits of songs I recognize and bits of songs I don't, all winding in and out of each other. Eventually he plays a tune so familiar to me that I instantly cringe.

'Oh no, don't!' I exclaim.

Theo grins evilly as his guitar twangs those notes that prompted so many hokey, faux-southern childhood performances. The song I couldn't escape, that chased me down school corridors. The song my mother had cursed me with when she chose my name.

Oh my darlin', Oh my darlin', Oh my darrrrrrlin' Clementine . . .

'This song is my villain origin story.' I scowl at Theo. 'This is what made me the neurotic wreck you see before you. This song following me around.'

Theo bursts out laughing. 'It's not actually a bad song. It could be worse . . . all my mates used to sing the Chipmunks theme tune at me.'

'The Chipmunks theme tune is *jaunty*,' I insist. 'Everyone loves it. And Theodore was everyone's favourite chipmunk too, so that's not even real teasing. My song is worse. Definitely worse.'

Theo fixes me with a look, and then he starts playing again. And this time when he plays, he plays it softer, slower, and when he sings all the hairs on the back of my neck stand up.

Now, somehow, the song isn't hokey at all; now it's raw and tender. He doesn't look at me, but the words that he sings wrap themselves around me like a caress. Surely, this is the least sexy song in the world? But somehow, somehow, Theo has changed it, made it into something lush and lovely and the way he sings my name over and over again has my breath catching.

When he finishes, the silence between us crackles, electric. In front of us, the sky is a molten flame above a silver sea.

'Maybe I like that song when it's you singing it,' I manage, and I sound so vacuous and breathy that I cringe.

'I like everything best when it's with you,' Theo says simply.

I shiver.

'Cold?' Theo asks. I nod.

Theo puts his guitar down by his side and wraps a hand around my wrist, moving himself so he's sitting behind me, his legs either side of mine, my back pressed against his chest.

He grabs another blanket off the sand and pulls it around his shoulders, clasping it in front of me so that we're wrapped up together in a little cocoon. His body radiates warmth; I can feel the steady *thud, thud, thud* of his heartbeat, and as I sit there in the cradle of his arms, we don't talk, we don't say anything at all, we just watch the sun finally dip down below the horizon.

Chapter Twenty-Seven

When we make our way back up to the house it's dark and Theo uses the torch on his phone to guide us. We walk close together but not touching, and yet my whole body is aware of him. I know that something has changed between us, and that when we get back inside we're going to have to talk about it.

I feel both terrified by that thought, and wildly elated. Because I'm *done*. I'm absolutely done with ignoring, and repressing, and being sensible. I have no idea if I will regret letting anything happen between me and Theo, but it seems pointless to continue worrying about it when it's abundantly clear that something *already has*. Now, it's just about acknowledging that, and working out what the hell we're going to do about it.

Theo opens the back door and moves to turn on a lamp. The sudden burst of light feels like a shock, and I blink, temporarily dazzled. When I open my eyes again, Theo stands in front of me.

'Clementine,' he says, his voice hoarse. That's all, just my name, and it hangs there in the air between us.

I honestly don't know who moves first.

Maybe it's both of us at once, because we crash into each other with enough momentum behind us to have me rocking back on my heels, and what happens then is not sweet or slow or considered. It's a frenzy – his lips hard on mine, my tongue in his mouth, his hand gripping the back of my head. He makes a sound, a desperate sound that turns my knees to liquid as I press myself against him, wanting *more.* And, dimly, over the heat and the need and the hunger, I'm aware of a feeling flooding my whole body, rushing through my veins. Relief.

Thank God, it seems to say. *Finally.*

I lean into his body like I'm trying to melt into his bones.

I have no idea how long this goes on for – it could be minutes or hours or whole lifetimes – before a sound suddenly punches through into the moment, shrill and relentless.

My phone, I register. *My phone is ringing.* I pull back slowly from Theo, dazed. His eyes are unfocused, his chest heaving. I realize that his hand is up my shirt and mine is down the front of his jeans.

'Theo,' I manage. 'We . . . I . . .' I can't get any further because my brain is still lagging behind. My brain is too busy being the world's most enthusiastic cheerleader – doing somersaults straight into the splits and chanting *Kiss! Kiss! Kiss!* – to do anything useful like stringing words together.

Theo gathers his wits first. He drops his forehead to mine,

just for a moment, eyes closed as he takes a deep, steadying breath. Then he wrenches himself back, away from me.

'Too fast,' he manages, his voice sandpaper. 'We need to talk first.'

'Yes,' I agree dimly. 'Talk first.'

'You should get that,' he says, and I'm totally distracted by his hands doing his jeans back up. I want those hands all over me. I want those jeans on the floor or on fire, I don't care, I just want them off him.

'What?' I say.

'Your phone, Clemmie,' he laughs, rueful. 'You should answer your phone.'

'Oh, right.' I try harder to get a grip on reality, and then I pull my phone out of my pocket and answer it without looking at the screen.

'Hello?' My voice is all breathless and husky. Theo combs his fingers through his rumpled hair. I watch his arm flex. His mouth is pink, his lips swollen.

'Clemmie?' a man's voice says.

'Yes?' I don't immediately recognize the voice and I pull the phone away to look at the number, but it's not in my contacts.

'I thought you weren't going to answer,' the man says, his voice low, almost a purr. 'I'm glad you did. I wanted to wish you a happy birthday.'

And that's when I catch up, that's when I realize who it is, whose voice is in my ear.

'Sam?' I croak, and across from me Theo freezes.

'Yeah, it's me. I got your number off Ripp, been trying to

work up the courage to call you, and then I saw your sister post about your birthday on Instagram and it seemed like a sign from the universe, you know?'

I swallow. Theo reaches out, cups his hand around my elbow.

'Why are you calling?' I ask.

Sam chuckles, and I hate that I remember that sound, that I used to love it, find it sexy and charming. Now it makes my stomach turn.

'It was just really great running into you,' Sam says, and his tone is intimate, cajoling. 'And I haven't been able to stop thinking about you. You looked good, Clemmie, really good, and it got me thinking about the way things were with us. I know it was a long time ago, but I just instantly felt that spark, you know? I felt twenty again, and I wondered if I could take you out . . . see if we were as good together as I remember. I think we could have a lot of fun.'

'You . . . you're calling to ask me out?' Theo's fingers tighten on my elbow but I barely register it, because I am busy being consumed by a burning-white fury. There's a moment of silence before I combust. 'Are you fucking kidding me?' I spit.

There's another pause. 'Wait . . . what?' Sam says, and I don't know if he's playing dumb or if he's really that stupid and genuinely bemused.

'You want to go out for a drink? See if shagging me is as good as it was when I was seventeen? Absolutely go fuck yourself, you toxic piece of shit. I hope you die alone and get eaten by cats. Actually, cats are way too good for you, I hope you get eaten by . . . by . . . slugs!' I slam my finger down on the screen to end the call, and then I throw my phone across the room, letting out a roar of anger that comes from somewhere deep inside me.

I don't think I even realize Theo is still in the room with me for several minutes. I feel like I have pins and needles all over my body, like I can't get enough air in my lungs.

Then Theo's arms are there, gently guiding me to the sofa, pushing me down so that I'm sitting. He disappears, and then returns moments later. He kneels down in front of me, brushes a few strands of hair gently away from my face, holds up a glass of water.

'Take a deep breath,' he says. 'And drink this.'

I sip the water, realize that I'm shaking, feel myself start to settle back into my body.

'I can't believe that just happened,' I say finally. 'That did just happen, right?'

Theo is still on his knees, worry written all over his face. 'Yes, that happened.'

'He . . . he . . .' I can't finish the sentence, can't believe that Sam has intruded here, here *again* in this house.

'Clemmie,' Theo says softly, taking the glass of water away, holding my cold hands between his and rubbing them gently. 'It's okay. You're okay.'

'Yeah,' I say. 'I'm okay. At least this time I managed to say how I really felt.' I chuckle weakly.

There's relief in Theo's eyes as his mouth tips up. 'Yeah, I don't think you left much room for ambiguity there.'

'Did I say I hoped he got eaten . . . by slugs?'

'You did.' Theo's smile grows. 'It was a very intimidating threat.'

'I suppose it *would* be very slow,' I agree.

'*So* slow,' Theo says solemnly. 'And slimy too.'

'Yeah,' I exhale. 'He deserves all the slime.'

There's a beat, two, and then Theo asks, quietly, 'Do you want to tell me about it?'

I nod, gesture to the sofa. Theo gets up and sits beside me. I pull my knees up to my chest, wrap my arms around them. 'I think I should have told you earlier,' I say. 'Should have explained . . .'

Theo stops me. 'You don't owe me an explanation. You don't owe me anything. If you want to tell me I'd like to understand, but if you don't, then there's no pressure. None.'

I smile quaveringly at that. 'It's not a big secret, exactly,' I sigh. 'It's just not a very nice story, and I don't like telling it.' I think about it. 'And to be honest, part of me feels, I don't know . . . *foolish* to still be carrying it around. I don't know why I can't let go of it, something that happened so long ago. It's obvious Sam doesn't even remember it.'

'I don't know what happened,' Theo says, 'but I know there's nothing foolish about the way you think or feel.'

'I'd better tell you the whole story before you go making assumptions like that.'

Theo shakes his head. 'I don't need to hear it to know whose side I'm on, Clemmie. I'm on your side, always.'

I swallow past the lump in my throat and decide it's best

just to jump straight in, not to give myself an excuse to chicken out. 'I met Sam when I was seventeen,' I begin, nervously wetting my lips. 'I was on a night out with Serena and Lil and he came over to chat with us, but somehow it ended up being just the two of us, sitting in a corner, talking until two in the morning.'

I think back to that night, to the way it had felt, Sam singling me out. The weight of his full attention had been powerful, had made me feel important.

'He was good-looking, charming, and – though I didn't know it then – he was the drummer in this up-and-coming indie band, just starting to get noticed. He had a magnetism about him, people were drawn to him, and he was interested in *me*. Shy, bookish, ordinary me.'

Theo makes a noise of protest at this and it makes me smile. 'As I saw myself at the time, anyway. And you have no idea what seventeen-year-old Clemmie was like.'

'She loved weirdly sexy medieval literature and she had an unhealthy interest in Ryan Gosling despite his extremely average looks, which speaks to her benevolence. And seventeen-year-old me would have been her best friend,' Theo says firmly.

I laugh then, a proper laugh, and some of the heaviness I'm feeling shifts. It makes it easier to carry on.

I take a deep breath. 'I gave him my number that first night and he called me the next day and the next and the next. He made me feel like I was the most amazing, desirable girl in the world.

'Even when I found out he was a musician it didn't bother me. I thought he was nothing like Ripp. He was so considerate; he listened to me, talked to me about books and music and art. He was a few years older and everything felt so grown-up. First love I suppose.' I wince. Theo stays quiet, his expression hard to read.

'Then he started taking me out, partying more. I was underage but no one ever checked when I was with the band. They would play and I'd watch and then afterwards Sam would come and put his arm around me, call me his girl, let everyone know how lucky he was to have me. God, I bought into it completely,' I scoff, thinking – for maybe the billionth time at this point – that I must have been an idiot.

'Why wouldn't you?' Theo asks. 'From what you're telling me anyone would have. We're all romantic disasters at seventeen.'

I eye him doubtfully and Theo clearly reads my expression.

'Hey, just wait until I tell you about my first girlfriend who was so nice when she was breaking up with me that I still thought we were together three weeks later when she stuck her tongue down Darryl Simmons's throat,' Theo says. 'But there's plenty of time for my romantic disasters. We're talking about you.'

'Right,' I nod, making a mental note to get the full story later, and feeling an irrational gut punch of jealousy and anger towards a nameless teenage girl.

'So, we were going out a lot. Sam always insisted I went with them, said he didn't want to spend time away from me, said it was no fun for him if I wasn't there too.' I fiddle with the hem of my shorts, remember how stunned I'd been by the idea that there was someone who simply couldn't bear to be parted from me. I mean, you didn't need the years of therapy I had undergone to hear the foghorns screaming '*DADDY ISSUES!!!!!*', but hindsight is a bitch, isn't it?

'At first it *was* fun,' I continue. 'Then, one day the paparazzi started turning up, taking Sam's picture when we arrived or when we left. Just a photographer or two, not a big deal. Like I said, his band was taking off. They had fans. I didn't love it, but I understood. I tried to just stay out the way, hide behind Sam when the cameras flashed.' My palms are starting to sweat now, knowing we're approaching the more difficult bit.

'Then, one night there were more paparazzi there than usual, and one of the photographers shouted my name ... well, actually, not my name, but *Clementine Harris*, and the next day *I* was there, in the papers. I remember the headline: A RIPP OFF THE OLD BLOCK'.

Theo makes a sound somewhere between a laugh and an outraged splutter.

'I know!' I wince. 'Actually *offensively* bad writing apart from anything else. But there it was: this whole story about how Ripp's daughter was a party girl, shagging a musician. After that there were more pictures, more cameras everywhere we went and honestly it was just *so* messed up. In ways that I didn't fully understand at seventeen, but *now* ...' I blow out a breath. 'They'd try and take pictures up my skirt, catcall me, or shout questions about my sex life, anything to get a reaction out of me. At the time I didn't think of myself as a child, but I was, really, only seventeen. You're so vulnerable, aren't you? Right on the edge of adulthood and not sure what to do with it. The way they talked to me . . .'

Theo's stoic look is strained now.

'It was *awful*. I was so unhappy. It really messed me up. I started having crippling panic attacks, didn't want to leave the house, and Sam kept saying they were all bastards but that we shouldn't let it stop us living our lives, that *we* knew it was all bullshit, so who cared? I wanted so badly to keep him that I just agreed, and it kept happening and it got worse and worse.' I'm talking faster now, the words pouring out of me.

'They kept taking more and more pictures, choosing shots where Sam would be holding my arm looking like he was supporting me, or where I'd be looking wild and upset by them. I stopped eating, made myself ill. Eventually they ran this story about how I had a drug problem, and how my dad was distraught about it all and trying to get me into rehab.' I blink indignantly at Theo here. 'And I never *touched* drugs. I mean, *once* I ate a hash cookie with Lil and Serena and I spent the whole night curled up in a ball thinking that words were shapes that were trying to squash me, and every time Lil or Serena spoke it was a deliberate act of attempted murder. So that pretty much soured me on the whole experience.'

Theo clears his throat. 'What happened after that story came out?'

'I mean, thank God this was before social media really

took off, but I was still scared that the university I was going to were going to hear about it, that it was going to completely destroy my life, so I went to Ripp.' I grimace. 'Big mistake. I *begged* him to talk to the papers, get them to back off, tell them that none of the stories were true. He just shrugged it off and told me it would all die down soon enough and not to let it bother me. He even made a joke about how I was finally showing everyone that I was my father's daughter, as if at last I'd done something to make him proud. I felt like I was going mad.'

'Fucking Ripp,' Theo mutters, only endearing himself to me more.

'Yeah. I was so angry with him, but Sam told me it was wrong to hold this stuff against Ripp, that I shouldn't let my relationship with him be destroyed by childish hurt feelings.' I rub my fingers against my forehead.

'In hindsight, he was pushy about it, saying he'd talk to my dad with me, that he'd be there, that he wouldn't leave me to face this alone, but at the time I thought he was being supportive. We had lunch together, the three of us, and Sam was on top form, charming the pants off Ripp, laughing, bonding over how much he loved Ripp's music, how much he admired him – which you know Ripp was just eating up. And I sat there, *miserable*. I couldn't do it, couldn't get past everything with my dad. I so rarely asked him for anything, it seemed cruel to withhold help when it would cost him so little, it felt too much like he'd abandoned me *again*.'

I blink back sudden tears. Theo mutters more swear words

under his breath, and shuffles a little closer to me, though I don't think he's even aware he's doing it.

I take a deep breath. 'The day Sam and I split up, he told me that Ripp had offered him a job as the drummer in his band. I was totally thrown, and I asked him not to accept. I couldn't understand why he would even consider it when he knew how complicated my relationship with my dad was, how hard it would be for me.' I hesitate here, because this part of the story is one I haven't told anyone except Ingrid – not even Lil and Serena.

'He . . . he said that I was being selfish. That this was his big chance. He told me that he wasn't going to be another person whose dreams were destroyed by me. I didn't understand what he was talking about, until he spelled it out. He meant my mum, that she'd given up her career for me, to protect me. That she'd given up *her* dream, and it was all my fault.'

Theo gets abruptly to his feet.

'Fuck.' He's angry now. '*Fuck that guy.* He actually said that to you? But you know that's bullshit, right?'

I smile weakly. 'I mean, I know it's not my fault I was born,' I say. 'But Sam was only saying something I'd already thought myself. And I've had a lot of therapy so it's not that I think it's my *fault*. It doesn't mean I don't still feel guilty.'

'What? Why?'

'Well, you know, the press went nuts when Mum and Ripp got divorced, the whole three babies thing. I think if she'd stayed in the business it would have been even worse, the attention on us. I can't imagine she'd have wanted that. And her and Ripp split up, so she was basically a single mum. I don't see what choice she had, really. And it's still hard for me – with the music – when my mum sings . . .'

Understanding dawns in his eyes. 'Have you ever spoken to her about it?'

I shake my head. 'No, maybe I will one day, but I don't know . . .'

Theo sits heavily back down on the sofa. 'What happened after that?'

I grimace. 'Believe it or not, things got worse. The news of the breakup leaked. We had paparazzi at the door; I felt I'd dragged everyone into my mess. My mental health took another hit. It was all quite . . . traumatic. The fact that Sam was working with Ripp now made the story bigger. In the end my mum stepped in. I finally came clean with her about what had been going on. I'd been doing my best to hide how badly I was handling things from, well . . . everyone. She got Uncle Carl to speak to the papers, and then Ava got involved too, started threatening everyone who even breathed near me with all sorts of legal action. That's how we found out . . .' My stomach twists, a memory of how I had felt the day it had all come out, the day Ava had had to sit me down at the kitchen table and break it to me.

'It had been Sam all along. He'd told the press about me and about who my dad was; he told them where we would be and when, helped stage the worst of the pictures, sold them fake stories about me. He'd done it all to boost his profile, get his name out there.'

'He . . . did *what*?' Theo sounds stunned.

'Yup. Everything had been a big lie. He'd known who I was from the start, had his eye firmly on the prize. I tried to talk to Ripp about it, but Sam smoothed it all over, made it seem like I was some hysterical teenager, upset about being dumped. Mum offered to get involved, but – honestly – when Ripp wouldn't take *my* word for it, I just couldn't bear to have anything to do with either him or Sam any-more. They were welcome to each other. So Sam got what he wanted, while I ran up here to hide and wallow, totally devastated.'

Theo sits silently for a long moment, stared at his hands. The muscle in his jaw keeps ticking. 'That was when you were up here with Granny Mac for the last time?' he asks finally.

'Yes, and you know how awful that was.' I sigh. 'But even when I was the world's worst house guest – either snapping at her or haunting the place like a sad ghost – she took care of me. She got Lil and Serena to come up and do the ritual. She knew all about our witchy games, and I think she was pretty desperate at that point. But it did help; it was . . . cathartic. We cast the spell and then we buried it here in the garden with all the other spells we'd ever cast. It felt final, momentous. Lil and Serena made wishes for me as well as a curse on Sam, just to get me to do something hopeful. It was the first time I started to feel better. It took me a long time to get back – medication and lots of therapy, but it started there.' My eyes are wet now and this time I let the tears fall. 'I never even thanked Granny Mac for making it happen.'

Theo pulls me into his arms, and I crawl into his lap, letting him wrap himself around me. 'I'm so sorry, Clemmie,' he murmurs into my hair. 'I'm so sorry that happened.'

'It was a long time ago,' I say against his collarbone.

He only tightens his grip on me.

We sit like that for a while, until I feel the tension start to ebb out of my body, until I soften against him, my head nestled in the crook of his neck, my hands tucked around his waist, pressed between his back and the sofa cushions. He strokes my hair and my breathing slows, my eyes flutter closed. I've never felt so safe, so comforted.

The next thing I'm aware of is that I'm being hauled around like a sack of potatoes.

'Gah!' I flail, smacking Theo in the face.

'Fuck!' he exclaims, trying not to lose his grip on me and sinking his fingers hard into my hip.

'Ow!' I squeal. 'Put me down!'

'Why are you trying to kill us both?' Theo puffs, setting my windmilling feet down on the stair above the one he's standing on.

I take a second to reorientate myself, grab hold of the banister before glaring at him. '*Why* are *you* carrying me up the stairs?'

'Because you fell asleep. It was supposed to be a tender

moment, but I think you've broken my nose,' Theo grumbles, lifting his hand to his perfect nose and checking for damage. I eye Theo's face, which, aside from being a bit pink (I am no lightweight no matter how many bicep curls you do), looks absolutely fine.

'Next time just wake me up,' I say.

'Oh, if only I had thought of that!' Theo smacks his palm against his forehead. 'No, wait, I did try – very gently – to wake you up, and you *growled* at me.'

'I did not!'

Theo is laughing now. 'Yes, you did. You drooled on my T-shirt and then you growled at me, and honestly I was afraid you were going to start biting me again next, so I *very chivalrously* decided to carry you up to your bed.'

'Is it chivalrous to point out when a woman has drooled on you?' I ask, turning and climbing up the rest of the stairs, Theo behind me.

'Imagine if you'd broken my nose, Clemmie,' he says from over my shoulder. 'You wouldn't be getting any more flowers from David then.'

'Oh! My flowers.' I spin back. 'I need to put them in water.'

I'm standing at the top of the stairs now, but Theo is still a step below me. Our faces are almost level, and I get to enjoy a close-up view of his amused expression. Our lips are almost level too, and that is even more distracting.

'I put the flowers in water earlier,' he says, and I watch his mouth form each word.

'Oh, good.' I lick my lips, and something flares in Theo's gaze.

The moment stretches, heavy with promise.

I move aside so that Theo can climb the final stair, which he does, his whole body brushing up against mine.

'Well,' I say, and then no other words seem to happen. My heart picks up again, pounding. We haven't talked about the kiss yet. The whole Sam thing was obviously a mood-killer, but where do we stand now? Should I invite him into my room?

Theo takes a step towards me, crowding me back against the door to my bedroom. *Oh my God*, my body screams. *This is it!!!!*

'Goodnight, Clemmie,' he says softly, leaning forward and brushing a kiss across my cheek, an all-too-brief moment of contact. 'And happy birthday.'

Then he turns and walks towards his own bedroom.

'Oh, yes. You too,' I squeak, flustered. 'I mean, not happy birthday to you, because it's not. Your birthday, I mean. But goodnight to you . . . too.' I think I hear Theo chuckle as he closes the door behind him, clearly no longer in any hurry to rip my clothes off.

My head crashes back against the door and I close my eyes in mortification.

Super cool, Clemmie. It looks like thirty-three is off to an auspicious start.

Chapter Twenty-Eight

For two days Theo acts as if *nothing* has happened. He's not awkward or distant, if anything he's sweeter than ever – the first morning when I come downstairs it's to find not only the flowers David sent me in a vase, but more daisies sitting in a jam jar next to my computer. He insists on cooking dinner for me by himself, and it's not even a complete disaster. He emails a bookshop in Alnwick and orders me a parcel full of the children's books they recommend.

But he doesn't say a single word about Sam or the kiss.

And that's *fine*, obviously. I'm taking it all in my stride. So we shared the most earth-shattering kiss in the history of human mouths, and I unburdened my soul to him, and he seems to have forgotten all about it. So what? Big deal. I'm not going to let a little thing like that faze me. At least that's what I tell myself when I accidentally wash my hair with bubble bath, go to the shops wearing two different shoes, and walk into the fridge when Theo unexpectedly enters the kitchen.

Totally unfazed.

In fairness, Theo has been very busy writing – I've heard the muffled evidence coming from behind his bedroom door, and while he's still been a bit reticent to talk about it, I get the sense he's leaving here with the shape of a whole album at least. I know Serena has booked him a studio in LA in a couple of weeks' time to record and that he feels excited about it. Which is great news for me because – despite actually doing very little – everyone is delighted with me. (Except David. David considers my work to have been *acceptable*.)

I have plenty to keep me occupied in these last few days as well, because while Theo is busy not talking about anything that happened between us, he's *also* not talking about the fact we only have two days left before we leave Northumberland. But David certainly is. David has a *lot* to say about it.

I think he's looking forward to getting Theo back to himself soon, and there is a long list of stuff that needs to be packed, and another long list of arrangements that need to be made for moving furniture, equipment, and Theo himself. I seem to spend half the day fielding phone calls from David, removal companies, and the airline because Theo's guitars need some insane insurance policy before they can be shipped back to LA.

So, after days of silence on the subject, I think I can be forgiven for the undignified squeak that escapes my lips when Theo says, very casually over dinner, 'I think we'd better talk about what we're going to do about us once we leave Northumberland.'

'What we're going to do about us?' I manage once the squeaking has finished.

'Yes, Clemmie.' Theo sounds impatient. 'We are leaving in two days, you know. We have to have this conversation some time.'

'*What?*' I exclaim, managing to sound both baffled and pissed off at the same time, which is exactly how I feel.

'About us,' Theo says, gesturing between us with his fork. 'Me and you. Us.'

'What about *us*?'

'Well, what did you think?' Theo says airily. 'That I was just going to jet off to Los Angeles with no plan in place for when we'd see each other again?'

As that was exactly what I had been thinking I decide to keep my mouth shut.

Theo casts a sideways look at me and puts his fork down. 'There's actually something that I wanted to ask you.' He looks flustered, a flush touching his cheekbones. 'One of the reasons I agreed to come to the UK for this writing session was because I needed to be around this week anyway. Lisa's getting married.'

'Your sister is getting married?' I frown. 'When?'

'On Saturday.'

'Saturday as in five days from now?' David had been cagey about when Theo himself was flying back to the States and I guess this was why. I have a dim memory of Theo mentioning a family event way back at Serena's party.

Theo nods. 'Yeah, it's a whole big four-day thing from

Thursday to Sunday. I'm flying back to LA on the Sunday afternoon. I wondered, well, I thought, maybe . . . I hoped you might . . .'

'Sort out your hotel?' I finish for him. 'I'm surprised David hasn't already. You've left it a bit late. Wait . . .' I eye him suspiciously. 'David *does* know you're not going straight back to LA, doesn't he? Because if you think I'm going to help you hide from him so you can keep funnelling Maltesers down your neck then—'

'Clemmie!' Theo interrupts, half-laughing, exasperation writ large in his eyes. 'Yes, David knows I'm going, and no, I don't want you to book me a hotel. Jesus!' He scrubs a hand over his face.

'Oh, sorry,' I say. 'It's just I've been sorting out a bunch of stuff like that this week and—'

'I'm trying to ask you out,' Theo blurts.

I blink.

He clears his throat; the flush deepens. 'I wondered if you'd be my date. To my sister's wedding.'

My jaw must be hanging open, because after a moment Theo says, his tone almost sulky, 'You don't need to look at me like that; it's not that strange.'

'You asking me to go to your sister's wedding as your date?' I repeat. 'It's actually *pretty* strange, given that you kissed me two days ago and then haven't said a word about it since!'

'Well, neither have you!'

Huh.

'And I've been waiting, being patient, not pushing or rushing you, trying to *show* you how I feel. Isn't that the romantic way of doing things?' Theo adds. 'Honestly, it feels like sometimes you're actively *trying* to thwart me.'

I start to choke on a sip of water. 'Thwart you? How was I supposed to know? Maybe next time use your words.' I wheeze, the word *romantic* ringing in my ears.

'I'm using them now.' Theo smiles, hands me a napkin, equilibrium returning. 'So, will you go to the wedding with me? Please?'

'I . . .' I hesitate. 'I can't just turn up at your sister's wedding. Does she know you're bringing a date?'

'I actually asked her if I could bring you weeks ago,' Theo says, the colour back in his cheeks. 'I just didn't have the nerve to invite you.'

I frown. 'How many weeks ago?'

His eyes meet mine. 'About five weeks ago. After you bit me then told me you wanted to lick my dimple. I hoped that these were signs you weren't totally indifferent to me.'

I blush, torn between mortification and whatever the warm feeling uncurling in my belly is. 'You want me to go with you as a date?' I say slowly. 'A romantic date? Or a friend date?'

'I suppose technically it's both,' Theo shrugs. 'I'm happy you're my friend, but I'm asking you to go as more than that.' He smiles again. 'Is that clear enough for you? I don't want there to be ambiguity about my intentions.'

'Your intentions?' I repeat, still trying to catch up with

what is happening and why Theo is suddenly talking like Mr Darcy.

Theo reaches over the table and wraps his fingers around mine. His hand is big and warm and just the touch of it quickens my pulse. 'I need you to know that I'm glad you told me about you and . . .' – he hesitates here, a look of distaste flickers over his face – 'your ex,' he manages. 'Because it means I understand better why this is complicated for you, why we need to take it slowly, why you need to be able to trust me, and that part of that is being completely clear and honest with you. So, yes, those are my intentions: to take you to my sister's wedding on a romantic date. I want us to be together. If you want to.'

I look down at our hands. 'I do want to,' I say quietly, 'but . . .'

'Ask me, Clemmie,' Theo urges, squeezing my fingers. 'Whatever it is, you can ask me anything. I won't keep secrets from you.'

'It's just that . . .' – I struggle for the words – 'in the past, I think you've been more . . . not that there's anything . . . I only . . .'

Theo slumps back in his chair. 'This is about my *vibrant sex life*, isn't it?' I'm relieved to hear the note of teasing in his voice.

'Yes,' I admit.

'Right,' Theo scrapes a hand across his chin. 'Let's just get it all out on the table, then, shall we?'

'Okay,' I say, trying not to look queasy while internally bracing myself for what is about to come.

'Well,' Theo muses, 'my first relationships – as you know – were your standard disasters. I was shy and awkward, and I didn't realize at the time that that made me just the same as every other teenager faking my way through secondary school. Then, when I was eighteen, I auditioned for The Daze and I got in.'

'I feel like you're brushing over a lot of stuff there,' I say.

'Not really.' Theo shakes his head. 'I was a total music geek. School orchestra, church choir, the whole lot. I spent most of my lunch breaks hiding out in the music classroom, telling myself I was giving off a moody and creative vibe while actually memorizing the lyrics to "Tubthumping". My teacher heard about the audition and convinced a couple of us to go. The whole process was a blur. Honestly, I was so nervous, I barely remember it.'

He sighs. 'Things happened very fast for us – not through any real combination of skill and talent. It was a "right place, right time" thing and the guys who put the band together were incredibly savvy. Anyway, it's true that when we first started out, I did not behave well. Suddenly I was a big deal, and men and women were literally throwing themselves at me and I started buying into the hype. The headlines that got written about me then were mostly true and I couldn't have cared less. I wasn't looking for anything serious – why shouldn't I have a different partner every night? Why not just say yes to all of it? I wasn't hurting anyone; I didn't break promises, because I didn't make them.'

Theo grimaces. 'I don't love that I was that person, but

I was eighteen years old, and an absolute idiot, thrust into a completely insane situation. I doubt most grown people would like to be judged by the person they were at eighteen, but for me it's difficult because I feel so wholly unconnected to that guy. Ten years later I was in my twenties but I felt like an old man. I was sick of it, sick of *myself.* I started having therapy, which helped a lot, then a couple of years later I met a girl – Cyn, and we started dating.'

I try to betray no flicker of emotion at these words.

'As you know, we were together for almost five years,' Theo continues, 'and during that time I was in a totally monogamous relationship, but that was when all my chickens came home to roost. The press had branded me a playboy, a womanizer. A dickhead, basically – and they weren't wrong then, but *now* there was no changing it. Every time I was near another woman there were photographs of us and headlines about how I was cheating, how Cyn and I were breaking up and getting back together. It was relentless. In the end we did break up – not because of that.' Theo looks thoughtful for a moment, taps his fingers against the top of the table. 'Or at least not totally because of that. Cyn was great – she trusted me – we'd just grown apart, we were both busy with work, always travelling, trying to snatch time together. We knew it wasn't right, that neither of us were in it for the long haul, that we were better as friends.'

'And then?' I ask.

'After that, it was more of the same – more rumours, more stories linking me to every singer or actress you can think of.

I basically stopped dating altogether – how *could* I really date someone in a situation like that? I wasn't a monk, but I was pretty close, not that you'd know it from my reputation or the way people write about me.' He shrugs, but I can tell the nonchalance is forced. 'I stopped trying to fight it, to explain myself. It's easier just to let people think what they want. I brought it on myself, after all. Now I have to live with it.'

I remember then, the look on his face the night of Serena's party, when she'd asked him if he had to sleep with everyone he met. I know he likes Serena, respects her, and I know that comment hurt him. I know, because I saw it. I just didn't know Theo then, not like I do now.

'So when you said you hadn't had a one-night stand in over a decade . . .' I trail off, turning the words into a question.

'That was true.' Theo's dimple appears, and the sight of it makes me happy. 'Not until this beautiful, tequila-swilling redhead whirled in on me hiding at a funeral, told me she'd just called down an ancient curse on her ex-boyfriend and then propositioned me. I was a goner from the start.'

And I know that every word out of his mouth is the truth. I don't even preface it in my mind with a '*maybe I'm an idiot for believing him, but . . .*'. I simply believe him.

'And *then*,' – Theo clutches at his hair in mock despair – 'picture it, if you will . . . this dream woman, she sneaks out on me! Leaves me a three-line note with the wrong name at the top and disappears. Now, some might call that karma.'

'Some might,' I agree, and I can feel a big, dumb grin spreading across my face.

There's a matching one on Theo's lips. 'But, fate steps in – I run into her again and we're about to be marooned in the middle of nowhere together for six weeks. I'm delighted.' Theo holds up his finger. 'Only, guess what? Her entire history means that she'll never see me as anything but a sleazy musician who charmed her into bed, and anything that I do to try and prove otherwise only strengthens the case against me – I'm a flirt, a charmer, every word I say has an ulterior motive.'

'Sounds like a real pickle.'

'Yes, it is!' Theo exclaims sternly. 'Because I'm so totally gone over her, more attracted to this woman than I've ever been to another human being in my life – like a fucking horny teenager – and if I give *any indication* of that, she will believe I am a tremendous sex pest. So for the first week I can't be in the same room with her. It's humiliating. Whenever she touches me, I think I might die. I'm a disaster. I'm convinced this whole idea was a huge mistake. I'm *mortified* that she thinks I'm a diva who gives a shit about what brand of mineral water I drink.'

'You *are* a diva!' I'm laughing now, elated.

'Right, maybe I've been made more aware of the things I've taken for granted for a long time,' he concedes, 'but you made me feel like you expected me to start throwing furniture if I saw a single red M&M.'

I laugh harder at that, and Theo is smirking. 'Anyway,' he carries on, 'the point is, I thought this girl wasn't interested, and that was fine. I was trying to be respectful of that, to keep a lid on my own feelings, but then she got high on painkillers and told me repeatedly and graphically how attracted to me she was—'

'No, I didn't!' I gasp.

'You did!' Theo laughs harder now. 'When we got back from our trip to the pharmacy. I woke you up and you were just babbling the filthiest stream of consciousness I've ever heard. There was something that I didn't understand about parallel parking and then some *extremely* explicit details about what you'd like to do to me and what you'd like me to do to you, and then you passed out again.'

'Oh my God.' I cradle my flaming face in my hands.

'Don't be embarrassed, Clemmie. I told you that you'd be great at writing smutty fan fiction.' He nudges my elbow. 'It was hot stuff, except for the part where you sneezed into my hand before I could pass you a tissue.'

'I don't even think I believe you.' I peep at him through my fingers and he's grinning wickedly.

'I swear it's true,' he says. 'But it made me think that maybe you did like me too, or maybe you *could* like me.' He shrugs again. 'I don't really know – I was a mess over it – but I couldn't keep away from you after that. Because being with you is the most fun I've ever had, and even if nothing else ever happens, just sitting on the sofa watching TV with you is the best part of my day.'

There's a pause. I look down at the plate in front of me, where my dinner has gone cold. Deep down I know there are a dozen other things we should talk about, a list of obstacles that stand between us and any sort of real relationship that is a mile long, but right now I don't want to think about those things. I don't even want to acknowledge those things exist. So I don't.

'That was quite a speech,' I say a little breathlessly. 'I guess after all that I'd better go to the wedding with you.'

'Really?' He smiles wide and gets to his feet. Coming to stand next to me, he reaches for my hand.

I tip my face up to look at him. He's so beautiful it hurts. 'Yes, really. You know how much I love party food.'

Theo tugs on my hand, pulling me up so that we're standing flush against each other. His arm locks around my waist, my pulse is racing, my breathing ragged, my body feels so hectic I'm afraid I might actually swoon, which would only further Theo's argument that I'm trying to thwart him.

'We're going on a date?' Theo asks, his lips millimetres from mine. 'A real date?'

I swallow, nod.

'*Finally*,' he breathes. Then his mouth comes down on mine, soft and sweet. When he pulls away only moments later, I make a sound of protest. Theo's eyebrow lifts. 'Any ideas how we should spend our last two days here?'

I brush my lips against his neck, which is met by a low growl of approval. 'Mmm.' I tip my head to the side. 'Maybe one or two. Tell me, how much do you remember about these *extremely* explicit details?'

'Everything, Clemmie.' Theo smiles. 'I remember everything.'

Chapter Twenty-Nine

The first time, we don't make it to the bedroom. We don't even make it to the stairs. The first time it's up against the wall in the living room and it's fast and desperate, completely without finesse. By the time Theo buries himself inside me it feels as if we've had six weeks of painfully slow foreplay and neither of our bodies care to mess around.

Theo's jeans are undone, my skirt is up around my waist. I want his shirt off, but I can't stop kissing him long enough to make it happen and I settle for bunching the fabric in my fist, my other hand roaming over his warm skin.

He reaches in his pocket and pulls out a condom.

'You just carry condoms around in your jeans?' I ask, eyebrows raised.

He huffs out a laugh, kisses me again. 'Lil handed them to me with a knowing look before she left the other day.'

I pull back. 'My *sister* snuck you condoms? That's . . . that's . . .'

'I know. But instead of dwelling on it, let's just be grateful.' He presses against me and I moan.

'Yes,' I manage, 'grateful. Very grateful.'

His first thrust has me gasping into his mouth. He moves his hand to my thigh, holding my leg, higher, tighter around his hip as he grinds into me over and over. I am stretched, full. Every sensation is too strong; my skin feels hypersensitive, each brush against it a flash of light. When his fingers dip between our bodies it only takes the lightest touch before I shatter, laughing and crying out gibberish as the orgasm sweeps through me.

He presses his face into my neck, his own rhythm faltering as he reaches his climax.

'Fuck, Clemmie!' he exhales against my overheated skin. 'Fuck.'

We stand still for a moment, breathing hard. I realize my eyes are closed, and when I peel them open it takes a second for Theo's face to swim into focus. He has a swathe of deep pink brushed across his cheeks; his eyes are wide. His hands rest on the wall either side of my face, and he leans forward, presses soft kisses across my cheekbone, down the side of my jaw.

'That was ... a little faster than I had intended,' he mumbles.

I laugh, the sound high and airless. 'I don't think either of us were in a position to draw things out.'

He groans, pushes his hips forward, still hard inside me. I make an answering sound of agreement.

'Right,' he says, clearly attempting to muster some self-control. 'Let's at least make it upstairs next. I intend to take my time, and I've spent six very long weeks dreaming about you in my bed. Or your bed. Really any bed.'

'Bed sounds good,' I agree thickly, though I band my arms tighter around him, pull his head down for a long, lingering kiss that escalates quickly to a clash of hands and teeth and tongues.

'Bed,' Theo growls finally, pulling away from me, cold air rushing in between us. He deals with the condom, zips his jeans back up. 'I'd sling you over my shoulder but I learned my lesson about trying to carry you up the stairs.'

He takes my hand, kisses me again, and again, and again. We move slowly, each step interrupted by these long, intoxicating kisses, and I'm rubbing myself against him totally without shame, searching for the friction my body craves. This time we make it as far as the stairs, before I am pushing him down, straddling him, greedy fingers tangled in his hair, his tongue in my mouth.

'Stop, stop,' he says, and I freeze.

'Clemmie. We cannot have sex on the stairs,' he says sternly. 'We are grown-up people, only steps away from a comfortable bed. If we don't move, I'm going to do some serious damage to my back, get carpet burn in unmentionable places.'

Oh God, stern Theo is such a turn-on; my grabby little hands are already reaching for him of their own accord.

His eyes darken and then we're kissing again, and I think we really are going to have sex on the stairs – even though Theo is right and it is deeply, deeply uncomfortable – because peeling even a millimetre of my skin away from his feels like it is simply not an option.

Then his arm is under my legs and he's lifting me and my hands are wrapped around his biceps as the muscles there tighten and, *oh, his arms, his arms!* And somehow he has us both back on our feet. Before I can utter a word of protest, he grabs my hand and drags me up the last of the stairs, practically flinging me through the door to my bedroom – which is the closest – and onto the bed.

'Clothes off. Now,' he manages, already stripping off his T-shirt.

I wriggle out of my top and bra – my skirt and underwear having been discarded along the way – and lie back, too turned on to be self-conscious about my own nakedness, too busy taking in every bare inch of Theo's insane body, the way he's looking at me with an unholy light in his eyes.

'This time,' he growls, 'we're doing things *slowly*.' My toes curl up at the deep note in his voice, and then he climbs on the bed, moves over me and now that there is nothing between us, now that we are skin to skin, I think I am going to die of the pleasure of it.

And then his mouth is everywhere.

'I'm obsessed with your skin,' Theo mutters, then he lifts his head, frowns. 'That sounded wrong. Not in a creepy serial-killer way. I don't want to *wear your skin* . . .'

'Shut up, weirdo,' I giggle, squirming under him.

Theo grins, goes back to pressing open-mouthed kisses over my chest, down my ribs. 'You're so soft,' he sighs, his breath skating over me, making me shiver. 'So, so soft. You taste so good. I want to bite you.'

'Again, with the serial-killer vibes,' I gasp, and he chuckles as he moves so that his lips are at my thighs, and he bites me gently, a scrape of his teeth.

'Oh my God, Theo,' I pant a minute later. 'Please. Please. Please.'

'So. Fucking. Polite,' Theo punctuates each word with a kiss. 'Tell me what you want, Clemmie. Everything you want.'

It's a perfect kind of torture, and true to his word, Theo draws it out, taking his time, until I feel like I'm going to lose my mind, until I am incapable of words and dimly aware that I am making noises I have never made before. The world shrinks down to the touch of his fingers, his tongue, and when he finally lets me come I feel all my muscles lock, my body bows off the bed.

'Oh my God,' I whisper, my heart pounding in my ears. 'Oh my God, oh my God.'

Theo pulls me to him in a tangle of sweaty limbs, a pleased smile on his face. 'That was even better than I remember, and I've been remembering it *a lot*.'

'Oh really?' I grin.

His arm drifts over my waist, turning me away from him, my back to his chest. 'Yes, really,' he says softly, his lips against the shell of my ear. 'But do you know what has been tormenting me for weeks? Lying there, just on the other side of this wall?'

'What?' I ask, breathlessly, pressing myself back against his erection, eliciting a groan of appreciation.

'The vibrator Serena sent you. Have you been using it?'

'Yes,' I say, then add the full truth in a whisper. 'I was thinking of you.'

Theo flips me onto my back, looms over me, and he looks half-wild now. His teeth flash in a feral smile. 'Show me.'

So I do.

It's hours later when we finally stumble downstairs, looking like we've both (barely) survived some sort of sexy tornado.

It's the middle of the night and we're in the kitchen. I am wearing Theo's T-shirt and making scrambled eggs and toast.

Theo is leaning against the counter, completely naked because 'we could have been doing this for weeks, Clemmie. We could have been naked together *for weeks*. I'm never putting on clothes again and neither should you. Y*ou* should definitely *always* be naked from now on.'

'I'm not going to cook eggs naked,' I say firmly. 'It feels . . . unhygienic and potentially dangerous.'

'Who needs to eat?' Theo exclaims expansively, snaking an arm around my waist and nuzzling my tangled hair.

'We do!' I huff. 'I think we probably just burned ten thousand calories. If we don't eat something and hydrate, my body might turn to dust.'

'Hmmm, wouldn't want that,' Theo agrees, taking the plate I hand him. 'And I think I like seeing you in my clothes *almost* as much as I like seeing you naked.'

I blush, which is ridiculous, given everything that has just happened between us, but I can't help it. I don't think any of this has really sunk in yet.

We eat our eggs at the kitchen counter mostly in comfortable silence. Theo clearly realizes he's ravenous after all because once he's finished his he starts trying to scoop food off my plate and I'm forced to threaten him with a kitchen utensil.

'Careful where you're waving that thing!' Theo yelps.

'This is another reason to put on clothes,' I smile sweetly.

'I can't believe you're complaining about my lack of clothing,' Theo sighs, getting to his feet. 'The shine is off already. You've had my body and now you're tiring of me.'

Even though his tone is joking, I know him well enough to hear the tiny, truthful fear at the heart of those words.

I stand as well, wrap my arms around his waist and squeeze him tight, plant a kiss on the perfect pectoral muscle in front of my face. 'I honestly don't think I could ever get tired of you, Theo.' I smile against his skin. 'Yes, I think you're *unbelievably* hot and you've potentially ruined sex for me forever, but I *also* think you're sweet and clever and funny and extremely, extremely silly, which is maybe my favourite thing about you.'

'Really?' He looks down at me, and there's a vulnerability in his expression that makes my heart squeeze.

'Do I really think you're extremely silly?' I go up on my tiptoes, kiss the corner of his mouth. 'Yes.' I take my courage in my hands. 'I'm totally mad about you. Full of very big feelings.'

His hands at my waist, he lifts me off my feet, spins me round. When my feet touch the ground again I'm laughing, and he catches my mouth with his. 'Very big feelings is good,' he whispers. 'Now, let's go back to bed.'

The next morning I wake up in Theo's arms. This time we shower together. This time nobody leaves.

PART THREE

Chapter Thirty

Two days and an obscene number of orgasms later, Theo and I pack the last of his stuff into his fancy car. When Theo insists I drive with him and I ask him what I am going to do with my own car, I do not appreciate his mournful sigh and answer of, 'Just take the handbrake off and let the sea take it; it's given all it can.'

Fortunately, Petty has roped Lil and Serena in to come and sort out the house once we leave, and oversee putting all of her stuff back in place before any holiday guests arrive. I am certain my sisters have agreed to this as a ruse so that they can come and check in on me and Theo, but Lil *has* offered to drive my car back down to London so I am not about to look that gift horse in the mouth.

'Nice love bite.' Serena greets me dryly at the door, at a disgustingly early hour of Thursday morning. 'Tell me again about these purely friendly feelings you have for Theo.'

I flush, pulling at my T-shirt in an effort to cover up the mark next to my collarbone. I'd accused Theo of living out some *Blood/Lust* fanfic fantasy and he certainly hadn't denied it. And, to be honest, I hadn't really minded.

'Holy shit, Clemmie,' Lil whispers, awed. 'You're, like, *glowing*. Your skin is radiant. I think you're surrounded by some sort of sex mist.'

'Um, *gross*.' I wrinkle my nose. 'Please don't ever say *sex mist* again, you creep. So, yes, okay, I may have some news . . .'

Serena stalks past me. '*Please*,' she says. 'The sexy writing was on the wall when we were here last week.'

'Are you angry?' I ask nervously, following her through to the now empty living room. I've been sort of dreading Serena's reaction, especially given the very legitimate claim of unprofessionalism she could level at me.

Serena eyes me narrowly. 'Because of the job? No. Whatever happened here, Theo had some sort of creative breakthrough, so everything worked out. But I did have to hear from David that you were going to his sister's wedding before you texted us asking for help. And now here we are clearly bursting into the middle of your love nest. Not cool, Clem.'

'Yeah,' Lil chimes in. 'You're always supposed to tell us these things first. You know we'd have your back. We're your people.'

'I know,' I sigh. 'I—'

This is the moment Theo chooses to enter the room, and my sisters spin on him as one furious, intimidating entity, like something out of Greek mythology with two heads and one dark agenda.

'Theodore,' Serena snaps, pure ice.

'Hey, S. Hey, Lil,' Theo greets them easily.

'Don't *hey* us.' Lil's eyes narrow. 'We're only going to say this once.'

'Say what?' Theo glances at me, clearly confused.

This is a feeling I share, but that doesn't last long when Serena steps right up into his personal space, pokes one polished, blood-red nail into his chest. 'If you hurt our sister, in any way at all, if you cause her to feel the least bit of upset, a tiny *quiver* of discomfort, you will find yourself with only fond memories of your manhood.'

'*Serena!*' I squeak, mortified.

'No, Clemmie,' Lil says, her voice softly menacing. 'You've been hurt too many times. We should have done this in the first place.' Then she looks Theo dead in the eye and slowly draws one finger across her throat, her face a terrifying, emotionless mask.

'Fuck, Lil!' I exclaim. 'That is the scariest thing I've ever seen. What is the *matter* with you? You two seriously need to calm down.' I turn to Theo. 'I did not ask them to do this. I don't even know what this is, except an effort to horribly embarrass me.'

'*Imagine*, your sisters embarrassing you in front of your new . . . whatever the fuck Theo is.' Serena's smile is like a knife. 'Not so fun when the shoe is on the other foot, is it?'

'That was totally different,' I mutter. 'And as far as I remember we didn't threaten to *maim* your new girlfriend.'

The horrifying expression drops from Lil's face in an

instant and she is all smiles again. 'That's the look I gave Sophie Ritter before our under 16's championship tennis final and she definitely peed her pants a bit.'

Theo doesn't look worried, only amused, and he says, calmly, 'I would never do anything to hurt Clemmie. Never. She's the most important person in the world to me.'

'Awwwwww.' Lil clasps her hands together, caving immediately.

'We'll see' is Serena's answer, backed up by another daggering glare. 'Anyway,' – she turns back to me – 'we brought all the stuff you asked for.'

'Thank you.' I slump in relief, accepting the fancy Louis Vuitton luggage that certainly doesn't belong to me.

'You can't turn up with your stuff in a carrier bag,' Serena sighs, taking in my expression. 'This thing is at a *very* swish hotel, Clemmie.'

'A nice bookshop tote is not a carrier bag,' I argue. 'More importantly, did you pack plenty of options?'

'I did,' Lil chimes in.

'Thank you. Theo has been very unhelpful about what the vibe is.'

Theo shrugs. 'I don't know what to say. I'm wearing a suit. Lisa's wearing a big white dress. What other information am I supposed to have? I already told you what I thought you should wear.'

'I am not meeting your family at your sister's wedding in a gold sequin mini dress that barely covers my crotch.'

Theo's eyes flicker as they skate across my face and down

my body. 'You looked so hot in that dress, and I wasn't allowed to appreciate it at the time.'

Our gazes clash and I feel my pulse tick up, heat pooling in my belly.

'I'm going to throw up,' Serena says flatly.

'*Sex mist*,' Lil whispers, eyes wide again.

'Just relax,' Theo says, reaching up to rub my back soothingly. 'Whatever you wear will be fine. You'll look beautiful.'

Serena snorts. 'Telling Clemmie to relax, that's a good one.' She smirks at me. 'Remember when Lil tried to get you to meditate?'

I groan.

'What happened?' Theo asks, eyes lit up.

'She got even more stressed out.' Lil throws her hands in the air. 'Who gets more stressed out while meditating?'

'Okay, you keep saying this, but it *was* stressful,' I insist. 'He said we were going to move through relaxing all the different parts of our body but he started with the *top of our heads*. How do you relax the top of your head? That's not a thing! Do you all have secret muscles I don't know about? I kept trying but it was like the wires weren't connecting, and then by the time I gave up on that he was already down to the knees and I'd missed a lot of crucial relaxation and I didn't know whether to just carry on or try and go back.'

Theo is laughing along with my sisters now, and he presses his face into my neck, the gentle huff of his breath warm against my skin. 'You're my favourite,' he says.

'I'm glad you're all amused, but there's nothing strange about being anxious about meeting your . . .' – I sift through a list of possible word choices and lose confidence – 'Theo's family for the first time.' The clothes thing probably doesn't seem like a big deal to them, but I want so badly to get everything right. Things with Theo and me are so fragile that the smallest mistake could send everything crashing towards disaster. At least what I wear is something I can control, and that thought feels like a key in my hand.

'Look, if it's worrying you, we'll sort it out, but I promise that you could turn up in a bin bag and *your Theo*'s family are still going to think that you are the best thing that ever happened,' Theo says firmly. 'And I've met all *your* family and they love me!'

'That's true,' Lil beams.

'Jury's still out,' Serena mutters, but I'd swear she seems to be softening slightly. When Theo grins at her affectionately she barely glares at him.

'Anyway,' – Theo slings an arm across my shoulder – 'we need to get going or we'll be late.'

'Right, okay,' I agree, feeling the nerves really kicking in now. It's not just meeting Theo's family that's freaking me out, it's that we're leaving our precious bubble. Together. I have no idea what that looks like.

Going into the real world means that, surely, we are going to have to deal with some of the many, many things that I have been trying really hard to ignore. Things like the fact Theo lives on another continent. The fact that he's famous. The fact that millions of people want to know what he ate for breakfast (two Pop Tarts, half a bag of Haribo, and three chocolate Hobnobs, because the past six weeks have created a monster and he wanted '*a last hurrah before it's all wheatgrass again*'). The fact that we haven't actually discussed *any* of this.

'I can *hear* you overthinking,' Theo says, taking the bag from me and heading out to sling it in the car.

I want to ask him if he's thought about this enough, but I bite my tongue. I'm not sure what answer I want.

'It will be great,' Lil says, pulling me in for a hug. 'You'll have so much fun.'

'And if you don't then you can send up the bat signal and we'll come,' Serena adds, wrapping her arms around the two of us.

I feel some of the tension leave my body. They're right; it will be fine. And if it's not fine, then my sisters will be there.

'Let us know when you arrive,' Lil calls, waving as I climb into the car beside Theo.

'Okay,' Theo says, slipping his sunglasses on and putting the car into reverse. 'I have the first episode of that true crime podcast you mentioned, or the next chapter of the audiobook you've been forcing on me. I did not think I would be so invested in regency romance, but here we are. That shit is so buttoned-up, it's sexy.'

I snuggle back in the seat with a smile. 'I knew it. But maybe we could listen to some music? Something you like?'

'Really?' He looks at me in surprise, but he sounds pleased.

'Yeah,' I nod as we drive away from the house that has kept us cocooned and safe for the past six weeks. My stomach lurches but I keep my words steady. 'Maybe it's time to try something new.'

Chapter Thirty-One

We're halfway to the hotel when Serena calls.

'Just wanted to give you a heads up that we've had someone poking around outside the house with a camera,' she says after I put the phone on speaker so Theo can hear.

'Paparazzi?' Theo asks, his eyes sliding to mine for a moment. My stomach dips.

'I think so,' Serena huffs. 'He had the requisite darting ferrety features and long lens adored by tabloid trash and perverts alike.'

'Could have been a bird watcher,' I say hopefully. 'There are lots of rare birds around.'

'My sweet, sweet summer child,' Serena sings. 'I love your optimism. Never lose it.'

'Yeah, yeah, okay. Not a bird watcher, I get it,' I grumble.

'It doesn't matter anyway, because you're not here, are you? He had to satisfy himself with pictures of me having a frank conversation with an inept delivery driver, who Lil then had to make a cup of tea for while he practically wept into her shoulder. Jesus, why do people need so much coddling? I'm surrounded by incompetents.'

'It's your burden to carry,' Theo says. 'Thanks for letting us know. Looks like we picked the right time to get out of Dodge.'

'You certainly did. I wonder if he's still out there,' Serena muses. 'I could turn the garden hose on him.'

Theo smirks. 'Sounds like you've got it handled. Can you let David know, too?'

'Will do,' Serena says and cuts off the call.

'Are you okay?' Theo asks me.

I shift in my seat. 'I guess so. I don't like how close that was, but like Serena says, we're out of the way now.' I watch his face closely. 'What about you? Are you okay?'

'Me?' He taps his fingers on the steering wheel. 'Sure.' When I stay quiet, he glances over and gives a short laugh when he meets my eye. 'Okay, I'm annoyed. I don't like thinking about photographers at Granny Mac's house because of me, but we avoided any major disasters.'

'What about now? Are you worried they'll follow you to the wedding?' I feel that lurch in my stomach again at the thought.

'I'm always worried where my family's involved,' Theo says with a lightness I'm certain he doesn't feel. 'But there's no reason to think it will be a problem. And the hotel has security. It's not vulnerable in the same way the house was. They're plenty used to dealing with celebrities. It will be fine.'

I'm not completely sure if he's trying to convince me or himself, but when he takes my hand and presses his lips to it, just as he had on my birthday, I try to ignore the tight feeling in my chest.

Despite Serena's warning, I had underestimated the reality of Lisa's wedding venue. Almost four hours later, we pull up a long, gravelled drive lined with tall, sentry-like poplar trees, all slender elegance, providing a canopy of soft, bright green. Birds are singing. The light is actually *dappled*.

When we finally reach the end of the drive, we turn a corner and the view of the hotel opens up in front of us.

'What in the Jane Austen is this place?' I ask, dazed.

'Yeah,' – Theo glances up – 'I think they used it in one of the *Pride and Prejudice* films or something. Lisa's mad for that stuff.'

The building is a dream, all tall Georgian windows, climbing greenery and pale honey-drenched stone. There's a wrought-iron conservatory attached to one side of the hotel, flowerbeds spilling over with frothy pastel-coloured roses, and an enormous lawn mown in such perfect lines of alternating light and dark green that I half wonder if someone's been out with a ruler and cans of spray paint.

Theo pulls the car to a stop, and as we get out, a woman in a smart black suit and impossibly high heels clips down the front steps.

'Mr Eliott,' she says warmly, and she almost manages to maintain a perfect air of professionalism, but when Theo smiles and holds out his hand to shake hers, there's the tiniest catching of her breath.

'I'm Cassandra,' she says, 'the hotel manager, and I'll be overseeing everything this weekend. We're going to make sure your sister and her fiancé have a perfect wedding.'

'That's all that matters, and please, call me Theo.' He turns to me, wraps his hand around mine, pulling me forward. 'And this is my guest, Dr Clementine Monroe.'

'Hi,' I say shyly, and I sense Cassandra's curiosity, even as she greets me smoothly. It's in the way her eyes linger on me, the way I feel her making a quick inventory of my person. That feeling of uneasiness grows as several other staff members arrive, a younger woman to move the car, and a pair of men in their twenties to collect our bags. These three are less skilled at hiding their interest, and Cassandra's smile grows slightly strained as they blush and stammer, and cast a lot of wide-eyed glances Theo's way and several at me, too.

Theo takes it all in his stride, obviously used to it, and I try to force myself to relax. After all, they're not being rude or difficult. It's not *bad* . . . it's just weird. In an abstract way I know that Theo is very famous, but I'm so used to thinking of him as *my* Theo that it's jarring to realize that he belongs to all these people too.

With a sinking feeling I realize how familiar this all is, how the looks and the strangled buzz of excitement used to follow us whenever I was with Ripp. For a moment I remember how it felt to hold *his* hand while people stared and whispered, and inched closer to us, how it made me want to crawl out of my skin and hide.

Thankfully, I'm not given too long to dwell on that because a tiny body comes storming through the door at a hundred miles an hour screaming, 'UNCLE THEEEEEEEEEEO!!!!!!'

And then the strange mood is broken as Theo's four-year-old niece hurls herself into his arms, and he is laughing and spinning her around.

'Hannah-banana!' Theo groans. 'When did you get so big?'

'When you were away,' the little girl answers earnestly. 'I got big because you only saw me on the computer and so you must have thought I was very small.' She holds her fingers apart to indicate how tiny computer-screen Hannah was.

'Very true,' Theo agrees. 'Now, let me introduce you to someone very special. This is Clemmie.'

'Hi, Hannah,' I say with a little wave.

Hannah looks at me consideringly. 'Why is she very special?' she asks Theo. Her tone conveys her doubt over this assessment.

'Because she's the best at telling stories,' Theo says. 'And because she does magic spells.'

'You do?' Hannah's eyes widen.

I nod. 'With my sisters. Ever since we were little.'

Hannah's eyes grow rounder as she considers the possibility that the decrepit old hag in front of her was ever a child. 'Okay,' she nods. 'I will go with her, then.' Her tone is regal and she holds out her hands to me, flinging her upper body forward with serene confidence that someone will always catch her. Theo is forced to bundle her quickly into my arms.

I grab onto her, and she clings to me like a koala, pressing a hot cheek to mine and whispering loudly in my ear, 'Will you teach me to do a spell?'

'What kind of spell do you want to do?' I ask.

Hannah's answer is immediate. 'One that turns Oliver into a bunny. I think a bunny would be more fun than a brother.'

'Hannah, are you— Aaaaaaah! Theo! You're here!' A small, brunette woman, who must be Lisa, with a baby – presumably the much-maligned Oliver – strapped to her chest, appears in the door screeching over her shoulder, 'Mum! Mum! Theo's here!'

'Teddy!' A shriek comes from inside and then another woman – silver-haired and elegant – barrels outside. Theo's dad and Lisa's future husband follow.

And suddenly Theo is surrounded by people hugging and kissing him.

Oliver lets out a wail of protest.

'See,' Hannah mutters, casting a darkling glance at the baby. 'They told me a baby brother would be fun, but he doesn't do *anything*.'

'Mmm,' I hum in agreement. 'Babies aren't terribly useful, but they do grow up, you know.'

'I s'pose,' Hannah sighs gustily.

'Mum, Mum, stop!' Theo is laughing as she smothers his face in kisses.

'My Teddy bear!' she coos. 'So tall, so handsome.'

I snort, and Theo's eyes slide in my direction.

'Muuuuum!' he whines, embarrassed.

'What?' Her eyes widen as she takes in his face. 'Theodore! You need a shave! This is how you turn up to your sister's wedding? Looking like a scruffy reprobate?'

I snort louder.

His mum looks over at me and smiles, though the smile is smaller, more polite. 'You must be Clementine,' she says, stepping forward. 'I'm Alice, and this is my husband, Hugh.' She tugs Theo's dad forward and when he smiles I notice he has the same heartbreaker dimple in his cheek as his son.

'It's nice to meet you.' I can't shake their hands because I'm still holding Hannah but I sort of bob my whole body which I realize instantly is a totally weird thing to do.

Theo slips his arm around my waist, tickles Hannah's feet. 'Did you just *curtsey*?' he whispers gleefully in my ear.

'Shut it, *Teddy bear*,' I hiss between clenched teeth.

'Right, right.' Lisa claps her hands. 'Theo, you can sort out getting all the stuff up to your room and then I'm sure Dad can find something useful for you to do. Mum and I are taking Clemmie with us to the spa.'

'What about me, Mummy?' Hannah asks.

'You're going with Uncle Theo,' Lisa says tranquilly, already bundling Oliver into her fiancé Rob's arms.

'I can show you my bridesmaid dress,' Hannah says happily as I lower her to the ground, her hand slipping into Theo's and tugging at him impatiently. 'Did you know bridesmaids are the most important bit of the wedding?'

He shrugs at me, a rueful grin on his face, and I feel a moment of panic at having my Theo-shaped security blanket ripped away already, while I try to remind myself that I am a functioning adult, capable of talking to other people in lots of different situations.

As I watch him disappear inside, Lisa's arm comes around my shoulder and she squeezes gently. 'The best thing about it being my wedding weekend is that people keep trailing after me with alcohol. Let's go and have a drink, shall we?'

'Sounds good,' I smile weakly.

Not too long later, Lisa, Alice, Lisa's best friend, Cara, and I are reclining in soft white leather massage chairs inside a long brick building that has been converted into a spa. Outside the tall glass doors bees dip drowsily through the Victorian walled garden. The room is draped in a hazy web of golden sunlight, everything from the floors to the furniture is in soft shades of white and cream, and the overall effect is of floating serenely in a cloud. The air smells like lavender; the chair is digging pleasantly into the muscles in my back; there's a glass of something sparkling and alcoholic in my hand; and my feet are soaking in a basin of warm, scented water scattered with rose petals.

I think it probably takes a special skill to be tense in such a situation, but I'm doing a great job. Mostly because of the three sets of eager eyes trained on me.

'So, you and Theo . . .' Lisa looks at me over the top of her glass.

'Yeah,' I say weakly. 'It's . . . new.'

'He seems very taken with you.' Alice's words are casual but I can sense the steel behind them. 'It must be serious for him to bring you to the wedding. He hasn't introduced us to anyone in a very, very long time.'

I'm not sure how to respond to that. 'I care about him a lot' is what I settle for.

'I hope so,' Alice says, the sharpness less covert now. 'He's not as tough as people think. I'd hate to see him have his heart broken.'

'We're all just a bit cautious, you know,' Lisa says almost apologetically, 'with Theo's . . . life being what it is. There have been plenty of people happy to take advantage of him.'

I'm starting to feel a much deeper sympathy for Theo over his encounters with my sisters now. 'Mmm,' I say, wiggling my toes. I wonder how much Theo has told them about my own history. 'I know a little bit about that. My father is a musician.'

'Is he?' Alice's eyebrows lift.

'Anyone we'd know?' Cara asks idly, topping up her glass with the chilled wine sitting beside her in an ice bucket.

I grimace. 'Er . . . probably. His name's Ripp.' I never really know how to introduce my dad, but the single name usually seems to do the trick and today is no exception.

Alice chokes spectacularly on her prosecco. 'Your father is Ripp Harris?' she finally croaks.

'Holy shit!' Cara exclaims, sloshing her perfumed foot

water everywhere. 'He's actually quite fit for an older man,' she adds ponderously.

'Cara!' Lisa hisses.

'What?!' Cara's words have a slightly slurred edge. 'It's a compliment. That's in her DNA. She's got hot genes. Hot old guy genes.'

Don't love that, but I maintain a stoic silence, try to keep the polite smile frozen on my lips.

Lisa turns to me. 'I'm so sorry; this is the down side of being fed mimosas from the moment you wake up.'

'It's fine,' I say.

'No, it's not,' Lisa insists. 'People do that to me all the time with Theo and it's like, "*The man is my little brother. Will you please put your tongue back in your mouth?*"'

'Ripp Harris,' Alice says a little dreamily. 'I had all his records when I was a teenager. Saw him in concert once.'

Lisa's head thuds against the back of her chair and she lets out a pained groan. The gesture reminds me so much of Theo that my smile is genuine.

'Alice?' A woman with luminous skin and a perfect manicure appears from behind a gently swishing screen door. Her voice is hushed and I worry for a second that she's going to try to get me to meditate again. 'If you'd like to come through to the treatment room?'

Theo's mum glides off, leaving me and Lisa behind. Cara is lying back in her seat, eyes closed, and the odd snuffling sound issuing from her lips indicates that she is not exactly present with us.

'Ripp Harris is your dad,' Lisa says, shaking her head. 'What's *that* like?'

'We don't really have much to do with each other,' I explain. 'But I just . . . you know, I *get it*. How weird it can be, being related to someone like that.'

There's a flicker of shared understanding between us, a pulse of recognition.

'Yeah,' Lisa says, letting out a deep breath. 'It is pretty weird. When you're not the famous one, but you're sort of . . . famous-adjacent. Not that we're not proud of his success,' she adds quickly. 'But it's probably good that you have an idea what you're getting yourself into. I have to admit, when Theo told me you weren't in the business, I was a bit worried.'

'Sure,' I agree. 'It's quite a full-on thing.' I say the words easily enough but they're accompanied by a ripple of anxiety, the worry I can feel like a living thing crawling under my skin. I take another deep gulp from my glass.

'It *is* full on,' Lisa says. 'When Theo joined the band, I was at uni, having a great time, and then boom!' She mimes an explosion with her hand. 'Suddenly *everyone* was talking about him. His face was everywhere. When we went out, they played his music. People found out he was my brother and they wanted to be my friend, wanted to know if I could hook them up with tickets or introduce them. It happened so fast, I couldn't get my head around it.' She looks sad for a moment. 'I was just starting to be my own person, you know. Then I wasn't; I was only Theo's sister. I hated it so much.'

'That must have been difficult,' I say softly.

'I don't think I handled it great, to be honest.' Lisa sighs. 'I gave Theo a hard time. I wasn't really thinking about how it was for him – he seemed to be having a great time. I just felt like he'd tossed this weird grenade into my life and then buggered off on some rock-star tour of the world.' Her eyes widen. 'God, sorry! That's a lot to unload on you when we've only just met.'

'No, not at all,' I smile. 'I get it, I really do. I'm not sure we're built to handle stuff like that.' I lean back and close my eyes for a moment. 'In a funny way it must have been harder for you. I never knew anything different. The very fact that I was *born* was just part of the Ripp Harris circus. For you it was all normal . . . until it wasn't.' When I open my eyes, Lisa is looking at me with a sympathy that has me awkwardly clearing my throat. 'But like I say, Ripp isn't really in my life anymore anyway.'

'Do you mind me asking . . .' – Lisa hesitates — 'is that because of all the press stuff? I know from bitter experience how hard that can be. Theo's done his best to shield us from it, but the paparazzi are wild. It was especially bad at the beginning.'

'Partly, I suppose. Mostly it's Ripp stuff. Let's just say he's not exactly made for fatherhood.'

'Not like Theo, then. He'd be a great dad,' Lisa says and then she flushes. '*Oh my God*, I'm so sorry, I didn't mean that you and Theo should start making babies.' She winces. 'Jesus, I sound like Mum. I just meant Theo is such a good guy.'

I laugh then. Mostly because I feel comfortable with someone who's clearly as skilled at putting her foot in it as I am. 'Theo is a good guy,' I agree. 'The best. It actually really took me by surprise, how kind he is.'

Lisa looks pleased. 'Yeah, he creeps up on people like that. I mean, don't get me wrong, he's been a massive famous star for over half his life so he can be wildly out of touch with reality at times. But he's also very thoughtful. Comes from being a shy music nerd when he was growing up, I guess.'

'Have you seen him try to work a washing machine?' I ask.

Lisa giggles. 'Obviously not, because when I see him, if he doesn't have David wiping his bum, then Mum is there fussing over her little baby. Let me guess, he turned everything pink?'

'Worse; he absolutely boiled this beautiful cashmere jumper that definitely cost more than my car. It's only wearable by Ken dolls now.'

'I'm surprised he didn't try and fit in it anyway,' Lisa snorts. 'Loves wearing those insanely tight T-shirts to show off all his muscles.' She shudders.

'Mmmm,' I agree, unable to hide my approval.

'Ewwwww!' Lisa bats me on the arm. 'Clemmie!'

'Hey,' I shrug. 'What can I say? He's got a nice . . . pair of arms.'

'Just when I thought we were going to be friends,' Lisa teases, and I feel a glow at the words.

We sit for a moment in comfortable silence, only interrupted by the odd snore from Cara.

'I actually think Theo has been really lonely lately,' Lisa says finally. 'I'm glad he's found someone who makes him happy.'

'You guys don't get to see him much?' I ask.

She shakes her head. 'Hardly ever. He's pretty good about FaceTiming and stuff, so Hannah knows who he is, but he's just so busy . . .' She trails off. 'Last time I actually saw him I was barely pregnant with Oliver. We weren't even sure if he'd make it for the wedding, what with his schedule, so the fact that he came for the whole weekend and brought you with him . . . it really means a lot to all of us.'

I frown in confusion. 'I don't think there's any way Theo would have missed this,' I say. 'As far as I know he planned this whole album-writing trip around it.'

Lisa looks surprised. 'He did? No, I don't think so. At one point he was really vague about whether he was going to be in the country or not.' She looks down at her toes. 'I mean, I don't want to sound ungrateful. Look at this place, I can't believe we get to have our wedding here and, you know, that was all him. I think I could have told him I wanted to get married on the moon and he'd have found a way to make it happen, but I would have been gutted if he hadn't been able to make it.'

Although I have gooey feelings about Theo (or – let's face it – David) sorting out his sister's wedding, something about what she's saying doesn't feel right to me.

'But he did come,' Lisa says brightly. 'And he brought you, too. So there's plenty to celebrate.'

'Absolutely,' I agree, lifting my glass. 'Here's to you and Rob and a lifetime of happiness.' Lisa clinks her glass against mine.

Cara lets out a sort of spluttering snore and then lurches up in her seat. 'Woooo! Wedding bitches!' she slurs, lifting her own glass before collapsing back again.

Lisa and I exchange a look. Then both of us burst out laughing.

After that, it's much easier to relax.

Chapter Thirty-Two

Later, when I am bundled into a golf cart and dropped back at the main building after the full-body massage Lisa insisted I have, I am pleasantly buzzed on sparkling wine and utterly drunk on pampering. I am all warm and malleable, like well-kneaded dough that's been left on a sunny windowsill.

'Theo's paid some stupid amount of money so we get unlimited treatments,' Lisa said, several glasses deep, after we had bonded over everything from Ryan Gosling (dreamy) to our love of teaching (Lisa is a primary school teacher) to how wildly overrated afternoon tea is ('I mean, what am I? *A child? A doll?* Just give me a normal-person-sized sandwich,' Lisa expounded, waving her arms while I hissed, 'Yes, yes, *exactly*.').

'We can just have anything we want,' she gestured around the spa, a frenzied look in her eyes. 'It's absolutely mad and I feel like we need to try and get him his money's worth. I've had my eyebrows threaded, my eyelashes tinted, my face peeled. Mum and I did a sound bath this morning with a woman called Acorn.' She looks shiftily from side to side before whispering,

'Then later a very muscular Swedish woman waxed my pubes in the shape of a heart. It's been a surreal sort of day.'

I realize once I reach the main building that I have no idea where I am going and also that I am only wearing a fluffy dressing gown over a pair of pants. This had seemed fine in the spa, but now, as I am confronted by Cassandra in her power suit and her clackety four-inch Manolo Blahniks, I admit to feeling a bit under-dressed. Upon reflection, I'm not actually sure where my clothes have *gone*.

'Dr Monroe,' – Cassandra smiles like my sartorial choices are impeccable – 'you and Mr Eliott are in the Bluebell Suite. I can have Caleb show you the way if you like?'

'Yes, thank you.' I try to sound as though I belong as I take in the beautiful, polished floor that looks like a shiny chess board, the tasteful wood panelling and velvet furnishings, the leafy potted palms, and the enormous carved wooden staircase. This place is gorgeous, and Lisa told me that the whole hotel is all theirs until Sunday. We're having a family dinner tonight before the guests start arriving tomorrow, then there's the rehearsal for the family in the church and the big rehearsal dinner, before the wedding itself on Saturday.

Caleb leads me up the thickly carpeted stairs (the feeling of which between my toes brings me to another soberingly pertinent question . . . *where are my shoes?*) and down a hallway papered in foiled brocade before depositing me outside an enormous door with a discreet gold plaque engraved with the words 'Bluebell Suite'.

When I open the door I am confronted by the glorious

sight of not only the most luxurious hotel room I have ever seen, but of Theo Eliott sprawled across the four-poster bed taking a nap. I actually feel my heart squeeze with the gladness of seeing him after only a couple of hours apart, which even I will admit is a bit much.

'Hey,' he murmurs, sleepily, happily, as I clamber up on the bed beside him. 'You've been gone ages.'

'I've been bonding with your sister,' I say. 'And I've lost my clothes. Not exactly the introduction to your family that I was expecting.'

He huffs out a laugh. 'They sent your clothes and your shoes up a while ago.' He pulls me tight against him, snuggling into me, burying his face in my hair. 'You smell good,' he says, his hands already going to the belt of my dressing gown.

'A woman called Acorn rubbed oil all over me,' I say, stretching like a cat under his touch.

I feel him smile against my throat. 'Lucky old Acorn.' He parts the dressing gown, his fingers brushing a trail down my chest that his lips are all too happy to follow.

And then, after several languorous and very blissful minutes, in a voice full of heat and laughter: 'Is that . . . a heart?'

'We have to get ready for dinner,' I say later, when I am lying with my head on his chest. His fingertips run lightly up and down the bare skin of my arm, and I love the feel of them – the rough callouses from hours and hours of playing guitar, drifting over me like I'm something precious.

'Can't we just get room service?' he groans.

I prop myself up on my elbow and fix him with a look. 'No, we can't. They're doing some fancy eight-course menu for us all, and your family are excited to spend time with you.'

'I'm excited to see them too,' Theo says, wrapping a long piece of my hair around his finger, 'but no man in his right mind would willingly leave this bed with you in it.'

'It is a very good bed,' I agree, and I sit up. 'But I think it will be really nice for you all to be together.' I clear my throat, a little awkward. 'Lisa actually said something I didn't understand. About you and the wedding.'

'Oh, yeah?' Theo continues to play with my hair, but I can tell immediately that he's being shifty.

'Yes, she said that at one point you maybe weren't going to be able to make it to the wedding. But you told me you'd organized everything so you could be here.'

'Oh, that.' He flops back down against the pillow.

'Yes, that,' I say, poking him in the side. 'Spill it.'

'It's not a big deal,' Theo mumbles. 'I just . . . wanted to give her an out.'

'An out?'

Theo sighs. 'Look, I'm trying really, really hard not to scare you off right now because I know we're something new and it's delicate, but sometimes being part of my life isn't the easiest.'

'I don't understand,' I say slowly.

'Yes, you do.' Theo scrubs his hand over his face. 'Of

course you do. You understand better than anyone. When I'm around, things can get hectic. Lisa's wedding should be all about her. I guess I wanted to give her the option . . . I mean, to let her out of inviting me without making things awkward.'

I'm quiet for a while as I think that over. It's not as if I can pretend I don't know what Theo's talking about; it's one of the big fears about our relationship that I can't bring myself to face head on. But, still, what he's saying feels wrong. 'I just don't think she would ever have chosen to be without you, Theo,' I say finally.

'Maybe, but she doesn't always get a choice about when my stuff spills over into her life and I wanted her to get to decide this one.' He says the words on a sigh, and I think about what Lisa said, about how it felt when Theo joined the band. How her life changed.

'Sometimes it's easier to just keep my distance, so that they don't have to deal with all the shit around me. I mean look at tonight,' Theo carries on, sounding sad. 'She could have had all her friends here – we've got the whole hotel booked until Sunday but it's just us for dinner because she doesn't want to have all the . . .' – here he waves his hand around – '*fuss* that I bring, and I can't blame her.'

I pick up my pillow and thwack him in the face.

'Ow!' comes Theo's muffled exclamation. 'What was that for?'

'Because you're an idiot,' I say. 'Hasn't it occurred to you that your family just want you to themselves tonight because they rarely get to see you? They're so happy you're here,

Theo. Your mum and Lisa both told me that. Several times. In between the very light, polite threats to my person if I hurt you.'

The pillow is still over his face. 'Huh,' he says finally.

I swallow a smile. 'Yeah, *huh*. Idiot.'

He throws the pillow back at me. 'Stop calling your boyfriend an idiot.'

I still. 'Did you just call yourself my boyfriend?'

Theo rolls his eyes. 'Of course I did, Clemmie. Don't tell me we need to have a talk about it like we're teenagers.'

'Um, I do think it's the sort of thing we should probably have a conversation about. You can't just *decide* something like that.'

'Like what?' Theo raises his eyebrows. 'That we're in a relationship? I thought we'd already agreed. We're sleeping together, aren't we?'

'Well, yes, but that doesn't necessarily mean . . .'

'Yes, it does,' he says firmly, and he's got his hot, stern voice on again. 'I don't want to even pretend that this thing between us is casual. We talked about it beforehand; we talked about our feelings. We are both adults. I'm *in* this. I'm with you. So if you feel differently then please tell me now.'

He takes my hand in his and looks up at me earnestly. It feels like all my organs are rearranging themselves. There's fear and joy all muddled up together, but I know he's right about this – whatever is between us is not casual. The way I feel about him is much too big for that.

'It's not fair making me have this conversation with you when you've got no clothes on,' I grumble.

His dimple appears. 'I have to make the most of every advantage.'

'I don't feel differently about it,' I say in a small voice. It's not the most eloquent expression of feeling, but it clearly does the job because Theo pulls me on top of him and then it's far, far easier to *show* him how I feel.

I lean down, catch his mouth with my own, kiss him slowly, gently, as if we have all the time in the world. His hands come up to frame my face, and he pulls me closer, his tongue caressing mine. There's a hum of pleasure and I'm not sure if it comes from me or him; it seems to echo through us both. This kiss is slow and sweet and filthy all at once. It's an act of tenderness, of possession, and I feel the now-familiar need at the heart of me, the need that seems to have no end, no matter how close we are, no matter how many times we do this, as if I won't be satisfied until I've totally consumed him.

'Now who sounds like a serial killer?' he laughs up at me after I try disjointedly to vocalize this thought.

'I thought it was quite romantic,' I insist, pressing one more soft kiss to his lips.

'Hey, if you're saying you need us to spend all our time pressed together with no clothes on, I will support you in that,' Theo says.

'Selfless of you.' When I pull away, he makes a sound of protest and it's my turn to laugh. 'We have to get up!' I say firmly, extracting myself from his limbs. 'We have to get ready for dinner. We already covered this. Stop being distracting.'

Theo's only answer is to hold his pillow up to his face and let out a string of muffled curse words.

Now, as I scramble out of bed, I can finally get a proper look at the rest of the room. The enormous bed is draped in a canopy of pale, pale blue, and at the foot of it (about a mile away from the world's fluffiest pillows) is a long sofa in a slightly darker blue velvet. This faces the two tall windows with far-reaching views of the countryside. There's a large, marble fireplace, all neatly laid with firewood despite the fact it's summer, and a couple of companionable armchairs arranged in front of it. There's a door off to one side, and I wrap myself back in my dressing gown so that I can explore more.

'Oh my God, this bathroom,' I moan, taking in the gleaming white tiles, the deep, roll-top bath, the two sinks, the waterfall shower big enough for six people. The floor is warm under my bare feet. 'When I die I want to be buried in this bathroom.'

'Not sure a bathroom-slash-graveyard will really fit with their luxury aesthetic,' I hear Theo comment.

When I come back to the bedroom, I find Theo sitting up, his hair standing on end. The crisp, white bedsheets pool around his waist. It's quite the view.

'What's this?' I point at another door, refusing to be diverted.

Theo yawns. 'Oh, that's the dressing room.'

'Oh, of course. *The dressing room,*' I say, pushing the door open. 'Just like they have in the Premier Inn.'

The dressing room is actually like a big walk-in wardrobe, one wall covered in mirrors, the rest in built-in shelves and clothing rails. There's a glass dressing table that looks like something from the 1920s. Serena's Louis Vuitton suitcase stands in the corner, but all of my things have been unpacked and organized. Rich people are strange – do they just feel no embarrassment over a stranger rooting around and folding their sensible Marks and Spencer knickers? Hanging on the rails are several dark garment bags.

'Are these all the suits David sent for you?' I yell. 'Didn't realize you needed so many options, princess.'

'Actually, they're not,' Theo says, appearing behind me gloriously naked. 'They're the things David sent for you.'

'For me?' I frown.

'Mmm.' Theo's already wandering away, back towards the bedroom, and I follow. 'You said you were worried you wouldn't have the right thing to wear, so I asked David to send some things for you when he was organizing my suit. That way if Lil didn't pack something you like then there would be other options.'

'You organized that?' I ask.

Theo shrugs. 'I don't think I deserve the credit; all I did was mention it to David.' He looks at me. Frowns. 'You said you were stressing about it. I didn't want you to be stressing about it. But you don't have to wear any of them if you don't like them.'

'Oh,' I say. I remember his words earlier. *If it's worrying you, we'll sort it out.* Maybe it wasn't a huge effort on his part but I feel a lump in my throat at the fact that it wasn't just a hollow reassurance, that he actually *did* something. 'Thank you.'

'Don't thank me,' Theo smirks. 'If it was up to me, you wouldn't wear any clothes this weekend.'

'Not sure that would go down great in the family photos.'

Theo wraps a fluffy white towel around his hips.

'What are you doing?' I ask.

'You heard my mum.' Theo rubs a hand across his chin. 'I'm going to have a shave.'

'Y-you're going to have a shave?' I repeat. 'Like that?' My eyes dip to his bare, muscled chest, over his stomach, the v-shaped lines disappearing below the edge of the towel.

'Ye-es,' Theo says slowly, bemused. 'Clemmie, why do you look like you're on drugs?' He steps closer, tips my chin up with his fingers. 'Your pupils are enormous.'

'*It's happening*,' I whisper in response.

'What's happening?' he half-laughs.

'Can I watch?' I breathe.

'You want to watch me shave?'

I shiver, don't say anything, only nod.

Amusement lights his eyes. 'Sure, weirdo. You can watch me shave.'

'Don't call your girlfriend a weirdo,' I say as I trail after him, and then I don't have the opportunity to say anything else for a long time.

Chapter Thirty-Three

We manage not to be too late for dinner, and I am glad because Theo's family really are delighted to see him. He sits across from me, between his mum and his sister, and Alice keeps putting her hand on his arm, as if reassuring herself he is really there.

We're eating in the conservatory on the side of the hotel that will host the rehearsal dinner tomorrow and then the reception on Saturday. Right now there are fifteen of us sitting at a long table in the middle of the room: Rob and Lisa, Alice and Hugh, Rob's mum, dad and step-mum, two older brothers and their partners, as well as Cara, Lisa's other bridesmaid Sophie, and Rob's best man and his wife.

Hannah and Oliver, Rob's nieces and Sophie's daughter are all being looked after by the on-site babysitter so that the grown-ups can enjoy the beautiful, tiny plates of food that are served paired with large glasses of wine.

It's dark outside and there are candles all around us. In the flickering glow of their flames we talk and laugh and eat and I get to hear plenty of stories about Theo's childhood. Lisa and Rob have been together since they were at school, so fortunately everyone here has had enough Theo exposure not to be overwhelmed by his presence. I realize that I had been bracing myself for that, but so far – apart from Sophie's slightly frozen expression – things have been relaxed, normal.

'Oh my God,' Lisa screeches after I bring up the story Theo told me when we first met. 'Colin the poltergeist! I had totally forgotten about him!'

'Well, I hadn't,' Theo grumbles. 'You scared the shit out of me.'

'I used to re-arrange all his FIFA trading cards when he was asleep, and then tell him Colin had done it.'

'Lisa!' Alice chides. 'I didn't know about this.'

'She told me it was because Colin had a thwarted football career – that he died before he could play his first match for Manchester United,' Theo says.

Rob chokes in his glass of wine. 'Devious,' he grins appreciatively, draping an arm around the back of his soon-to-be wife's chair.

'*Then*, she started leaving footballs everywhere.' Theo pouts. 'Like, hundreds of them kept turning up.'

'Is that what that was about?' Hugh looks outraged. 'We thought the neighbour's kids kept kicking them over the fence. I had to have a word with Dominic about it. He must have thought I was going mad.'

Lisa is laughing so hard there are tears streaming down her face. 'That was Cara.'

Cara smirks. 'I *borrowed* them from the school's PE cupboard.'

'I started thinking that I was going to be smothered to death by the things in my sleep.' Theo sighs dramatically. 'I still can't watch Man U play without experiencing traumatic flashbacks. I was being gaslit by my own sister, living in an Alfred Hitchcock film.' He shudders.

Everyone is laughing now, and I nudge his foot under the table with mine. He grins at me, winks, and for a second I feel like we haven't left the bubble at all. Maybe the bubble is just us.

The next day I spend the morning exploring the grounds of the hotel while Theo hangs out with his family. They invited me to join them, but I made an excuse about having to do some work so that they got a couple of hours alone. As nice as they've been to me, I know how precious this time with Theo is to them.

He comes to find me when his parents and Lisa head off for the ceremony rehearsal at the church, and we walk around the gardens hand in hand. It's a bit cooler today, and I'm happy to lean into Theo's side.

'Ooh, there's a croquet set,' I say as we make our way across the lawn.

'Don't you think you're taking this whole regency romance thing too far?'

'Those sound like the words of a man who is afraid he's going to be destroyed.'

'Er, I think you'll find I'm amazing at croquet,' Theo huffs. 'Bring it on.'

It then transpires that despite our confidence, neither of us actually knows how to play croquet. Theo invents his own rules, which he keeps accusing me of breaking, as well as an elaborate forfeit system that turns the game into an increasingly dirty makeout session. I can't even pretend to be annoyed.

'I'm just saying,' Theo opines as we make our way back towards the hotel where some of the guests are already arriving, 'next time, *strip* croquet. Think about it.'

I get ready for dinner while Theo showers. I'm even more grateful for David's intervention, because Cara told me that the dress code for tonight and tomorrow is 'red carpet glamour' and that the floral tea dress I'd been planning on wearing to the rehearsal dinner wasn't going to cut it.

'I mean, look at this place!' She had gestured around us in clear disbelief. 'It's where film stars get married. None of us will ever be anywhere so fancy again so all the guests are going right out. I've got a designer bodycon dress that I found on eBay for tonight, and Lisa let me choose my bridesmaid's dress, thank God. It's classy as fuck.'

The clothes David arranged certainly fit the brief. As I unzip the garment bags I am confronted by half a dozen of the most beautiful, eye-wateringly expensive designer dresses you could imagine, and each one is in my size (something that I had been dubious about when I saw the labels). I run my fingers over the beads, the tulle, the sequins, before settling with a happy sigh on a dark, emerald green silk gown.

At first glance it's deceptively modest, high at the neck, long sleeves, cinched in at the waist with a softly draped skirt spilling down like ink to the floor, but the skirt has a split that bares my right leg up to the thigh when I move. It's like a sexy sneak-attack and, I swear, it makes me feel like Angelina Jolie.

My hair falls down my back in mermaid waves, courtesy of the YouTube tutorial Lil sent me and then spent forty minutes talking me through on FaceTime. My lipstick is the exact juicy red of the apple that took out Snow White.

As I stand in front of the mirror, I know I have never looked better. It's not just the dress that probably cost as much as a deposit on a small flat (though I'm 100% sure that's not hurting), but my skin is glowing (thanks, Acorn), my eyes are bright, I can't stop smiling, my posture is loose. Maybe it's the sex mist as Lil called it, but I think it might just be that I'm happy. Down-to-my-bones happy.

When I'm ready, I walk back through to the bedroom and come to the sort of grinding halt that should be accompanied by a record scratch.

Theo is wearing a tuxedo.

All the air has vacated my body.

And I'm not the only one staring. He has frozen in the middle of fussing with his silver cufflinks. His lips are parted, eyes wide.

My gaze slides over him: his dark hair brushed back, his

clean-shaven face, the immaculately tailored black jacket over the fine white shirt stretching across broad shoulders. His perfectly tied bow tie is like the ribbon on a present, and I itch to go and undo it, to tug that strip of black silk until it comes apart in my hands. I can almost hear the rasp it would make as I eased it away from his throat, how those shirt buttons would fly open under my fingers. Any immunity that I thought I had built up to his good looks has been officially obliterated. He's so gorgeous it gives me a toothache.

I'm breathing hard, and I can feel my cheeks flush.

Theo takes a step towards me. Stops.

'You look . . .' He trails off, his voice rusty.

'Yeah. You too,' I manage.

'I can't touch you,' Theo says carefully. 'Because if I touch you, I'm not going to be able to stop touching you, and I cannot be late for my sister's rehearsal dinner.' He pauses. 'Right?'

There's something hopeful in his voice that makes me laugh. 'That's right. They're doing canapés and cocktails outside and we're already late. They'll be waiting for us and people will *definitely* notice you are missing. We should go.'

'Okay,' Theo sighs. 'But later. Later I'm going to have a lot to say about you in this dress.'

'I'm not going anywhere.' I smile, feeling suddenly shy.

Theo's throat bobs. He doesn't say anything, just nods, then holds out his hand.

I slip my fingers into his and the two of us head out the door and downstairs in a fraught silence that seems only to lessen its grip slightly as we get further away from a bed and closer to civilization. By the time we hit reception I feel more like a human and less like a walking bag of uncontrolled hormones, but I'm still careful not to look directly at Theo in case I end up accidentally climbing him like a tree in front of his friends and family.

The place is much busier than it has been, with a few guests who have obviously driven up after work to check in to their rooms ahead of the dinner. I catch a glimpse of Cassandra, behind the desk, directing various staff members with an elegant wave of her hand like a virtuoso conductor, completely at her ease.

It's a short walk around the side of the hotel to the patio where pre-dinner drinks are being served. Lisa said around fifty guests were joining us for dinner and to stay over tonight and then about the same again were coming tomorrow for the wedding. We join the crowd, walking across the gravel paths which are proving a challenge for those in spiky high heels. I have never mastered walking in high heels so today for once I actually feel quite smug in the pair of flat, gold sandals I picked up last summer in the supermarket. Sure, they might have cost £12 and be made out of plastic, but I'm not the one sinking into the driveway like I'm unsuccessfully traversing the Fire Swamp in *The Princess Bride*.

I start to feel the eyes on us, the people nudging one another, the whispers. Theo is wearing his sunglasses, but they're not really a miraculous Clark Kent/Superman disguise transforming him in the eyes of strangers. Unsurprisingly, I was always way more into Clark than Superman. When I say this to Theo, he smiles.

'Typical you to fancy the handsome nerd.'

I nod, trying to ignore the interested stares. 'That is my type.'

'Well, lucky for you I'm a handsome nerd who looks great in Spandex. So you don't have to choose – the best of both worlds.'

'You're so full of yourself, Eliott.' I bump him with my hip.

Of course, lots of people actually know him, and we stop often so that he can introduce me to friends or more distant family members. He's polite, engaging, quick to smile, but I know him better now, know that he's not as relaxed as he seems. I see the way his smile shows off his teeth, but not his dimple. I feel his hand tighten in mine, hear the way he talks – his words smooth as a pebble skipped across water, and I realize that for all the charm and warmth he exudes he doesn't give himself to everyone. Not the way he does to the people he really cares about.

'Excuse me.' One of the guests approaches us nervously; she's probably in her mid-thirties, wearing a spangled purple gown that looks like a grown-up prom dress. Cara was not lying about how dressed up people were getting: it's like the Oscars red carpet out here.

'I'm really sorry to bother you,' she continues breathlessly. 'I hope this isn't really rude, but I'm such a big fan, I wondered if you would mind taking a picture with me?'

Theo smiles with his teeth again. 'Of course,' he says lightly, 'that's so nice of you to say. Are you a friend of Lisa's?'

'I actually work with Rob,' the woman says. 'They're such a lovely couple.'

'They are,' Theo agrees.

'I love your dress,' I tell her. 'Would you like me to take the picture for you?'

'Oh, yes, thank you.' She hands me her phone and I snap the photo. Theo literally looks like he's stepped out the pages of *GQ* magazine; the woman's smile is wide and disbelieving as he loops his arm around her shoulder.

When she thanks me again and wanders off with a dazed expression I realize that the floodgates have opened now, and there's a small, awkward crowd surrounding Theo as each person plucks up the courage to approach him next.

Every time, Theo seems surprised, delighted, only too happy to meet them, but I can see the tension in his jaw, the way his eyes slide over to where Lisa and Rob are having their photos taken by the professional photographer, blissfully unaware. The relief he feels in that moment, that he's not somehow stealing attention from her, is obvious.

'Do you want to be in the photo?' a younger guy asks at one point and I realize that he's trying to work out if I'm *someone* worth meeting. After all, I am here with Theo.

'Oh, no,' I say awkwardly, 'I'm just the photographer tonight.'

'I think she might be that one from *Game of Thrones*,' I

hear him say to his friend as they lope away, and I stifle a giggle that borders on the hysterical.

'You okay?' Theo asks quietly, his hand resting on the small of my back. 'I know these things are a lot . . .'

I look up at him, at the worried crease between his brows. 'I'm good,' I say, and it's mostly the truth.

I can see how much it means to all these people to meet him. I can see how careful he's being to give them something that will make them happy. How they'll go home and tell their friends, '*You won't believe it. I met Theo Eliott in real life, and he was so nice.*'

It's bringing up memories of being with Ripp, and Sam too, that don't feel great, but I'm still aware that it's different. Theo doesn't live for it the way they did, and his eyes flicker to me often, measuring, checking in with me. I realize with a pang that when I was in this situation with my dad, I always felt like he wanted me to fade into the background, that I couldn't exist for him because every fan he met was the most important person in the room – after himself of course. I don't feel that with Theo.

With Theo, I'm the most important person in *any* room.

'Mostly, I'm interested in snagging some of these canapés before they're all gone,' I say, placing a hand over my stomach. 'I'm starving.'

Theo grins, and then insists we track down every member of the waiting staff so that we can try and compare each different offering. When I tell him I prefer the mushroom tartlets to the miniature lemon cheesecakes he tells me firmly that I'm out of my tree and stuffs another cheesecake bite in my mouth. I'm half laughing, half-choking when I see the wedding photographer has captured the moment.

'You guys are so cute,' she smiles, before moving on,

'Yeah, we are,' Theo beams, hooking his arm around me and pressing a kiss to my temple. I squeeze my eyes shut, worried that he's going to see my whole heart in them.

Chapter Thirty-Four

It's not long afterwards that we go in for dinner. We're sitting with Theo's family and I feel myself relax as that sense of being on display disappears. After we've eaten, Lisa swaps seats with Theo to sit beside me. She looks incredible in a long, sequined pink dress.

The tables have been cleared though people are lingering over coffee and drinks. There's a band who've been playing soft, jazzy covers through dinner, but who are moving on to something more upbeat now. Cara is beginning to drag people up to dance.

'If this is the rehearsal, I can't wait to see the place tomorrow,' I say to Lisa.

'I know it's all ridiculous,' she grins, 'but it seemed mad not to let all our friends make the most of the hotel.'

'It's not ridiculous at all. All these people love you and they're so excited to celebrate you and Rob. You can feel it in the air; it's lovely.'

'I'm so glad you're here,' Lisa says, and she squeezes my hand.

I squeeze back. 'Me too,' I say honestly.

Later, I wander outside to cool down, pressing my hands to my flushed, pink cheeks. It's dark now, and the stars are out, scattered across a velvet black sky: the splintered light from the mirror ball inside multiplied by infinity.

There's a handful of people out smoking and vaping, and I lift my hand in greeting to them before carrying on further into the grounds, away from the noise and the lights, just for a minute, just to catch my breath.

Down one of the gravel pathways is an archway cut through a tall hedge, and beyond that a small, private garden with a stone bench. I sit down with a grateful sigh. The high shrubbery encloses the space, and I feel my shoulders relax. It's fun being here, but it's a lot of people, especially after the solitude of the past six weeks.

There's a crunching sound as someone else walks down the path, and I don't even wonder for a moment who it might be, so sure it's Theo – the only other person I want to see right now. I left him sitting with his mum, a sleeping Oliver in his lap, his face pink and happy.

'Here you are,' he says, stepping through to my hiding place.

'Here I am,' I agree. 'You didn't have to worry about me; you were having a nice time with your mum.'

He saunters over, his hands in his pockets. 'She took Oliver and Hannah up to bed,' he says, sitting down next to me. 'Good luck to her. The baby finally fell asleep. Hannah's still going strong.' He tips his head back, closes his eyes for a moment.

'That's because you were slipping her all those sweets that are *supposed* to be wedding favours for tomorrow.'

His mouth tugs up. 'Hey, that's what uncles are for.'

'Winding children up and then leaving someone else to try and wrestle them into their pyjamas?'

'Exactly,' he nods. 'All the fun, none of the responsibility. It'll be different when I'm a parent. Might as well make the most of it.'

The image of Theo holding a little dimpled baby temporarily cuts off the blood flow to my brain. I might have to put my head down between my legs.

'Do you want children, then?' I ask casually. Or at least, I aim for casual, but it definitely comes out too squeaky to pull it off.

'Yes, I think so,' he says, his face still tipped up, away from me.

'Lisa said she thought you'd make a great dad,' I say.

He chokes on a laugh, winces. 'Oh God, sorry. I thought it would be Mum trying to not so subtly make the case for more grandchildren.'

'It was actually in the context of a conversation about Ripp.'

'Oof. Not sure that's better.' He picks up my hand, presses a kiss to my palm. I curl my fingers like I'm planning to hold on to it forever.

'I'm having a nice time,' I say. 'I really like your family.'

'They love you.' Theo turns to me now, and his eyes glitter, stars there too. 'Lisa's already told me she'd choose you over me if we ever split up. Mum and Dad want to know if you'll be coming for Christmas.'

My heart squeezes. 'Christmas is almost six months away,' I say.

'I know,' Theo sighs, sounding almost sad about it.

We're quiet for a while.

'I've never made plans with anyone before,' Theo says softly, 'but you make me want to buy a five-year diary just so I can write your name on every page.'

I laugh, the sound bright and scattered in the darkness. 'I love you,' I blurt, because at this point *not* saying it is a lot harder than saying it. I feel like I swallowed the sun and I'm trying to hide it from everyone, including myself.

Not anymore.

Theo exhales softly, a sound of relief. He pulls me across his lap, wraps his arms around me, presses a kiss next to my ear. 'Clemmie, I am so in love with you,' he whispers.

Then he kisses the pulse at my neck, the corner of my mouth, my eyebrow, my throat. Soft, sweet touches of his lips against my skin that make me feel cherished, even as they set my heart pounding. By the time our mouths meet, we're both breathing heavily. My lips open under his and his hand cups my calf, moves up over my knee, all the way up to the top of the split in my skirt, his touch warm and heavy. I reach up, pull on his tie and it unravels in my fingers just the way I'd imagined.

'Do you think Lisa will be upset if we miss the rest of the rehearsal dinner?' I ask huskily.

'She and Rob actually slipped away twenty minutes ago,' he murmurs, his thumb brushing the inside of my thigh in a way that has me taking a sharp intake of breath. 'And honestly, I think I deserve a medal for turning up at all, given the way you look in this dress.'

'It's a very nice dress,' I pant, his fingers skating closer to the edge of my underwear.

'It is,' Theo agrees amiably. 'Let's go and take it off you.'

Chapter Thirty-Five

'Come to LA,' Theo says later when we are wrapped around each other in bed. My green dress is pooled on the floor, his tuxedo is scattered around the room at various interesting stopping places.

My heart stutters. 'I can't.' I wiggle away from him. 'I can't just follow you around. I have to sort my life out. I need to get serious about job applications, contact anyone who might be able to help. Maybe take on some sessional teaching.'

'You don't have to come on Sunday,' Theo says, pulling me back close. 'Come in a week or two. For a visit.'

'You'll be recording then,' I say against his chest.

'I want you there.'

'How can this possibly work?' I whisper it, hardly wanting to say the words aloud. 'When we live over five thousand miles apart?'

It's one of the questions I've been too scared to ask, but we've run down the clock. There's no time left. Theo leaves on a private flight in less than forty-eight hours. I feel like even asking the question is removing the pin from an emotional hand grenade, but he doesn't flinch.

'It will work because we'll make it work,' he says calmly. 'We'll see each other as much as we can and once you figure out what you want to do and where you'll be based then I'll be based there too.'

I prop myself up on my elbow. 'What?' I ask, startled.

'Sorry, is it too soon to talk about getting a place together?' Theo rolls on his back, smacks his palm against his forehead. 'God, I have absolutely no cool around you, but we can slow everything down. We don't have to talk about that yet, or at all, if you're not ready.' He's rambling slightly now, nervous.

'It's not that.' I shake my head, consider. 'Okay, it's not *just* that because, yes, it is fast, but we've been living together for weeks and I'm sort of dreading that part being over . . .'

He sits up, his expression hopeful. 'Really? So we can talk about it?'

'Yes, we can talk about it.' I frown. 'But what did you mean about being based where I am? Wouldn't you want me to come to LA?'

'I mean, sure, if you wanted to,' Theo shrugs, 'but if you do decide you want to teach or whatever, you won't have a huge amount of say, will you? As long as I can get to an airport I can be based wherever.'

'But . . . won't that be . . .' I hesitate, unsure. 'I mean, won't it be really inconvenient? You've got a life in LA. You can't just leave that behind.'

It's Theo's turn to frown. 'You're doing what my family

do,' he says finally, and he sounds annoyed. 'Holding me to such a low standard. Firstly, any inconvenience is relative because – and I don't wish to sound like a massive dickhead here – I am quite well-off and I can afford to spend the time and money on travelling. But secondly, and more importantly, why do you think I *wouldn't* inconvenience myself for you? Why wouldn't I compromise? Why wouldn't I do the harder thing? You're worth taking trouble over, Clemmie.'

'Oh,' I manage.

'Yeah,' he says. 'And you're lucky I didn't throw *my* pillow at you for that one.'

I laugh, collapse into his chest, relief pouring through my veins. 'You do sound like a massive dickhead,' I snort. '*Quite well-off,* indeed.'

Theo responds by tickling me until I beg for mercy.

'So where does that leave us for now?' I ask once I've recovered.

'Maybe you can fly out to LA to visit in a couple of weeks, and then once the record is done, I'll head to London and we can make a plan from there?' Theo suggests, like trotting around the globe really isn't a big deal.

I sigh. 'Tragically, we can't just live in a house by the sea like two little mice. We were always going to have to re-enter the real world some time.'

He glances at me, rueful. 'I loved living in that house with you.'

'Well, I understand you're a man of means. I'm sure Petty

will give you the friends and family discount any time you want to take a trip down memory lane.'

'Six weeks every summer, tell her to put it in the calendar.'

'For someone who doesn't usually make plans, you're getting pretty good at it.'

'I like the way the future looks right now,' he says.

'Me too.'

'And I suppose when we're apart we'll just have to have plenty of phone sex,' Theo muses. 'I haven't done that since the dawn of video chats.'

'Well, it's nice for couples to try new things together,' I say.

'Speaking of which,' Theo's eyes darken, 'all those mirrors in the dressing room have given me a couple of ideas . . .'

'I'm listening.'

The next morning I prise my eyes open just after ten and force my aching body up and into the shower while Theo sleeps. All these late nights of mind-blowing sex are taking their toll, not that you'll hear me complain . . . well, except about the fact that I need to wear another high-necked dress today thanks to Theo's continuing interest in my collarbones.

It's a beautiful day for a wedding, all blue skies and marshmallow clouds, and I pad through to the dressing room, blushing at the sight of the handprints on the mirrors. I'll have to clean those off before housekeeping arrive or I'll never be able to look Cassandra in the eye again.

I brush out my damp hair at the dressing table and then creep back through to wake Theo.

'It's almost eleven,' I say, pulling away when he tries to tug me back into bed. 'There's only an hour and a half until the wedding. We slept in late.'

'How long can it possibly take to get ready?' Theo murmurs sleepily, not relinquishing his hold on the belt of my dressing gown. 'Five, ten minutes? That leaves us a good eighty minutes to fill. I can get an awful lot done in that time.'

'I know that,' I laugh. 'But while you might be able to get ready in ten minutes, I'm afraid us lesser humans take longer.'

'You look insanely beautiful just as you are,' he insists.

'Right, well, as I'm not turning up to your sister's black-tie wedding in a dressing gown with wet hair, let's just agree to disagree on this one.' I move back round to my side of the bed and unplug my phone from the charger.

'Oh, shit,' I say, my eyes widening. 'I've got eleven missed calls from Serena.'

Theo makes a sound of concern but I'm already dialling.

'Clemmie?' Serena sounds pissed.

'Yes, hi, are you okay?'

She lets out a long breath. 'Of course I'm okay. Are you okay?'

'Er, yeah, I'm fine,' I say and I look over at Theo, bemused. He shrugs. 'I'm with Theo. It's the wedding today.'

'Oh my God,' she says, dazed. 'You don't know? How do you not know?'

'Know what?' My heartbeat picks up. 'What's happened? Is everyone okay?'

There are a few clunking noises, the murmured sound of voices as Serena moves away from wherever she is. When her voice comes down the line it's soft and gentle. That's how I know something is really wrong.

'Okay, Clemmie, don't freak out,' she says soothingly.

'Don't ever start a conversation that way!' I exclaim. 'Now I'm definitely freaking out.'

Serena makes a noise of exasperation and it makes me feel a bit better. 'Look,' she says, 'it's nothing to panic about, but there are some . . . pictures doing the rounds.'

'Pictures?' I'm totally lost now. 'Pictures of what?'

'Pictures of you and Theo. They got picked up online early this morning and it's turning into a bit of a story. The PR people here were supposed to have been in touch with Theo about it already.'

'Theo just woke up,' I say, and I put the phone on speaker so that he can hear.

'Okay, don't need the details on *that*.' Serena takes another deep breath; I think it's some sort of calming breathing exercise, but it's making me want to scream. 'It's good that I got hold of you. We think there might be some paps waiting outside the hotel and we're a little worried some of them may try and sneak in with the guests.'

'Paps?' I repeat, bemused. 'You mean paparazzi? Here? At the wedding?'

I glance over at Theo and his hands have fisted the bedsheets.

'Yes,' Serena says, 'because of you and Theo. The pictures.'

'Right,' I say slowly, trying to sound calm for Theo's sake. 'I mean I suppose they were going to find out about us some time but I didn't think they'd come *here* . . .' I trail off.

'There must be some other reason for them to be here,' Theo says, his voice rough. 'They wouldn't bother if it was something innocuous. This isn't a celebrity wedding. What aren't you saying, Serena?'

'It's not just you two being together.' Serena's voice has gone soft again, and I know I'm going to hate whatever comes next. 'It's the pictures, they're pretty . . . errr . . . salacious.'

'*Salacious*?' I snort in disbelief. 'I don't think you've ever used that word in your life. What are you talking about?'

'They're extremely fucking horny, Clemmie!' My sister snaps, the thread of patience she's been clinging on to clearly frayed right through.

Theo almost falls off the bed.

'What do you mean?' I croak.

'Just . . . make sure you talk to hotel security right away. I'm stuck in meetings here, but I'll call back as soon as I can. And tell Theo he needs to answer the fucking phone. It's all going to be fine, okay? I promise.' She hangs up then, but the anxiety in her voice leaves an icy feeling spreading through my chest.

As soon as the call disconnects, I type Theo's name into the browser on my phone and the articles pop up immediately.

THEO ELIOTT AND RIPP'S DAUGHTER CAUGHT IN STEAMY CLINCH, the first headline screams. I click through and there are the pictures.

'Oh my God,' I whisper, feeling all the blood drain from my face.

'What is it?' Theo asks, his voice tight. He leans over to look at my phone.

'It's pictures of us from last night,' I say, the words flat and empty. 'From when we were in the garden.'

The pictures are slightly blurry, but you can see enough. I'm straddling Theo on the bench, his hands are all over me. In one of the pictures my head is thrown back, my face a mask of pleasure, his lips on my neck; in another we're kissing and his hand is pushing up my skirt, my bare leg wrapped around him. There are more, each one a clear shot of an intimate moment. In some of them they've strategically placed an emoji to censor part of the image – which actually has the effect of making them look even more explicit.

The one that really punches me in the chest isn't even one of the *salacious* ones: it's Theo cradling my face, looking at me with stars in his eyes because I've just told him I love him. That moment was *ours*, and I feel like someone has stolen it.

No wonder the press are here. My heart is beating fast, and my mind is swimming with memories of my previous encounters with these people. The flashing cameras, the cruel, jibing words, the intense vulnerability, having to see lies splashed about with absolutely no control over any of it. The fear, the panic, it's all still there, waiting inside of me, like a long-dormant volcano ready to erupt.

But it's not just that. It's Lisa's *wedding day*. And it's about to be ruined. Because of me. I look over at Theo and I think the stricken expression on his face must mirror my own.

'Fuck.' Theo hisses a breath between his teeth, hauling himself out of bed and grabbing his phone. He stalks through to the dressing room and slams the door behind him. It muffles the sound but I can already hear him talking to David. '. . . Just make sure we get a load of extra security here, right now. I am not having paparazzi crashing my sister's wedding, David. How did this happen?'

I stay where I am, sitting on the edge of the bed, and keep clicking. Whoever took the photos is quoted too. 'He brought her to his sister's wedding and it's definitely serious. They've been all over each other the whole time.'

There is one major difference from the last time I found myself in the public eye: now the news cycle is twenty-four hours, and everyone in the world can join in.

WHO IS THIS UGLY BITCH? is the top comment underneath from someone called TheosGirl42.

Please, he'll be bored of her in a week, says another. She's not even pretty.

We all know Theo and Cyn belong together! #Thyn has over 2,000 likes and counting.

The comments from total strangers pile up and up and up, and I feel them like a physical weight, crushing me. I shouldn't keep reading but I do, scrolling through page after page of abuse.

My phone starts going wild with notifications. They've found my social media now, and even though all my accounts are private someone has obviously given the press access and I start seeing pictures from my Instagram popping up too. It's another tiny betrayal, another moment of wondering who it is I can't trust. I have approximately seven thousand friend requests and it looks like everyone I've ever encountered is reaching out to check in with me, which would be nice if the interest wasn't so rabid.

Already, it's clear the photos are everywhere, and most of the accompanying articles refer to me as 'Ripp's daughter, Clementine Harris'. It looks like the old stories never truly died because I see myself being described over and over again as a 'troubled party girl' who had 'disappeared from the public eye to seek help'. There's even speculation Theo and I met in rehab. My stomach starts churning faster.

I spot a new photo, one where I'm wrapped up in a black coat, looking dishevelled and alarmed, my hand lifted up to shield me from the flash of a camera. It's the photo of me leaving Theo's hotel the day after the funeral, when the paparazzi had been camped outside. The breathless headline above reads, THEO ELIOTT AND CLEMENTINE HARRIS, A TIMELINE: EVERYTHING WE KNOW ABOUT THEIR RELATIONSHIP SO FAR.

There's a knock on the door and I get up to open it. Lisa stands on the other side, her hair is swept up in a chignon and she's wearing a white satin dressing gown with the word BRIDE emblazoned on the pocket. Her face is pale.

'Oh my God, Clemmie.' Her eyes fill, threatening to ruin her make-up. 'I'm so sorry!'

'You don't have anything to be sorry about,' I exclaim quickly, pulling her through the door. 'I'm the one who's sorry. It's all my fault.'

'I just can't believe that someone at our wedding, someone I *know*, would do something like this, selling photographs of you . . .'

'It could have been anyone, Lisa,' I say numbly, wanting to reassure her. 'Someone who works at the hotel, someone who works for one of the suppliers, anyone could have taken those pictures. Theo and I weren't exactly in a locked room.'

'Do you think so?' Lisa looks miserable. 'It's making me feel sick, not knowing who to trust. I can't believe this is happening, today of all days.'

Theo emerges from the dressing room, and he's wearing jeans and a T-shirt. He strides towards his sister, pulls her into his arms. 'Everything's going to be taken care of,' he says tightly. 'I've got David coordinating with the hotel security now, and we're bringing some extra guys in, just as a precaution.'

'Extra security?' Lisa looks stunned. 'Why?'

Theo's eyes slide to mine over the top of Lisa's head. 'Just to be on the safe side,' he says, keeping his tone light. 'We don't want any photographers bothering your guests, not on the biggest day of your life. Speaking of which, shouldn't you be getting ready? Or are you planning on being fashionably late?'

'I just wanted to come and check on you,' Lisa says, taking a step back so she can scrutinize Theo's face. 'Make sure you were both okay.'

'We're fine,' Theo says. 'But I'm just going to nip downstairs and have a quick word with Cassandra before I get changed.'

'He's lucky he only has to put on a suit and that's the job done,' I say mechanically. Theo and I exchange another look and I can tell he's relieved that, like him, my priority for now is making sure Lisa is okay.

Lisa gives a watery chuckle. 'That's true,' she says. 'I've been getting ready for three hours already.'

'Right.' Theo hooks his arm around her shoulders, steering her towards the door. 'So let's get you back in the make-up chair so that Rob doesn't think you've gone all *Runaway Bride* on him.'

He's still chattering away to her as the two of them leave the room. He casts a worried look at me over his shoulder, and I try to stretch my mouth into the shape of something that feels vaguely like a smile. If the frown on his face is any indication, I do not succeed.

When the door closes I stand, frozen for a moment, one question circling round and round in my head: *What are we going to do now?*

Chapter Thirty-Six

My phone rings again, and this time it's a video call. Like the Avengers, the mums have assembled, though their base is around our kitchen table. They are all wearing the same expression – a perfect blend of worry and fury.

'How are you doing?' Ava asks, her voice sympathetic. 'Serena caught us up on everything.'

'I'm . . .' I tilt my head, as if trying to get my thoughts and feelings to settle down. 'I think I'm just overwhelmed right now. It all feels like a bad flashback to last time. Seeing the pictures . . . There's a lot of adrenaline. I'm . . . still shaking.'

'I can understand that, but this isn't the same thing, okay?' Ava's voice is firm.

'I knew that if Theo and I got together then eventually we'd have to deal with the press.' I sit down on the blue sofa. 'I didn't want to think about it, but I knew. I just had no idea it would be . . .' – I gesture widely – '*this*.'

'From what Serena has said it's a perfect storm of things.' Ava is calm. 'A slow news day, Theo's recent absence from the press, the stories about him being in rehab, your father, the photos—'

I grimace here, and Mum grabs the phone, her face suddenly close to the camera. 'Darling, don't worry about those. We've all been caught up in a moment, and you actually looked very beautiful, the pair of you, like a Pre-Raphaelite painting.'

'Muuuuum,' I groan. 'You cannot say things like that about photographs of me and my boyfriend getting off with each other.'

'It's just sex, Clementine,' she says placidly. 'Everyone does it.'

'Not in the side bar of the *Daily Mail*, they don't.'

'Your mum's right,' Petty says, drifting back into view. 'It was very Dante Gabriel Rossetti but, you know, less *mournful*. That green dress.' She sighs, dreamily. 'I think it's trending on Twitter.'

'Green dresses really are so powerful,' Ava agrees.

'And with the red hair?' Petty pretends to swoon. 'Get out of here.'

'I don't think any of you understand how serious this is,' I snap. 'I'm trying to get a job for one thing.' I feel hysteria rising inside me. 'And now those photos are out there. Me half dressed with a rock star's hands up my skirt. Who's going to hire me?'

'It's hardly like you've got an OnlyFans account,' Mum says cheerfully. 'Your privacy was invaded! Not that in this day and age an OnlyFans account is anything to be ashamed of either . . .'

I close my eyes, not at all sure I want to be distracted from the current crisis by how deep my mum's knowledge of OnlyFans runs. 'I don't think that matters.'

'So we'll get the pictures taken down,' Ava says.

'How?' I ask.

Her mouth thins. 'I haven't ironed out the details yet, but we'll make it happen.'

'I just can't believe this is happening again,' I say finally. 'These pictures of me, out in the world ... I know I'm not seventeen anymore, but I feel exactly the same. So helpless. So *violated*. I hate it.' A tear spills down my cheek.

There's a sound in the doorway, and I look up to find Theo standing there. I can only assume he heard what I said because he looks like he's swallowed a rusty razor blade.

'Hey,' I say softly.

'Hey.' He tries to smile, but can't quite pull it off. His posture is taut as a bow string.

'The mums are on the phone,' I say, holding up the screen so that they can all greet each other.

Theo's eyes anxiously scan my face, and it's easy to see the concern swimming in them. 'I spoke to the PR people and they don't think we should comment at this point,' he says and then hesitates. 'But there have been a couple of developments.'

I don't like the sound of that. 'What sort of developments?'

He clears his throat. 'Um, well, there's this ...' He moves around the sofa and gives me his phone. Our fingers touch and his usually warm hands are ice cold.

I look down at the screen.

'*Theo Eliott's secret marriage*,' I read aloud. 'What is this?'

'Just keep reading,' Theo looks pained.

'Oh my God,' I scroll down. 'This is *madness*.' There are two photos in the online post, both taken on the beach in Northumberland. In the first Theo and I are deep in conversation at the edge of the water, in the second we're walking away from the camera hand in hand. I know exactly when this was, another of our private moments, splashed around for people to see.

'"I saw him with her a few weeks ago,"' I read aloud. '"He introduced Clementine as his wife. They seemed really in love."'

Theo shifts uncomfortably.

'This is that girl who stopped us on the beach!' I exclaim. 'She doesn't mention that you also told her you weren't Theo Eliott in the first place. *Jesus*.'

'Yeah, unfortunately it's been picked up by a couple of websites.' Theo scrubs his face with his hands. 'I don't think it will be a big deal; this is like the third time they reckon I've got married in secret.'

'A secret bigamist? Where do you keep all your secret wives?' I ask.

'In the attic,' Theo smiles wanly, and when I smile back it's the first time I feel a moment of calm in the storm.

'I don't understand how they found out about Ripp so quickly, though,' Theo frowns. 'It's not like you ever introduced yourself to anyone as Clementine Harris. There's not really anything online that links the two of you.'

'I told your sister and your mum,' I say slowly, 'in the spa, but they'd never . . .'

Theo shakes his head. 'No way, never.' He thinks about it for a moment. 'Wasn't Cara there too?'

'Yes, she was.' I feel sick. 'Do you really think that she'd do this? She's Lisa's best friend.'

'No.' Theo sighs, runs a hand through his hair. 'I mean, I don't think so anyway, but I absolutely believe she'd blab about your dad to anyone who'd listen.'

Yes. I think. *I could see that.*

'What's the other thing?' I ask.

'What?'

'You said there were a couple of developments. So, first of all we've been married off . . .'

'Mazel tov,' Petty puts in from the phone where I'd almost forgotten about our audience.

'What's the other thing?' I ask again, ignoring this.

That tell-tale tic of his jaw means I know he's upset. 'It's . . .' He trails off, takes a steadying breath. His hand clenches at his side. His tone becomes clipped, business-like. 'It would seem that one of the more industrious journalists has dug into your past . . . with Sam.'

'*Sam?*' And there it is, the final tug of the rug from under my feet.

Theo nods, and even his nod is angry – a sharp jerk of his chin. 'A couple of the photos from when you were seventeen have resurfaced.' I start, and the pain that I see in Theo's face then is horrible. 'It looks like Sam's done an interview – or made some on-the-record comments at least.'

'An interview?' I say blankly. 'About me?'

'I don't know the details yet,' Theo says, his voice ice. 'But I have people working on it.'

'That piece of shit,' Ava's voice comes from the phone.

'No arguments here.' Theo turns to look at her on the screen. 'I'm about to jump on a conference call with my lawyers, and I wondered if you'd join, Ava?'

I don't hear Ava's response, too distracted by the wave of grief and anger and fear that swamps me. It's like what I felt at Granny Mac's house, but worse. It's not just a memory of what happened then; it's like it's all happening again *now* – like every bit of that pain and insecurity has come back as strong as it ever was. I'm flattened by it.

'He's pissed off about the phone call,' I say hollowly. 'He'll want to get back at me. He'll say things . . .'

'Hey.' Theo crouches down by the side of me, takes my face in his hands so I'm looking at him. I focus on those honey-gold flecked eyes. 'You didn't do anything wrong here. And he's not going to say anything to anyone, okay? I'm going to take care of it.'

He sounds so sure that it takes the edge off the panic crowding my body. 'Okay,' I manage.

'We're going to leave you to get ready for the wedding,' Ava says. 'Theo, send me the details for the call, okay?'

'Will do,' Theo nods, and we say our goodbyes.

A weighty silence fills the room.

'What should we do?' I say finally. 'Should we leave? I think I should go home.'

Theo shakes his head. 'I think it will make things worse – there are people camped outside and if we leave early, or even if you leave by yourself, there may be a bigger story. Plus I think Lisa would kill me.' He growls low in his throat. 'I can't believe this. I can't believe I've managed to bring this fucking circus to her door on the most important day of her life.'

'It wasn't just you,' I say bleakly. 'If it wasn't for me, and my connection to Ripp . . .'

'No, Clemmie.' Theo grabs my hand. 'This is all me. I can't—' Whatever he's about to say is cut off by the shrill ring of his phone. 'This is the lawyers,' he says, looking at the screen. 'I'll take this while you get ready. We'll go to the ceremony and duck out of the reception early, then I'll drive you home, okay?'

'Okay,' I agree weakly.

I go back to the dressing room, pull on my dress – a heavily embroidered lilac tulle halter neck that only an hour ago I'd been excited about wearing – with a mechanical indifference. I brush my hair, but don't have time to do much beyond French-plaiting it into a long braid.

My face in the mirror is pale and pinched. The glowing woman from yesterday has disappeared, and no amount of blusher and highlighter is bringing her back. There's a knock on the door and Theo appears. When did we start knocking? He's being careful with me, and I can hardly stand to look at him – scared of what I will see in his eyes.

'Are you ready to go?' he asks. He's changed into another suit, blue this time, with black lapels. He's as gorgeous as ever, but there's tension written in every line of him.

I get to my feet. 'Yes,' I say.

'You look beautiful.' His voice is soft.

'So do you.' I manage a small smile. There's a pause. 'This is going to be bad, isn't it?'

His expression tightens. 'It's going to be fine.' He takes my hand in his and squeezes my fingers just for a moment before letting go, and then we head out to the wedding.

Lisa and Rob are getting married at the small church in the grounds of the hotel – once part of the grand estate that belonged to some real-life Mr Darcy character. The birds are singing, the church bells ring, the sound cutting through jasmine-scented air. It's so lovely it feels like a joke. How can the world just carry on like nothing has happened?

As we near the church, the tickling sensation skitters across my skin. Heads turn. Whispers start. It's different from yesterday. No one seems to want to look me in the eye, but I can still feel the weight of their interest. They've all seen the pictures. Of course they have. Every single person here has seen what Theo and I got up to last night.

I remember how it felt the last time – when the papers had run stories about me being on drugs, and then I'd had to be out in the world with people I knew, school friends who had looked at me with a sort of gleeful fascination, strangers who did a double-take in the street, their curiosity slithering over me like an uninvited touch.

I plaster a fake smile on my face, but I feel like I want to throw up in one of the perfectly tended flowerbeds. The feeling only grows when we join Theo's mum in the church.

Alice's eyes betray her own worry as she greets us. I blink hard when she asks me if I'm okay. I hate that she's dealing with this on Lisa's wedding day, that I've caused all this drama for their family. I also don't love that she must have seen the pictures of me and Theo together . . . not everyone has Dee Monroe's laissez-faire attitude to these things.

'Today's not about us,' Theo says, and I nod in agreement. 'Let's focus on Lisa and Rob.'

'I can worry about both my children at the same time, Teddy,' Alice says. 'I'm your mother.'

'I'm so sorry this happened, Alice,' I manage.

She frowns. 'It's not your fault. It's those bloody vultures again. Are they really waiting outside the hotel? I'd love to go out there and give them a piece of my mind.'

'They'd enjoy that,' Theo says with a small smile. '*Theo Eliott's mum on the rampage.* I can see the headlines now.'

'I've been taking Tae Kwon Do classes in the village hall,' Alice mutters darkly. 'I could do some serious damage, you know.'

'Let's save the lawyers' fees and just rise above it instead,' Theo says. 'We can call you karate kicking the shit out of them Plan B.'

'Fine,' Alice grumbles. 'But don't you let them get to you, okay? No one blames you for this.'

Theo doesn't say anything, only nods tightly. I can tell he

doesn't agree, and from Alice's defeated look I'd be willing to bet she can too.

The ceremony itself is short but sweet. Hannah stomps down the aisle in rainbow tulle and fairy wings, stopping halfway to greet her next-door neighbour and ask why they haven't brought their dog. Then Cara and Sophie in sleek navy slip dresses dipping low in the back, looking, as promised, *classy as fuck*. Finally, Lisa floats down on Hugh's arm in flowing white silk.

The drama of the morning melts away for a brief moment. Alice, Theo and I all cry, but not as much as Rob, who blubbers like a baby. Oliver, the actual baby, is strapped to the best man's chest and wearing a tiny tuxedo onesie. He appears largely uninterested in anything except Rob's buttonhole which he is desperate to get hold of for the sole purpose of putting it in his mouth.

'See,' Hannah shout-whispers in my ear from our position in the front pew. 'Babies are so silly. Can we get a hamster instead?'

After the vicar pronounces Rob and Lisa husband and wife, we all head back out into the sunshine and shower them with sweet-smelling confetti made of dried rose petals. Lisa hugs me like we've known each other for years, and I squeeze her back, my eyes stinging.

'Are you crying again?' Hannah asks me suspiciously.

'No,' I say.

'Yes, you are! All the grown-ups keep crying.'

'I'm not crying, Hannah-banana,' Theo says.

'Funny how quickly those sunglasses went back on,' I mutter, dabbing carefully at my eye make-up. A waitress appears with a silver tray and I gratefully grab a glass of ice-cold champagne. Honestly, I can't believe I've made it this far into the day without a stiff drink.

'Is it time for ice cream yet?' Hannah demands, making a decision on her priorities; clearly, worrying about weeping grown-ups is not high on the list.

'When we've had our pictures taken,' Rob says, scooping her up into his arms. 'Before you spill ice cream all over your pretty dress.'

'Daddy! I'm not a baby!' Hannah screeches as he carries her away through the guests milling and drinking.

'There's going to be a bad-tempered fairy in all their photos,' Alice says fondly.

'I wonder if they make those wings in my size?' I say. 'I think it's a look.'

Theo is tense, scanning the crowd, but as the afternoon wears on it becomes clear that the security outside have done their jobs. No one is here who isn't supposed to be here. The sidelong looks and the whispers continue, but as Theo and I barely touch for the rest of the day, at least they don't have any further ammunition. I flinch at every flash of a camera, and I don't know if you've noticed this about weddings, but there are cameras *everywhere*.

We make it through lunch and the speeches, which pass in a blur, and my cheeks hurt from the effort of constantly smiling as though nothing is wrong.

The first dance rolls around and Lisa and Rob sway across the dance floor looking delighted with all their life choices, and when Alice and Hugh join them, Theo slips his fingers through mine and we dance too. His hand is tight at my waist, warm through the fabric of my dress, and I find myself gripping the lapel on his suit so hard my knuckles turn white. We don't talk, just sway gently to the music. I want to press my face into his chest and cry.

There's more dancing – a raucous, twirling 'Come on Eileen', a painfully earnest and very slightly off-the-beat attempt at 'All the Single Ladies', and they even play an old song by The Daze, which Theo suffers through good-naturedly while Lisa cackles and points at him.

Finally, Theo appears beside me and says the words I've been waiting to hear.

'We can leave now.'

Chapter Thirty-Seven

Alice cries when she hugs Theo goodbye and I know just how she feels.

Theo is quiet when we drive away from the hotel. The photographers have finally cleared off, presumably scared away by security or expecting us to be hunkering down in the hotel for another night. Theo and I haven't talked about why we're leaving early, about what will happen when we arrive at Mum's house.

Instead of talking, Theo lets an audiobook play, but the charming romance being read by a dashing actor does nothing to distract me. As the miles increase so does the heavy feeling in the car, but I can't work out what to do to dispel it. I feel exhausted. My thoughts are scattered like shrapnel. I can't hold on to anything long enough to make sense of it, can't really process anything that's happened in the past twelve hours.

I suppose I shouldn't be so surprised, but I'm genuinely not prepared for the photographers waiting for us outside Mum's gates.

'Oh, shit,' Theo says succinctly, his hands tight on the steering wheel.

Four or five of them surround the car as we wait for the gate to open at the bottom of the drive. There are flashes going off outside the window, and I hold my hand up to my eyes, a sound of distress coming out of my mouth. They're shouting, but I can't make out the words. Panic. Hands tingling, my breath catches, and I'm seventeen again.

'It's okay,' Theo says tightly. 'It's okay. It's going to be okay.' He says the words, over and over, like a chant, but I can't answer him, can't seem to speak as the gate finally swings open.

We shoot up the drive, away from them, and I close my eyes, tears leaking out the corners.

The car comes to a stop. Theo turns off the engine. The sudden silence is a blade hanging over us.

Theo's head lolls back against his seat. He closes his eyes for a moment.

'I have to go,' he says finally. 'I've arranged for them to move my flight to tonight.'

'You're going to leave?' I ask, and even though I had been expecting it, it hurts so much I flinch. 'Now?'

'If I go then this will stop,' he says softly. He lets the words linger in the air for a moment. A horrible truth.

'I've got a plan. I'm going to go back to LA and get my picture taken. I think that will get everyone off your back pretty immediately.'

'Get your picture taken?' I repeat.

Theo's throat bobs. 'With Cyn. We've done it for each other before, as a favour. We only have to stand side by side and people assume we're back together. The stories write themselves.'

'Oh.' The word is hollow. 'That's nice of her.'

'Clemmie.' He sighs my name. 'I don't want that part to be some tragic miscommunication, okay? It's a step in a practical plan. I'm telling you now because I want you to know that it will be a lie, an act. Cyn is just my friend. I don't want you to think, even for a second, that I want to be with anyone but you.'

'Then why are you leaving?' The words wobble as they leave my mouth.

He reaches out, brushes a strand of hair away from my face, the movement tender. 'Because I've been selfish with you,' he says. 'I knew you had reservations about this stuff and I wanted you so badly I didn't let it matter, didn't talk about it, didn't do enough to protect you. I told you I understood you needed to take things slow and I just . . . bulldozed you into a relationship, and that wasn't fair.'

He looks down at his hands, and his voice is rough. 'Typically, I am a pretty selfish person. But I can't be the reason you're in pain, Clemmie. I can't be the reason you're reliving your worst trauma. Seeing those pictures of you from when you were seventeen just about broke my heart. You were so young, and knowing what you went through, how you were treated . . . I heard what you said this morning and I saw the look on your face when we just drove through the cameras.' He winces, sucks in a sharp breath. 'I'll never forget that. And it was because of *me*. I think if you're being really honest this isn't what you want.'

'Of course *this* isn't what I want,' I say, trying desperately not to cry. 'But that doesn't mean I don't want *you*.'

The smile Theo gives me is the saddest smile in the history of the world. 'This *is* me. That's the problem.'

I'm too churned up to know what to say to that. Everything is happening so fast; hours ago we were happy. I know that I love Theo, but this situation is everything I've been afraid of. The worst of it is that he's not wrong. I knew from the start that I couldn't get involved with him for precisely this reason. How could I possibly live my life like this? But how can I possibly let him go?

'It's too much,' I say desperately. 'It's too much to think about. I can't untangle it. It's overwhelming. I need you to give me a minute to catch my breath here.'

'I know,' he says. 'It *is* too much. But I was leaving anyway, so let's just . . . take some space.'

'Space from each other?' It hurts to think about it.

'I think it's the right thing to do,' Theo says. 'For both of us.'

Then he leans over, presses his lips softly to my cheek. He makes a sound, low in his throat, and it takes everything in me not to grab him and haul him into me, to kiss him until he promises not to go.

Instead, I open the car door and clamber out, grab my suitcase off the back seat. Numbly, I watch as he drives away, watch until the car disappears, back behind the gates where the cameras flash once more. I watch until Theo Eliott is completely gone, and only then, standing alone in the dark, do I let myself cry.

The front door flies open.

They come storming out, a whirl of Armani (Serena) and lilac hair extensions (Lil), and I'm sandwiched between them, wrapped in their arms, back on solid ground.

'You're here,' I say on an exhale.

'Of course we're here.' Serena sounds furious.

'Who do we need to curse first?' Lil asks.

PART FOUR

Chapter Thirty-Eight

It's been four weeks since Theo left for LA. That's almost seven hundred hours of silence and five thousand miles worth of space between us. Not that I'm counting.

I have experienced all the emotions. All of them. Len and I were together for four years and our breakup was nothing to the pain of losing Theo. Four weeks later I still feel like someone is trying to cut my heart out of my chest with a spoon.

Somehow, Theo managed to get the pictures of us taken down from most places. It's the internet, so nothing ever really dies, but all the big news sites pulled them. Whatever Sam said never materializes either, and I have no idea how he did that, but I suspect it involved a lot of money changing hands.

As Theo predicted, the world lost interest in me the instant photos of him and Cyn hit the news cycle. I told myself I wasn't going to look, but of course I did, and when I saw him, his arm slung around her slim shoulders while she beamed up at him, her hand in the back pocket of his jeans, I screamed into my pillow for a solid ten minutes.

They looked great together. Perfect. And even though Theo had told me in no uncertain terms that it was simply a setup, it was too easy to imagine it was real. What made it worse was that I thought in other circumstances I could like Cynthie. There was something about her face, the dry voice I remembered hearing on the phone, that had me thinking we could be friends. Unfortunately, part of me wanted to run her over because she'd put her hand on Theo's ass, and that didn't seem like a great basis for friendship.

The news I've had about Theo has been through three sources, and I have clung to these fragments like an industrious squirrel gathering nuts for winter. The first is a phone call from Lisa the day after we get back from the wedding.

'Clemmie, I'm so sorry.' I can hear the sadness in her voice. 'I can't believe he left. I can't believe any of this happened.'

'It's not your fault,' I say, and my own voice sounds calm, empty. I'm cried out. 'I'm only sorry it had to happen when it did. Your wedding was so special, and you and Rob really deserved the perfect day.' And then, after a pause, 'Have you spoken to Theo?' It seems I do have some moisture left inside me, because tears gather in my eyes when I say his name.

'He's gutted, Clemmie,' Lisa says instantly. 'I've never heard him sound like that before. I—' She hesitates, and then she adds, softly, 'Please don't give up on him.'

'I think he's the one who gave up on me,' I reply sadly. And after that there's not much more to say.

The second piece of news I get is four days later and it comes, unexpectedly, in the form of an email from David.

Clementine,

Mr Eliott is requesting something called a 'Singing Hen' and I can find no information about what this may be apart from several disturbing YouTube videos. Might you be able to clarify?

David

Dear David,

I think you may mean a Singing Hinny, which is a traditional griddle cake from Northumberland. Sort of a flat scone with raisins. My Granny Mac used to make them. I'll attach the link for the recipe here.

Clemmie

P.S. How is he?

Clementine,

This recipe contains large quantities of butter and lard so I am confused as to when Mr Eliott would have had the opportunity to sample them, given his strict nutritional plan.

David

P.S. I would never discuss the personal life of my employer, nor is it my place to pass judgement on his emotional state. That being said, the man is currently demanding bizarre baked goods, refusing to leave his house, and has developed a worrying obsession with a rather maudlin teenage vampire drama. I will leave you to draw your own conclusions.

In a strange way, it is reassuring to know that Theo is as unhappy as I am, that he's obviously thinking of me. It makes me feel less like I imagined everything that happened between us.

I wonder if David will find someone to make him Singing Hinnies and if Theo will eat them remembering how I cooked them in Granny Mac's kitchen just to feel closer to her when the sweet smell filled the air. Or the way he burned his mouth because he was too impatient not to cram one straight in his mouth when I lifted it off the griddle and then blamed me for making it too hot when I laughed at him. Thinking about it makes my chest hurt.

The other person who talks to me about Theo is Serena. Two weeks after this conversation with David, she tells me Theo has been locked in the recording studio throwing himself into his work. The record label are delighted. My sister's feelings are, understandably, mixed. On the one hand she's delivered the undeliverable album, and on the other her sister's heart is broken. It says a lot about how much she loves me that she feels any qualms about this because she models herself quite earnestly on a frozen-hearted Disney villain and her bosses basically want to throw her a street party.

I decide to follow Theo's example, and I've been working too. I've finished a draft of my children's book (yes, I have reached the point where I can call it a book now) and I sort of love the way it came out. I email it to Serena and Lil, who message me a stream of consciousness as they are reading.

Serena: I always knew somebody would write a book about me one day.

Lil: OMG! I'm already obsessed. The grandma is Granny Mac right? I love how grumpy she is.

Lil: Just snort-laughed at the bit where Maree sets the shed on fire. So Serena.

Serena: That fire was very small and an accident and nothing has ever actually been proven. For any further comment I can refer you to my attorney.

Serena: This is everything. Angry girls are the best.

Lil: Nooooo. I just got to the mermaid. I forgot about the peanut butter sandwiches. This is making my heart hurt.

Serena: Hahahahahaha! Maree is such a badass. I love her.

Lil: Everyone knows Sass is the best character. I wish we could have done a spell to fill my hair with moonlight. Imagine me with MOON HAIR?? I would be unstoppable.

Lil: Clemmie, you are so clever. It is BEAUTIFUL. We are such powerful sister witches.
Serena: Agreed. You need to get this shit published ASAP so that other youngsters can learn from my/Maree's example.
Serena: We're shaping young minds here!!!!!

I'm planning to send the manuscript off to three or four agents who I think might like it. Maybe. I just have to go over it a bit more and dig out some extra courage first. Even in my current, emotionally shattered state, working on the book has felt like a lifeline. It's the first work I've done in a long time that feels *good*.

I haven't looked at my academic book, nor have I filled out any job applications. I don't know how to come to terms with my not wanting to do either. I'm so tired of it, the precarious nature of it all. I'm tired of working so hard for so long and having nothing to show for it. I can't summon any enthusiasm, a single spark of joy.

This is made worse by the fact that the end of the summer is in sight now, and I really need to make some sort of plan. I can't continue to ignore this problem, because – it seems to me – having a job and somewhere to live are the sort of very basic grown-up duties I shouldn't be failing in at thirty-three years of age. I've dedicated my entire adult life to academia and look where it's got me: sitting in my pyjamas in my mum's house, having an existential crisis.

'If you have any time to spare, I could use some help

with work,' Mum says, coming into the kitchen to fix herself a cup of coffee. 'We're organizing a big fundraiser right now and I'm spread way too thin with Sandy off on maternity leave.'

'What's the fundraiser for?' I ask.

'We're raising money for a programme we run, offering music therapy to refugees and displaced children,' Mum says distractedly, digging around in the empty biscuit tin. (What can I say, I'm eating my feelings.)

'Oh, that sounds interesting.' I lift my head.

Mum hums. 'The main thing is, I need someone to help with the organizational side of things. The vendors are all giving me a headache with their different demands.'

'Of course, I'd be happy to help,' I say. 'But tell me more about the programme.'

Mum looks at me in surprise. 'Really?'

'Yes, really.' I laugh. 'Why is that such a strange question?'

'It's not that.' Mum shakes her head. 'It's only . . . you've never seemed that interested in my work before.'

A wave of shame washes over me. 'It's not that I'm not interested. It's just . . . well, it's complicated, I suppose.'

Mum pulls out a seat across from me. 'What's complicated about it?' She frowns.

I could duck this conversation, but honestly, ever since I told Theo what Sam said, it's been on my mind. 'I . . .' I take a deep breath. 'I always felt guilty about your work, so I suppose I avoided talking to you about it,' I say awkwardly. 'Which I realize is really shitty of me.'

'Guilty? Why on earth would you feel guilty?'

'Because you had to give up your dream for me.' I squeeze the words out, knowing that I need to say them now. 'You gave up being a musician because you got pregnant, and I know that it's not my fault, but I always felt bad about it.'

Mum's face is a perfect mask of astonishment. Eyes wide, mouth hanging open. 'Wait . . . what?' She shakes her head. 'You think I gave up singing because I got pregnant?'

It's my turn to frown. 'Well, yeah. You stopped when you had me because of the way the press were hounding us and you were raising me on your own. Just when you were set to be the next big thing.' I'm explaining it but it feels weird; I mean, this stuff isn't news to her.

Mum taps the table with her fingers, looking into the distance for a moment. There's so much happening in her face I have no idea how she's feeling. 'Clemmie,' she exhales finally. 'I wish you had talked to me about this a long time ago.'

'You know how great I am at avoiding anything that makes me uncomfortable.'

She smiles sadly. 'I do know. You're so good at keeping things bottled up. I'm your mother and I had no idea you were carrying that around.' She takes my hand in hers, clasping it across the table. 'Listen to me. I love you with my whole heart but I didn't give up being a musician for you. I didn't give up my dream. I realized that *wasn't* my dream, so I quit.'

'You . . . what?' I manage.

Mum huffs out a breath. 'I mean I didn't *love* the press

stuff, and it would have been more difficult having a baby with me, but musicians have babies all the time. None of that would have stopped me if it was what I wanted – as long as you were safe and happy too. But after that first record came out, I was miserable. I'd spent years thinking it was going to be everything I wanted, and then I hated it. I felt so isolated and I didn't like all the politics that came with working with a big label. Your dad loved every minute of it; he was made for the whole scene, but I wasn't. My heart just wasn't in it at all.'

I'm totally stunned.

'The work I do now,' Mum says, and her mouth lifts in a smile, '*this* is my dream job. This is my life's work. I wouldn't want to be anywhere else. It just took me a while to figure it all out. Sometimes you have to take a risk, follow a fork in the road you didn't see coming, to end up where you belong.'

I blink. Oh God, I am having too many epiphanies at once. I feel like someone just downloaded a software update into my brain.

'You really didn't want to be a singer?' I ask, the words rough.

'Nope,' Mum says firmly. 'And I'll tell you something else: the last people I'd ever let make a decision for me would be those shitty little men with their cameras.' She pauses here, measuring her words. 'I know what happened to you as a teenager was extremely painful, darling, and if I could have protected you from that I would have done, but you can't let other people – people who have so little claim on your life – have control over you and your happiness. You can't let them make decisions *for* you.'

'You're talking about Theo,' I say flatly. 'But you sound like Sam. That's just what he would say to keep me with him, that we couldn't let the press stop us from living our lives.'

'The difference is that Sam was trying to manipulate you and get what he wanted,' she says. 'The words are right, but he used them to control you. You *can't* let the press stop you from living your life, not a life that could be filled with joy and love. I know it's hard to stop yourself from caring what they say and do,' – she pauses here to look me in the eye and make sure she has my full attention, that I'm really listening – '*believe me*, I really do know that, but at some point you have to let go of trying to control what other people think of you if it means you're standing in the way of your own happiness.'

I let the words sink in, feel them loosen the knot inside me just a little. They're not magic words that fix the problem, but they help; they give me room to breathe, to consider another way.

'And,' my mum says, almost casually, but she's not fooling me, 'I think rather than Sam's words you should focus on Theo's actions. He drew the press away, got straight on to his lawyers and threatened everyone with legal proceedings. He was like a man possessed doing whatever needed to be done to get those pictures taken down. That's not like Sam, who was a sneaky little bastard. Or your father for that matter, who has all the depth of a cheese sandwich. Ripp's a careless man, Clemmie, not a bad one. He doesn't *intend* to let anyone down; he simply doesn't *think*.'

She gives me another beady look. 'This isn't history repeating itself. Just because they share an occupation doesn't mean they *are* the same. Theo isn't anything like either of them, and for what it's worth, I think he's shown you that.'

I chew on my lip. 'I just don't know if I'm ready to put myself in the position to test that theory,' I admit. 'It feels like I would be making myself so . . . vulnerable.'

Mum laughs then, squeezes my hand. 'Darling, I have bad news for you. Falling in love is always about making yourself vulnerable. Even when it's not with a rock star.'

'Ugggggggh.' I drop my head into my hands. 'Why is it so hard?'

'I don't know,' Mum says. 'But I think that's why God invented therapists.'

Chapter Thirty-Nine

Another week passes before the event of the year: Lil-Fest.

It's been one more week of radio silence from Theo. After my conversation with Mum, I've started to wonder if maybe he's waiting for me to reach out to *him*. After all, he said he didn't want to be selfish, to push me into anything. Is it possible that he wants *me* to be the one to choose?

Once the thought occurs to me, it feels obvious. For weeks I've been assuming that Theo's lack of communication meant he didn't *want* to be with me, that he was trying to let me know it was over, but if I ignore the very loud voice of my own insecurities, if I stop comparing him to people who are nothing like him, I know that doesn't ring true.

Theo has been clear with me from the start. Before we were anything, even when I was calling him by the wrong name, Theo told me his *intentions*. Theo hasn't faltered. He told me that he wants me. Over and over and over again. He told me with words and he showed me a hundred different ways. I know that he cares about me like I know what day of the week it is.

I just need to decide what *I* want.

When I see Ingrid, I fill her in on what my mum said and then we sit in thoughtful silence for a long time. It is a softer silence than usual. Not a silence like a scalpel, but a silence like a deep breath.

'I think I'm scared of not being good enough,' I say finally. 'Of failing at things, coming up short, disappointing people. Even people I haven't met. Even anonymous commenters on the internet. But especially people I love.'

'What do you think will happen if you're not good enough?' Ingrid asks.

'They'll leave.' The answer is swift, unwavering.

Ingrid's head dips, and I get that buzz from doing a good job at therapy, even while realizing that this is exactly part of the problem.

'Theo left,' I say, pressing at the tender bruise on my heart. 'He did it for noble reasons, I know. Logically, I understand. But he left. And it hurt.'

'That sounds like something you should tell him,' Ingrid says. 'I think it sounds like something he would want to hear.'

Those words have been rolling around in my head. *Would* Theo want to hear that? Maybe. Theo has always seemed interested in what goes on in my head. (Actually, that's an understatement, because he once told me he wanted to '*crawl inside my brain and read it like a book*', which I informed him was somehow both sweet and psychotic at the same time.)

All this leaves me with plenty to agonize over, but for today I try to push everything else to one side. Today is about Lil.

Lil-Fest started on Lil's sixteenth birthday and it has only grown in scale and production value with every passing year. We hold it in the meadow at the back of the mums' house on the last weekend in August and as such it has always marked the bittersweet end of summer.

The first Lil-Fest was Lil and a few of her friends playing a set on a 'stage' which was actually a chalk outline on the grass, while we coated ourselves in body glitter and drank slightly warm cheap cider.

As Lil's and Serena's personal and professional circles grew, so did Lil-Fest. Now there's a real stage with enormous speakers, a line-up of whatever bands are in town at the time and want to come and hang out – some big names, some up-and-coming artists – a variety of food trucks and usually a couple of hundred guests.

The trees are strewn with fairy lights and handmade dreamcatchers, and this year one of Lil's mates is running yoga sessions in a small yurt that appeared overnight. We still cover ourselves in glitter, but the cheap cider has been swapped out for organic IPAs and cocktails in jam jars. Some years we do it in the rain and the mud (which Lil claims is actually more authentic), but today it's dry and warm, though there are several ominous-looking clouds on the horizon.

Given my aversion to live music, I have, in the past, spent as much of Lil-Fest as possible hanging out in the kitchen, or even sneaking off to my room, but this year I might actually make it down to the stage, might listen to some of the bands play. It's been a long summer and a lot of things have changed.

It's late afternoon and I'm sitting in a little alcove by the pond, watching guests file from the other end of the house down to the meadow where the stage is set up, psyching myself up to go and join them. My sisters appear at my side. Serena is holding a crown of sunflowers which she lays on my head. Lil hands me a pair of fairy wings. After I mentioned Hannah's to her she ordered them for all of us in an adult size especially for this event. Serena's are black and spiky, making her look like a vampire bride, and that is the only reason she has agreed to this.

'Good turnout this year,' I say, squinting out at the growing crowd as a young girl with a guitar sings wistfully into the microphone. 'Are you going to play?'

Lil's cheeks are rosy. She's wearing her own sunflower crown and it's a little crooked. 'Yep, soon I think because I keep drinking those pink drinks Ava mixed that taste like juice but they're making things a bit . . .' She pinches her thumb and forefinger together thoughtfully and I have no idea what the gesture is supposed to mean.

'She's already pissed,' Serena translates.

'Where are Bee and Henry?' I ask.

'Bee's at work but she might come by later,' Serena says with extremely practised nonchalance, and Lil and I exchange a look of amusement.

'Henry's coming later too,' Lil says. 'I'm pretty sure he's going to propose tonight.'

'What?!' Serena and I shriek in one voice.

'I know. Isn't it lovely?' Lil glows softly, suddenly angelic and alight with love. I blink, but I think actually it's just the sun hitting her body glitter. That and the wings.

'I found the ring last week – he's the worst at keeping secrets,' she says fondly, 'and he was a nervous wreck all morning. I just wish he'd ask me so I could put him out of his misery.'

'You're going to say yes?' Serena asks, stunned.

'Of course I am.' Lil is serene. 'He's it for me. I knew it the second we met. Just like I wished for.'

Serena makes a *harrumph*ing sound.

'That's wonderful,' I say, the words clogged with tears. 'I'm so happy for you, Lil. Henry is the sweetest and he loves you so much.'

'I know,' Lil says, totally secure. Then a frown flickers over her face. 'Speaking of big, soulmate love . . .'

'Yes, I've been thinking about that too,' I interrupt her. '*Big love, the unconditional, whole-hearted, soulmate kind*. That's what you said, isn't it?'

'Yes,' Lil nods while Serena makes fake barfing sounds.

'I had an epiphany the other day, in therapy,' I say, smiling at the memory. 'I mean, I've been having them all over the place recently, but I realized the other day that whatever happens, there's one thing I can count on: I already have that love. I have my soulmates, the ones who'll be there no matter what, who love me unconditionally. It's you two. You've always been there. No wish required.'

There's a stunned silence for a second as my sisters just look at me, then Lil makes a sort of wailing noise and throws her arms around my neck. Her hot tears hit my skin. 'I love you, sweet Clementine,' she whispers.

'Honestly,' Serena huffs, furiously trying to avoid eye contact, 'you two are so dramatic.' But she can't hide her sniffle, and Lil and I haul her in for a long and – thanks to three pairs of fairy wings – uncomfortable hug.

When we disengage, Lil looks determined. 'I think the three of us need to talk about Theo.' The words make me start.

'I thought we were going to wait.' Serena scowls at her.

My eyes dart between them. 'What are you two up to?' I ask.

Serena continues to glare at Lil, who looks unrepentant.

'We have something to tell you,' Serena says slowly. 'But I'm not sure this is the right time.'

'That's not ominous at all,' I grumble. 'Now you have to tell me.'

'It can wait,' Serena says firmly.

'No, it can't.'

'Ugh, fine . . .' Serena practically stomps her foot, but then she's interrupted by Lil.

'Oh, shit,' Lil breathes, looking over my shoulder.

Serena's eyes narrow as she also takes in whatever Lil has spotted. 'Did you know about this?' she asks.

'No, no, of course not,' Lil exclaims as I swing around.

Strolling across the garden towards us, all smiles, is Ripp Harris.

And just behind him is Sam.

'Lily pad!' Ripp says, grabbing Lil by the shoulders and kissing her on the cheek. 'Happy birthday, my beautiful girl.'

'What are you doing here, Dad?' Lil manages, her eyes moving to me.

'We're here to play Lil-Fest!' Ripp grins. 'I'm told it's the hottest gig in town. Your mum sent me an invite ages ago, and we were in the area so I thought I'd surprise you. The rest of the band are arriving soon.'

I think Petty sends Ripp an invite every year. This is the first time he's ever bothered showing up. Of course.

I can't tear my eyes away from Sam, who is looking anywhere but at me.

'What the fuck, Dad?' Serena says through gritted teeth. Ripp's smile falters, confusion writ large on his brow.

'What?' he says. 'What's the matter?'

'Why would you turn up here with him?' Lil demands, her hands on her hips.

'What are you doing here, Sam?' I ask.

Ripp's frown deepens.

Sam lifts his eyes to mine, and I can actually see the moment of calculation before the mask of charm descends. 'Clemmie, it was all such a long time ago. We were just kids. Don't you think it's time to let it go?' He looks at Ripp, sighs heavily, communicating a vague sense of exasperation.

'Oh, that's right,' Ripp chuckles, relaxing. 'You two used to be a thing back in the day. Come on, Clementine, if I was worried about bumping into an ex everywhere I went I'd never leave the house.' He laughs harder, and Sam joins in.

The intense, laser focus of my anger switches to my father in an instant. 'You do not get to chime in on this, Ripp. You're the one who hired the man who broke my heart, and who still seems to be doing his best to hurt me. Ask him who was giving fucking *interviews* about me a few weeks ago.'

'You both need to leave, Dad.' Lil says the words firmly.

'Right now,' Serena adds.

'What are you all talking about?' Ripp asks. He's not smiling anymore; his eyes are moving between me and Sam. 'What interviews?'

'Why don't you ask him,' I spit out.

'That's enough.' Sam looks pissed now and he moves towards me, reaches out to take my arm. I think he wants to pull me away so that this conversation can happen somewhere a lot less public.

He doesn't have the chance, however, because suddenly a very familiar voice yells, 'GET YOUR FUCKING HANDS OFF HER.'

Chapter Forty

We all turn as one, and there, striding across the lawn like an Austen hero with a face like thunder, is Theo, and I don't have time to process anything except the sweet, sharp spike of joy that cuts through me at the sight of him, before he's there, pulling Sam's hand from my arm and ploughing his fist into his face. Sam goes sailing backwards, straight into the pond with a tremendous splash.

There's a moment of stunned silence.

'Ow! FUCK!' Theo yelps, hopping up and down on the spot. 'I think I just broke my hand. Jesus! Owwww.' He cradles the hand he used to punch Sam, hissing in pain. '*Shit*, that hurts.'

There are a million things I want to say to him, but when I open my mouth all that comes out is, 'Is that the first time you've punched someone? I think you're supposed to put your thumb on the outside.'

Theo looks at me with exasperation. 'Yes, thank you, *Street Fighter.* Didn't realize you were such an expert. And when would I have punched someone before?'

'I don't know. At school?'

'What sort of school did you go to?'

'Should have just kicked him in the balls.' Serena examines her nails. 'Saves your knuckles.' Sam flinches from his position, still groaning in the water, and Ripp goes to pull him out, looking completely confused.

Theo and I stare at each other for a beat. 'What are you doing here?' I ask.

His eyes run over me like he's dying of thirst and I'm a tall glass of water. 'I'm playing a gig in London tomorrow. I have press today,' he says, and I feel my body drifting closer to him. 'I was going to stay away but I couldn't. I need to talk to you, I—'

'You're going to be hearing from my lawyers, mate!' Sam screeches, suddenly reminding me that we are not alone.

Theo's face, so close to mine – how is it already so close to mine? – looks as startled as I feel to find the rest of the world has not melted away, and that we are in fact being watched with interest by my sisters, my dad, and my ex-boyfriend, who is dripping pond water everywhere, clutching his nose, blood running freely down the front of his shirt.

Anger flickers in Theo's eyes, and he turns his tall body so it's between me and Sam. I get a hit of his clean, salt and citrus scent and my knees weaken pathetically. 'I'm not your *mate*,' he growls. 'And you deserve to have the living shit kicked out of you for how you've treated Clemmie.'

'Hear, hear,' says Serena, a bloodthirsty glint in her eye.

'No one is kicking the shit out of anyone,' I huff, tugging

at Theo's arm. Anger blooms and I narrow my eyes at him. 'I don't need you swooping in here, after disappearing for a month, punching people for me. If anyone gets to hit Sam in the face it should be me.'

'Too bloody right,' Sam yelps. 'Wait . . . what?'

I turn on him. 'And I thought I told you, you and I were done, Sam. Didn't I make myself clear the last time we spoke?'

'I'm going to sue the lot of you!' Sam splutters, casting a dark look at Theo. 'I think your boyfriend broke my nose.'

'He's not my boyfriend,' I say, and Theo flinches.

'Will somebody please tell me what's going on?' Ripp looks determined now, a flintiness to his gaze that I've never seen before.

'That piece of shit fed a bunch of lies to the press about your seventeen-year-old daughter, gaslit her and used her to get his name in the papers and a job playing for you,' Theo says coldly, extending his rage to include Ripp. 'That's what happened. And you did fuck all to protect her.'

'I didn't know anything about this,' Ripp blusters.

'Don't say that. I told you.' I cross my arms. 'You wouldn't believe me. You laughed it off.'

Something like shame flickers across Ripp's face. He turns to Sam. 'Is this true?'

'Of course not,' Sam says thickly, still holding his nose. 'I don't know why she can't get over a breakup that happened fifteen years ago. You know me, Ripp. I'm not that guy.' He turns to me. 'Look, Clementine, I know I hurt you when I ended things and for that I'm sorry, but you need to let go of this childish vendetta.'

'*What* did you just say?' I laugh, a hard sound of disbelief.

'I'm going to kill him,' Theo mutters, starting forward.

'Get in line, buddy,' Lil says through clenched teeth, the scary murder face on. Serena has to wrap an arm around her waist and physically hold her back from scratching Sam's eyes out. 'You're dead, you psycho!' Lil screeches, her fingers held out like talons.

'Sorry,' a new voice says, interrupting this very *Jerry Springer* moment. 'Is this a bad time?'

Everyone freezes.

'This *cannot* be happening.' I exhale, closing my eyes. When I open them it's to find Len hovering nearby, a pet carrier in his hand.

'Why are *you* here now?' I groan, my head in my hands. Perhaps this is some sort of cheese-induced nightmare, and if I try hard enough, I can wake myself up.

'Hello, Leonard.' Serena's eyes sparkle dangerously. 'How's the crotch? Any . . . *issues* down there?'

'W-what?' Len looks aghast as Lil cackles. 'Uh, your mum said I could find you out here,' he says awkwardly, turning to me and ignoring my sisters. He runs a hand through his sandy hair. His face is thinner, and he has new glasses. 'I didn't realize there was a party going on.' Len has always made an excuse to avoid Lil-Fest. He considers my family 'eccentric' and he said this often and in the kind of tone that made it clear that was a Very Bad Thing.

'You're Len?' Theo says, incredulously, and he looms, big and furious, blood still clearly running high from his confrontation with Sam.

Len takes a step back, and then does a visible double-take. 'Are you . . . Theo Eliott?'

'I'm your worst nightmare,' Theo growls.

It's an objectively hilarious thing to say so I don't think anyone can blame me when I crack up. Len eyes me warily, like I'm a lunatic. Theo's glance flicks to me, still angry but then, reluctantly, he starts to laugh too.

'I cannot believe you said that in real life,' I giggle. '*I'm your worst nightmare.* All right, Christian Bale. What a tough guy.'

'I am tough,' he insists. 'I just punched someone!'

'Yeah, and there were plenty of witnesses too.' Sam seems to have staunched the flow of blood now, but his nose does not look good. No one seems in a rush to offer him any kind of first aid. Or a towel.

'I don't know,' Serena muses. 'The only thing I saw was you falling over into the pond onto your own face.'

'Yeah, me too,' Lil puts in, her smile sweet. 'So clumsy.'

'Clemmie, I need to talk to you,' Len says nervously.

'No, *I* need to talk to you,' Theo insists.

'I need to talk to you too,' Ripp says, and part of me wonders if he simply can't bear to be left out.

'Er, *hello*?!' Sam exclaims. 'Is no one going to help me? I think we need to call an ambulance.'

'A Waaa-mbulance more like,' Lil mutters, delighted with herself.

I squeeze my eyes closed again. Take a deep breath. I don't know what sort of sick joke the universe is playing but I suppose the only way to get out of this living nightmare is to see it through. 'Right,' I say finally, pointing at Len. 'You first. What do you want?'

Chapter Forty-One

'Er, it's . . .' Len gestures to the pet carrier. 'It's the cat. I thought you might like him back.'

'You've brought Tuna?' I exclaim, rushing over to the carrier and peering inside to see the familiar grumpy face of my rescue cat staring back at me in mute disapproval.

'Well, it turns out he and Jenny don't really get on,' Len mumbles. 'Anyway, if you're happy to keep him I'll be on my way. Leave you to your . . .' – his eyes move from Sam's dripping form and broken face to Theo's glower, to my flower crown and sparkly purple fairy wings – 'party.'

'Can you take Tuna and leave him with my mum?' I ask, and with a beleaguered sigh and a wary look at the lot of us, he picks up the pet carrier.

'Fine,' he says. 'But, Clementine,' – his eyes flick around the group once more – '*as a friend*, I really think you need to take a good, hard look at the choices you're making.'

'I really don't give a shit what you think, Len,' I reply. 'But you're right . . . I do need to have a look at my choices.

I can't believe I wasted four years of my life on a man with the personality of a dry Ryvita because I was too scared to have an emotion. You can go now.'

And just like that the chapter closes on Len. Good bloody riddance.

Chapter Forty-Two

'One down,' I sigh. 'Two to go.' I turn to Theo. 'Would you mind waiting for me in my room? I need to sort this mess out.'

Theo hesitates, looks like he's about to say something, but then he nods. 'Sure, I'll wait for you.'

'Theo—' Serena starts, but he holds up his hand, his face steely.

'I'll wait for you,' he says once more, the words unyielding, not up for debate. It's that stern voice again, the one that I feel *everywhere*, and the squeak that Lil makes tells me that I am not the only one vulnerable to its effect. With that, Theo stalks off.

I turn slowly to face Sam. It feels like the moment in a film where the hero confronts the big, bad baddie. Only, the man in front of me isn't the villain in my story; that's giving him way too much credit. Standing here, shivering and wet, his artfully mussed hair plastered to his head, his expression like a toddler on the brink of a tantrum, he looks like what he is: pathetic.

'Sam, what you did, all those years ago . . .' I take a deep breath, ready to say the things I've wanted to say for such a long time. 'It honestly felt like you broke something in me. You hurt me so badly that it took me a really, really long time to get over it. And not because you were particularly special, or because our relationship was that great, but because your actions were so selfish, so needlessly cruel, that I still cannot even process how you looked at yourself in the mirror afterwards. Why did you do it? Why did you sell me out to the papers like that? Was it all just a big lie?'

He finally has the decency to look embarrassed. 'Clemmie, no,' he says awkwardly, lifting his hand to push his wet hair back from his face. 'It wasn't like that. You've got it all wrong.'

'You mean you didn't sell stories about me to the press, or arrange for them to take pictures of me?' I ask.

His eyes dart to Ripp, who is standing like a statue.

'This is all a big misunderstanding,' Sam says nervously. 'I might have reached out to some contacts when I was trying to get the band off the ground, but it wasn't about you, Clemmie. I was as horrified as you were when they turned their attention on you, but you know what they say . . . all publicity is good publicity, right?' He gives me a smile that I think is supposed to be charming. 'What we had was real, the feelings I had for you were *real*. I didn't know what was going to happen. It just got a bit out of hand.'

As the words come out of his mouth, I realize how little I care about them. It doesn't matter to me anymore why Sam did what he did or how he wants to justify things to himself. It doesn't even matter if our relationship was a lie, or if at some point he really did have feelings for me. For a long time I let myself think those things were important – that understanding the whys and hows of it all would help to fix something inside me that was broken. Now, I realize that Sam didn't break me. He hurt me, and I protected myself the best way I knew how: by folding myself up as small as possible.

Over the past few months, I've had to face up to a lot of things. Splitting up with Len, losing my home, losing my job, meeting Theo, going to Northumberland and being forced to confront all the ghosts there, learning the truth about my mum's decisions, dealing with the press again . . . every single thing has been like a crack in the protective shell I built around myself, letting the light pour in. It's been messy and painful but things have changed. *I've* changed.

'I think if we could just talk about it,' Sam continues, clearly feeling like he's back on solid ground now, 'I could explain. I never wanted to hurt you.'

'Sam,' I cut him off. 'I don't need to hear it. The past is the past, but a few weeks ago you were talking to the papers about me again. It's enough. We're done. You're not welcome here.' I take a step towards him, because apparently I'm getting a lot of closure in the space of ten minutes. 'And if I ever see or hear from you again, then *I'll* be the one to go to the press. The world is a different place now, and I think people would be really interested to hear *my* side of this particular story. I mean it. Go away, and stay away.'

Chapter Forty-Three

Serena and Lil decide to follow Sam and make sure he's really gone, but after seeing his face when I delivered my final threat, I honestly don't think I'll be having anything to do with him ever again. Ripp and I are left standing alone.

There's an extremely awkward silence.

'Well?' I say finally, with a sigh. 'What do you want, Ripp? In case you haven't noticed, I've got a lot going on right now.'

Ripp clears his throat. 'I-I'm sorry,' he says.

I wait, but that seems to be it. 'Right. For what exactly?'

He lifts a hand to the back of his neck. 'Er, for all the stuff that went on with Sam?' He says it like it's a question. 'Obviously I'll sack him.'

I blink. '*Now* you'll sack him?'

'I mean, to be honest, Clemmie, I was thinking about doing it anyway. He's not as good as he used to be.' Ripp twinkles conspiratorially, as if we're on the same side. 'And now that I hear what went on before . . . there's nothing else to be done, is there?'

Well, I suppose that at least explains why Sam suddenly wanted to get in touch and ask me out. Dating me had worked great to insinuate himself the first time around. What an unoriginal dickhead.

'So now that it's convenient for you, you believe me and you're going to get rid of him?' I let out a humourless laugh. 'Thanks a lot, Ripp. Father of the year yet again.'

Something flashes in his eyes and I don't know if it's anger or hurt, but I don't really care.

After another moment of silence, he speaks again. 'I think I probably deserved that,' he says quietly. 'I know I haven't been a good dad to you girls, but I do want to try to do better. Your sisters are giving me a chance. Why can't you?'

'Because I gave you chances,' I say calmly. 'Loads of them. And you let me down over and over again. You broke my heart. You made me feel like there was something unloveable about me that I had to fix. You may be my father, Ripp, but I don't *owe* you anything.' I can almost hear Ingrid cheering me on. Actually, she would never do anything so demonstrative, but maybe she'd at least be nodding her head a tiny bit.

Ripp looks stunned. 'Look.' His voice is unsteady. 'I'm so sorry, Clemmie. I never meant to make you feel that way. That's not how I feel at all. I love you. I love all three of you.'

He takes a deep breath, rubs his forehead. 'When Carl died, it was . . . like a wake-up call for me. I realized some things about myself, and my life, things I didn't like. I have regrets. Plenty of them. And I want to make amends. You're right that you don't owe me anything, but I don't want to leave things as they are until it's too late. I don't want you to hate me.'

I sigh. 'I don't hate you, Ripp. Maybe I did once, but I really don't anymore.' And it's true. When I look at Ripp now I see a flawed man who made some shit choices. But that doesn't mean I need to make concessions for him, or let him off the hook for hurting me. 'I just don't think I'm interested in having you in my life.'

I expect him to protest but he doesn't. He just nods. He looks older suddenly, smaller. 'Maybe I don't get to be your dad,' he says slowly. 'But I can still be here for you. If you need anything. If you want to talk. Whatever relationship we can build, I want it. It can be on your terms, Clemmie.'

I hesitate, thrown by this. It's surprisingly sensitive and totally out of character. It gives me a moment's pause. I thought I had Ripp Harris all figured out. Then again, it seems like a lot of things I thought I knew are turning out to be wrong.

'No pressure,' he says, holding up his hands.

Finally, I nod. 'Okay. I'm not promising anything, but I'll consider it. Maybe we can . . . talk.'

He deflates in front of me and instead of treating me to the Ripp Harris sparkle, he looks me steadily in the eye. 'You've got my number.' Then something lightens in his face. 'But now I'd better let you go. There's a young man in your bed-room and we rock stars don't like to be kept waiting!' With a wink he turns and saunters off. I sigh. I guess Ripp's journey towards emotional maturity is going to be a slow one. My eyes turn to the house. Watching Ripp go is easy. I don't know if I have it in me to see Theo leave again.

By the time I head up the stairs to talk to Theo, I am reeling from the emotional whiplash of the last hour of my life.

When I reach my bedroom door I hesitate for a moment and then knock.

'Clemmie?' Theo's voice comes, and I rest my head against the door, take a moment just to enjoy the sound of him saying my name in that rough, velvet voice. 'I don't think you need to knock when it's your own bedroom.'

I turn the handle and he's standing by my desk, looking at the bookcase. He's holding a *Baby-Sitters Club* book in his hands like it's some sort of precious relic. It's not lost on me that this is the place where everything started for us. It feels strange seeing him in this room again.

'Hi,' I say, and I worry that he can hear all the longing in my voice.

'Hi,' he returns softly, laying the book down. Now I have a chance to really take him in I notice there are circles under his eyes. Some of that sun-kissed gold has gone from his skin. His eyes skate over my face, studying me just as intensely as I'm studying him. I wonder what he sees when he looks at me. Can he tell how hard the past five weeks have been? The way the corners of his mouth pull down makes me think so.

'Theo, whatever this is . . .' I start.

There's a persistent, low buzzing noise in the room, and

it takes me a while to realize it's his phone, which must be in his pocket. The buzzing stops only to start again immediately.

'Do you need to get that?' I ask.

Theo looks pained. 'Yes, I do. I'm supposed to be on my way to this interview. I'm already late. People are getting . . . annoyed.'

'Is David on the other end of that phone?' I whisper, horrified, like this conversation may be bugged, which – knowing David – is worryingly plausible.

There's a deep voice ringing up from the bottom of the stairs. 'Mr Eliott? Mr Eliott, we have to go now.'

'Who's that?' I ask.

'My driver, Steve. David told him to carry me out over his shoulder if necessary to get me to the TV studio on time. I was about to barricade myself in the room. I'd try and fight him but he's got a much tougher face than Sam.'

'What are you doing here, Theo?' I ask.

'Honestly?' He looks at me and I nod. 'We were driving down the M40 and before I even knew what was happening I was directing Steve here. I know I said I'd give you space but—'

'That's not what happened,' I cut him off, and while my voice is steady it is laced with anger. 'You *left*.'

He swallows. Nods. 'I know. In the moment I thought it was the best thing to do.'

I rub my eyes. 'You didn't give me any time to sort through my feelings. You didn't give me a chance. You said you bulldozed me before, but leaving was another way of doing that.'

'I know,' Theo says again.

'Stop agreeing with me!' I snap. 'It's making fighting with you extremely difficult.'

He huffs a short choke of laughter followed by a sigh. 'I'm sorry. I'm so sorry I left. I'm sorry I'm not disagreeing with you. I *shouldn't* have left like that. I've been miserable over it. Lisa yelled at me a lot and she made the very astute point that leaving people in order to protect them is not the healthiest way of dealing with things. I've been doing it to my family for years, too. At the time I honestly thought I was looking after you, but ... maybe I was protecting myself. All this shit I bring into a relationship ... I think maybe I left before you could realize I wasn't worth the effort. Before you left me.'

I'm somewhere between laughing and crying when I say, 'It sounds like we've both been talking to our therapists.'

The ghost of a smile. 'I've been seeing mine a lot, even by LA standards.'

'Look,' I sigh. 'Whatever this is, you turning up today ... I can't deal with it right now. I feel like my brain and my heart have been shoved in a blender. I've just had confrontations with my ex-boyfriends, and my father. I'm not in a place to talk to you about this ...'

The phone buzzes again.

'Especially not with a ticking clock on the conversation,' I finish pointedly.

'That's fair.' Theo nods, tucks his hands in his pockets. 'I shouldn't have ambushed you like this. It was wrong.'

The phone buzzes again. 'Oh my God, just answer it!' I exclaim.

With a rumble of frustration, Theo does. 'Yes?' he says, clipped, his eyes still on me. 'I know.' There's a pause and while I can't hear David's words, I can hear the tone of his voice. It is . . . not calm.

'I *know*, David.' Theo pinches his nose. 'Yes, I do think this is an excellent example of my priorities. *You* were the one who said I should . . .' Whatever the interesting conclusion of that sentence may be I don't find out because it is cut off by the sound of indignant squawking.

'I agree the timing could be better,' Theo says calmly after a moment, 'but this is the situation we find ourselves in. Tell them I'm on my way. They'll just have to push my bit back. Oh, er . . .' – here Theo hesitates, flexes his right hand with a grimace – 'and can you make sure the doctor is on hand, because I've hurt my thumb. I don't think it's broken.' The squawking has stopped, but the frozen silence on the other end of the line rings out twice as loud. Finally, I hear David say something.

'Yes, *thank you*,' Theo replies acidly, 'I *am* aware that playing the guitar necessitates the use of my thumb; that's *why* I'm asking you to call the doctor. Just stop fussing, I'm leaving.' With this, he disconnects the call, scrubs his unbroken hand over his face.

'I really am sorry about this, Clemmie. I'm going to leave now. But you know where I am. Whenever you're ready to talk . . . *if* you want to talk, I'll be there. I'm not going anywhere.' He hesitates here. 'I mean, I am literally leaving now, but I'm not *leaving*.' He makes a slightly pained noise. 'How can I be so bad at this?'

The phone is buzzing again, but Theo ignores it for another long moment, staring deeply into my eyes.

'Mr Eliott?' The voice outside is closer now, footsteps pounding up the stairs.

Theo lets out a deep sigh of frustration, and then, like he can't help it, he leans forward, touches his forehead to mine, eyes closed just for a second as our breath mingles. It's only the slightest touch, the tiniest point of contact between us, but I feel it down to my toes. My body is having some sort of meltdown and my brain isn't far behind.

Then, he wrenches himself away with a soft curse. 'We'll talk later, okay?' he says to me. 'I mean, I hope we'll talk later. If that's what you want.'

'I'll think about it,' I say. He nods.

And with that, he's gone, jogging down the corridor.

'All right, I'm coming, I'm coming,' I hear him call.

'Mr Eliott, you're going to get me sacked,' his driver's voice murmurs. 'You said you only needed five minutes and that was an hour ago. I'm supposed to hog-tie you and stick you in the boot at this point . . .'

'I'm really sorry, Steve, but at least I left you the audio-book to keep you company. I told you you'd like it.'

'Yeah, that's true. I've just got to the bit where the Duke proposes . . .'

As the sound of their voices recede, I throw myself onto my bed. 'What. Was. That?' I ask the empty room.

'That's just what we want to know,' Lil's voice pipes up, and I turn to find her and Serena standing in the doorway. Lil is holding a disgruntled Tuna the cat in her arms.

'Seriously, Clemmie,' Serena says. 'What the fuck is going on?'

Chapter Forty-Four

The next day is another familiar annual event: recovering from Lil-Fest. And last night had been a doozy. After I told my sisters that I didn't want to talk about my feelings anymore, that instead I wanted to go downstairs and drink and dance until I couldn't feel my face or my feet, they had wisely agreed to put our conversation on hold.

When, half an hour later, Henry proposed to Lil live on stage, our fate was sealed. We toasted the happy couple until we were all glittering with champagne, and rather than dwelling on the emotional train crash that had taken place earlier, I decided just to be happy for my sister and to spend the rest of the night celebrating her.

Now it is gone midday and my entire body is protesting that decision. I manage to force my eyes open and realize I am lying face down on my bed. Tuna examines me with haughty benevolence from his position curled on top of my laundry.

When I try to roll over, something gets in the way and it

takes an embarrassingly long time to realize I have my fairy wings on over my pyjamas.

My bedroom door slams open, making me wince.

'Fucking hell,' Serena groans from the doorway. 'I think I might be dying.'

'Join the club,' I croak. 'Why do I have these stupid wings on?'

Serena laughs, but then clutches her stomach. 'You were adamant you wanted to sleep in them,' she says after a moment. 'I don't know why. I feel like it made sense at the time.'

She crawls into bed beside me. 'Why do we do this to ourselves every year?' I moan.

'Because we're idiots.' Serena's voice is muffled from where her face is pressed into the pillow.

'What did we do last night?' Lil's voice quavers from the doorway. 'I feel like I've been run over.' She comes to join us, curls up in the foetal position at the end of the bed.

'What are you doing here?' I ask. 'Shouldn't you be with your fiancé?'

'Henry's been up for hours. Apparently he's gone for a hike.' Lil shudders.

'Can't believe you're going to marry that psychopath,' Serena murmurs.

'I've got tea and dry toast,' Mum sings as she enters the room carrying a tray. This, too, is tradition, and we all groan and grumble as we gingerly sip tea and attempt to keep the toast down.

'We can't keep doing this,' I say. 'We're getting old. Hangovers last, like, a week now.'

'It was a good night though.' Lil winces. 'I think.'

'One for the books,' I agree. 'Our baby sister is getting married.'

'Even though I truly believe marriage is an outdated and patriarchal institution, I'm happy for you, Lil,' Serena says thoughtfully. 'Henry is actually a pretty good guy.'

'He's offered to make Serena a new fitted wardrobe,' Lil explains to me.

'Ah. I guess she needs the space, now that her *girlfriend* is leaving stuff at her flat.' I smirk.

'If I had the strength to lift this pillow, I'd hit you in the face with it,' Serena snarls. 'Now please be quiet so I can die in peace.'

We spend the whole day in bed, and after sleeping some more and eating the McDonald's that Henry brings back for us ('I told them you were a good guy, Henry,' Serena says), we have rallied enough that we are sitting upright on my bed and arguing.

'I'm just saying that Ryan Gosling was a very basic choice,' Serena says. 'It's not exactly an original teenage crush, is it? I think it would have been more character-building to pick someone less . . . obvious.'

'Says the woman with the Britney Spears posters,' I mutter.

'Britney is a visionary,' Serena huffs.

'Ladies, ladies,' Lil interrupts before Serena can launch

into her I-heart-Britney routine. 'Let's not fight. I'd like to remind you that we can all agree on one thing. One film that unites us all. One film which produced a myriad of crushes. The 1999 classic, *The Mummy*.'

'Oh, yes,' I agree emphatically.

'This is true,' Serena allows.

'Every single person in that film can get it.' Lil swoons back against my pillow.

'We should watch it right now,' I say. 'If anything can heal me, it's Brendan Fraser in those old-timey explorer clothes.'

'Yessssss,' Lil hisses.

I grab my laptop, and when I fire it up, an alert pops up. I've got an email from David.

Dear Clementine,

As you know, I take my responsibilities as an assistant very seriously. It would be extremely unprofessional for me to get involved in Mr Eliott's personal life, and I would never dream of doing so. The files I attach here are innocuous invoices for you to check over. If they are anything else then I can only apologize for what must be an unfortunate clerical error. I hope that you will take the time to consider these invoices carefully. I believe they are something special.

With all best wishes,

David

'I've just got the weirdest email,' I say, reading it aloud to my sisters. 'I have no idea what he's talking about. Special invoices?' I click on the attachment, which is a ZIP file. 'These aren't even documents at all; they're audio files,' I say, looking at the screen.

Lil makes a squeaking sound.

I intercept a sneaky look that passes between my sisters.

'What was that?' I ask suspiciously. 'Did you know about this?'

'Noooo,' Serena says slowly, 'but if they're what I think they are then you should definitely listen to them.'

Then, understanding finally dawns. '*Oh.*' A chill tingles up and down my spine. 'It's his album, isn't it?'

'Actually,' – Serena hesitates – 'I don't think it is.'

'Why are you all being so cryptic? What's going on here? Did you know Theo was in town?'

Lil caves first. 'We knew he had a gig in London tonight. We were going to tell you about it yesterday.'

'Did you know he was coming here yesterday?' I ask, my eyes wide. 'Did you know David was going to send me this?'

'No!' Serena jumps in. 'Theo definitely *shouldn't* have come here. He was supposed to be on the bloody *One Show*, announcing the new album, and he ended up being insanely late, squishing on the end of the sofa next to some bloke from *Love Island*. The fact that he went AWOL drove everyone at the office out of their minds. I set my phone on mute the second he appeared. I can't deal with any more Theo nonsense. My work is done; I wash my hands of him.'

'But, about the music . . .' Lil starts then trails off, looks at Serena and the two seem to have a fraught conversation using only their eyebrows.

'I was going to give you a copy myself,' Serena finally says, grudgingly. '*Even though I could have been sacked for doing so*,' she adds, shooting Lil a filthy look.

'You've heard it?' I say.

Serena rolls her eyes. 'Of course I've heard it, Clemmie. What sort of a question is that? If you know how to produce a record without listening to it then please do fill me in. We've signed some cartoon frog off YouTube and I'd love to get out of that one.'

'Your job is gross,' Lil mutters. 'What about artistic integrity?'

'It's not a crime to make money. What about getting off your high horse and letting people just enjoy stuff,' Serena snaps. 'It doesn't have to be that deep.'

'Stop it!' I exclaim. 'Now is *so* not the time for this!' My sisters appear chagrined for thirty seconds before sending each other death stares once they think I'm not looking. 'What about you?' I turn to Lil, bringing us back to the matter at hand. 'Have you heard this album?'

Lil's eyes slide away from mine. 'Not all of it.'

'And it's not the album,' Serena says again.

'I'm so confused.'

'Look, Clemmie,' Serena says breezily, 'instead of asking us about it, why don't we just listen to it? Then we can talk about it . . . after.'

I instantly feel like I'm going to throw up. Of course I want to listen to it. Of *course* I do. But I'm also scared – scared because the combination of music and Theo is a DEFCON 1 nuclear threat to my emotional safety. I know David wouldn't have given it to me, and my sisters wouldn't be acting like demented, shifty-eyed weirdos, if it didn't have something to do with me, and how can I ever, ever prepare myself for that?

'Clemmie.' Lil cups my chin between her two hands. 'You need to hear it. Trust us. Just press play.'

So I do.

Immediately the room is filled with a song that I recognize – the one Theo played for me, the one I called pretty. But it's so much more than that now. It streams from the speakers, lush and beautiful. It's not just Theo and his guitar anymore, but a whole band – an orchestra maybe, because I can hear strings too, soft and romantic. It's overwhelming, but not as overwhelming as when Theo's voice joins in.

That voice.

That smoky, sultry voice that burns through me like good whiskey, diffusing into softness and heat. And the song he's singing . . . it's about me.

Met her at a funeral,
Good thing I don't believe in signs,
Cause the moment that I saw her,
I knew that she was mine.
Oh, my Darling,
Oh, my Darling.

He doesn't say my name, doesn't have to. It hangs in the air, there in the lingering rhyme. He doesn't say my name but it feels like he's breathing it across my skin.

'Oh my God,' I whisper.

'Holy shit,' Lil rasps.

'Yup.' Serena sounds resigned.

After the first song, I think I may get a reprieve, but I don't. Song after lovely song, they're *all* about me. Hundreds of little inside jokes tease through the lyrics, references to sea shells, to label makers, to green dresses, toasted marshmallows, magic islands, and jam jars filled with daisies.

When a track starts that sounds different to the ones that have come before, not sweet or delicate, but with a pulsing growl of bass, a shriek of electric guitar, I feel my toes curl. The music builds. Theo's voice is low and wicked, the whole thing is a meticulous act of seduction.

'What's this one called?' I ask Serena.

'"Serial Killer",' she says, lifting her eyebrows when I choke on a laugh. 'And I don't think I want to know why.'

'If it feels like this, it's a wonder the two of you ever got out of bed.' Lil's eyes are round.

'Yeah, it feels like this,' I say distantly, every nerve ending in my body responding to the thrum of the music.

'Sex mist,' Lil murmurs, awed.

The song ends, but there's still more to come. 'Did he just . . . make a joke about *The Wife of Bath*?' I ask at one point, dazed. As well as the obscure medieval literature references, there's a song that I'm 99.9% sure is about our favourite couple in *Blood/Lust*.

I am startled again when, instead of Theo, another voice starts to sing. I turn wide-eyed to Lil, who only nods. It's the song they started writing in Northumberland, and Theo steps aside, leaves Lil space to shine. Her voice is sweet and dreamy, Theo's a soft echo, harmonizing with her, the two of them blending into something magic, his guitar the only other accompaniment.

Weird, wayward, wilful, wild,
Salt in the air, laugh like a child
Stars in our hair, a charm in our smiles
Write our names in silver sand.
Three sisters dancing, hand in hand.

The three of us sit, our arms wrapped around each other, as the music soars through the room. Even Serena and Lil who have obviously heard it before seem stunned into silence. It's such a tender, perfect expression of our relationship. I can hear Lil in the lyrics, feel our stories weaving around us, the history of who we are, who we've been to each other. I feel a wave of love for them that threatens to crush me, and I can't believe that Theo made space for this – a tribute to my sisters, my soulmates – in what is essentially the story of us. The rightness of it knocks me sideways.

After this there's only one song left. I'm honestly not sure my heart can take any more, but as Theo sings about heartbreak and mistakes, the final thread of my composure slips.

> *They can call me cursed if they want to,*
> *But if I had three wishes,*
> *Each one would be for you.*
> *You.*
> *You.*
> *You.*

And as his voice breaks on the last note, so do I. I cry in a way that I've never cried before, heavy, racking sobs that are painful and sweet. I lie with my head in Lil's lap, Serena's hand stroking my back, and I feel stripped clean, completely light.

It's a perfect love letter. And he wrote it just for me.

'He knows me,' I say dazedly. 'He knows all of me so well.'

'Jesus, Clemmie,' Serena says, scrubbing her eyes with the back of her hand. 'If you don't marry the man, I think I might have to.'

'Don't worry,' – I give a watery laugh – 'I'm already there.'

'Thank fuck for that,' Serena sighs. 'I'd make a terrible heterosexual.'

'But I'm so confused,' I say. 'Why did you say this isn't his album when it obviously is?'

Serena and Lil exchange another look. 'Stop doing that!' I snap. 'Stop *managing* me. Just tell me what's going on.'

'These are the songs that didn't make it onto the album,'

Serena says finally. 'He recorded a bunch and he decided to hold these back.'

I frown. 'There are more songs?'

Serena nods. 'It happens. Sometimes musicians write a lot and not everything makes it onto the record.'

'Are the other songs . . . are they about me?'

'No,' Serena tilts her head. 'Or, at least, there are a few generic ones about heartbreak. Most of them are actually written by someone else; Theo chose them from our catalogue.'

'That doesn't make any sense,' I say. 'Theo writes his own music. It's so important to him.'

'Hmmm.' Serena just makes a non-committal noise.

'There's still something you're not telling me,' I insist, and I look at Lil, who holds up her hands in silent surrender. 'Why would Theo use someone else's songs when he has these? I mean, I know I don't know much about music but . . . God . . . these, they're *incredible*, right?'

'Yes,' Lil says quickly.

'Yes,' Serena agrees.

'So, what . . .' I trail off. 'The album, the real album, is it better than this?'

Serena hesitates. 'It's fine,' she says. 'It totally does the job. His fans will be happy. The label is happy.'

'But Theo wanted this to be special!' I exclaim, frustrated. 'He was so upset about his last album. He knew he had something better in him, something great. He's been working on this for *years*. And you're telling me he's just not using it because . . . *Oh!*' The truth finally breaks through. 'He's not using them because they're about us. Because they're full of us. Because he knows I want to keep things private.'

My sisters both shift uncomfortably.

'I don't think it's for us to say what's going on in Theo's head,' Lil manages eventually. 'You should really talk to him about it.'

And even this makes sense to me now, the way everyone is being so careful not to put pressure on me. Even though it's killing them, they'll all let this beautiful thing disappear rather than put me in a position where I feel exposed.

'Well, fuck,' I breathe.

'What will you do now?' Lil asks, digging around for something to blow her nose on.

'I guess I'll go and get him,' I say. 'Can I borrow your car?'

Chapter Forty-Five

They offer to come with me but I need to do this alone.

'He's playing a small, secret gig in Shepherd's Bush to celebrate the album announcement,' Serena tells me as I strip out of my grimy pyjamas and try to make my hungover face look vaguely presentable.

'I'm so proud of you.' Lil squeezes me when we're at the front door. 'You deserve your happily ever after.'

'I think we all do,' I say.

'You're both being too mushy again,' Serena grumbles. 'Can we just get on with it so that I can head inside and eat a bacon sandwich? I've had to be disturbingly hungover for all this . . .' – she waves her hand in the air – '*emotion*.'

'Okay.' I take a deep breath and jangle Lil's car keys (there's no way I am risking taking *my* car for such an important journey). 'So there will be a ticket waiting for me at the door, right?'

Serena nods. 'Yep, all sorted. But you'd better leave if you want to make it in time to catch him before the show. He's on in . . .' – she looks at her watch – 'about an hour.'

I jump in the car, jittery with nerves and flying high on adrenaline. While this isn't the most practical plan, I don't care. After five weeks of painful agonizing, I'm ready.

Am I scared out of my mind? Yes. Am I going to risk my heart anyway?

You bet I am.

Because I love Theo Eliott, and right now I'm choosing him over being afraid. I am choosing a messy, beautiful, complicated life over one where I am safe but unhappy. Seeing Sam and Len yesterday made me realize even more clearly just how far I had shrunk my world down, how little I had let myself feel for so long. This summer has been an awakening. The fear that has been controlling me for so long doesn't get to have this.

My blood is pumping and I turn on the radio. They're playing a song I don't know but it's catchy and bright and I turn it up, up, up, roll down the windows and dance in my seat.

Almost an hour later, I pull into the car park in Shepherd's Bush and rush over to the venue. Theo will be on stage in only a few minutes, but there are a bunch of people still hovering around out the front. Serena told me that word of Theo's gig leaked a few hours ago and there has been a mad scramble for tickets. Evidently quite a lot of people who were unsuccessful have turned up anyway.

I push my way through the crowds towards the box office where a frazzled-looking man is trying to turn away wave after wave of eager fans.

'Excuse me,' I say, then I try again because, unsurprisingly, he doesn't seem too interested in listening. 'Excuse me. EXCUSE ME!'

Finally he turns to me, his expression grim, and I lean forward, lower my voice.

'My sister, Serena Ojo-Harris, organized a ticket for me to collect.'

'There are no tickets left for tonight's performance,' the man says with the tired, robotic quality of someone who's had to repeat themselves a lot.

'Oh no, I know. Um, but she's with EMC – the label? It might be under my name? Clemmie, Clementine Monroe?'

The man fixes me with another hard look and crosses his arms. 'Look, love, I've heard them all tonight so don't start. There are no tickets left. None. Please vacate the premises.'

'Oy, we're . . . err, we're with the record label too,' a young girl gasps, shoving me unceremoniously to one side. 'This is Theo Eliott's manager.' She points to her friend who looks about sixteen but tries to affect the appearance of a world-weary music manager who's seen it all.

'I said, clear off before I call security,' the man at the box office snaps.

'Oh well, at least we tried,' the girl says to me consolingly. 'Maybe he'll come out and do autographs later.'

I hover for a moment until I'm pushed aside by the next wave of hopefuls. Shit. I head back out to the front and pull out my phone, ready to call Serena. When I'm greeted by an ominously blank screen I realize that somewhere between here and home the battery has died. I left the house in such a hurry I didn't think to check. Oh, God. What do I do now? I don't even know a single person's phone number off by heart anymore.

I rub my forehead. Right. Okay. I can do this. I'm making a grand romantic gesture here. I will not be deterred.

That thought comforts me for another five seconds, until I realize I don't really have a lot of other options. Maybe I can sneak in? Sneaking into a music venue is not very Clementine Monroe behaviour, but this is the new me – bold! Fearless! On a mission for love!

I skirt casually round the side of the building. I stuff my hands in my pockets and for some reason start chewing on an imaginary piece of gum. I look up at the graffiti-covered concrete like I am simply a humble architecture student fascinated by the quality of the workmanship. It's only when I realize that I've started humming the *Mission Impossible* theme tune under my breath that it occurs to me I might not be pulling off the role of stealthy outlaw.

Also, I am far from the only person who has had this plan. There are tons of people crowded round the side and they're being held at bay by a small army of very serious-looking bouncers in black suits.

I check my phone again in case it has miraculously come back to life. Nothing. Without any more of a plan I go back round to the front of the venue, sit down on the edge of the pavement and stare at my hands.

It doesn't matter. I can call him later. It's not like this is the only chance I have to tell him how I feel. Even though the thought is logical, I feel a deep pit in my stomach. It's not just that I want to be with Theo *now*, it's that I wanted to *show* him that. I wanted to do something to make him understand. Serena's ticket was supposed to get me backstage; he was supposed to know that I was there, cheering him on. Way outside my comfort zone but proud of him and his work.

I can tell him that, I remind myself. *I can make him understand.*

That's when I hear a familiar voice.

' . . . and then maybe we'll see where the night takes us.' A pair of expensively distressed shoes step out of the car that has stopped in front of me and I look up, confronted by the last person I expect to see.

'Ripp?' My mouth drops open.

My father looks down to where I am sitting on the curb and frowns. 'Clemmie? What are you doing down there?'

The twenty-something blonde bombshell who's wrapped around him pouts. 'Riiiiiipp,' she whines, 'I thought we were going to see the show.'

'In a minute.' Ripp disentangles himself and holds out a hand to help me up. 'Why are you sitting out here on the pavement?'

'There's been a mix-up with the tickets. I couldn't get in,' I say, trying to ignore the death stares the woman he's with is sending me.

'Oh, now, that won't do,' Ripp tuts. 'Why don't you come in with me?'

'Do you have a ticket?' I ask.

He lifts his eyebrows. 'I'm Ripp Harris; I don't need a ticket. I'll just ask them to let you in.'

I scoff at that, dart another look at his date, which Ripp follows. For a moment I think he's going to suggest bringing her too, but clearly he's trying to make a go of this whole parenting thing.

'Sorry, love.' Ripp turns to her. 'Looks like I've had a better offer. We'll do it another night, yeah?'

Her mouth drops open. 'Are you being serious?' she screeches.

'I need to spend the evening with my best girl.' Ripp beams winningly at me, and I think in his universe this is an act of good parenting – choosing me over a date with a woman ten years my junior. I suppose he is turning down a shag for me. Not that I want to think about that.

'I cannot believe you are doing this, Ripp! We're done!' The blonde is quivering with rage.

'Now, don't overreact, Carlie . . .' Ripp soothes.

'It's *Marley*,' Marley snarls.

'Course it is,' Ripp agrees. 'Here,' he says, reaching in his pocket for his wallet to pull out a fat wad of bank notes. 'Why don't you call the girls, go have a night out on me. You deserve it, and there's no sense denying London the sight of you looking gorgeous in that dress, is there? I'll call you in the morning.'

Marley's face softens as she plucks the money from his hands. 'Fine,' she says, treating me to another glare (fair enough I suppose, though I think my father is the one who deserves it more). 'But you'll be making this up to me for a long time, Ripp.'

'You know how much I love making things up to you.' Ripp kisses her on the cheek and she giggles. I think my hangover is back.

With Marley disposed of, Ripp gives me his full attention. 'Shall we?' he asks.

He saunters round to the stage door where the men in suits are still holding back the crowd. Something in the way he moves has the crowd splitting before him, and I hear someone hiss, 'Holy shit, is that Ripp Harris?'

'Hey, Tony!' Ripp exclaims, moving towards one of the surly-looking men, all smiles.

An answering grin breaks on Tony's face. 'Mr Harris,' he booms from about seven feet up. 'Didn't know we'd be seeing you tonight.'

'Well, Tone, strictly speaking we're not on the list, but I was just passing by with my daughter,' he gestures to me. 'She's a pal of Theo's so we thought she could drop in and surprise him.'

'Not on the list?' Tony frowns.

'I'm supposed to be on a list,' I say a bit desperately. 'My name's Clemmie. My sister, Serena Ojo-Harris? She works for EMC.'

Tony lifts the tablet he's holding, and flicks across the screen. 'Sorry,' he says. 'Not on here.'

Ripp has been distracted, signing an autograph. 'It's all right, Tony. She can come in with me, can't she?'

Tony's gaze flickers between us as more people start pressing forward. Camera phones start flashing. 'Yeah, no worries, Mr Harris,' Tony says. 'If she's with you, that's fine.'

So, it seems I'm bringing my mostly estranged father along to my romantic gesture. This is officially the most bizarre experience of my life, so I suppose it's fitting.

'Cheers, Tone, give my love to Roberta and the kids, won't you?' Ripp sings cheerily as we sail past, and through to a badly lit corridor.

'Right,' Ripp says, rubbing his hands together and sniffing the air like a bloodhound. 'Follow me.' We begin to wind our way through the halls, past dressing rooms and what looks like a green room where several bored-looking men and women in suits are clacking on their phones.

Loud music fills the air, and I realize with a sinking heart that Theo is already on stage. 'We're too late. He's already started. I think we'd better just find somewhere to wait for him when he comes off,' I say nervously.

'Don't be daft,' Ripp says, getting in the spirit of things now. I know the look on his face. The buzz of being at a gig, the sound of the live music, the smell of sweat and beer . . . he's in his element. 'Don't you want to see what he can do? Follow me.'

And like Alice and the White Rabbit I decide to simply follow him down the rabbit hole. I mean, how much weirder can the day get? As we get nearer to the stage, the music gets louder and louder.

Various crew members rush past, looking busy, and about

half of them call out a greeting to Ripp. I guess he really is a familiar face around here.

'I sneak in to watch a fair bit when I'm in town,' Ripp says, clearly reading my mind. 'I like to see who's coming up. Sometimes I'll find someone who we can offer a support slot to, help get their name out. It's a tough business.' He shakes his head. 'Small venue for a man like Theo Eliott to play, but it sounds like they're a good crowd.'

He's not wrong. I can already hear the audience roaring their approval.

'Ripp, let me ask you something.' I put my hand on his arm, tug gently at his sleeve.

He comes to a halt. 'Sure, shoot, kiddo.'

'Say you wrote an album . . . the best thing you ever wrote, and it was all about Mum, or, I don't know, the woman you love, and it contained all these tiny little private details about your relationship. Would you release it?'

Ripp's brow crumples in confusion. 'I don't understand the question,' he says.

I laugh. 'Don't worry. I think you just answered it.'

We climb some stairs and then suddenly, there we are, right at the side of the stage.

And there *he* is. Theo. He's wearing a red silk jacket with nothing underneath it, and matching trousers. A baby blue electric guitar is cradled low on his hips, the strap slung around his neck. His fingers dance up and down the frets, silver rings flashing in the light, the ends of his dark hair damp with sweat as he flicks it away from his eyes.

His expression is intense while he croons into the mic, his eyelids drooping as that gorgeous gravel voice fills the air. I can't take it in. He's Theo and he's not. He stops singing for a moment, waits and lets the crowd scream the words back to him, a smile on his face. No one can keep their eyes off him.

'Wow,' I whisper.

'Yeah,' Ripp nods, standing close behind me. 'That kid's got the goods.'

'He does,' I agree, looking out at the crowd, how spell-bound they are, and instead of feeling queasy, I just feel proud.

Suddenly, the lights on stage shift and Theo's gaze slides in our direction. I realize a second too late that from his viewpoint I'm standing, spot lit, right in the middle of the stage entrance.

'Oh, shit.' His eyes burn into me and I gulp, lift my hand in a weak greeting.

Theo's own hands fall away from his guitar and he stops singing. Just stops dead. There's a moment of jumbled discord as the rest of the band try to work out what's going on, but Theo only stands there, eyes locked on me, and slowly they stop playing, too.

The entire auditorium of two thousand people falls silent.

My heart is beating so fast that I realize I am going to find out what it feels like to *die* of embarrassment. This is it. This is the end. I have just ruined Theo's gig. If this doesn't actually kill me, then Serena definitely will.

Some awkward chatter breaks out in the crowd, a hum of confusion. *Is this part of the show?* I know they can't see me, but I still feel exposed.

'Excuse me, folks,' Theo says, straight into the microphone. 'I'll be right back.'

And then he unplugs his guitar, places it in the rack beside him and strides off the stage, coming straight for me like a sexy, shirtless missile.

'Oh, shit!' I squeak again.

'Clemmie,' he breathes when he reaches my side.

'Theo, what are you doing?' I shove his arm, panicked. 'You can't just walk off stage in the middle of a gig. Get back out there!'

'What are you doing here?' Theo asks softly, completely ignoring me.

'We can talk about it later!' I hiss. 'Just go, go!'

He smiles, folds his arms across his chest. 'I'm not going anywhere until you tell me why you're here.'

I cast a desperate look at Ripp, and he grins. 'Don't worry, love, I've got this.' Then he saunters nonchalantly out onto the stage.

'Hello, London,' he purrs into the mic as the stunned crowd catch up with what's happening and start to go wild. 'I heard my mate Theo was having a party with two thousand of his closest friends.'

The audience screeches, delighted by this weird and wonderful turn of events.

'Now while he attends to some business, I wondered if you'd indulge me. It's been a while since I played for such a good-looking crowd.' And then, he picks up Theo's guitar, strums it a couple of times, and launches into one of his most famous tracks. The rest of the band share a brief *what the fuck is going on?* look, and then gamely start playing along. Soon the place is full of the sound of two thousand people singing a tune that *Rolling Stone* magazine ranked number nine in the top 500 songs of all time.

Of course, all of this is barely on my radar, because I'm so busy staring at Theo, who is smouldering at me with the shirtless intensity of a fallen angel.

'What are you doing here, Clemmie?' he asks again, his voice steady.

'I came because I love you, you idiot!' I hiss, smacking my palms against his chest and pushing him. 'This was supposed to be a romantic gesture, but you've utterly lost your mind, you—'

Theo, the wall of muscle, doesn't flinch. Instead he puts his fingers gently around my wrist, and tugs me so that I'm falling against him, and then he lowers his head and presses his lips to mine, cutting me off mid-rant.

Fireworks. There are actual fireworks going off in my bloodstream, sparks flying off my skin, everywhere he touches me. We're a safety hazard. We're going to burn this building to the ground.

Finally, I pull away.

'I'm still mad at you,' I say.

He lets out a long, slow breath. 'I know.'

'I heard the album. The real album.'

He starts. 'How did you . . . Did Serena give it to you? I *told* her . . .'

'She didn't,' I cut him off. 'I have my sources but they will remain secret.'

'I didn't want you to hear it, at least not now. I didn't want you to feel like I was – like *anyone* was – pressuring you to release it. I made something else for the label. I completely get why those songs shouldn't be out for just anyone to hear. I needed to write them, but only for you, for us.'

'You're an idiot,' I say.

'What?'

'You heard me. You making a beautiful piece of *art* about us is not the same as our private lives being splashed around the tabloids. If you don't release those songs, it will be . . .' – I cast around for the right words – 'it will be a sacrilege, Theo.'

'I don't think you understand.' Theo cups my cheek. 'If those songs come out, then people will dissect them; they'll write about them; they'll tear the lyrics apart and turn them into stories.'

I look into his eyes. 'Let them,' I say.

We just stand and stare at each other for a moment.

'I love you,' Theo exhales, his fingers tangling with mine.

'I love you, too.'

The kiss we share then is the fairy-tale kiss, the happily-ever-after, end-of-the-rainbow kiss. It's soft and sweet and full of promises that I know we'll both keep.

'I missed you so much,' Theo says.

'I don't think I want to be an academic anymore,' I blurt.

Theo blinks, but otherwise doesn't seem too worried by

the change of subject. 'Okay,' he says, smoothing the hair back from my face.

'It's been making me miserable for a long time,' I say, 'but I thought I had to stick at it, because I've put so much in. I didn't want to be a person who quit because it was hard. I thought it was too late to change my mind. I didn't want to be in my thirties with no idea of what I want to do with my life . . .' I trail off.

'And now?' Theo asks gently.

I let out a deep breath. 'Now, I think maybe it's okay not to have everything figured out. Now I think maybe I don't need to prove anything to anyone . . . maybe I'd just like to try . . . being happy.'

'I'd like you to be happy too,' Theo says, and he wraps me in his arms, tucks the top of my head under his chin and gives me one of those perfect hugs. 'I want you to be happy more than I want anything else in the world. Even more than I want David to stop force-feeding me kale.'

I press into him, hold on tight for another second, then draw back. 'What would make me happy right now would be for you to go and finish this concert.'

He kisses my nose. 'You've got it. But when I'm done, we're leaving here together, okay?'

'Okay,' I grin. 'But only because you look so good in that suit you've scrambled my brain.'

He kisses me again, so thoroughly that my knees dissolve like water. He steadies me. Grins.

'Later,' he promises.

'Later,' I agree.

Theo is still laughing as he bounces back on stage, joining Ripp for the last couple of verses of the song he's performing. It seems my father has had no trouble at all vamping for the crowd, and they cheer and stomp their feet in appreciation.

'Ripp Harris, ladies and gentlemen,' Theo says, leading the applause as Ripp takes a bow.

Ripp appears beside me, panting and happy like a Labrador.

'Did you two sort things out?' he asks.

'Yeah, we did.' I nudge his shoulder with mine. 'Thanks.'

'No worries. Good show, this.' His eyes sharpen. 'Do you think your Theo might like a guest spot on the next tour?'

'You can always ask him,' I say lightly, utterly confident in what my boyfriend's answer will be.

'Okay, okay,' Theo is saying, settling himself behind the microphone with his guitar, once more. 'Now, as some of you may know, yesterday we announced my new album, and I thought maybe I could give you a bit of a sneak peek at one of the tracks. What do you think?'

The crowd go wild.

Theo strums his guitar. His eyes slide over to me, and his voice dips as he says. 'This one is for the woman I love. It's called, "Oh, My Darling".'

And while he plays, I don't feel scared or overwhelmed at all. I feel like I've come home.

Epilogue

Nine Months Later

'I suppose I shouldn't be surprised that your boyfriend is trying to sneak you out of here early,' Serena sighs, 'but I wish he'd be more subtle about it.'

'I don't know what you mean,' I say from my position, upside down and slung over Theo's shoulder.

'It's not like this is the actual wedding, S,' Theo grumbles. 'And I've been in LA all week. Have you *seen* Clemmie in this dress?'

'Put my sister down, you degenerate,' Serena insists, and with a sigh Theo lets my feet slide to the floor. The fact that my whole body presses against him on the way down is just an added bonus for us both.

'I thought she'd be more relaxed now that the album's out,' I whisper to Theo, adjusting the neckline of my pink dress which is, admittedly, a little on the low side.

It seems that, yet again, the bigger boobs spell has been hard at work.

'She won't be happy until we've swept the Grammys,' Theo says, distracted by the view he has straight down my dress and clearly not displeased with the situation.

'Which we will.' Serena flicks her hair with satisfaction. 'Multiplatinum in two months? It's my best work yet.'

'I think I had something to do with it, too,' Theo protests, his warm hand curling around the back of my neck in a way that has me sighing with pleasure.

Serena obviously hears because she lifts a warning finger. 'The two of you need to keep it in your pants for the rest of the rehearsal dinner.'

We're in a luxury eco lodge deep in the Cornish countryside where tomorrow Lil and Henry will get married in the woods under a chuppah that Henry built himself.

Theo had a gig last night so he could only fly in right before the event. After the wedding we're driving up to Northumberland for six weeks. I'm deep in the edits of my book which is being published next year and, true to his word, Theo booked Granny Mac's house for the same six weeks that we were there last year.

David is unimpressed by the whole situation, especially because Theo has given him the six weeks off as paid holiday and his long-suffering husband is dragging him off to the Bahamas. David has described this scenario as 'a living nightmare', but Theo insisted it would be good for him. We have compromised on proof-of-life updates three times a week. Theo is gleefully looking forward to forty-two days of unfettered access to Dairylea Dunkers. The man truly has the palate of a five-year-old.

He's also happy because for one of the weeks, he's booked a nearby house for his family to come and stay, and I just know they're going to love it. Hannah is especially excited about being at the site of our witchiest adventures. Upon meeting her, Serena instantly identified a kindred spirit, while Lil intoned, 'The magic is strong in this one.' Hannah was of course delighted, though – for now – Oliver remains disappointingly human.

Fortunately, my time is pretty flexible these days. I'm doing a mixture of freelance copy-editing and work for my mum's charity to subsidize my tiny publishing advance and scrape together a reasonable salary. I'm going to start teaching creative writing classes with kids from one of Mum's initiatives in the autumn, and Lisa's going to be my glamorous assistant. I still don't have it all figured out, but I'm enjoying what I do and that's what really matters.

And the fact that I get to go and spend six weeks in my favourite place with my devastatingly beautiful, kind, funny, extremely silly boyfriend is quite the bonus, too.

'I thought you were practically the patron saint of hot sex,' I point out to Serena now.

'I am!' Serena insists. 'I'm just saying let's have a little *class*. An hour, two tops, to celebrate our sister and then you kids can go crazy.'

'If you guys want to go and have sex that's fine with me,'

Lil beams, drifting over. 'Actually, Henry and I can point you in the direction of a very handy linen cupboard.'

'I swear, next time we cast a spell I'm asking for ten million pounds.' Serena swigs her champagne. 'You horny toads are living proof that we have serious magic in our blood.'

'And you're not?' I ask, raising my eyebrows and glancing over to where Bee is laughing with our dad. Serena and Bee are taking things slowly, keeping things casual because that's what suits them both, but that doesn't mean the arrangement isn't making my sister disgustingly happy.

'Well, I for one am extremely grateful for your magical abilities.' Theo pulls me close, plants a kiss on the top of my head as I lean back into him. 'Though after that article about Sam, I'll admit I'm feeling increasingly sorry for Len. You lot don't mess around when it comes to a good curse.'

I smirk. A couple of months ago Sam was in the press. Actually, a few stories came out about him after Ripp kicked him out the band, stories about what an obnoxious jerk he is mostly, but this one – a damning story featuring several of his exes who spilled the beans on his mediocre love-making – has been especially entertaining.

'Serves them both right,' Lil smirks. 'You don't mess with our sister.'

'I'll drink to that.' Serena lifts her glass.

'To the Weird Sisters,' I say. 'Sisters, soulmates, best friends.'

We clink our glasses together and sip champagne. Lil drags Serena off to talk to a friend of hers, winking at Theo and me over her shoulder.

gets a mention, and for once I know I will not miss anyone. I am truly, sincerely, from-the-bottom-of-my-heart grateful to all of you. Thank you so much for helping to make the book you hold in your hands. It means everything to me.

Thank you to Jess Mileo, who held my hand and kept me sane, and made me feel extremely powerful. I appreciate you!

My huge thanks to the whole team at ILA, who are well on the way to helping me achieve world domination. Your passion and enthusiasm for this book in its earliest stages was a huge deal for me. I will never, ever forget it. Thank you for the champagne and introducing me to the grumpy office dog who I will be putting in a book asap.

Thank you to all my international publishers and translators. Your kind words and enthusiastic pitches have made me feel like the luckiest woman on the planet. Getting to work with all of you is such a privilege, and I can't believe my words will be translated into so many different languages.

Thank you to my earliest readers, Keris Stainton, Lucy Powrie, Lauren James, and Sarra Manning. All writers who I admire enormously, your support and enthusiastic messages made a very scary process much easier to navigate.

Thanks, as always, to my friends and family who have to put up with me while I write books – a generally thankless task, so this opportunity to show my gratitude is very welcome! Of course, my biggest thanks to Paul and Bea. There are no books without you. I love you so much, it's embarrassing.

Finally, thank you to my readers, old and new. To the gorgeous, loyal, extremely kind readers who have been with me from the start. Thank you for your support. Thank you for recommending my books, for reading them with your mum/daughter/sister/gran. Your stories and your messages have made me so happy. And to my new readers, hi! I'm so happy to meet you. I think we're going to have a lot of fun together.

Thank you to everyone at Simon & Schuster UK who helped us to publish *Under Your Spell*

Editorial
Molly Crawford
Mina Asaam
Gail Hallett

Production and Operations
Karin Seifried
Mike Messam
Isabelle Gray

Copyeditor
Federica Leonardis

Proofreader
Victoria Denne

Design
Pip Watkins

Finance and Contracts
Maria Mamouna
Isabel Ireland
Meshach Yeboah
Keely Day

Sales
Madeline Allan
Heather Hogan
Jonny Kennedy
Lydia McCallum
Dominic Brendon
Mathew Watterson
Katie Sormaz
Rachel Bazan
Robyn Ware
Rich Hawton

Marketing
Genevieve Barratt
Sarah Jeffcoate

Publicity
Sabah Khan
Harriett Collins